Continue
Laughing

Also by Carl Reiner

ENTER LAUGHING
ALL KINDS OF LOVE

Continue Laughing

Carl Reiner

A BIRCH LANE PRESS BOOK
PUBLISHED BY CAROL PUBLISHING GROUP

A Birch Lane Press Book
Published by Carol Publishing Group
Birch Lane Press is a registered trademark of Carol Communications, Inc.
Editorial Offices: 600 Madison Avenue, New York, N.Y. 10022
Sales and Distribution Offices: 120 Enterprise Avenue, Secaucus, N.J. 07094
In Canada: Canadian Manda Group, One Atlantic Avenue, Suite 105, Toronto, Ontario M6K 3E7
Queries regarding rights and permissions should be addressed to Carol Publishing Group, 600 Madison Avenue, New York, N.Y. 10022

Carol Publishing Group books are available at special discounts for bulk purchases, sales promotion, fund-raising, or educational purposes. Special editions can be created to specifications. For details, contact: Special Sales Department, Carol Publishing Group, 120 Enterprise Avenue, Secaucus, N.J. 07094

Manufactured in the United States of America

10 9 8 7 6 5 4 3 2 1

Library of Congress Cataloging-in-Publication Data

Reiner, Carl, 1922–
    Continue laughing / by Carl Reiner.
        p.   cm.
    "A Birch Lane Press book."
    ISBN 1-55972-273-8 (hardcover)
    1. Young men—United States—Fiction.   2. Comedians—United States—Fiction.   3. World War, 1939–1945—Fiction.
I. Title.
PS3568.E4863C66   1995
813'.54—dc20   94-44308
                                                                  CIP
                                                                  r95

For Estelle, Rob, Annie, Lucas,
and my brother, Charles Reiner,
who thought I should be an actor

✦

"Every actor in his heart believes every
bad thing printed of him."
—Orson Welles

Thank you, Bruce Shostak, Dan Strone, Barbara Scher,
and George Shapiro for your encouragement, diligence, loyalty,
and insight.

Part 1

David Kokolovitz swished his foam-laden, single-edged Gem razor through the hot water in the cracked porcelain basin as he peered into a bathroom mirror that was in serious need of resilvering. He carefully evened his sideburns, smiled his patented crooked smile, and checked his face for handsomeness. It was apparent to him that in the last three years he had gotten quite a good deal better looking. His face had not harvested a serious pimple in almost two years, his cheekbones had somehow become more defined, and his wavy brown hair, which he now lovingly combed, had started to organize a definite hairline, not unlike Ray Milland's. Today was the day he had decided to do whatever was necessary to bring to a close his career as a full-time delivery boy and part-time actor so he could become a full-time actor. Today he would notify his boss, Mr. Foreman, that Friday would be his last day delivering sewing machines for the Foreman Machine Works. Later, he would inform Margie Skulnik that for the next few months they would not be spending their weekends together going to the movies or picnicking at the Bronx Zoo or trysting behind the Milton Morganthau Mausoleum at Woodlawn Cemetery. And tonight he would walk into John Marlowe's dressing room and inform the old man that Saturday night would be his farewell performance as Donald Meadows in *The Bishop Misbehaves* at the Marlowe Theatre. And lastly, before he left the apartment that morning, he would try to convince his parents that his decision to pursue a career as an actor was a thoughtful and irrevocable one.

"David," he heard his mother's shrill voice order as he enhanced one of the waves in his hair with the back of a wet comb, "you can comb your hair later! There are other people in the house who would like to use the bathroom!"

He marveled at his mother's power to see through locked doors, an occult gift he attributed to her Romanian-Gypsy heritage. The moment he unlocked the door to leave, his sixteen-year-old sister dashed in, slammed down the toilet seat, and kicked the door shut.

"Marcia," Mrs. Kokolovitz screeched, "toilet seats don't grow on trees! You break another one, you can make in the park! Now hurry up, you'll be late for school! David," her voice now back to normal, "I'm making you a bull's-eye."

Only when Mrs. Kokolovitz was pleased with her son's general behavior did she offer to make for him an egg fried sunny-side up in the hole torn out of a piece of white bread.

"Sorry, Ma, but I don't have time," he called out as he rushed to his room to grab a shirt and his worn New York Giant's baseball jacket.

"No time for a bull's-eye?" she called after him, pulling a slice of limp Wonder bread from the loaf.

"I have to get to work a little early today," David explained as he approached the kitchen. "I have to talk to Mr. Foreman about something."

"About what kind of something?" she asked suspiciously.

"About finding someone to replace me in the shop."

"And why," she asked, digging a hole in the bread, "should Mr. Foreman find someone to replace you?"

A horrible hacking cough preluded the arrival of David's father.

"If you're making that egg for me, I don't want it," Sam Kokolovitz said as he struggled into his Indian-patterned flannel bathrobe. "I'll just have some toast and jam."

"Ma, don't make the bull's-eye. I told you I didn't have time for breakfast."

"Don't change the subject," she answered as she dropped a pat of butter into a hot cast-iron frying pan. "What's happening that you want to quit your job?"

"You're quitting your job?" his father interjected as he chain-lit his second cigarette of the day. "David, you're not enlisting in the army, I hope."

"No, Pa."

"Where are you rushing, son? You can't wait till they draft you?"

"Papa's right," Bertha agreed as she gingerly placed the yolk of the egg into the hole of the sautéing white bread.

"Who knows," Mr. Kokolovitz managed to say between coughs. "Maybe somebody'll shoot that Hitler bastard and they won't need you altogether."

"And maybe," his mother said, basting the bull's-eye with foamy butter, "if you don't stop smoking, your lungs will bust!"

"Don't change the subject, Bertha. We're not talking about my lungs, and for your information, my lungs are fine."

"Hocking up phlegm every morning in the toilet for a half hour is fine by you, Sam?"

"I don't cough from cigarettes," he argued while coughing. "I cough because I have a catarrh."

"Don't blame your guitar, Sam. You cough because you smoke like a chimney?"

"Ma, Pa," David interrupted, "can I explain to you why I'm leaving Mr. Foreman."

"Who's stopping you, so explain!" his parents said, speaking together.

"I went for an acting audition yesterday, and I was offered this job with a professional Shakespearean touring company."

Before his parents could mount their objections, he pressed on. "I'll be playing different colleges and high schools for four months, and they're going to pay me thirty dollars a week!"

"Someone is going to pay you," his father asked disbelievingly, "thirty dollars a week to act in a Shakespeare play? You never acted Shakespeare before."

"Sam," she explained, coming to his defense, "in the play that David is acting in now, *The Bishop Behaves . . .*"

"Not *behaves,* Ma," David patiently corrected. "It's *mis. Mis*behaves."

"All right, in *The Bishop Misbehaves,*" she conceded. "David has been acting with an English accent, and nobody can tell he wasn't an Englishman."

"Bertha, you need more than an English accent to act in Shakespeare. You need feeling."

"Feeling?" she argued. "David had plenty of feeling last night on the telephone when he recited the whole balcony scene from *Romeo and Juliet* to what's her name."

"Margie, Ma! You were listening in when I was talking to Margie?"

"Not only me. The whole building was listening in! What do you expect when you recite Shakespeare at the top of your lungs at two o'clock in the morning?"

"Where was I, Bertha?"

"In bed snoring. I tried to wake you up so you could hear him. It was so beautiful I almost cried." She sighed as she gently slid the sizzling bull's-eye out of the frying pan and onto one of her few remaining unchipped dinner plates. David was not surprised by his mother's supportive attitude; she was his biggest fan.

"You really think it had feeling?" David said, dipping a piece of the fried bread into the runny yolk.

"I'm telling you, David, when I woke up and heard such beautiful language, I thought Papa had left the radio on and I was hearing the *Lux Radio Theatre.* You sounded just like what's his name?"

"Ronald Colman?"

"No, the other one, what's his name? You know him. He played that fellow in that movie with Basil Rothman?"

"Rathbone, Ma."

"That's right, but what's the other fellow's name who played with him, the handsome one with the mustache? You know, Robin Hood!" Bertha snapped her fingers and grimaced. "The one who played Robin Hood! Flink!" she cried, slapping her hands together. "Harold Flink! You sounded just like him."

"That's Flynn, Ma, Errol Flynn!"

"What's the difference, you sound like him," she cooed as she placed a glass of chocolate milk before him, "and with such feeling. I'm not surprised that someone wants you in their Shakespeare play."

"Plays, Ma, four plays. It's a repertory company. Do you know what that is?"

"Do I know what repertory is?" his father asked boastfully. "Listen, before you were born, I sat in an orchestra seat and saw Eva LaGallienne in *The Wild Duck* at her own repertory theater! That woman, every week, sometimes twice a week, she performed a different role in a different play, so don't tell me about repertory!"

Both his parents were leaning the right way. The signs were encouraging.

"Ma," he said, jamming a forkful of yolk-soaked bread into his mouth, "this is the best damn bull's-eye I ever ate."

"Don't curse," she admonished.

"Oh, Ma, Pa," he offered casually, preparing to drop the bombshell, "did I tell you that this repertory company was going on tour?"

"No, you didn't."

"You mean," his father ventured cautiously, "it's not like Eva LaGallienne where she played different plays in one theater?"

"It's more exciting, Pa! We do different plays in different theaters."

"Different theaters?" his mother asked timorously. "But we'll be able to go and see you act. I mean, like when we took a subway to the Marlowe Theatre in Manhattan."

"Well, I don't know, Ma. These theaters are all over—"

"So where is all over?" she asked suspiciously. "Brooklyn, Queens, Staten Island? Here in the Bronx, I hope, so we wouldn't have to travel so far."

"Bertha, look at your son's face with the crooked smile. He's not talking about the Bronx and Staten Island. You're not talking different boroughs, are you, David?" Mr. Kokolovitz challenged as he took a deep drag from his half-inch cigarette butt. "You're talking different cities. Am I right?"

"Well, Pa, the tour isn't set yet, but I'm told that we'll be playing colleges and high schools in Georgia, Alabama, South Carolina, Tennessee—"

"David, you are not going to quit your job at Foreman's," his mother commanded, "and you are not going to those terrible cities!"

"They're not terrible, and they're not cities Ma. They're states!"

"David, don't correct me when I'm talking!" she ordered sharply. "I don't care if they're countries; you are not going! It's enough that your brother's in North Africa. I don't need two sons away from home."

To underline the finality of her dictum, she angrily snatched the fresh Camel cigarette from her husband's mouth just as he was about to chain-light it.

"Sam," she screeched, "stop with the smoking already!"

"Dammit, Bertha!" he bellowed. "Look what you did!"

In pulling the unlit cigarette from her husband's mouth, Bertha had inadvertently torn a patch of skin from inside his lower lip.

"Do you see, Sam," Bertha lectured, "what can happen to a man from smoking!"

"I see," he growled, licking his injured lip, "what happens when a woman doesn't mind her own business."

"David, you want to be an actor? Be an actor," she said, ignoring her husband. "Did I ever try to stop you?"

"Yes!"

"Never! When did I ever try to stop you?"

"Ma, when I told you that I was going to act at the Marlowe Theatre, you said, 'Over my dead body.' "

"Oh, sure," she admitted begrudgingly, "before I saw you act on the stage, but after the show, didn't I tell you that you were the best one?"

"You told the whole audience," his father mumbled, holding a handkerchief against his lip. " 'That's my son David wearing the tails,' she yells. 'In the program he's Don Coleman, and he was the best one!' "

"He *was,* Sam! You didn't think he was the best one?"

"Yes, but I didn't holler and create a disturbance."

"You said it yourself, Sam. If you have a good product, it pays to advertise!"

David smiled, gulped down his chocolate milk, and headed for the front door.

"Where are you going, David?" his mother yelled as she followed after him. "What are you going to do?"

"What I have to do, Ma. Join the Avon Shakespearean Company."

In making his exit, David closed the apartment door just forcefully enough to illustrate his resolve. He waited in the hall for an explosion that did not happen.

"The Avon Shakespearean Company," he heard his father muse. "Sounds very classy, Bertha. It must be a legitimate enterprise if they can afford to pay an actor thirty dollars a week."

David strained to hear his mother, who was speaking uncharacteristically softly.

"Sam, how can he travel out of town for four months? He doesn't have the right clothes, and if he did, he doesn't have a valise to put them in."

David smiled, listening to his parents behave like his allies instead of parents.

"Sam, you'll go down to Kraft's Luggage and buy one of those black whad-dya-call-it bags; you know, it has two compartments, and it folds over."

"A Gladstone bag?"

"Something like that. You'll get one for David."

David ran the five blocks to the 179th Street el station thinking, One down and two to go.

No matter what time David arrived for work at the machine shop, Mr. Foreman would announce loudly how many minutes late he was. Today, eager to tell Mr. Foreman of his plans, David arrived two minutes early, hurriedly unpadlocked the heavy metal door, rushed into the shop, and started to sweep the floor, just seconds before his boss arrived.

Mr. Foreman eyed David suspiciously. "My assistant is planning to leave early again tonight?" he asked, trading his copy of the *Daily News* for a grease-stained denim apron.

David never thought of himself as Mr. Foreman's assistant, but as a temporary, underpaid delivery boy. Mr. Foreman, on the other hand, dreamed of his becoming a first-class, low-salaried repairer of millinery sewing machines and, God willing, a potential son-in-law. Mr. Foreman had once actually arranged for David and Leona, the youngest and prettiest of his four plump daughters, to meet accidentally at a delicatessen where he knew David would be eating. He had invited David to sit at their table as his guest, and for the length of the lunch, Mr. Foreman watched silently as his highly intelligent, bespectacled daughter delicately ate her sliced-turkey sandwich while searching desperately for just one thing that she and David had in common. There was one, a common anger at her father for arranging the embarrassing meeting.

"Mr. Foreman," David blurted out after twice clearing his throat, "I have been offered a well-paying job as an actor, and I'll be leaving here at the end of the week."

"You mean this?" Mr. Foreman asked, staring at David with unblinking eyes, his face ashen. "What you said?"

"Yes, of course."

Mr. Foreman turned his back on the ingrate, picked up a sewing machine that needed servicing, slammed it down onto the metal worktable, and for the next hour paid attention only to forcefully hand-grinding a new steel shaft while humming an angry version of "I'm Forever Blowing Bubbles."

"You know, Mr. Foreman," David said, feeling guilty, "my friend Marvin might be interested in the job."

"Your friend Marvin? That idiot who was fired from Acme Printing upstairs for burning down the shop?"

"He wasn't really fired, Mr. Foreman. He was just laid off until the shop is rebuilt."

Mr. Foreman pushed past David and picked up his circa-1930 standing telephone and unhooked the earpiece from the cradle.

"Operator," he shouted into the mouthpiece, "give me, please, Buckminster 5146 . . . Did your son Larry find a job yet? . . . Good, can he start today? . . . Send him right down!"

On his way back to his bench, without displaying any emotion, Mr. Foreman ordered David to go home.

"Now?" asked David incredulously. "I'm willing to work out the week. I mean, I could show this Larry around and teach him to—"

"Teach him what? How to come in ten minutes late every day and leave ten minutes early to go act on a stage for free? No, thank you, David. I'll teach him. You pack up your things and go."

David knew there was nothing he could say that would make Mr. Foreman understand why he had to go. He grabbed up his belongings, which included a comb and a dog-eared copy of *The Actor Prepares,* by Stanislavsky, and left.

He stood on the sidewalk and looked up at the aged, grime-encrusted sign that read: Foreman Machine Works. Through the half-opened shop window David glimpsed a sad-faced man staring down at him. How could I, he thought, spend five days a week, ten hours a day, for more than a year in a cell-like space, with this morally decent, opinionated, illogical, penurious slave driver and leave without at least saying so long? He decided that he could not.

"S'long, Mr. Foreman," he shouted up to the old man, and waved. "I'll send you a postcard from Georgia."

Mr. Foreman was about to reply, "Save the two cents," but realizing the postcard would contain news of the professional acting career of his all-time favorite delivery boy, he relented.

"I can't stop you from sending postcards, David," he shouted down. "It's your money."

David found a seat for his subway ride to Margie's house and smiled at his good fortune. Not only had he found a seat, but when he called her from a phone booth, he learned the great news that her mother would not be home that afternoon. He could feel his penis start to react and immediately willed it to desist. Once upon a horrible time, on a stiflingly hot summer day when he was sixteen and had just started working, he had been caught by this human phenomena and experienced the most horrendously embarrassing moment of his young life. Standing in a steaming, humanity-packed subway car, he had tried desperately to keep his erection from rubbing up against the buttocks of a tall, devastatingly attractive, young college student. He had bent himself out of shape sucking in his gut in an attempt to keep any part of his pelvis from touching any part of the girl's behind when an obese woman, who was standing back to back with him, bent over to retrieve her shopping bag and inadvertently pushed David hard against the lovely student. She immediately recognized evil when it touched her and began screaming at the top of her lungs, "You disgusting pig! May God strike you dead!"

To this day David could will his penis to stand at ease simply by conjuring up the sound of the shrill voices of the two irate women passengers who whacked at him with their heavy pocketbooks, shouting for a policeman to "arrest this no-good, rotten rapist!"

Now, sitting in an almost-empty subway car, David's thoughts drifted to Margie's mother, Mrs. Skulnik, who was very fond of David and too often told him so. Though not as pretty as her daughter, she had the same hypnotic green-blue eyes and a voluptuous body which she moved in a way that embarrassed and frightened David. He strongly suspected that this forty-three-year-old platinum-blond flirt was out to seduce him. Why else would she tell him some of the things she did?

"David, would you believe," she once asked while he was waiting for Margie to dress, "that my lovely daughter and I wear the same-size brassiere? Maybe I fill mine out a little more, but we wear the exact same size everything, from panties to garter belts. Isn't that amazing?"

More amazing, he thought, was that she told him the reason that she and Mr. Skulnik were no longer married.

"Three years ago, right before the high holidays," she related casually, "I stopped off at my husband's fur factory just before closing time, and I found him involved with one of his models, if you know what I mean by *involved*. That was it for me, David. That kind of behavior I do not accept, and I asked him to leave."

What Mrs. Skulnik had omitted saying was that the naked model trying to hide herself under her half-nude husband was not a model at all but her plain-looking older sister, Francine.

As David briskly negotiated the five blocks from the subway station to Margie's apartment building, he was deep into one of his recurring sexual fantasies. He pictured Margie greeting him at the door wearing her new black patent-leather pumps, a black brassiere, and no panties.

As he passed a florist shop, he thought for a moment of buying a dozen red roses, but his raging libido and the high price of roses discouraged the thought. However, the romantic in him prevailed, and he sprang for a twenty-cent bunch of lilacs.

With the flowers hidden behind his back, David pressed the buzzer to the Skulnik apartment and silently rehearsed his impression of Ronald Colman as François Villon in *The Vagabond King*. His heart pounded as he heard the clicking of Margie's high heels.

"Who's there?" a girlish voice sang out.

" 'If I were king, more than red roses to your fair feet I would bring,' " David answered like Colman (Villon) in *The Vagabond King*. "I would thee bring white lilacs, and not only to thy fair feet . . .' "

Before he could say, "But to thy fairer breasts," the door opened, and there stood Margie's mother, in high heels and a skin-tight satin slip.

"David," she gushed, "it's you? Please excuse my attire. You know, David dear, I could have sworn it was the Vagabond King himself at the door. You sounded exactly like Ronald Colman. How do you do that?"

"Do what?" he joked, the flowers still hidden behind his back. "That's my natural way of speaking."

"Of course." She laughed throatily. "That's why you changed your name to Don Coleman."

Mrs. Skulnik gestured for David to enter and immediately smashed all his hopes for an afternoon of sex by announcing that her daughter was out.

"But I'll be happy to entertain you until she returns, David darling."

He froze as she smiled coquettishly and moved toward him. When she was almost up against him, she reached out, encircled him with her arms, and grabbed hold of the lilacs.

"David, you're hiding flowers behind your back. Don't tell me, let me guess. Are they lilacs? They smell like lilacs."

"Yep, they're lilacs," he admitted, hoping she would release him.

"I have a very sensitive sense of smell," she said giggling.

David thought, This lady with no dress on is keeping her arms around me much longer than necessary.

"They are lilacs," she said as she brought them to her. "Oh, how sweet. Shall I put them in water?"

"No, Mrs. Skulnik, don't put them in water," David said, rescuing his lilacs. "I'd like to hand them to Margie as they are. When will she be back?"

"Very soon. She took my dress to the cleaners to be pressed. I have a heavy date for lunch today, and at my age I try to look as spiffy as I can."

"You look pretty spiffy right now," he said.

David could have kicked himself for telling her that, for while his words were still hanging in the air, Mrs. Skulnik put her naked arms around his neck and planted her full red lips on his full, sweaty ones. He was sure that most of the neighbors on the floor heard the resounding smack their lips produced when he finally pulled away.

"I hope," she cooed, "that Margie appreciates what a romantic feller she's got. *Ooh,* if I were a few years younger and not such a moral person, I would try to steal you away from Margie."

And if I were few years younger, he thought, I'd invite you to my bar mitzvah and have my mother deal with you. He prayed that Margie would return with the damned dress and save him from an embarrassment which was mounting precipitously as Mrs. Skulnik sat on the couch and crossed her magnificent legs, legs that looked exactly like

Margie's. All Margie had to do to get David into a state was to cross and display them just as her mother was doing now.

"Come sit by me, David," she coaxed, smoothing the cushion next to her, "or should I call you by your stage name, Don Coleman?"

David gave her permission to call him Don and was about to say that he preferred to stand when Mrs. Skulnik unceremoniously jerked him down onto the couch.

"Now tell me, Don," she said, clutching his hand, "when I leave for my appointment—and don't think I'm prying, but I *am* Margie's mother, and since her father doesn't seem to take an interest, I have to do double duty. What I'm asking, Don dear," she continued coyly, capturing his other hand, "when I go to my luncheon and you and Margie are alone in the apartment, what will you two do to pass the time?"

Mrs. Skulnik actually fluttered her eyelids and smiled at David while awaiting his response.

"Oh," he said offhandedly, "we'll probably crack open a box of Mallomars and listen to those new Harry James records Margie got for her birthday."

"Really, Don?" she asked innocently. "I can't believe two young people wouldn't take the opportunity to do a little more than that while Mama's away."

"Oh, well," he joshed, "sometimes we might jump up and dance a fandango."

"Cheek to cheek?" She laughed, and then, still clutching both of David's hands, Mrs. Skulnik, in one swift move, lifted him off the couch, placed one of his perspiring hands on the small of her back while pressing his other one against her breast, and swaying sensually, she hummed Larry Clinton's "My Reverie" badly off key into his ear.

It was taking superhuman concentration for David to keep his easily motivated penis from reacting to the feel of her soft left breast, against which she was pressing his imprisoned right hand. He tried once or twice to put some air between their cheeks and pelvises, but each time, Mrs. Skulnik pulled him closer to her.

" 'Only a poor fool, caught in a whirlpool,' "—she sang the lyrics softly and awfully in his ear—" 'of romance would be so cruel . . . as you are to me . . .' "

She hummed a few more bars and then, remembering the final lyrics, sang them with a burst of emotion.

" 'So love me . . . as you loved me in my reverie . . . Make my dream a reality . . .' " In her zeal, as Mrs. Skulnik reached the frenzied climax of the song and sang " 'Let's dispense with formality,' " she negotiated a fancy turn and a sudden deep dip that caught her unsuspecting partner completely off balance. Unable to release himself from her embrace, David fell backward onto the floor and pulled his reluctant partner down on top of him. She made no attempt to get off and used the opportunity once more to kiss him smack on his mouth.

"If someone"—she tittered—"should walk in now . . ."

It was at this moment that Margie, carrying her mother's dress, blithely entered the room. The sight of the grotesque human tableau on the living-room floor froze Margie in her tracks.

"How disgusting!" she shouted, flinging her mother's dress at her. "How could you do such a thing?"

"Listen, Margie," David explained, quickly springing to his feet and to his defense. "Your mother and I were dancing . . . We have never . . ."

"Oh, David, I'm not talking to you," Margie screamed as she retrieved the dress and reflung it at her mother. "That is horrible, Mother, just horrible!"

"Young lady," Mrs. Skulnik replied quietly as she rose to her feet, "I will not allow you to speak to me like that! I *am* your mother, and you *will* respect me! Now look and see what that stupid, out-of-control anger of yours has done," she said, picking up the dress from the floor and waving it in her daughter's face. "You have ruined the only dress I have to wear to my luncheon today!"

"And you, Mother dearest, ruin everything!" Margie shouted, snatching back the dress and ripping off a sleeve. "No wonder Daddy left you!"

Feeling terribly out of place during this ultrapersonal mother-daughter heart-to-heart, David quietly began to inch himself toward the door.

"David," Margie demanded, "do you have any idea what my mother was doing with you?"

"Sure," he said naively. "Dancing."

"Is that what you think she was doing, David?" she snarled as she ripped off the other sleeve. "Just dancing?"

"Well, no, she was humming, too."

"And why do you think she—?"

"David," Mrs. Skulnik interrupted, "she has no right to interrogate you like this."

"Oh, don't I, Mother dearest?"

"No, you don't. Now Margie, you will stop this minute!"

"I will stop, *Mother,* as soon as you *stop teasing my friends!*" she screamed as she ripped her mother's dress to shreds.

Mrs. Skulnik stared menacingly at her daughter before retrieving the remnants of her flowered chiffon dress and storming from the room.

At home, David had witnessed and participated in loud family fights, but no one had ever slammed anything as violently as Mrs. Skulnik slammed her bedroom door. The resultant shock wave actually caused David's heart to skip a beat. Except for movies with Bette Davis or Joan Crawford, he had never seen anything so awesomely dramatic. I'm in a melodrama, he thought, cast in a role that I'm totally unsuited to play. He stood by helplessly, thinking, How the hell did I get into this dumb drama, and who is this girl that I've pledged to love forever and who has promised to marry me in five years, or sooner, if I became a star? How could sweet, tender Margie suddenly turn from June Allyson into the Cat Woman? He stood transfixed as he watched her metamorphose again from a snarling, ripping predator into a pitiable, meowing, lost kitten. Seeing her now, lying on the carpet, curled up into a fetal ball and weeping what seemed like honest tears, he wondered whether it would be adult to just fold his tent and steal away rather than stay and try to comfort her. Maybe, he thought, even though sex couldn't possibly still be on her agenda, I should say a kind word to her—if I can think of one. How much of a risk would I be taking if I leaned over and said, Howya doin', honey? She's unarmed. While pondering his options, he heard a a small voice speak his name.

"David," Margie said, picking herself off the floor, "I want to talk to you—in my room." The moment Margie ordered him to her bedroom, David's adrenaline kicked in, and two quick scenarios flashed before him. Margie would either kick him in the balls or rip off all his clothes and smother his naked body with hot, wet kisses.

An audible whimper escaped from him as he caught sight of her inviting, sleep-rumpled queen-sized bed. He became aroused at the thought of how Margie's beautiful body twisted and turned the previous night to make all this appetizingly delicious dishevelment. The idea of lying with her among the rumples was abruptly dispelled by the sound of a bottle of Tweed toilet water crashing against a wall.

"I had to do that," Margie explained, "and I hope you know why I did it."

"Oh, I do," David lied. "I sure do."

"Why?" she demanded.

"Why what?" he stalled.

"You don't know, do you, David?"

"Sure I do," he insisted as he reached for the doorknob.

"Don't lie to me, David. You don't know what I'm talking about," she cried out. "And why is your hand on the doorknob? You don't want to know, do you?"

"I absolutely do," he said, backing away from the door.

"David," she announced as she flung the door open, "you can leave if you want."

"I'll be happy to leave, I mean, if that's what you want."

"What I want," she pleaded as she slammed the door shut and locked it, "is for you to understand why I tore up my mother's dress and why I threw her bottle of toilet water against the wall."

"I think maybe," he ventured cautiously, "that you're mad at your mother for flirting with me and forcing me to dance with her and kissing me."

Margie flung her hairbrush against the wall.

"You didn't see her kissing me when you came in, did you?" he rushed to explain. "I shouldn't have told you. It's my fault."

"Your fault, your fault!" she screamed wildly as she rushed at him.

To ward off what looked like a major physical assault, David threw his arms up in front of his face.

"Nothing is your fault, my darling David," she cried, flinging her arms around him with such force that the bones in his neck cracked.

"Thank you, God, for sending me David Kokolovitz to love and understand me," she cried out as she showered his face and neck with wet kisses.

David had no choice but to put his arms around her and fight back, with tighter hugs and squeezes and deeper, wetter kisses. Within minutes, two of his fantasied images had come true. He was naked and lying in Margie's cozy, Tweed-scented, rumpled bed, *and* he had been kicked in the groin. Inadvertently, Margie had kneed him there when she lovingly but without warning tried to push her thigh between his legs. With an abject apology and her sweet, warm lips, she attempted to heal his "boo-boo" by gently kissing every part of his body but the part she had accidentally bruised. Margie had vowed that she would never kiss that part of a man unless that part belonged to her husband or at the very least her fiancé. David had made no such vow about kissing that part of a woman, and during their passionate foreplay, he was strongly tempted to experiment. He found himself spending an inordinate amount of time licking her belly button and the area just above her pubic hair, and he sensed that had he gone for it, Margie would have been receptive, but he could not risk her thinking that he was a pervert, the current opinion of the gang of guys who hung out in front of the neighborhood candy store.

David reluctantly retreated from the taboo territory and went back to nuzzling Margie's full, warm breasts. Aroused as he was, David did not feel at ease climbing on top of Margie, and he froze when he heard Mrs. Skulnik moving about the apartment. He kept throwing quick, nervous glances toward the door, hoping to climax before Mrs. Skulnik burst in with a policeman and had him arrested for contributing to the delinquency of a minor. Margie would not be eighteen for two weeks, and each time he had sex with her, he worried that he was breaking not only God's law but a federal statute as well. With his mind so filled with fear and guilt, he climaxed even more quickly than usual and a very few moments later was reaching for his jockey shorts. Margie, who had been lying quietly and observing him, suddenly reached out, grabbed the shorts out of his hands, and pleaded with him to lie down next to her for a little while longer.

"You know what I'd rather do," he suggested, playfully wresting his shorts back from her. "Go down to the deli and share a corned-beef sandwich with you, my treat. I've got some very, very exciting news to tell you."

"You've enlisted in the army?" she asked fearfully.

"Much more exciting than that," he boasted, pulling on his trousers.

"The marines! Oh, David, not the marines!"

"No, not the marines," he joked as he picked her brassiere off the floor and playfully tossed it at her.

"The air corps?"

"Something even more thrilling than dropping bombs on Nazis. Let's just say that it may be the best thing that's happened to me in my whole life," adding hastily as she started to pout, "Except for you, Margie! I'll tell you all about it at the deli."

After accepting the fact that David would tell her nothing until they reached Hitzig's Delicatessen, Margie dressed quickly and ushered David through the living room and past her mother, who was sitting stiffly in a hard-back chair, staring intently at her new, mahogany-cabineted Magnavox, superheterodyne radio and pretending to be engrossed in the tribulations of *One Man's Family.*

David waited in the hall and was amazed to hear Mrs. Skulnik sounding calm and civil.

"I suppose, Margie darling, that after noshing a greasy, corned-beef sandwich," she said, turning down the volume on a Rinso commercial, "you won't want to eat the lovely tuna-fish salad I've just finished preparing for our lunch."

My God, her mother heard everything, David thought. What a strange lady! She knew her daughter and I were screwing in the bedroom, and instead of coming in and throwing a bucket of cold water on us or bashing my ass with a broom, like most mothers would, she's in the kitchen making tuna-fish salad. David peeked into the apartment and saw Margie pick up a glass-sculptured mermaid from the coffee table, wondering whether she planned to throw it against the wall.

"Mother darling," Margie trilled sweetly, hefting the heavy glass sculpture, "since I'm never coming back to this apartment, ever, I'm taking my mermaid with me."

With that, Margie whirled around, stomped out of the apartment, and joined David in the hall.

"I love this so much," she explained as she caressed the mermaid's torso. "My daddy gave it to me for my birthday, and since *I'm never coming back here, ever!*" she screamed for her mother's benefit, "I couldn't leave it there."

Before her mother could react, Margie steered David toward the stairway. He wondered as they ran down the three flights to the lobby what the hell Margie meant when she screamed out that she was never coming back, ever. Did she really mean never, ever, or was it just something she always threatened when she and her mother had a dress-ripping fight. David waited till they were in the street and heading for Hitzig's Deli before broaching the subject.

"Margie, what did you mean when you yelled out that you were never coming home again, ever?"

"Just what I said, I'm leaving for good."

"C'mon, Margie, where are you going to live?"

"With you," she said matter-of-factly, and ran off down the street.

David let Margie get twenty paces ahead of him before shouting, "You can't live in my house!"

Margie smiled at him and raced ahead. He could have caught up with her, but at this moment he was not sure what he wanted. He had never seen Margie behave this way before, but as he trotted behind her toward the restaurant, he could not help marveling at how beautiful she was and how gracefully she ran on those long, perfect legs. I'm a lucky guy, he thought, to be in love with a girl like that who has told me so many times how she loves me more than anybody in the whole universe. He thought, too, about how really little he knew about this strange girl with the long, wavy blond hair and sensational figure who less than five months ago had come backstage after seeing him perform in *The Bishiop Misbehaves* and told him what a wonderful, brilliant actor she thought he was and how attractive he looked onstage and how handsomer he was in person. She's perceptive, she's honest, and she has taste. What more do you have to know about a girl? So she's a little emotional; so what? She's beautiful, and she's exciting, and she's the only girl I know who lets me make love to her almost anytime I want. What if she's a little crazy? She's more beautiful than she is crazy. I'm not going to find anyone better.

He found his girl sitting on a soda case in front of Hitzig's, laughing hysterically.

"The expression on your face, David, when I said I would live with you, it was priceless."

"So you were just kidding?" he asked.

"I'm starving." She smiled devilishly and danced into the restaurant and over to the sandwich counter where the five-foot-two Hitzig was dropping a fifteen-pound cooked brisket of beef into a top-loading steam cabinet.

In thirty years of loyal and uninterrupted service the old, dented metal box had steamed thousands of fat-laced slabs of Hitzig's renowned corned beef and equally acclaimed peppered Romanian pastrami. Except for a bearded eighty-five-year-old man who bent over his glass of hot tea, David and Margie had the restaurant to themselves. It was only ten-thirty, but the morning's activities and the seductive aroma of the steaming meats made David ravenous. When he heard Margie blithely order two very lean corned-beef sandwiches, he vigorously explained that it was the fat that gives the corned beef its taste.

"And it's the fat," Margie countered, "that gives women those big behinds. Would you like me to end up with a behind like my mother's?"

David had found Mrs. Skulnik's behind quite sexy but wisely chose not to comment.

"Oh, by the way, Margie," he began casually, "in all the excitement this morning I didn't get a chance to tell you the good news. Well, first off, I quit my job at Foreman's . . ."

Before David could tell her why, Margie smacked him hard on his shoulder.

"Oh, no, no," she cried. "David, tell me you're joking! You didn't quit your job, did you?"

"I did, but it's nothing to get upset about, Margie."

"Why didn't you tell me this before I told my mother that I wasn't coming back. David, I was counting on that money!"

"What money?"

"Your salary!"

"My salary?" David's voice rose an octave. "You were counting on my salary for what?"

"For the little apartment I was going to rent," she explained, sinking into a chair. "I'm not going back to my mother. You heard me tell her that, didn't you?"

"I thought you were just saying that because of what happened."

"Yes, David," she snapped, "but I wouldn't have said it if I knew that you didn't have a job."

"Fifty cents!" Hitzig said as he placed the steaming sandwiches on the counter.

David paid and carried their lunches toward a table.

"What my mother did to you," Margie said, trailing after him, "she's tried to do with every boyfriend I ever brought home."

"She didn't do anything to me, Margie."

"She never does anything, David. Do you know what I mean when I say she never does *anything?*"

"Well, sure . . ."

"No, you don't, David! Do you know why my father had an affair with my aunt Francine?"

"I didn't know that he did."

"Everybody knew. After I was born, my mother decided to become a virgin again."

"Really?" an embarrassed David joked. "How did she do that?"

"My mother is a sick woman, and if I don't get out of the house, I'll become just like her. You understand that, don't you, David?"

All David understood was that he had suddenly lost his appetite for the beautiful, fatty corned-beef sandwich that sat before him.

"Margie honey," he began gently, "you didn't let me finish what I was telling you. The reason I quit my job is because I accepted another job with a Shakespearean touring company."

A second after the word *job* fell from his lips, an ear-piercing screech escaped from Margie, followed by a glass crashing to the floor.

"Oi gevalt! I dropped my glass of tea," the old man rasped. "Who's screaming like that?"

"How much money a week will they be paying you in this new job?" Margie asked eagerly.

On learning what David's weekly salary would be, she let out another high-decibel shriek, but this time the old man had no glass to drop.

"A zoo," he muttered, "she belongs in a *zoo.*"

"Wow! Thirty dollars a week for four months? David, how much does that come to?"

"Oh, roughly"—he could not resist boasting—"about five hundred and twenty-five dollars."

When David saw Margie's eyes widen, he wished that he had kept his big mouth shut. He clenched his body and waited to hear the plan she'd hatched and which he was sure to veto.

"Oh, David, David, David," she screamed, *"Now we can get married!"*

Margie's explosive proposal elicited a snide *"Mazel tov"* from the old man and a barely audible "Wha?" from David. He spent the next ten minutes trying to stop Margie from alternately hugging him, jumping up and down in place, and loudly insisting that a town-hall wedding this Saturday afternoon and a week's honeymoon at Niagara Falls was a perfect plan.

"Margie, listen to me, will ya?" he said, grabbing her shoulders. "I'm leaving Sunday for a tour of the South, so I can't do any of the things you're asking me to do! Can you understand that?"

"I got it!" she screamed, jumping up and knocking over her chair. "I'll go with you, and we'll get married in Atlanta! Oh, David," she squealed as she wrapped her arms around his neck, "we'll be like Scarlett O'Hara and Rhett Butler! Wouldn't that be romantic?"

David knew better than to disagree with a person who was hanging from his neck and kissing him hard and repeatedly. She was obviously possessed and had to be handled delicately. With all the theatrical skills at his command, he agreed that getting married where Rhett and Scarlet did was a "swell idea and really, really romantic."

"You know, Margie," he said, putting his hand on her shoulder and sounding like old Judge Hardy giving sage advice to his son Andy, "if you were to ask most people what they thought about a boy and girl our age, in love and in our financial position, running off to Atlanta to get married, I think they'd say that it was a really stupid thing to do."

"Who cares what they say? What do you say, David?"

"I'd say," David said, looking into her eyes and using his deepest, most serious voice, "that those people sure made a lot of sense."

"And I say, David, that you don't really love me."

"Of course I love you."

"You're not serious!"

"I am serious."

"David, if you were serious, you wouldn't be doing your impression of Lionel Barrymore."

"Lewis Stone," he corrected. "Lewis Stone played Judge Hardy."

"David, you were talking like Lionel Barrymore."

"You're wrong, Margie. I don't do Lionel Barrymore!"

"Why do you have to impersonate anybody when I'm talking about our future together?"

David had no answer, or none that Margie would have liked. He simply apologized and suggested that they eat. A slightly nauseated David toyed with his sandwich while Margie hungrily attacked hers. With her mouth filled with corned beef, she laid out an extraordinarily detailed plan for the rest of their lives. For their immediate future she suggested a small but beautiful wedding in an Atlanta synagogue.

"And David, if there are no synagogues in Atlanta, then we'll find a nice Jewish judge to marry us, and after our honeymoon, I'll go back to the Bronx and furnish a darling little inexpensive one-room apartment with money that you send from the part of your salary that you don't need for food and incidentals."

As she continued, David, who had a fixed smile on his face, began to wonder who this prattling person was, this girl whom he thought he could not live without. "Of course, we won't have children," she announced blithely, "not right away, anyway, or who knows, maybe never."

It was during this last part of Margie's litany that David realized that he did not love Margie nearly as much as she loved him. He started to question what there was about her that he loved. Certainly he loved the way she was built and the way she always said yes to sex and the confident way she told him that someday he would be a big Hollywood star. As he stared forlornly at his untouched sandwich and heard how his young life was being mapped out for him by a person about whose judgments he had serious doubts, he realized that from then on he must be exceedingly careful. Whatever I say, he thought, it must be positive and contain a sizable loophole through which someday I may have to crawl. Unfortunately, Margie concluded building her air castles before David had created that all-purpose magic comment.

The best he could muster was: "Hey, Margie, you're amazing. Just now, when you were making all those plans, I swear you looked and sounded just like Carole Lombard!"

As David turned down the cluttered alley leading to the stage door of the Marlowe Theatre, he suddenly became saddened by the thought that in a week he would be leaving this nest of theatrical security to join a strange new company where it was likely that he would no longer be "the best one." It was not only his mother's opinion, but he sensed that Mr. Marlowe agreed that he was something special. He had never actually complimented David on his acting ability, but in the theater's ten-year history, Don Coleman was the only actor to have asked Marlowe to be paid and actually got the old man to agree to do so. David never had the pleasure of boasting about this singular honor because of a pact he made with Marlowe on that memorable first payday.

"Don, my boy," Marlowe had threatened as he stuffed a sealed envelope into David's jacket pocket, "if ever you divulge to anyone that I am giving you this money, you will be summarily fired."

David had no fear of being fired, for his replacements were apprentices who, talentwise and heightwise, would be unacceptable to Marlowe's six-foot daughter, Angela.

For the past year David had enjoyed being the biggest fish in a small pond, but now he wondered about the size of the fish in the big, new pond and how deep the water might be. It could well be that he was getting in over his head, but this disquieting feeling left him as soon as he knocked on Mr. Marlowe's dressing-room door.

"Larrimore, goddamit," he heard Marlowe bellow, "I told you I don't want to be awakened until the half hour! Now that I'm up, bring me a fresh bottle."

"It's not Larrimore," David explained." It's Don Coleman."

"Well, come in and shut the door," he bellowed.

David was always amazed at how this unpleasant, bent seventy-nine-year-old man could, with minimal makeup and a quick hair brushing, transform himself into a sober, benign, and handsome English bishop.

"I'm glad you dropped by, boy. I was about to send Larrimore to fetch you."

During the previous evening's performance David had come a hairbreadth away from stepping on one of the old man's biggest laugh lines, and he was sure that Marlowe was going to remind him again that killing a star's laugh was an unpardonable theatrical sin.

While Marlowe was taking a swig from the cough-medicine bottle that held his evening's supply of Jack Daniel's, David started to apologize.

"What happened last night in the second act, Mr. Marlowe, was that a man in the first row coughed just as you said, 'Poppycock,' and I didn't think the audience heard you say, 'Poppycock,' so I didn't think they'd laugh."

"But they did laugh."

"I know," explained David eagerly, "that's why I hesitated and split my line in two."

"And that is why you are the only member of my company who gets a weekly pay envelope. Tonight, Don, my boy," he continued after taking another swig from his bottle, "during the curtain call, I want you to do something for me, if you will."

"Oh, I will, sir. What is it?"

"Don, you know when I step forward to thank the audience and say, 'If you liked our little show, knock on your neighbor's door and tell them about it, but if for some reason you didn't like it, don't knock'?"

"Yes, sir," David answered having no idea what the old man was getting at.

"Well, while the audience is laughing and I am bowing, I want you to step forward, hold your hand up, and ask for silence, but don't start talking before the laugh starts to die down."

David was completely confused. He had often heard Mr. Marlowe instruct the entire cast not to move a muscle during his curtain speech and final bow. I can hear your eyeballs move, he would say, so if you want to remain a member of this company, you will keep your eyes riveted on me until the curtain is down!

"Mr. Marlowe," David asked as the old man took another pull from his medicine bottle, "what am I supposed to say?"

"You will say, 'Ladies and Gentlemen,' " Marlowe began, storing the bottle in the pocket of his bishop's frock, " 'today is the seventieth birthday of our beloved director and founder of the Marlowe Theatre of the Performing Arts, and I would appreciate it if you would all join me and the rest of the cast in wishing him another seventy years of health by singing Happy Birthday, Mr. Marlowe.' Here, Don, I've written it down. I trust that you will learn it and say it exactly as I've written it, and most important, it must sound spontaneous and heartfelt. Do you think you can do that?"

"I'm sure I can, Mr. Marlowe, but what about Angela. I mean, Miss Marlowe? Won't it sound better if your daughter did it?"

"My daughter is a ham! If she did it, it'd sound rehearsed and insincere. Don, you do it!"

To indicate that he would brook no further discussion of the matter, Mr. Marlowe turned his back, unzipped his fly, and shuffled to the sink. Legitimate theaters built during the turn of the century had no private toilets except in the star's dressing room, and since the star's toilet had been broken for years and the old man refused to spend money to repair it, he shamelessly peed in the sink whenever the urge came upon him.

Riding a sudden and unexpected wave of confidence, David blurted out, "Sir, I thought I should tell you that after Saturday's performance I'll be leaving the show."

David knew he was in trouble when he heard the flow of urine stop abruptly. He stood motionless and watched the old actor turn his head toward him while keeping his hips over the sink.

"Sir, I've been here for a year, and this opportunity to go with a Shakespearean repertory came along and —"

Marlowe's fiery stare stopped David dead. He then turned his back and finished urinating.

"Don, I am sorely disappointed," the old man said, zipping up his fly, "that you would stoop to this!"

"Stoop to what?" David asked ingenuously.

"Oh, come, boy, you know and I know that there is no Shakespearean touring company" Marlowe laughed, "You want a raise, don't you? Pretty circuitous way of asking for one. Okay, Don, I hear you. Now, none of the other cast members know about our little arrangement, or have you gone and blabbed about it?"

"No, sir," David said, trying to keep the sarcasm out of his voice. "I have told no one that you pay me one dollar a week."

"Good, good, Don," the old man said, patting David on the arm. "That kind of loyalty deserves to be rewarded. Although I am a little baffled as to why you would invent this touring-company thing just to ask for a raise. By God, if anyone deserves a raise, you do, and I'm sorry that you had to dissemble to get it."

"I didn't dissemble, Mr. Marlowe," David shot back, assuming that dissemble meant lying. "I didn't invent the touring company to get a raise."

"Well, whether you did or not, Don, my boy, as of this week," the old man said, growing expansive, "I am going to fatten your pay envelope substantially."

David had no thought of accepting Marlowe's offer but, curious to know what Marlowe meant by substantially, asked, "How much were you going to fatten my envelope?"

"By twenty-five percent," Mr. Marlowe announced as he unsheathed an El Producto cigar, "and I think that is more than generous."

"Twenty-five percent?" David shouted. "You're offering me a quarter raise?"

"That's right," Marlowe answered, misreading David's response, "and keep your voice down. Yes, you'll be getting a dollar twenty-five a week, and I trust you will continue to keep it our little secret!"

Anxious for the old man to know how ridiculous he thought the offer was and trying to remain civil, David explained that he had been offered thirty dollars a week to act in the repertory company. On hearing this, Marlowe turned his back to David, lit his cigar, and stared at the ceiling.

"Don Coleman," he said resignedly, "because I feel that you have the potential to be a truly fine actor, I am willing to overlook your little ploy and make you a very generous but final offer. Don, if you promise never to come up with any more transparent schemes to extort money from me, I will add another twenty-five percent to my first offer."

"Mr. Marlowe," David protested, "I am not trying to extort money from you. I was offered thirty dollars a week to—"

"Two dollars and not a penny more!" boomed Mr. Marlowe. "Take it or leave it! Just know that by taking this money you will have lost my respect. Now get out of my sight."

David started to respond, but Marlowe threw up his hands and waved him off. David turned to leave, but before he could escape, Marlowe grabbed his arm and spun him around.

"And, Mr. Coleman," the old man growled, his face a few inches from David's, "at the curtain call tonight, you are relieved of the honor of leading the audience in the salute to my birthday. I will do it myself. Now go!"

During David's last week of performances, the old man ignored him completely and went out of his way to say a perfunctory but pleasant good night to every member of the cast but the blackmailing, traitorous ingrate of a leading man. In spite of this leprous treatment, David dared, after his last performance, to knock on Mr. Marlowe's dressing-room door and ask if he might come in. He was prepared to thank Mr. Marlowe for the wonderful opportunity he had given him, but before David could speak, the old man, as he had done every Saturday for months, pushed a small envelope into David's pocket. Ordinarily, David did not take the envelope out of his pocket until he was a safe distance from the theater but this evening he retrieved it immediately, tore it open, and handed one of the dollar bills back.

"This really isn't mine, Mr. Marlowe," David explained as Marlowe eyed him suspiciously. "I'm sorry there was a misunderstanding, but I wasn't asking for a raise when I told you about the touring company. I really was offered that job."

Marlowe fingered the dollar bill and glowered as David started for the door.

"Just a moment, young man!" Marlowe roared. "Come back here! Take the damned money, you earned it!"

This action produced the only moment of sentiment that the two of them had ever experienced together. David would remember, too, the feeling he had when he discovered that penurious, old John Marlowe had not returned his dollar but had replaced it with a brand-new five-dollar bill. David was shaken. From this fine old actor he had received the greatest compliment of his young career.

Carrying his new and bulging Gladstone bag and wearing a broad-shouldered, double-breasted blue serge suit that he had bought at Ripley's for $12.50, David Kokolovitz picked his way through the morning crowd of commuters in Pennsylvania Station to the information desk, where he learned that the train to Atlanta was leaving on track 14. When David arrived at the gate, he was stunned to see a flushed and worried Margie Skulnik obviously searching for his face in the crowd. What is she doing here? he thought. Just a few hours ago, didn't I bid her a long, emotional farewell and promise to write her every day and call every other week? So why had she come to Penn Station when they had agreed that it would be easier for both if she didn't? It couldn't be that she had made the long subway ride from the Bronx just to deliver the box of Schiller's pastry that she now held gingerly by the strings.

"David," she screamed on spotting him, "I have something extremely important to give you."

Cheese Danish isn't that important, David thought as she raced to him and handed over the grease-stained box. From the intense look in her eyes David surmised that there was something beside pastry stimulating her.

"The Danish," she explained as she fished excitedly in her oversized purse, "is a present from my mother, who said she hopes bygones can be bygones."

Margie squealed as she retrieved an unprepossessing piece of white tissue from her purse.

"This, David," she announced as she lovingly unfolded the paper and displayed a shiny gold ring, "is for you!"

"What is it?" he asked, knowing full well what it was.

"It's a friendship ring, David. I got it at Sharf's Jewelry!"

"It looks like a wedding ring."

"That's what *I* said," she admitted, "but Mr. Sharf said a ring could be anything you want it to be. Well, I want it to be a very, very, extra-special friendship ring."

"You shouldn't have," David protested.

"I wanted to. I felt so bad that night when you gave me this," she said, extending her hand to display the fifty-cent silver-plated snake ring that he had presented to her after their first sexual encounter, "and I never gave you anything in return."

"No, Margie, you've given me a lot," David said, thinking of all the times she had said yes to him.

"Please, David, please," she pleaded, her big eyes looking up at him imploringly, "put it on."

"I can't take this," he said, examining the ring. "It's genuine four-teen-carat gold. It must have cost a fortune."

"I bought it on the installment plan," she explained excitedly. "Only twenty-five cents a week!"

"For how many weeks?"

"What's the difference, David, it's only a quarter." She giggled, taking his right hand. *"Ooh,* I hope it fits."

David watched helplessly as Margie isolated his ring finger and slipped the wedding band smoothly past the first knuckle, quickly discovering that no matter how she jiggled and forced it, the ring would not go over the second one.

"If only I had some soap," she prayed.

Settling for spit, she suddenly rammed his finger into her mouth and ran her warm, wet tongue up and down and around the ring, unaware that she was embarrassing and arousing him. She retrieved his wet finger and tried vainly to force the ring past his reddening knuckle. She accelerated her efforts when the platform conductor sang out: "Boooaaarrrd!"

"Wait a minute, will ya?" a panicking Margie shouted back. "I almost got it on!"

Informed by the pain in his finger and worried about missing the train, David reclaimed his hand and wrenched the ring off.

"Margie, face it," he said, handing her the salivaed ring and moving toward the gate, "it's too small. Why don't you take it back and exchange it for one that isn't so expensive, maybe one that's silver-plated and looks more like a friendship ring."

When he dropped his bag to show his ticket to the conductor, Margie grabbed David's left hand and with cobralike speed, effortlessly slipped the gold band on his ring finger.

"There, it fits like a glove," she announced triumphantly as she threw her arms around David's neck and kissed him with a verve and passion that, in a less public environment, David would have enjoyed immensely. They stayed glued to each other's mouths until a second "Boooaaard," shrilly delivered a foot from their ears, caused them to spring apart. As David walked briskly along the platform and boarded the monstrously long train that was waiting to transport him to his new life, he wondered whether there was any way he could not have promised a begging, tearful Margie that he would never, ever, remove her ring from his finger.

From the moment the train pulled out of Penn Station, David's attention shifted from the ring on his finger to his new and exciting surroundings. David, who had ridden on subways and elevated trains all of his young life, was amazed to see how different New York looked from the window of a real railroad car. While appreciating the new and fascinating sights that passed by outside, David became drawn to one inside the car and seated directly in front of him. It was a beautiful head of sparklingly clean, straight golden-blond hair that was being brushed by the delicate and graceful hand of its obviously proud owner. He became mesmerized watching the ivory brush engraved with the initials H.K. slide smoothly through the long, silky tresses. David thought, Probably doing the recommended one hundred strokes. He'd seen Margie brushing her hair, but not with the verve and dedication of this young girl. Her hair seemed young, so he assumed that she was, too. He knew he would ultimately see her face, but he was enjoying the mystery. He was suddenly in Hitchcock's *Thirty-nine Steps.* How to make this beauty turn around? I could, he thought, go to the toilet and sneak a look on the way back. No, not very suave. I'll just tap her on the shoulder and say, Miss, you can stop brushing; your hair is perfect! While considering his options, a strand of her blond hair floated down and came to rest on his knee. He felt a sudden excitment as he looked down at the long golden thread lying on his blue serge trousers. Gingerly, he picked it up and examined it. He smiled and thought of his mother. "Again you were with that Margie!" she would admonish him every time she found a blond hair on his clothes. "David," she'd say, "it's not healthy to be with a girl so often!"

David held the single strand of hair between his thumb and forefinger and, while contempating his next step, impulsively reached forward and held it in front of the girl's face.

"Pardon me, miss," he said, "is this lovely strand of spun gold yours?"

David had to assume that his lighthearted attempt at humor had failed when the stranger shrieked in terror, bolted from her seat, and ran whimpering up the aisle, tripping and falling twice before she arrived at the lavatory. David immediately started to perspire, wondering what he had done to provoke such behavior. When he dared to look up, he discovered that his fellow passengers did not seem at all concerned that a girl had just screamed and dashed madly to the toilet. I guess, he thought, passengers on railroad trains are more blasé about things than people who ride the subways. Feeling responsible for the girl's condition, David considered knocking on the lavatory door and apologizing but worried that it might make things worse. More than ten minutes had passed since she ricocheted her way up the aisle, and he wondered what the hell she was doing in there. How long should it take a normal person to realize that a playful stranger had made a bad joke? She's probably not a normal person, he concluded. He pulled a small, fat, leather-bound book from his canvas knapsack and thought, I'll study one of the plays that I'm supposed to get familiar with. The casting director, Mr. Case, had told him that this season the company would be performing four plays, *As You Like It, The Taming of the Shrew, The Comedy of Errors,* and *Hamlet. The Comedy of Errors* seemed appropriate to him. This blond fruitcake, he reasoned, might be soothed if she saw him studying Shakespeare.

The day he was accepted into the company, David had skipped his lunch hour, rushed to a secondhand bookstore, and for thirty-five cents bought this brittle, dog-eared, leather-bound, complete works of the Bard that was marked to sell for $1.25.

David glanced up to see three of his fellow passengers standing at the lavatory door, impatiently waiting for the blond hysteric to finish her ministrations. He sighed in sympathy, put his thumb into the indent that read, *Comedy Error,* flipped the book open and read:

THE COMEDY OF ERRORS

SCENE: *Ephesus*

Act I

SCENE I: *A hall in the* DUKE's *palace.*
Enter DUKE, AEGEON, Gaoler, officers, and other attendants.
AEGEON: Proceed Solonius to procure my fall / And by the doom of death end woes and all.

After reading those first few lines of the play, a few gnawing questions arose in David: Where the hell is this Ephesus? Is it a real country or one William Shakespeare invented, like Freedonia was invented for the Marx Brothers' *Duck Soup?* And how do you pronounce AEgeon, and why are the first two letters of his name capitalized, and what did AEgeon mean when he said, "Proceed Solonius to procure my fall"? David read a half paragraph of Solonius's reply and became deeply concerned about having to memorize and speak lines that made little or no sense to him. This was definitely going to be a major challenge to his career as a Shakespearean actor. Immmediately, he comforted himself by remembering that he had gotten this job by doing an emotional and flawless performance of Romeo's balcony-scene soliloquy. It was during that audition, when his adrenaline was flowing, that he first realized what Romeo actually meant when he said, "He jests at scars that never felt a wound." David hoped that in the coming weeks of rehearsal he would continue to have that kind of revelation. He wondered if the Selwin brothers expected him to know the meaning of all the lines he would be reciting and how they would react if he were to ask them to explain what they meant.

David reread AEgean's opening lines and was deep in concentration, wrestling with the meaning of Solonius's long-winded reply when he heard the soft, sweet voice of an angel.

"Are you Don Coleman?"

Without moving his head from the book, David looked up slowly to see who had spoken to him. Less than a few dozen people in the world knew of the existence of Don Coleman, and he was thrilled that one of the people who knew of him owned a sirenlike voice and the most beautiful face he had ever looked upon. Framing this blemish-free, milky-white visage was long, silken blond hair which cascaded down the back of the seat in front of him. He immediately recognized the hair as belonging to the girl who, fifteen minutes ago, he had caused to become unglued. He was thankful that her insanity was temporary and was about to apologize for frightening her when she spoke again.

"You *must* be Don Coleman."

"If I must, I must," he said hesitantly, hoping the small attempt at humor would not produce the same effect that his last one did. "How did you know my name?"

"I was told"—she smiled as she pushed a handful of her lustrous hair from her remarkable face—"that someone named Don Coleman might be on this train, and when I saw you reading Shakespeare, I knew it had to be you. Mr. Coleman, you *are* traveling to Atlanta to join the Avon Shakespearean Company, aren't you?"

"Yes, I am, and obviously you are, too, Miss . . . uh?"

"Troy," she said, extending her dainty white, ringless hand toward him. "Helen Troy," she added with a wide, breathtaking smile.

"Helen Troy"—he smiled back—"that's a beautiful name."

"It's not my real name," she admitted. "I changed it for the stage."

"Me, too," David rushed to confess. "Don Coleman is my stage name."

"Mister Coleman," she said, sliding into the empty seat beside him, "may I sit with you for a little while?"

"Yes, you may, Miss Helen Troy. You know, that name really suits you."

"Well, thank you, kind sir," she said, pulling all of her hair to the right side of her head and exposing her left ear. "My real name is not at all good for the stage."

David stared at her naked alabaster ear and thought, That's the kind of ear poets write odes to.

"Helen," he said, doing his best Groucho impression, "I'll tell you my name if you tell me yours."

"All right, Don. It can't be worse than mine. Are you ready?"

"Ready," he shot back.

"You first," she insisted as she let her hair fall back over her perfect ear.

David had misgivings about telling her that his real name was David Kokolovitz. From the clear way she spoke and her general mien, he assumed that she was not Jewish and suspected that she might be anti-Semitic. June Simpson, in his high school graduation class, who looked very much like this Helen Troy, had actually said to him when he asked her for a date, "Even though you're the nicest Jewish boy in the class, I wouldn't feel right going out with you."

"My real name is David Kolovitz," David said, shortening his name by one internal syllable. "Make that Kokolovitz," he added guiltily. "It's been so long since I've used it, and you can see why."

"Yes, I can see why," she agreed, "and I think it's wise that you changed it. I'll bet people always mispronounce it."

"Right, and they're always asking me to spell it, and it's embarrassing, because I'm really not that sure of the spelling."

"My real name is Katherine Kunts, and the problem I have," she continued gaily, "is that when I say it, it makes some people laugh, mainly men. They'll snicker and say something like 'Are you pulling my leg?' or, 'You must be kidding.' "

"And you have no idea," David asked, astounded at her naïveté, "why these men snickered?"

"Well, I imagine they thought Kunts is a silly-sounding name," she answered innocently, "although none of the girls at school ever laughed at it, and those girls were always ready to make fun of anything."

"What school is that?"

"Edgewater. It's a Presbyterian all-girls' school. You don't find my name silly, do you, Mr. Coleman?"

"No, not at all silly. In fact, it's sort of, uh, romantic."

"Really? No one ever told me that before."

David found it hard to believe that no one ever told her the accepted meaning of her name.

"Would you care to know," he asked, venturing to go where obviously no man or woman had ever gone before, "why men sometimes snicker when you tell them your name?"

"Do you know?"

He looked into her large, trusting eyes and weighed his options. He could tell her the truth and risk sending her into hysterics again, or he could tell her he didn't know what Kunts meant and thereby deny himself a potentially memorable experience.

"I think," he began cautiously, "that the reason some guys snickered is because there's a slang word just like it."

"What does it mean?"

"Well, it's a street word," he continued professorially, "that's often used in the, uh . . . street by rough types . . . to refer to a woman's, uh, privatest part."

"You mean," she said skeptically, "that Kunts means vagina?"

"Two!" David corrected. "Your name is plural."

Helen Troy stared at David in disbelief, then sat back in her seat and became rigid. David was about to apologize for carrying the bad tidings when she wheeled on him.

"I cannot believe that what you have told me is true."

"It's true," David mumbled.

"If it is, Mr. Coleman, then perhaps you can explain to me why my parents or my sisters or my friends or the teachers at Saint Mary's never bothered to tell me what you have just told me?"

"Maybe they didn't know," David responded. "Where're you from?"

"Canandaigua!" she challenged.

"That could be it!" he explained. "It's New York slang, and maybe nobody up there in Cana—"

"Contrary to what you may think of upper New York State residents, Mr. Coleman," she proudly instructed, "we have some degree of sophistication. We do own radios and read newspapers."

"I know. Canandaigua is a real up-to-date town," he lied, "but that slang word is not the kind you'd read in a newpaper or hear Jack Benny use on his radio program, but even if it's only known in New York City, I think you did a real smart thing by changing your name, and I honestly think that the name you chose is absolutely a stroke of genius. When I first saw you, I thought, and this is going to be hard for you to believe, I thought, My God, that girl is so beautiful. She looks like I always imagined Helen of Troy must've looked. Now, I wouldn't blame you if you said I was lying, because it does sound like bull I'm trying to hand you."

"I didn't think you were handing me bull manure, Mr. Coleman," she said, tossing her golden locks, "but maybe you'll think I'm handing you some when I tell you that my middle name is Helen and I was born in Troy, New York, and my Uncle Charles always called me Helen of Troy even when I was small, and I certainly didn't look like her then."

"Well, you certainly look like her now," David said, studying her face.

"You're being kind," she said coyly.

"No, I'm not. I'm being honest. Heck, if I owned a thousand ships and wanted them launched, you'd be the face I'd hire."

It took an uncomfortably long time for the small joke to register, but ultimately her face broke into a smile, and she told him that he was very clever.

"Mr. Coleman, I'm so glad you're going to be in Atlanta," she gushed, extending her hand. "I do hope we can be friends."

"I'm sure we can be friends, and who knows," David said playfully as he took her hand in both of his, "we might even be lovers."

When he read prehysterical panic in her eyes, David dropped her hand, patted his Shakespeare tome, and quickly explained, "Onstage lovers is what I meant. Like Petruchio and Katharina in *The Taming of the Shrew* or Orlando and, uh, what's her name in *As You Like It.*"

David observed that the panic in Helen of Troy's lovely eyes had turned to distrust, and he fought to make her understand that he was not flirting with her.

"I've got a girlfriend. See!" he said, pointing to the ring that had been forced onto his finger less than an hour ago.

Helen frowned and stared at the luggage rack overhead.

"I know this looks like a wedding band," he rushed to explain, "but my girlfriend said that the jeweler told her it was a friendship ring. She—"

"Rosalind!" Helen interrupted sharply.

"No, Margie," he countered.

"No, Rosalind in *As You Like It*. That's the character's name that you were searching for. I don't know who's going to play that part. Mr. Selwin just told me to familiarize myself with the whole play. Why did you think her name was Margie?"

"I didn't. Margie is the name of the girl I—"

"I think the other girl's part is Celia, but I'm not sure," she admitted. "It couldn't be Margie."

David decided there was nothing to be gained by setting the record straight and mumbled, "Yeah, you could be right, It's probably Celia."

"Well, why don't we find out," she said, snatching David's book from his lap, and finding the play. " 'Rosalind,' " she read loudly with an unconvincing English accent, " 'daughter to the banished duke and Celia, daughter to Frederick.' There!" She smiled triumphantly as she snapped the book shut and handed it back to him. "I knew it wasn't Margie. Margie doesn't sound like a name Shakespeare would use."

With the same dedication she used to get her flawless hair to look more perfect, Helen Troy stood up and smoothed out nonexistent wrinkles from her clinging jersey dress, moving her hands over her extraordinary body while regaling him with a never-ending list of the plays, poems, and monologues she had committed to memory. David was impressed by what he saw during her body-caressing exercise and could not help comparing Helen's figure to Margie's. He concluded that physically it was a toss-up. Helen Troy had movie-star hair, eyes, and face, Margie had a rounder and more alluring bosom, and although he could see only a bit of Helen's ankles, he had to assume that since Margie's were the prettiest legs in the world, they had to be better than this strange, talkative Canandaiguan's, who, like it or not, was going to be a part of his life for the next four months.

"I may not be the best actress in the world," she admitted as she concluded listing the things she had memorized, "but I do have a wonderful memory."

As she settled back in her seat, David decided that since he and Helen Troy would be working together it might be a good idea to find out what it was that so agitated her earlier.

"Miss Troy?" he said as softly as he could. "I think I owe you an apology."

She spun her head around so sharply that David was sure he had spooked her, but when he saw her mouth set in something resembling a smile, he breathed a sigh of relief.

"Please call me Helen," she said sweetly, "and why do you think you owe me an apology?"

"For scaring the daylights out of you."

"When did you do that?"

Boy, he thought, what an unexpected question coming from the self-proclaimed Queen of Memory.

"When I," he dared to remind her, "tried to return one of your beautiful hairs?"

"Oh, that. I'm sorry, Don—may I call you Don?"

"It's only fair."

"Don, I apologize for my behavior, but every so often, when someone touches me a certain way, I lose control."

"I'm sorry. I didn't know."

"It's not your fault. I wasn't always like that. It's just something I can't seem to shake."

"If you don't know why this happens," David suggested as delicately as he could, "maybe if you go to a—"

"I don't have to go anywhere," she interrupted, turning her body and bringing her face close to his. "I know why it happens. About a year and a half ago," she said, now speaking in a breathless whisper, "a man with a lovely speaking voice . . . very much like yours, tapped me on the shoulder and said that I had dropped my wallet. Well, when I started to turn to him, he grabbed my arms, pushed a gun against my throat, and told me to be quiet. Then he raped me."

"Gosh!" was all the response a completely staggered David could muster.

For the next few minutes, speaking forthrightly and without being asked, Helen Troy offered an explicitly detailed account of what she called "the most horrible and nightmarish experience of my life." In a detached, reportorial manner she recounted the entire assault, replete with the rapist's sadistic orders and embarrassingly graphic descriptions of what the rapist forced her to do. She described calmly "the devastating emotional and physical pain" she had to endure for the eight hours the ordeal lasted.

"Do you know, Don," she confided, "that you're the first person I have ever told this story to?"

"Really?" David stammered, "I'm honored. I mean—"

"Promise me," she pleaded, "that you won't tell another living soul what you have just heard. I don't want people to look at me and then think of me only as someone who has been raped."

David promised that he would keep her confidence, adding an ineffectual "I'm sorry, I really am."

"Thank you, Don," she whispered. "Someday, if I feel strong enough, I'll tell you the whole story."

"You mean . . ." he said, shaking his head in amazement, "that there's . . ."

Helen nodded sadly and then turned and settled back in her seat.

For the remainder of the trip to Atlanta, exchanges between David and Helen were minimal, limited to an occasional nod or smile or a "How're ya doin'?" Their most intimate contact came when he politely turned down a large macintosh apple she offered him. Why did I do that? he wondered. I'm starving. It's been hours since I've finished my mother's Spanish omelet sandwiches and Margie's cheese Danish. Why did I refuse a perfectly good apple?

David spent most of the trip to Atlanta either reading Shakespeare or trying to understand why he didn't take the damned apple. David was aware that there were many things in this world that he did not understand, and on his first day away from home, he added two more: Katherine Kunts and most of what Shakespeare wrote.

The Avon Shakespearean Company had remained solvent for most of its twenty-year existence due to the miserly managing of Harold and Raymond Selwin. Each fall season, by offering a menu of four beautifully costumed and acceptably acted productions, the brothers were able to enlist as benefactors most of the Deep South's culture-minded citizens. In his day, Harold Selwin, the handsomer of the two brothers, was considered to have star potential. His debut performance as the dashing Mercutio in John Barrymore's production of *Romeo and Juliet* received glowing reviews, and he was on the verge of a major career when, during the dueling scene at a matinee performance, he suffered a stroke and collapsed onstage. Subsequently, he regained limited use of his arms and legs, but the left side of his face remained immobile. All of this history David had learned from Clifford Case, the casting director who hired him, and David was thinking about it as the train pulled into the Altanta station.

Standing on the platform, waiting to meet the train, was a five-foot three-inch ferret of a man holding a handwritten sign that read Avon Shake Co. With minimum enthusiasm and politesse, the nervous little man with a leonine mane of gray-blond hair welcomed each new company member with a cursory handshake.

"I am Raymond Selwin," he announced in a deep, resonant voice that belied his 104-pound frame. "Just leave your luggage where it is and Beauregard will collect it."

"Y'all call me Bo," grunted a six-foot-four giant as he snatched David's bag from his hand.

"In five minutes, with balletic agility, Bo was able to collect all the actors' luggage and strap it securely onto the roof of a nine-passenger, wood-paneled, 1936 Chevrolet station wagon. After ushering everyone into the dusty, fender-dented wagon, Raymond Selwin took a healthy swig from his silver hip flask and settled himself behind the wheel.

"Before I answer any of your questions," he announced as he banged his foot on the clutch pedal and shifted the car into gear, "why don't we all say who we are. For those of you who don't know, I'm the co-owner and codirector of the company, and I'm happy to welcome you."

"I am August Shuttleworth, and I am not happy!" the bent old man seated directly behind Mr. Selwin declaimed. "I had to buy my own railroad ticket. Your representative, Mr. Case, did not send me one as he promised he would, and I'd like to be reimbursed for it."

"You will be reimbursed, sir," Raymond answered, jerking into second. "I'll inform our bookkeeper."

"You won't have to inform anybody if you give me money now," August Shuttleworth shouted. "I have been burnt before, Mr. Selwin, and once burnt—"

"Bo," Raymond Selwin ordered resignedly, "make out a check to Mr. Shuttlecock."

"It's *worth,* Mr. Selwin," August corrected as he leaned forward. "It's Shuttle-*worth,* and if it's all the same to you, I'd prefer cash."

Looking at August Shuttleworth's lined face in the rearview mirror, Raymond Selwin sighed wearily, thinking as he dug some money out of his pocket to give to the old fart, Just what this company needs, an eighty-year-old pain-in-the-ass malcontent.

As each actor introduced himself, David, who was in the rear seat of the station wagon, had only a back-of-the-head or profile view of his new male colleagues, but with this sparse information, he concluded that he might not be the handsomest guy in the bunch but he was definitely the most non-Aryan looking. Seated next to August Shuttleworth was one of the Aryans, who announced clearly and proudly that his name was Gaylord Morley. David thought, If that's his real name, real accent, and real hair, then he will probably get all the best parts. The seat next to Gaylord Morley was occupied by a girl with unkempt, mouse-brown, wispy hair who had to say her name three times, the first time because she spoke too quietly for anyone to hear and the second and third times because August Shuttleworth was too vain to wear his hearing aid.

"Speak up, speak up, Maggie!" August Shuttleworth scolded when he finally heard her. "We're going to be doing Shakespeare, and we want to be heard in the balcony, don't we? Now, Maggie, say your last name again. I didn't get it."

"Kulkas," she shouted, "and you didn't get my first name, either. It's Peggy, not Maggie!"

"Peggy?" he chided, giving her arm a friendly pat. "I think Maggie suits you better."

"And I think that Shuttle*cock* suits *you* better."

David was startled by the way Peggy emphasized cock. He had never before heard a girl use that word before so openly and with such good humor. He liked that. He also liked the sound of Peggy's soft voice, but he did wonder if it was strong enough to carry in a large theater. He wondered, too, what her face was like, having gotten only a fleeting glimpse of her when she slipped into her seat.

When an affected English-accented voice rang out from the rear— "Hello, people, I'm Helen Troy"—Gaylord Morley spun around, repeated his name, and held out his hand, which Helen warmly took in both of hers. As they held hands and agreed that meeting each other was a great, great pleasure, David experienced an unexpected sense of relief. He had assumed that he would be the one Helen Troy would be leaning on for her emotional security. After all, he was the one who taught her that her family name meant vagina, and he was the one she had sworn to secrecy about being sexually molested by an armed rapist. He was aware, too, that if she leaned on him too hard or too often, it would take superhuman strength for him to remain faithful to Margie Skulnik. Better, he concluded as he toyed with the ring on his finger, that she lean on Gaylord.

In the backseat of the station wagon, sitting between Helen Troy and David, was a thin, bored red-haired fellow who, with a three-pack-a-day resonance in his voice, announced that he was Eugene O'Neill.

"So as not to confuse me with that other guy," he added, lighting up a Camel, "call me Gene."

"Damn!" David exploded, slapping his hands together. "Two Eugene O'Neills in one company! What's the odds of that happening? Okay, Gene, you spoke up first, so I'll change my name to David Kokolovitz. No, wait, better make that Don Coleman. I think Beauregard's last name is also Kokolovitz. Right, Bo?"

Bo, whose bulk took up the two seats next to the driver, turned slowly and menacingly pointed a long, gnarled finger at David.

"You back there," he said in a Georgia-accented and surprisingly high pitched voice, "Mah name is Delahousay and not whut you said."

"Oh, sorry," David said, hunching his shoulders. "I thought it was Kokolovitz."

Bo stared at David for an uncomfortably long time before his heavy-lipped mouth broke into a gap-toothed grin.

"Y'all funnin' us," Bo said, slapping the back of his seat. "At's whut y'all wuh doin', wu'nt it?"

David, smiling broadly, admitted that he was "funnin'."

"Ah get it." Bo chuckled. "Beauregard don't fit with that for-eigner-soundin' name you said. 'At's damn funny."

So that he'd be able to spring this damn funny joke on his drinking buddies, Bo, for the remainder of the journey to the hotel, insisted that David teach him how to say Kokolovitz and "some more of those funny-soundin' Jew names."

David felt an odd sense of anticipation as he entered the once-elegant lobby of Atlanta's famous Hotel Tallulah. He had never before stayed at a hotel, and as he strode to the registration desk beneath the carved rococo arches and past the chipped but still-majestic marble pillars, he started to feel giddy. Hey, he thought, I'm walking through the same kind of lobby that Cary Grant and David Niven always walk through in their movies. Of course, the stars never carried their own bags. Knowing that it would cost him at least a nickel tip, David wrestled his bag away from a sixty-five-year-old bellboy and arrived at the front desk just as Raymond Selwin called his name and held out a key to-ward him.

"Don," Raymond said, checking a list, "you're in room 312. That's a single, and it's a dollar fifty a day."

Swift, probing glances were passed between the cast members when Selwin added, "Double rooms are two dollars, so if any of you want to pair up, you can each save fifty cents a day."

"I'm all for that!" August Shuttleworth cackled lasciviously, dis-playing a set of uneven, unbrushed yellowish teeth. "Now which one of you attractive gals wants to save yourself fifty cents a day?"

"Shuttleworth!" Raymond Selwin shouted disapprovingly. "You're in room 320, and settle down!"

As Raymond Selwin continued calling off room numbers and handing out keys, David noted that Eugene O'Neill and August Shut-tleworth were to be his third-floor neighbors. Helen Troy and Peggy Kulkas would be a floor below, occupying rooms 212 and 216, respec-tively, while Gaylord Morley, by fate or design, was assigned room 214, which David assumed was right smack between the two girls. Of course, David conceded, the handsome blond guy's going to get the best parts, why not the best room.

"This will be our home base for the next sixteen days," Raymond Selwin announced. "Rehearsals will be held in the Grand Ballroom, and since you have the formidable task of memorizing and rehearsing three plays in two weeks, we'll start work tomorrow morning and every morning at seven A.M. sharp and continue through to eleven P.M. You'll have a half hour for lunch, which the company will provide. However, you are free to buy your own lunch, which will probably cost you twice as much as what we will be charging you."

"For dinner," he pressed on, "you'll have forty-five minutes and be on your own. A list of clean, reasonably priced, fast-service restaurants in the area will be posted in the ballroom, and I recommend that you use them. For those who might want a snack before retiring, there's an all-night coffee shop right around the corner on Peachtree. Have a good night's sleep, everybody. I'll see you all in the Grand Ballroom at seven A.M."

Raymond Selwin turned sharply on his heels while delivering the last instruction and hurried from the lobby, leaving behind him a dazed, leaderless group of hungry, malcontent actors who at this moment were unsure of how to proceed with their lives. August Shuttleworth, having spent most of his life with traveling road shows, was the only one who knew what he had to do.

"If you will all excuse me," he announced, picking up his half-century-old carpetbag, "I am going up and soak these old bones in a tub of hot water, and you, Maggie dear," he added suggestively, encircling Peggy's slender waist, "are more than welcome to join me."

"Oh, fiddle-de-dee," Peggy drawled, fluttering her eyelids. "I wish I had known, but I went and soaked my bones last night. Sorry, Mr. Shuttlecock."

The old man took his arm from around Peggy's waist and whispered to David as he walked away, "That young lady will never know what she's missed."

Peggy's kittenish impression of Scarlett O'Hara tickled David, and he controlled an urge to hug her and say a word or two to Mr. Shuttleworth, whose propositioning a girl who could be his granddaughter repulsed him.

"There, my friends," Eugene said, his freckled Irish face in a bored expression as he blew a puff of smoke in the direction of the old actor, "you have a fine example of a genuine dirty old man in action. And Peggy, I suggest that you watch him like a hawk. He's definitely after your eggs."

"Folks, I've worked with old Gussie in stock," Gaylord Morley interjected, "and I assure you he's quite harmless, but how about this little lady. Did she ever handle the old coot beautifully? Hey, I'm starved! What say, gang, we drop our bags in our rooms and then all go out for a snack. Synchronize your watches and meet me here in nine minutes."

As the group cheered Gaylord and his great idea, David thought, Boy, just by complimenting Peggy, which I thought of doing, and suggesting we all go out for a snack, he's suddenly become our fearless leader. However, when Gaylord announced that the hamburgers and Cokes were his treat, David realized that he had hastily misjudged a man who possessed true leadership qualities.

Hanging askew on one of the filigreed elevator doors was a Temporarily Out of Order sign. The dog-eared sign had hung there for three months, waiting for the new owners to take over the hotel, which they were planning to do as soon as arrangements were made to relocate or evict all of the deadbeat residents.

In its seventy-two-year history, the Hotel Tallulah, formerly known as Harrington House, had gone through several incarnations. In its heyday, the stately, four-storied, red-brick edifice played host to the most fashionable and wealthiest of southern aristocracy. In the early 1930s, along with the rest of the country, Harrington House fell on hard times and was rescued from imminent demolition by Miss Tallulah Keenan-Forrest, a woman of rare beauty and intelligence. She renamed it the Hotel Tallulah, and for fifteen years, by paying her legitimate taxes and whatever reasonable bribes the local government officals requested, Madam Tallulah was able to successfully operate the cleanest and most frequented whorehouse in the county. When Madam Tallulah died in 1934, she bequeathed the rundown hotel to Flo and Lil, the two remaining hookers-in-residence. Unfortunately, Madam Tallulah left nothing to pay for the taxes and the hotel's upkeep. Flo and Lil were still fairly attractive and earned just enough from their profession to afford the bare necessities of life. With the present room rentals and the seventy-five dollars they received for the use of the ballroom, they had just enough money to allow "those lovely actors and actresses to finish practicing their Shakespeare plays" before the bank foreclosed.

After climbing three flights of stairs and inspecting his room, David learned that besides there being no elevators, there was also no hot water—or cold, for that matter. When David went to wash his hands, all that the nickel-plated faucet would expel was a series of spurts that rarely connected. He dried his hands on a tattered towel that had lost its fluff years ago.

David's spacious walnut-paneled bedroom boasted two large windows, one curtainless and one paneless, although boarded up. Lying on the sagging mattress of the unmade bed were two grayish-white un-

ironed sheets, a frayed blanket, and a disreputable-looking, stained pillow. David had seen enough movies to know that a chambermaid was
supposed to make up a guest's bed but surmised that here he was expected to be his own servant. Instead of being daunted by the seedy
room and the unappetizing bed, David felt strangely exhilarated by it
all. Even the sight of a tiny mouse scampering across the floor and es-
caping under the door did nothing to dampen his spirit. He thought, If
my mother saw that mouse running around the room and the bed I'm
going to sleep on, she'd call a cop to drag me home. But she's not here,
and I'm doing what I've always dreamed of doing, acting in a professional theater company and getting paid a real salary! He couldn't wait
to write Margie and explain how excited he felt to be on the road, living
in squalor.

David's stomach growled when he swung his suitcase onto the bed.
It reminded him that his host and leader had ordered everybody to
meet in the lobby in nine minutes. With two minutes to go and the clear
image of a juicy medium-rare hamburger dancing in his head, David
grabbed his jacket and headed for the lobby.

Coming down the stairs at a hungry man's pace, David almost
bowled over an attractive middle-aged woman.

"What's your hurry, young man?" she asked sweetly. "Whoever
she is, I'm sure she'll wait for you."

"I'm sorry," he explained, recovering the purse he had knocked
from her hand, "but I'm meeting some people in the lobby. We're
going out for a bite."

"Oh, that's wonderful," she said, fishing inside her red patent-
leather purse. "Would you be a darling and bring back a ham sandwich for me?"

Before David could decide if he wanted to be a darling, she took
his hand and pressed a dollar bill into it.

"On white with lettuce, tomato, and lots of mayonnaise. I'm in
317, and I'm a night owl," she added flirtatiously, "so just knock, Mr
. . . uh?"

"Coleman," he said, using his stage name comfortably now, "Don
Coleman."

"I'm Flo, and you won't forget the mayonnaise, Mr. Coleman?"

"I won't," he said, nervously fingering her dollar bill.

Wow, he thought as he barreled down the stairs, what beautiful
cleavage, and does she ever smell good. Was it his imagination, or had
the scent of Flo's potent perfume followed him down three flights of
stairs and into the lobby. Ten feet behind, Eugene O'Neill, who was in
David's flower-scented wake, wondered why this seemingly straight
actor smelled like a gardenia.

"Pardon me," Eugene said, tapping David on the shoulder, "but are you aware that you smell like a Turkish whorehouse?"

"It's not me"—David laughed, sniffing the dollar bill in his hand— "it's this dollar. It came from one of the hotel guests."

"Who is this guest who douses her money with aphrodisiacs?"

"She said her name was Flo," David answered, wondering what an aphrodisiac was.

"Redhead, about forty, short skirt, large mammaries?"

"That's her. D'you know her?"

"No, Donny boy," Eugene whispered conspiratorially, "but I'd be happy to."

Someone tapping insistently on a plate-glass window drew their attention to the front door. Standing on the street outside the hotel was Gaylord, gesturing to David and Eugene to join him and the girls.

As the five young actors started down the dimly lit street, Helen Troy slipped her arm through Gaylord's, announced cheerily that she could eat a horse, and then spontaneously burst into song. With Gaylord in tow and doing an enthusiastic but embarrassingly bad imitation of Judy Garland singing "We're off to see the Wizard, the wonderful Wizard of Oz," the two skipped their way down an imaginary Yellowbrick Road. David, by seeing the movie a half-dozen times and skipping up and down Tremont Avenue for hours with his friends Lenny and Shlermy, had mastered the cute crossover walking steps and was dying to show them how the number should be done. He was about to ask Peggy to be Dorothy to his Tin Man when Eugene O'Neill stepped up and offered her a cigarette.

"Those two happy campers," Eugene whined à la W. C. Fields as he struck a match, "are making me bilious. I hope neither of you are planning to skip after them."

Not wanting to appear square, David pooh-poohed the thought.

"I was," Peggy admitted, "but I won't if it'd make you throw up."

"You're very thoughtful," he said, offering her a light.

David felt a sense of isolation as he watched Peggy puffing on her cigarette. He thought, Eugene and Peggy have smoking in common, Helen and Gaylord have their blondness, and what I have is in the Bronx, a thousand miles away.

David sat on the outside seat of a corner booth eating his first southern-style hamburger, which, at fifteen cents, was three times as large but nowhere near as satisfying as the five-cent, soft-bunned White Castle miracles he loved dearly. He started to feel an uneasiness about his future. Eating an unsatisfying hamburger loaded with foreign-tasting sweet relish was depressing, and listening to Gaylord and Eugene intelligently discuss the sad state of the theater and the sadder state of the world was intimidating. That they were, respectively, five and six years older than he explained why they were more knowledgeable and sophisticated, and it augured badly for his place in the company.

Ambling back from the diner, Gaylord Morley and Helen Troy, arm in arm, were once again leading the way. Peggy Kulkas and Eugene O'Neill followed closely, with David lagging ten steps behind the pack and feeling alone and redundant. They had started walking back as a threesome, but Peggy and Eugene became deeply engrossed in a discussion to which he could make no contribution. They had both gone to Catholic schools and were trading stories about mean nuns and their creative disciplining. When they arrived at the hotel, Peggy was so absorbed in Eugene's tale of a sadistic Sister Elizabeth that she suggested that Eugene come to her room to continue recounting it. David was astounded at how casually Peggy made a suggestion that reeked of impropriety.

Gaylord and Helen waved good night to their colleagues and settled into a cozy corner of the lobby to continue talking about the theater and their dreams of starring on Broadway.

Following behind Peggy and Eugene as they mounted the stairway to their rooms, David observed that Peggy had a tight, attractive behind and quite shapely legs, notwithstanding the deep, one-inch, oval-shaped divot that was missing from the calf of her left leg. He was dying to ask Peggy if Sister Rebecca, a nun who walloped her in the face for talking during mass, was the one who was also responsible for gouging out the piece of flesh. Before reaching the second-floor landing, Peggy stopped short.

"Don," she said contritely, "Eugene and I have been very rude. We've been chattering away and have completely ignored you."

"Oh, that's all right," David lied. "I was interested in your stories. I had some rotten things happen to me in school, but no nun ever locked me in a closet for seven hours."

"Well, you were lucky," she said smiling, "you went to a school with nice nuns."

"Obviously, Don," Eugene chimed in, "you didn't go to school in Pittsburgh."

"No, the Bronx."

"The Bronx?" Peggy asked eagerly. "Not Saint Martin of Tours?"

"No, Saint Martin of Tremont," David joked. "My uncle Martin Meyerwitz. He's not really a saint, but he takes such crap from my Aunt Rose that my father says they should make him one."

David was relieved that Peggy and Eugene laughed. He felt a niggling sense of guilt for allowing them to think that he was Catholic. He had never hidden that fact that he was Jewish, but it always secretly pleased him when a Gentile assumed that he wasn't or, when they found out he was, told him that he didn't look Jewish. He was also pleased now to hear Peggy invite him to join her and Eugene in her room.

"Well, I don't know," he said, seeing Eugene arch his eyebrows and frown menacingly in his direction.

"C'mon, Don, it'll be fun," she urged.

"I'm pretty tired, Peggy," David said, faking a yawn. "I'll just go and deliver this ham sandwich."

As David stood before the door to Flo's room, without being aware he was doing it, he straightned his tie and checked his fly, the ritual he always used before going onstage. He took a deep breath, raised his hand, and jumped back a foot when the door opened before he could knock. Flo stepped forward, bringing her cleavage to rest inches from his face. Nestling in it was a huge silver cross. Boy, David thought, I am in the land of the Gentiles. Catholics, blondes, and crucifixes everywhere. Not since he pretended to read from the Torah at his bar mitzvah six years earlier had he felt so Jewishly Jewish.

"Here's your ham sandwich and your dollar, madam," he said in his best stage diction. "One of the actors paid for it."

"Well, if that's not the sweetest thing," she cooed. "D'y'all like to come in for a li'l ole visit?"

"I have a seven o'clock rehearsal tomorrow morning." he apologized, wondering what she meant by a "li'l ole visit." "Maybe another night."

"Dahlin', I always say," she said, running her tongue slowly across her lip, "a bird in your hand is better than no bird in my bush."

"That's interesting," he said, realizing that the woman with the crucifix on her chest was a hooker, "but I gotta get some sleep."

"Well, if you can't sleep, you know my room number," she said, blowing him a kiss.

The Grand Ballroom of the Hotel Tallulah was really a misnomer. It was no longer grand and had not been used as a ballroom since 1929 when Madam Tallulah threw a glittering New Year's Eve party to usher in that year of great promise and portent. Today the ballroom reflected none of its glory days. The enormous crystal chandelier that once filled the elegant ballroom with brilliant light from its dozens of bulbs now struggled to do the job with four sixty-watters.

When David opened the fifteen-foot-high, mahogany-paneled doors and stepped into the cavernous, dimly lit room, he was surprised to discover that he was alone and early.

It was clear from Raymond and Harold Selwin's posture and demeanor when they arrived minutes later that Harold was the more important brother. It seemed to David that Raymond Selwin had lost a lot of his personality since last night. His foot-and-a-half-taller brother Harold had a star's aura about him. He sported a gold-tippped cane and wore a black woolen cape, which, with one hand and the panache of a bullfighter, he swooshed from his shoulders and draped over one of four folding chairs Raymond had just carried across the room and placed there. This Harold Selwin, David thought, has even more style than old John Marlowe. It was not obvious that the left side of Harold Selwin's face and body were partially paralyzed. His still-striking profile, coupled with a large dash of vanity and an extraordinary acting ability, enabled Harold Selwin to use his impairment for dramatic effect. The slight quiver in his deep, gravely voice gave a riveting emphasis to everything he said. When he beckoned David to come closer to him, David quickly obeyed.

"Young man," he whispered, "tell me your name, clearly and with authority."

Clearly and with authority, David mused. I'll give him my Orson Welles. No one ever sounded clearer or more authoritative than Orson when he signed off on his Mercury Theater radio show with "I am your obedient servant . . . Orson Welles."

"I am," David answered, pitching his voice as deeply as it would go, ". . . Don Coleman."

"Now, I want you, Mithter Coleman," Harold Selwin continued, speaking slowly and quietly, "to repeat what I thay, uthing the exthact rhythm and emphathith."

So concerned was David about making a good first impression that he did not notice that Harold Selwin spoke with a pronounced lisp.

With a regal flourish, Harold Selwin raised his good arm above his head and, with his hand trembling noticeably, started to recite pedantically, in a mellifluous, quivering voice, the opening lines of *King Richard III*, which were "Now is the winter of our discontent / Made glorious summer by this sun of York."

Determined to follow Harold Selwin's direction to the letter and not unaware that he was mimicking a man who, ten years earlier, had suffered a massive stroke, David raised his arm above his head exactly as the old man had and proceeded to imitate precisely the subtle trembling of his hand, the contorted mouth, the quivering voice, and the articulated, fluttering lisp.

"Now ith the winter of our dithhcontent," David emoted, spraying saliva as his mentor had. "Made glorioth thhummer by the thun of York."

David felt satisfied that he had delivered a perfect impersonation of Harold Selwin's readings. The trembling hand and the subtle raspberry sounds the old man made with his tongue when he lisped, David assumed, were brilliant acting choices Mr. Selwin made to enhance the character of King Richard. Stunned by David's display, Harold Selwin turned to confer with his brother, who at that moment was having a life-threatening coughing fit, a condition brought on by trying not to laugh at the fartlike sounds David made impersonating his brother's lisp. An angry Harold Selwin studied David's eager face and decided that the neophyte had not been making fun of his impairment but was simply a blithe idiot with an uncommon gift for mimicry.

"Mithter Coleman," he repeated to unfreeze a petrified David, "thinthe my brother theems unable to get his cough under control, would you be tho kind and thet up four more chairth in a themi-thircle."

David, realizing what he had done, immediately grabbed a folding chair and snapped it open. He was deeply mortified and remained so until, in the men's room, he described to a bemused but sympathetic Eugene O'Neill how he had mimicked Harold's Selwin's "performanth of *King Richard the Thhhird.*" Later, at dinner, when he saw Peggy double over with laughter and spitting out french fries as he lisped his way through King Richard's speech, David's feeling like a schmuck all but left him. He never appreciated before how entertaining and endearing self-deprecation could be until Peggy kissed him on the cheek and told him how funny he was.

Harold Selwin had ordered eight chairs, and David knew of only five actors beside himself that would be at the meeting. He wondered who would be sitting in the extra chairs and whether they would be competing with him for leading parts. Gaylord Morley and Eugene O'Neill were competition enough. At two minutes of seven, David felt a sense of relief when one of the massive, doors creaked open and he saw a short, plump, bespectacled young man take a tentative step forward and inquire if he were in the right place. Raymond, who was busy coughing and lighting a cigarette, beckoned for him to come in. David watched this smiley, open-faced actor click his way across the hardwood floor on leather heels and thought, Looks like a nice guy, like one of the gang from the neighborhood back in the Bronx. Might be someone to pal around with if I don't hook up with an actress.

When the young actor spoke forthrightly, with a thick southern accent, David knew immediately that this boy wasn't from the Bronx.

"Hi, I'm Christian!" he said, offering David his hand.

"And I'm Jewish!" David countered as he shook it.

The confused look on Christian's face lingered for a short, uncomfortable moment before his mouth broke into a sweet smile.

"I'm sorry, couldn't resist," David hastened to apologize. "I'm Don, Don Coleman."

"You never have to be sorry for making people laugh," Christian said, his smile now broadening to show a mouthful of baby teeth set in an expanse of pink gums. "Y'all really Jewish, Don?"

"Yep, and y'all really Christian, Christian?"

"In name only"—he laughed—"according to my mama. My last name don't suit me, neither, but I'm stuck with it. It's Priestley," he said, pumping David's hand, "Christian Mather Priestley! Now ain't that a damn load of goodness for one man to be cartin' around?"

Christian Mather Priestley's southern drawl was so profoundly thick that David had to strain to understand what he was saying. Why in the world, David thought, would the Selwin brothers engage an actor who spoke like this? He couldn't possibly handle the elegant and poetic speeches of Shakespeare's characters. David was rudely roused from his musings by Christian Priestley's fleshy face suddenly appearing inches from his own. Being short, myopic, and vain about wearing his thick-lensed glasses, Christian often found himself talking into people's nostrils.

"D'y'all mind if I sit next to you, Don?" he drawled, giving David a potent whiff of his breakfast. "You're the only member of the company I've met."

"Be my guest," David said, leaning back to avoid Christian's bacon-and-egg breath.

David was hoping to keep the seats on either side of him available for Helen Troy or Peggy Kulkas, or perhaps for a new, attractive female member of the company.

Within moments, the other actors straggled into the ballroom and quickly chose their seats. Unhappily, David found himself wedged between Christian Priestley and August Shuttleworth. Eugene and Peggy took seats to the right of Christian, and Gaylord and Helen sat to Shuttleworth's left. From Eugene and Peggy's sedate behavior, David suspected that they had spent the night together, and from the way Helen and Gaylord were chattering away, he was sure that they had not.

"Don, my boy," Eugene said, winking as he passed by, "I trust Flo enjoyed your ham sandwich."

"I didn't hear any complaints," David boasted, not wanting to appear unworldly.

Facing the semicircle of actors, an impatient Harold Selwin stood by and watched Beauregard cross the length of the ballroom carrying a massive, thronelike chair he had appropriated from the hotel lobby. Harold Selwin lowered himself into it and with a flourish pounded his cane on the parquet floor to cue his brother, Raymond, to formally introduce him.

"Ladies and gentleman," Raymond proclaimed loudly as he stepped forward, "the founder and artistic director of the Avon Shakespearean Company, Mr. Harold Selwin."

After making his introduction, Raymond left center stage for his brother and disappeared into the shadows. David was impressed by how Harold, who had remained seated when his name was announced, took on a regal bearing by simply filling his lungs with air, subtly tilting his chin forward, and raising his hand to stop the perfunctory applause which, out of supreme guilt, David had started.

"I thank you," he said quietly, "for your kind rethepthion. And now to work!"

Harold then raised his cane and beckoned his brother, Raymond, to take over.

"My brother," Raymond began, "expects wonderful performances from each and every one of you, which ultimately you will give. I must warn you, however, that in the coming weeks," Raymond vowed, blowing out a dense cloud of smoke, "you will find yourself working harder than you have ever worked in your life."

Harold pounded his cane on the floor and nodded his head in agreement. All of the actors were raptly attentive except for August Shuttleworth, who was clipping his nails.

"Your days will be long and arduous," Raymond promised, "and you will often be rehearsing one play in the afternoon and performing another at night. It can be, as you may suspect, physically exhausting. However," he continued, his voice rising in intensity as smoke seemed to billow from every hole in his face, "if you can resist complaining to each other about how hard you're working or how much your muscles and bones ache and instead keep your mind and your energy focused on your goals as an artist, you can turn what seems like debilitating exhaustion into blessed exaltation!"

As Raymond continued to outline the details of the grueling schedule and the amount of pain they would have to endure, David was impressed by the astonishing vocal power of this 104-pound, chain-smoking emphysemiac. Suddenly, David felt like he was Ruby Keeler in *Forty-Second Street* listening to Warner Baxter trying to convince him that in life there was no more noble endeavor than rehearsing until you dropped dead.

"Give us just three things," Raymond pleaded, his voice trembling with emotion, "dedication, diligence, and punctuality and we will give you a theatrical experience you will never forget. I promise you that in years to come you will remember these sweat-filled days as being the best days of your lives."

Satisfied that he had sufficiently inspired the cast, Raymond put his cigarette to his lips and sucked up into his lungs the last half inch of smokable butt.

"And now, ladies and gentleman," Raymond said from behind a cloud of smoke, "if there are no questions, I will continue."

"I have questions," August Shuttlworth shouted. "When the hell are we going to get some hot water? I'm out of clean underwear, and don't tell me I can wash 'em in cold water, because cold water don't get the job done!"

"Beauregard!" Raymond ordered, knowing that Bo had left the room, "you tell the engineer that Mr. Selwin will not tolerate another day without hot water and if that boiler is not fixed today there will be consequences."

Before anyone realized that Raymond had been talking to a shadow on the back wall, he bulled on.

"So, people, except for Miss Mary Deare Prueitt, a lovely local actress who will be joining us later this morning, our company is complete."

Hearing the name Mary Deare Prueitt made David smile. He wondered if she could possibly be as lovely as her name.

"We have a massive amount of work to do today," Raymond announced, tamping out his cigarette butt. "I am going to assign the roles you will be playing in all four of our scheduled productions. Except for *Hamlet,* which we will be doing later in the season, I suggest you start learning your lines immediately. I have here," he said referring to a slip of paper, "the casting for *As You Like It,* which we will start rehearsing this morning. For the role of Orlando . . ."

Before David had a chance to actively pray for the role, he heard Raymond say, "Orlando will be played by Don Coleman." A few seconds later, he struck gold again with the part of Antipholus of Ephesus in the *The Comedy of Errors.* He wondered, though, how Eugene O'-Neill, a freckled redhead and three inches shorter than he, could possibly play Antipholus of Syracuse, his identical twin brother. The next casting was a big disappointment. In *The Taming of the Shrew* he would be playing Lucentio and the Tailor. Lucentio can't be much of a part, he reasoned, if I have to double in the role of the Tailor, and how important is a role that's designated simply as the Tailor? His hopes of getting another lead were dashed when he learned that in *Hamlet* he would be playing King Claudius. He thought he still might have a shot at Hamlet since none of the other actors were announced to play Hamlet, either.

"I'm going to pass out your sides for all four plays," Raymond said as he reached into a shabby briefcase and retrieved stapled stacks of yellow paper. "Now, how many of you are not familiar with sides?"

Christian and Helen raised their hands.

"This is not the full play," Raymond explained, holding up an oblong pack of paper that measured four-by-five inches, "just your speeches. You do not have the speeches of the other characters in the play, but you do have the last four words they say before your character speaks. So listen carefully, and when you hear those four words, that will be your cue to say your lines. Guard these sides well, because if you lose them, you will be charged to have them replaced."

David had learned when working for Marlowe that using sides saved the management money, but it did nothing to help an actor understand what the play was about.

For the rest of that morning, with sides in hand, the new members of the repertory company sat in a semicircle and gave voice to their characters. During this process Harold Selwin remained seated in his high-backed chair and would pound his cane on the floor whenever an actor misread a line or delivered it without energy or understanding. Raymond would then reread the offending line with the proper rhythm, inflection, and meaning and have the actor mimic his reading. Often, Harold would have them read it over and over until he was satisfied that they had gotten it right or was convinced that they would never get it right. Harold seldom banged his cane whenever Gaylord, Eugene, or David read their lines, and when he did, Raymond had to correct them but one time. August Shuttleworth, who had played Duke Frederick many times, spoke his lines acceptably well, but because of his hearing problem, he had to be prodded each time his cue came. David thought that Peggy read the part of Celia beautifully, but Raymond stopped her repeatedly to tell her that if she cared that anyone past the first row would hear Shakespeare's immortal words, she would have to speak up. After the third or fourth reproof, an impatient Harold Selwin banged his cane on the floor and shouted, "For God thaketh, Mith Kulkath, you have big, beautiful, healthy lungth. Uthe them!"

David was shocked that Harold Selwin would dare to refer to Peggy's breasts like that. All eyes were on her as she walked up to him. With a sneer on her face, she pointed a finger in his face and shouted, " 'I'll hang on every tree'! / That shall civil sayings show: / Some, how brief the life of man.' "

David was amazed at how cleverly Peggy told the old man off by using the lines from *As You Like It.*

Howard Selwin glared at her for a moment, then banged his cane on the floor.

"Yeth, yeth, girl," he shouted, pointing at her bosom, "thath what thothe lungth are for!"

When it came Helen Troy's turn to read Rosalind's speeches, she delivered them loudly, clearly, with authority, and in a grating, monotonous singsong that put David's teeth on edge. David was surprised not to hear loud cane banging from Harold. It was Raymond who stopped her, and after listening attentively to his interpretation of how Rosalind's lines should be spoken, Helen smiled knowingly, thanked Raymond for his marvelous direction, and proceeded to singsong them back exactly as before. Before Raymond could stop her again, Harold interrupted by smartly rapping his cane against his brother's leg.

"She'll be fine, Raymond," he said gently while staring at Helen. "My dear, you show great potential, and after rehearthal I will work with you perthonally."

It was apparent to everyone that the girl had a dead ear and no rhythm, but it mattered little to Harold, who was smitten by her beauty.

From the first moment David saw Helen he felt that he was in the presence of one of the world's true goddesses. Now, with every line, her beauty and goddessness faded, and by the time the reading of the play was over, David had become completely depressed. Orlando, he learned, was not as good a part as he had expected; most of his scenes were with Rosalind. In one of the scenes he had little to do but sit quietly on a rock for what seemed like eternity and suffer through Helen Troy's tuneless, roller-coaster rendition of Shakespeare's faultless iambic pentameter. He dreaded the prospect of being similarly assaulted every time they had to perform the play, and it was all he could do to keep from screaming, "God, please make her shut up!"

Forcing actors to learn and rehearse three of Shakespeare's plays in two weeks would, by any standards, be considered cruel and inhuman punishment, but to Raymond and Harold Selwin it was a financial necessity. Their solvency depended on getting these plays in front of paying audiences as soon as possible, however slovenly the production.

During this period there was little sleeping, no leisurely dining, and a minimum amount of showering. After grueling seventeen-hour days, no one seemed to notice the musky odor that most of the actors carried with them, or if they did notice, they were too tired to care.

Mary Deare Prueitt arrived a day late, but the Selwins chose not to rebuke her, for she was not only the daughter of a state senator but also one of the two members of the cast who would not be getting paid. Christian was the other, and the only one who was *paying* for the privilege to act in a professional company. When Mary Deare Prueitt swept into the ballroom and glided across the floor, David thought, This can be trouble. She was nowhere near as pretty as Helen Troy, but there was something about her that was unsettling and strangely irresistible. He ruled out the lovely, large, lacey, white picture hat she wore and the shapely but slightly bowed legs that, thanks to the backlighting from the open ballroom doors, he was able to glimpse through her sheer, billowy organdy dress. As she came closer, it immediately became clear why her presence was making him nervous. It was the shape of her eyebrows and the tilt of her nose, the fullness of her lips and the way her mouth went up at the corners—and her smile! A broad, sunny smile that framed a set of perfect, even white teeth. My God, he thought, this is uncanny! Except for her magnolia-laced southern accent, her jet-black hair, lavender eyes, and her darling bowed legs, Mary Deare Prueitt is the spitting image of every girl I ever wanted to make love to!

"Hi, I'm David," David said, trying to remain cool, "or rather, I was David. I'm Don now, Don Coleman, and I have to tell you," he continued hesitantly as he fingered Margie's ring, "that I have a girl-friend in the Bronx who's a dead ringer for you."

"Y'all think she's pretty?" Mary Deare asked kittenishly.

"Oh, yes, very pretty." David smiled, holding out his hand. "She gave me this ring. Her name is Margie."

"Oh, double drat!" Mary Deare pouted.

"Double drat?" David smiled.

"Yes," she explained, "drat that I'm not the only girl in the world who looks likes me and double drat that she went and hooked a cute boy who I was hopin' was available. So," she said, turning sharply to Christian Priestley, "who are you?"

"I'm Christian Priestley and I don't have a girl who looks like any-body. In fact I don't have a girl."

"Well, Christian honey," she said, tapping the tip of his nose, "we'll be on the lookout for one for you."

David felt that telling Mary Deare that he had a girlfriend was the decent thing to do. However, on hearing the suggestive way she said he was a cute boy she was was hopin' was available, he wondered if in this instance doing the decent thing was also doing the stupid thing.

After observing the cast members rehearse for just a few days, it was apparent to David that Eugene O'Neill was the actor with the most intelligence; Peggy Kulkas, with the most honesty; August Shuttle-worth, with the most experience; Helen Troy, with the most annoying voice; and Mary Deare Prueitt, with the most charm, sensuality, and delightfully enticing bow to her legs. Christian Priestley was certainly the most patient and amiable. Harold Selwin had ordered Christian to learn all the male parts except Hamlet in all of the plays and not to expect to rehearse any of them until after the company was on the road. In the meantime, Christian would be the company stage manager and property master. Gaylord Morley was definitely the actor with the most panache. Panache was a word David did not know until he heard Eugene ask Gaylord if he could borrow a cup of it from him.

"I really stunk up Petruchio today," Eugene explained. "I just couldn't get my feet untangled."

From that David assumed that panache meant grace and elegance, which Gaylord oozed. Until that time David didn't realize that he had some of that stuff, too. He sensed that since he required much less attention than his colleagues, the Selwins were pleased with his work. His gift for impersonation made it easy for him to copy Raymond's suggested readings. By the second week David was feeling so secure in his acting that he was no longer concerned about not understanding 50 percent of what he was saying onstage. At rehearsal several days before his debut performance in *As You Like It,* David was in the process of adding a pinch of Ronald Colman to Orlando's best and longest speech when Beauregard barged in.

" 'Scuse me, Don, for stompin' on your purty actin', but Mr. Selwin wants y'all at the warehouse right now. Station wagon's out front and ready to roll."

The cast bolted from the ballroom, raced through the hotel lobby, and piled into the station wagon. Any respite from their confining schedule was welcome, even a five-minute drive to a warehouse. It was in this huge, damp dungeon where the scenery and costumes were stored that David and his fellow actors first learned that besides acting in the plays, the male members of the cast were expected to double as stagehands. Raymond Selwin dropped this bomb matter-of-factly, as if the information were common knowlege. There were mild rumblings of discontent, but no one voiced an objection until Gaylord and David learned that their assignment as high-men required that they climb twenty-foot ladders and screw large "sky hooks" into ceilings. Gaylord balked because of a chronic back condition, and David yelped because of his monumental fear of heights. In a touching display of company spirit, which surprisingly still existed after long days of ultra-togetherness, Eugene and Christian volunteered to be the highmen. They would scale the tall ladders if David and Gaylord agreed to carry in the heavy canvas scenery and get it ready to hang. David was disillusioned to learn that in place of realistic wood-frame sets, he would be acting for a company that used ratty painted-canvas backings.

"People," Raymond called, "as actors, you are all aware how important it is to know your lines, but for us it is equally important that you also know how to load and unload scenery, so for the next few hours, Beauregard will instruct you how to set up a stage. All right, let's get to it!"

After learning how to unfold and unroll the ratty canvases, Bo handed them each a monkey wrench and told them to assemble a thirty-foot-long pipe by joining together five shorter ones. Gaylord had never in his life used a monkey wrench or even touched one.

"They didn't tell me I was going to be a friggin' plumber," Gaylord grumbled as he fought to join together two sections of rusty pipe.

"Who'd figure," David groaned, struggling to straighten out a huge, wrinkled canvas, "that we'd be acting in front of this crappy-looking scenery."

David dropped his wrench when he heard Raymond Selwin's voice boom out, "That crappy-looking scenery, Mr. Coleman, was painted for the great Southern and Marlowe Company by Mister John Colesworthy, a world-renowned muralist who, for your information, had also been commissioned by Buffalo Bill to paint the cycloramas for his Wild West Show, but I don't expect you've ever heard of any of those people."

"Well, I never heard of Colesworthy, Mr. Selwin," David admitted, "but I've heard of Buffalo Bill—everybody has—and I know about Southern and Marlowe, and I really do admire them, especially Marlowe."

"Mr. Coleman," Raymond Selwin sneered as he walked up to him and blew smoke in his face, "I am sorry to say that I do not appreciate your humor."

"I wasn't being funny, Mr. Selwin. I really admire them."

"Well, then, why don't you tell us all about Southern and Marlowe and why you admire Marlowe in particular."

"Be happy to," David said cockily, winking at Eugene. "Uh . . . Southern and Marlowe, they were these . . . uh, actors, big Shakepearean star actors who toured the United States for years—I think it was from . . . uh . . . oh, about the 1880s until the late 1920s. They played the biggest theaters in all the major cities. Southern and Marlowe were married and were the first big stars to bring Shakespeare to small western cities and towns. They'd play their whole Shakespearean repertoire for an audience of cowboys and ranchers, and farmers, too, and they'd eat it up. They'd go wild for plays like *Hamlet* and *Macbeth* or any play where they could hoot and holler at the stage and hiss the villains and cheer the heroes. I guess E. H. Southern and Julia Marlowe ran the biggest hit Shakespearean touring repertory of all time, and Julia Marlowe I've heard was considered one of the most beautiful and brilliant Ophelias ever."

Eugene, stunned by his colleague's knowledge of obscure theatrical history, applauded wildly but stopped abruptly when Raymond glared at him.

"Yes, she was brilliant and beautiful," Raymond allowed begrudgingly, "and she had no problem acting in front of these magnificent works of scenic art, which, Mr. Coleman, I'll thank you never again to refer to as crappy scenery."

Raymond Selwin turned, glared at Eugene again, and then strode angrily to the other end of the warehouse.

"Hey, Don," an impressed Eugene asked, "where the hell did you learn so much about Southern and Marlowe?"

"At Yale, I majored in bullshit. No, actually," David admitted, "Mr. Larrimore, a hundred-year-old stagehand at the Marlowe Theatre, told me about them. He'd toured with them for most of his life. This Julia Marlowe was an aunt of John Marlowe, this guy I worked for, and when Southern and Marlowe retired, Julia Marlowe willed Mr. Larrimore to her nephew."

"Mr. Coleman, we are joining pipes together now." Raymond's voice echoed across the dank warehouse. "We are not jabbering!"

At the other end of the warehouse, standing with Raymond amid several antique steamer trunks were Helen, Mary Deare, Peggy, and a jolly-faced, three-hundred-pound woman who was unlocking one of the trunks. Every square inch of the old hump-lidded trunks were plastered with stickers designating the towns and cities to which they had traveled. The only unstickered spaces remaining were on the lids where the names Southern and Marlowe were emblazoned in bold, Wells, Fargo–style lettering.

"People," Raymond called loudly, "stop what you're doing for a moment and come to me!"

David and Gaylord, happy to leave their rusty pipes, dropped them with a clatter and ran to join Raymond and the girls.

"Packed in these trunks are the costumes you will be wearing onstage for the next three months. Fifteen years ago, my brother and I bought this magnificent wardrobe from the Southern and Marlowe estate, and I trust that you will treat these historic raiments with the respect and reverence they deserve."

Raiments, David thought. Boy, today's my day for new words.

"Some of you will be wearing the costumes that were, some thirty years before, actually worn by these two brilliant actors."

"Thirty years!" David whispered softly to Eugene. "I hope somebody had 'em dry-cleaned."

"To answer our resident comedian, who has yet to learn the difference between a real whisper and a stage whisper, at the start of every new season, all of our wardrobe is thoroughly dry-cleaned and freshened. Does that allay your fears, Mr. Coleman?"

David smiled goofily and nodded.

Raymond turned to the obese woman at his side and announced, "This is my wife, Faith, who will be giving you your costumes for all the shows but *Hamlet. Hamlet*'s wardrobe will join us in three weeks. You will try on all of your costumes right now, and if you gave our casting director accurate information about your size and weight, no adjustments should be necessary. You will each share a trunk with one other member of the company, and everyone will be responsible for keeping his or her costumes fresh and tidy and to make any minor repairs that become necessary."

With that last instruction, Raymond beat a hasty retreat and left his wife to handle the actors.

"Who's playing Bianca in *The Shrew?*" Faith asked.

"Me, me, I'm playing Bianca!" Peggy shouted, becoming giddy over the prospect of putting on the exquisite, tight-bodiced knockout of a gown Faith pulled from one of the trunks.

Peggy was not alone in her excitement. All the cast members, in their fashion, *ooohed* and *aaahed* and squealed their approval of the costumes they were handed.

"Now, today you will try on all of your costumes and practice getting in and out of them," Faith announced. "And we'll start with the ones you'll be wearing for *The Comedy of Errors.* I'd like to check those, as you'll be performing that first."

For the next half hour, from opposite ends of the warehouse a medley of giggles, shrieks, and comments echoed from the two makeshift dressing rooms that Beauregard had fashioned from old theater flats.

"God, this is magnificent!" Gaylord shouted as he modeled the robe he was to wear as the Duke of Ephesus. "It's me! I'm never taking it off."

"It fits, my dress fits! Hey, Mom," an elated Peggy shouted. "Now I can go to the prom!"

"Gang," David announced loudly, sniffing one of his wool tights, "Mr. Selwin did not lie. My stockings smell like dry-cleaning fluid!"

David was terribly impressed by the lushness of the velvet jackets he was to wear and only discovered that his jacket was really a doublet when Faith shouted at him, "Mr. Coleman, you're dragging the sleeve of your doublet on the floor."

He had always thought a doublet was the short pants that were worn over the tights. He was so excited at the prospect of prancing around in his magnificent crimson-red doublet and hose that he forgot for the moment that he was also a stagehand with pipes to wrench. He loved his puffed-sleeved velvet doublets but cursed at the matching wool hose. After much tugging and groaning, David finally struggled into his very tight tights, only to discover that the crotch was a foot below his own and no matter how much he stretched the wool to conform to the length of his long legs, it inevitably returned to its original length. He complained to Eugene, who was having his own war with tights that were miles too long. Eugene, who was five feet ten, had told the casting director that he was six feet because he had heard from a six-foot-tall alumnus of the company that the Selwins only hired actors who'd fit perfectly into their costumes. David, on the other hand, had told the truth. He was six feet two but didn't think to mention that most of his height was in his legs. Eugene and David were relatively friendly, but when they mutually got the idea to trade tights, their bond thickened.

Gaylord was the first to don his full costume and was obviously pleased with the way he looked. Christian, who sadly had no costume to try on, watched enviously as Gaylord strutted about.

"Oh, Grandma," Christian joked, "what muscular calves you have!"

"So you better watch your ass, Little Red Riding Hood!" Gaylord replied, playfully hitting him on the shoulder with his plumed hat.

When David and Eugene donned their identical Antipholus costumes, added their blond pageboy wigs, their embroidered gold headbands, and adjusted their posture, they looked remarkably like twins.

"It's amazing what wigs and costumes can do," Christian offered, "but shouldn't you do something about your legs?"

"We did. Eugene and I traded tights."

"Well, Don, the tights didn't do it. Eugene's got legs like a stork, and yours are like a ballet dancer's."

"We'll put a note in the program," Eugene chided. "Antipholus of Syracuse had polio as a child."

"Damn if he doesn't have better legs than I," Gaylord remarked as he circled David. "Did you ever study ballet, Don?"

"No." David laughed and then clapped his hands. "Eugene, I've got an idea! What if we put like a falsie on your calf?"

"Don, my boy, I have never worn a falsie before, but if you can find me a pair—"

"I can," Christian said as he raced off. Moments later, he returned triumphantly, waving a pair of falsies.

"They always have these in the wardrobe department," Christian said excitedly. "Now pull down your tights and I'll tape them on for you."

Reluctantly, Eugene acquiesed, and within minutes the calf enhancements were in place.

"They look great," Christian gushed as he stepped back to admire his work. "If I were you, I'd wear them all the time."

"Is he shittin' me, Don?" a skeptical Eugene asked. "Do they really look all right?"

"We're a perfect match!" David said, standing beside Eugene, "no one would ever guess that one of us is wearing false tits on his legs."

At the dress parade, all of the cast members assembled in the center of the warehouse where Beauregard had set up a stage light. It was apparent to David that these costumes were not made to be worn by amateurs. Except for August Shuttleworth, who refused to put on his costume, all of the men looked dashing and all the girls, radiant. David had expected that Helen Troy would be the most beautiful, and she was, but it was Mary Deare Prueitt, in an extremely low cut dress, who grabbed his attention. This couldn't be the girl who, during rehearsal, wore dungarees, a University of Georgia football jersey, and stuffed her hair under a golf cap. In the form-fitting silk gown they had given her to wear as his wife, Adriana, she had turned from Rebecca of Sunnybrook Farm into a voluptuous version of Snow White. It was her long, shining black hair lightly brushing the top of her snowy-white bosom that did him in. To stop the throbbing in his ears he tried unsuccessfully to turn his eyes away from her remarkable chest. He was completely captivated and began to tremble when he saw this beautiful southern belle approaching him.

"Well, Antipholus honey, look how they dressed up yo' mama. Think you'd like a roll in the hay with li'l ole Adriana?"

It was all he could do to stay in control when she put her arm through his and whispered in his ear, "Hey, Donny, why'd you keep those sexy legs of yours hidden from me all this time?"

Taking his life in his hands, David whispered back, "For the same reason you kept that great hair under a cap and covered those breasts with a football jersey."

"You're all right, Bronx boy." she laughed, punching him on the arm. "You and I're gonna play nice together on this tour."

For the third day in a row an expectant Margie opened her mailbox and found that there was no letter from her David. From the romantic moment at the train station when she jammed her ring on his finger, she considered that they were betrothed and started referring to him as "my David."

Since arriving in Atlanta, David had written her a letter a day, but after a perfect record of eleven straight days, the letters suddenly stopped. On that eleventh day, when she received a picture postcard of the Hotel Tallulah that had room only for a cursory note, Margie had a premonition that something was wrong. At first, she accepted the fact that because it was a postcard he could not write all the personal things he usually did. She also conceded that what he did write on the card— "Margie, I'm too busy to even go to the toilet"—was true, but after four days she could not believe he was still that busy.

"I know his habits," she cried to her mother, who could not console her. "He's very regular, and I don't care how busy he is. By now he must have gone to the toilet a dozen times. Why couldn't he have taken his pad and pencil in with him and written to me while he was sitting there? Something is wrong, Mother! I know it."

She now started to think that the reason David did not send her any money from his salary was not because he would not be paid until after the first week's performance but because he wasn't going along with her wedding plans.

Margie ran to her room, locked herself in, and started to reread all his letters, searching for a clue to his behavior. She quickly scanned through the descriptions of how well the rehearsals were going and what a good and speedy director this Raymond Selwin was and how he missed her even more than a fatty pastrami sandwich. She slowed down to reread what he had to say about all the cast members. He had written much about what a really interesting guy Eugene O'Neill was and how funny he was and how Eugene and a girl named Peggy had hit it off and how beautiful and boring his leading lady Helen Troy was and how her voice sounded like chalk on a blackboard and what a bore an old guy named Shuttleworth was and how he made lewd remarks and propositioned all the girls in the company. He spent one whole letter telling about his roommate, the handsomest guy in the company and the one with the most panache. It worried her a little that he would use a word that she had never heard him use before and would have to look up. She had mentioned in a return letter that he sounded different and hoped that he didn't change too much, because she loved him just the way he was. He wrote many times about Helen and Peggy and a lot about a gentle giant named Bo who once picked up the back end of a station wagon while he and Christian shoved a broken jack under the axle. She reread the letters and noted that only once, early on, did he mention Mary Deare Prueitt, and then only to say that she was a little bowlegged and one of those spoiled rich belles who flirt with everybody but was probably very nice and had a kind of relationship with Christian, who was also a real open and friendly type. It was the phrase "kind of a relationship" that sent her antenna up. It meant to her that Mary Deare Prueitt, a flirty, rich Gentile bitch was really unattached and after her David.

She considered getting on the train to Atlanta to see if her awful promonitions were true but instead opted to write her intended a very long, emotional letter.

In the auditorium of Anniston High School in Anniston, Alabama, the curtain rang down on the premiere peformance of *As You Like It,* and although some of the cast stumbled over a line or two and August Shuttleworth, who had trouble hearing his cues, twice spoke his lines while Gaylord was still emoting, David felt that the afternoon was a triumph, at least for him. He remembered all of his lines, and the scene for which he and Eugene had choreographed an elaborate and violent-looking wrestling match had the young audience a-whoopin' 'n' a-hollerin'. He was especially pleased at how the audience responded to him during the curtain calls. He felt that he received as much applause as anyone in the cast except Helen Troy, which was no surprise given the noisy reaction from the boys in the audience when she made her first entrance. She looked breathtakingly beautiful in her costumes and especially sexy in the one when she masqueraded as a man and showed the rowdy crowd how her long, shapely legs looked in tights. What flabbergasted David was how tolerant they were of her stilted acting and her grating, ear-shatteringly loud voice. On their first onstage exchange in the play, David wondered why she was screaming at him. For a fearful moment he thought she was having another fit of hysteria, like the one he provoked on the train, until he recalled Raymond Selwin's preshow instructions to the cast.

"The words of William Shakespeare," Raymond Selwin had instructed solemnly, "are among the greatest ever written and deserve to be heard by every member of this audience, including the student who may be sitting in the last row of the balcony. I beseech you, for Shakespeare's sake, for my sake, and for God's sake, *project, project, project!"*

Helen had obviously taken Mr. Selwin's words to heart, and during the course of the play, as she gained confidence, her voice increased in volume, and when she *projected* the final lines of Rosalind's epilogue, she sounded to David like the fight announcer at Madison Square Garden:

"If I were a woman'," she bellowed, " 'I would kiss as many of you as had beards that pleased me, complexions that liked me and breaths that I defied not; and, I am sure, as many as have good beards or good faces or sweet breaths will, for my kind offer, when I make curtsy, bid me farewell.' "

Weird as it sounded, it apparently paid off, because dozens of young men in the audience stood up and shouted, "I bid you farewell, honey," "Hey, I got a sweet face," "I got no beard, honey, but I'll grow one if you kiss me!"

What amazed David was that this rowdy audience had actually understood Shakespeare's words well enough to respond to them.

As soon as the curtain fell on this first performance, Eugene did something that David thought strange and humorous. He tilted his plumed hat to a rakish angle and, facing the back of the curtain, did a little tap dance while singing in a soft tenor voice,

> "Pax vobiscum . . . (tap tap tap) . . .
> Et cum spiritu tuo . . . (tap tap tap) . . .
> Ite missa est . . . (tap tap, ta ta, tap tap)!"

David later learned that Eugene was tap-dancing to the Latin prayer that priests intoned at the end of mass. David joined the act as soon as he learned the routine, and Peggy, who at first thought it sacrilegious, relented, and for the rest of the run, after every final curtain, the Avon Trio performed their ritual *Pax Vobiscum* song-and-dance act.

All performances were scheduled to begin at two-thirty in the afternoon, which required that the scenery be loaded into the school auditoriums by seven o'clock in the morning and be hung, lit, and ready by noon, in time for Raymond Selwin to rehearse the young drama students who had been chosen to play the half-dozen small speaking parts and also the nonspeaking roles of townsfolk and spear-carriers. Harold Selwin traveled ahead of the company and at each high school prepared the students by showing them where to stand when they delivered their lines and how to stand stock-still when other actors were talking.

Since the company performed only one-night stands, most of the actors' days were spent loading and unloading scenery into and out of Bo's ton-and-a-half truck, piling in and out of the station wagon, and traveling to the next school. Sleeping and eating were not considered priorities. Raymond Selwin no longer drove the station wagon, having been replaced by Christian, who now added chauffeuring to his other duties. Raymond was happy to be relieved of the awesome responsibility of driving while half-drunk, and now, as a passenger in Bo's truck, he could concentrate fully on his drinking.

The caravan traveled as little as forty miles a day or as much as three hundred, and today, because of bad scheduling, they would have to drive through the night for almost four hundred miles in order to get to Columbus, Georgia, for the next day's performance of *The Comedy of Errors.* It was a crowded station wagon, but everyone seemed content with the seating arrangement. Mary Deare chose to sit in the front seat between Christian and Shuttleworth. Gaylord and Helen were content to be in the middle seat, and in the backseat were the Avon Trio—Peggy, Eugene, and David. It was a good arrangement for David, as Peggy and Eugene slept cuddled, leaving him plenty of room to stretch his long legs. He would gladly have given up the leg space to have had somebody to cuddle with. It was at these times that he allowed himself to muse about which of the girls in the company he would like to be holding in his arms. Mary Deare, he decided, would be his first choice.

As they were loading up for the trip, David surmised that something had happened between Gaylord and Helen which caused them to lose their lust for chatting with each other. By explaining that sitting so close to the windshield frightened her, Helen cajoled Eugene and Peggy into exchanging seats with her, which put her in the rear seat with David.

"Well, look at this." She giggled, "I'm back with my old train pal. I hope you're happy with the new arrangement."

David would have preferred to say, "No, I'd much rather Mary Deare sat here," but ever the gentleman, he told her that he was delighted.

By two o'clock that morning, the only sounds heard in the old station wagon were the squeaking of the right rear wheel, Gaylord's resonant snoring, and the munching of celery, which Christian chewed to keep himself from nodding off at the wheel. David had been asleep for more than an hour and had been dreaming that Margie and he were in Penn Station and she was licking his finger, trying to suck off the wedding band that she had forced on it. He awoke with a start when he felt his hand being squeezed by a warmer hand which instinctively he knew did not belong to him. He was further startled to see a head of blond hair lying in his lap. It belonged to Helen Troy, and he assumed that in her sleep she had unknowingly fallen there. He hoped that without awakening, she'd release his hand, roll off his lap, and never know she had used his genitalia as a pillow. The palm of her hand was atop the back of his, her fingers laced through his and holding them in a death grip. Boy, he thought, this girl really sleeps tense. They remained in this position for some time, and although her head was lying heavily against his groin and he could feel her warm breath on his thigh, he somehow was able to remain a perfect gentleman. He was surprised to discover that he was capable of this kind of control. Finally, she stirred, and with their hands still locked, she reached up and scratched her nose with his forefinger. He held his breath as she raised her head from his lap, and after much twisting and squirming, she rolled onto her side thus giving David a view of her perfect profile. Still clutching his hand, she lay quietly for a few moments, breathed a few deep breaths, and then, without warning, gave David one of the biggest surprises of his budding sexual life by casually guiding his hand into her blouse and under the straps of her brassiere.

He would never have guessed when they started on this trip that one of his hands would end up inside Helen Troy's blouse, and he certainly could never have imgagined that this sleeping beauty with the movie-star figure was flat-chested. How could this ravishing blond goddess, who had all the boys at Anniston High drooling, have absolutely no bosom? At first, he thought that his hand might be resting on her upper chest, but when he felt a fair-sized nipple pressing into the palm of his hand, he knew where he was. My God, he thought, she's wearing falsies! Maybe the ones Christian taped to Eugene's calves came from one of Helen's costumes. He tried to hold as still as possible while he contemplated ways to extricate his hand without embarrassing himself or Helen. David glanced at Gaylord, who was snoring louder than ever, and wondered if his falling out with Helen had anything to do with his discovering that she wore falsies.

While he speculated how long he could keep his hand in this position without cramping, a sudden bump in the road rocked the wagon and brought grumbles from the sleeping group, a whispered "Sorry, folks" from Christian, and much position shifting. Strangely, Helen did not move, but her grip tightened, and suddenly David felt his hand being used as a Ouija Board pointer, moving slowly, in very small, sensual circles across her nipple, around her chest, and finally arriving at her other breast. Oh, my, he thought, she's having an erotic dream.

After a few more moments of Ouija boarding, David could feel a major problem arising. As his hand was moved from firm nipple to firmer nipple, it had become impossible for him to keep his involuntary, base emotions in check. With her head lying heavily in his lap, he was petrified that she would be awakened by his growing erection. Miraculously, she was not. From what he could see of her face, she appeared to be having a wonderfully restful night. From time to time she would relax the grip on his hand, but would soon retighten it and, with his help, go back to fondling herself. He had never before caressed such small breasts, and as the night wore on, he learned something that he would remember for all time: He loved fondling breasts, no matter the size. It was also on this trip that he discovered that he could function fairly well with practically no sleep. At daybreak Helen awoke and sat up. He was astounded at how unperturbed she was when she discovered where she had been lying.

"Oh, look at me." She giggled. "I'm lying in your lap. Now, however did I get here? I am so sorry. I hope I didn't disturb your sleep?"

"He was even more astonished at how she seemed not to notice that when she sat up, he had slipped his hand out from inside her brassiere.

"Oh, look at the mess I made of my blouse. I'll have to borrow Faith's iron."

David smiled and glanced furtively at her bosom, which once again seemed to be like the rest of her, perfect.

At six-thirty that morning the caravan arrived in Columbus, and the company members wearily went about their appointed tasks. The men were dropped off at the high school to start setting up the stage, while the women, chauffeured by Mary Deare, the only licensed driver among them, searched first for a diner where they could order breakfast and then for suitable, cheap sleeping accommodations for the cast.

Before setting up the stage, David and Eugene would first tackle the distasteful job of retrieving their wardrobe trunk, which contained both actors' costumes and the tons of perspiration those costumes absorbed during the previous night's performance. Because of the volume of sweat that the two of them generated every night, David and Eugene learned never to open their trunk in an enclosed area. They would carry it to an open field, and, at the count of *un, deux, trois,* they'd throw open the lid and run as far away from the offensive odor as they could. When they thought it safe, David and Eugene, with hankies covering their noses, would gather up their costumes, and quickly throw them over clotheslines they had set up for the daily air-freshening process.

During the performance of *The Comedy of Errors* that afternoon, David, feeling fairly secure in his part, took the time to stand in the wings and watch all the scenes he was not in. He was particularly interested in seeing Mary Deare perform Adriana's emotional speech in the second act and watched in awe as this southern belle, speaking without a trace of her native accent, delivered Shakespeare's words with such telling effect that he felt his face flush.

> "I am possess'd with an adulterate blot;
> My blood is mingled with the crime of lust:
> For if we too be one, and thou play false,
> I do digest the poison of thy flesh,
> Being strumpeted by thy contagion.
> Keep then fair league and truce with the true bed;
> I live unstain'd, thou undishonored."

My God, I'm in love! David realized as he watched her perform. From the first moment in the ballroom when he saw her walk toward him wearing that sheer dress, something started to happen to him, and now, when she so movingly said, "For if we too be one, and thou play false, / I do digest the poison of thy flesh," he felt that she was speaking to him. Without fully admitting it, he had always wanted the two of them to be one. And damn if he didn't "play false" with her when he told her that he had a girlfriend. The moment the words were out of his mouth, he had regretted uttering them. He really wanted to say, "I had one until I saw you." He wasn't quite sure how Adriana's words "I do digest the poison of thy flesh" pertained to him exactly, but since they met, he'd been feeling nauseated, like he'd been poisoned by eating bad fish. Could it be that she picked up his feelings about her and wanted to digest the poison of his flesh? Maybe she was in love with him too. When they met, hadn't she told him he was cute and asked him if he was available? If she only knew how, last night in the back of the station wagon, he had wished that it was *her* hand clutching his.

Captivated by her loveliness and spurred by her brilliance, David proceeded to give one of his most energized performances, thinking, If only we were playing *Romeo and Juliet* tonight, we'd show Leslie Howard and Norma Shearer how it should be done.

The audience reaction during the curtain calls was very good, particularly for Mary Deare, who seemed stunned at the response. Immediately after doing their *Pax Vobiscum* tap dance, David rushed to the girls' dressing room to tell Mary Deare how powerfully she had affected him, but she wasn't there, and no one knew where she had gone.

"She's still in costume, and Bo wants us to have our trunk ready in half an hour," Helen Troy said, "so if you find her, don't keep her."

"I won't," David said, thinking that if he found her he'd love to keep her.

"Better get moving, Don," Helen sang. "We have another long ride tonight."

David sensed something flirtatious in the way she said *we* and wondered again if she had not pretended to be asleep last night.

After making a quick search of the auditorium, David heard what sounded like a dog whimper. He followed the sound to the balcony, where he found Mary Deare sitting on the top step of the middle aisle, hugging her knees and crying softly. He approached her warily, reasoning that anyone who climbed to the top row of the balcony to cry must want to be alone.

"Hi, I hope I didn't startle you," he ventured.

She raised her head and looked up at him with lavender eyes that glistened with tears. No girl had ever before looked at him the way she was looking at him, and it made him feel both uncomfortable and wonderful.

"Oh, Don!" was all she managed to say through sobs as she stretched out her arms and wiggled her fingers at him. He couldn't believe that she was inviting him to hug her, but what else do such fingers mean? He kneeled in front of her and waited for her to put her arms around his neck before embracing her. He was dying to kiss her but decided against it, as he had no idea why she was hugging him. Maybe she needed comforting because she had gotten a telegram saying her dog, Fido, had been run over. Whatever the reason, David was happy to be where he was, in heaven. She held him tight and continued to whimper for a little while and then fell silent. After several noncommunicative moments, David sat beside her and started to rock her gently, humming Brahm's lullaby, a song that his father used to play for him on his flute at bedtime when he was little. When the song ended, she sighed, kissed his cheek, and whispered, "Oh, Donny, thank you!" Then, wiping her face with the palms of her hands, she stood up, took David's hand in both of her wet ones, and assisted him to his feet.

"You know somethin', Donny," she said, standing one step below him and looking squarely in his eyes, "you're purty."

"Purty?" he jeered. "You better look again."

"I'm lookin'," she said, putting her hand under his chin and scrutinizing his face, "and you're right! You ain't purty, you're gorgeous, and I love the way you hum!"

She gave him a half smile and then pulled up her gown and raced down the steep balcony stairs so fast that David feared she'd trip and go flying over the rail.

"Donny," she said, turning to him at the foot of the stairs, "I love acting. I love everything about the theater!"

He stood transfixed as he watched her disappear down a stairwell, wondering what the hell had just happened between them, if anything. Could she possibly be feeling any of the things for him that he was feeling for her? She did say she loved everything about the theater, and he was part of what she loved. She did kiss him on the cheek and thank him, but wouldn't she have done that to anyone who happened along and comforted her? He decided that she wouldn't. She must like me, he thought. She said I'm purty, and she likes the way I hum and she called me Donny! Nobody has ever called me Donny! These small, affectionate hints were all the encouragement that David needed to start some full-scale courting.

By the time David got back to the stage, Eugene had disassembled the pipes and had the backdrops all rolled up.

"Don, old shoe, I hope you have a good reason for leaving me to do all this shit by myself."

"I have the best reason!" he whispered, grabbing his arm. "I'm in love!"

"Me, too," Eugene said dryly. "Not Peggy, I hope."

"No." David laughed. "Mary Deare. Is that crazy or what?"

"It's crazy."

"Why is it crazy, Eugene?"

"Because she's engaged to be married."

"How do you know?"

"Peggy told me."

"Who told *her?*"

"Christian."

"How does Christian know?"

"Christian knows everthing; that's his job." Seeing the pain in his friend's face, he added, "Mary Deare confided in him."

That night, as he lay in a lumpy bed beside Gaylord, who was snoring more noisily than befitted a handsome leading man, David's mind lingered over Eugene's upsetting news and all the events of the last twenty-four hours. First the weird encounter with Helen Troy in the back of the station wagon, and now the emotional experience in the balcony with a girl he discovered he loved during the second act of that night's performance. Why, if she's going to get married, he had asked himself many times in the last two sleepless hours, did Mary Deare, when she was sitting in the balcony sobbing her heart out, invite me to hold her in my arms? Maybe, he thought wishfully, she was upset because she was planning to dump her fiancé because he won't let her be an actress and she hugged me because she needed support and strength to call off the marriage. Breaking off a relationship is a really difficult thing to do. This last thought nudged his conscience and crisply brought to his attention the ring Margie had given him. He was not aware that while thinking of Mary Deare he had twisted it off his finger and now held it in his hand. He tried to close his eyes and nap for the few remaining minutes of the morning, but a nudge from his conscience rolled him out of bed, and he sat down at the tiny desk in the dollar-a-day rented room and wrote a newsless, guilt-relieving "I'm so darn busy—will write more soon—love ya, hon" postcard to Margie, a note with more hurtful information written between the lines than good news in it.

By consuming mugs filled with the black coffee Bo had brewed in his truck, Bo and Christian readied themselves for the fairly long trip to Hogansville, Georgia, where later that day the company would perform *The Taming of the Shrew*. Raymond Selwin was lying in the cab of the truck, having drunk himself to sleep. The company would not eat breakfast until Bo spotted an open roadside diner. The two vehicles always traveled in tandem in case either of them broke down, which they did often. Among Bo's many indispensable talents was his ability to change flat tires in minutes and to repair anything that had moving parts. Bo was one of the primary reasons that the Avon Shakespean Company rarely failed to make a scheduled appearance.

As David dragged his tired body and his Gladtone bag to the station wagon, he could not believe he was the first one there.

"Where the heck is everybody, Christian," David said as he hefted his bag onto the rack atop the wagon. "Weren't we supposed to load up at six-thirty?"

"Yes, we were. You're the only one who's on time, Don," Christian chided, smiling lewdly. "Anxious to try out the new seating arrangement, are we?"

"New seating arrangement?" David said hopefuly. "What new—?"

"Hey, Don," Christain said, gulping his coffee, "you didn't know that Mary Deare will be riding in the backseat with you?"

"No, I didn't," David said, fighting to contain his excitement, "How'd that come about?"

"Mary Deare asked me, and I said it was all right with me."

"She did?"

"Yes, and I said if it's all right with Helen, and she said, under the circumstances, it was fine with her."

David's brain raced to divine what Helen meant by under the circumstances. Did she mean that she knew his hand was on her breast the night before and didn't want it to happen again, or had Mary Deare told Helen that she had fallen in love with him.

"But I thought," David said casually while his pulse raced, "Helen said she was afraid to sit that close to the windshield."

"She is."

"And she's willing to swap seats with Mary Deare?"

"Oh, no, Don. Helen's staying put. You'll have two lovelies keeping you company back there. Lucky guy!"

"Yeah, lucky," David said, his heart sinking. "Christian, you said 'under the circumstances.' Uh, what was the problem?"

"Well," Christian said, looking about furtively, "it's a groping problem."

"Groping?" David asked, feeling guilty even knowing that the groping he did last night was forced upon him. "Who groped who?"

"Shuttleworth!" Christian whispered. "Anytime Mary Deare's ass is within reach, he grabs himself a handful. Even in his sleep last night he struck. Horny old bastard."

David clucked disapprovingly while in his head he transposed Christian's words Mary Deare's ass to Mary's dear ass.

Within minutes a weary group of players with bags in hand straggled to the wagon. David and Mary Deare exchanged meaningful smiles as David took her bag from her and hoisted it onto the rack. While Christian was securing the luggage, Gaylord, Eugene, and Peggy, aware of the new seating arrangements, silently climbed into the wagon and took their places. Shuttleworth, who had been told but didn't hear, got into the front seat, and when Mary Deare moved toward the rear, he grabbed onto her skirt.

"Whoa, little lady," he said, never having heard her name. "You're up here with me."

"Not anymore," Mary Deare shouted, yanking her skirt away. "I've been reassigned."

"Gonna miss your company, little lady," Shuttleworth shouted.

"Well, I'm not going to miss your gropin,' li'l old man," Mary Deare said with a big smile, speaking too quietly for him to hear.

David followed Helen into the wagon, giving her the opportunity to choose her seat. He hoped that she would take one of the window seats, but Helen chose the middle one with such certitude that he sensed she knew his feelings for Mary Deare and wanted to keep them apart.

Moments after the caravan started rolling, everyone but David fell sound asleep. He looked past Helen, whose head was resting uncomfortably against the back of the seat, and then over to Mary Deare, who smiled at him, cupped her head in her hand, closed her eyes, and leaned against the window. He thought, Would that I were a glove upon that hand—or at least the pane in her window. He smiled at the silliness of his paraphrase of Romeo's lines and closed his eyes to remember the rest of the soliloquy. Shakespeare had taken a firm toehold in David's psyche and would remain there for the rest of his life. David slept deeply for seventeen minutes. He was startled awake by Christian's unwelcome voice.

"Praise the Lord! Bo has found us some fooo . . . oood!"

David rubbed his bleary eyes and looked over to Mary Deare, who had been prominent in his dreams, and was startled to see her staring at him quizzically, her head cocked to one side and nodding toward his crotch. He looked down and once again found a blond head nestled there.

"It's Helen." David shrugged, whispering embarrassedly, "I didn't know she was there. I should wake her, shouldn't I? I mean, she's probably hungry."

Without moving her position, Helen opened her eyes slowly and muttered, "Where am I?"

"In the lap of luxury, honey," Mary Deare quipped.

"That's funny." David laughed, pleased that Mary Deare could see the humor in the situation.

"I do apologize, David," Helen said girlishly as she sat up. "I just keep falling into your lap, don't I? Now, how does that happen?"

"Why don't we all figure that out at breakfast," Mary Deare said, rising from her seat.

The hungry actors tumbled out of the station wagon and descended like locusts on Ma Sissy's, an unprepossessing, six-stooled country diner where, for fifteen cents Ma Sissy herself cooked up a breakfast of farm-fresh eggs—"Which way y'all want 'em?"—four strips of bacon, a mess o' grits, buttered toast, and a cup of chickory-blended coffee. David never looked foward to a meal more eagerly, for besides being ravenously hungry, he ended up sitting on the porch at a rickety table for two, having breakfast with Mary Deare. It was here, between bites, that David was finally able to tell her how moved he had been by her performance the other night.

"When you did that speech in the second act, Mary Deare," he said, relishing saying the Deare part of her name, "I felt the hair on my neck stand up like it does every time I hear Caruso sing 'Vesti la giubba.' "

"It's so strange your saying that, Donny, because when I was on-stage speaking those wonderful words," she said dreamily, a forkful of grits poised at her mouth, "I felt like I had floated out of my body. It was scary, and I think that's part of the reason I became so emotional last night. I do want to thank you for letting me cry on your shoulder. That was so sweet of you, Donny." She popped the grits into her mouth. "By the way, what's that Vesty la Jew thing you said before that perks up your l'il ole neck hairs?"

"Vesti la giubba. He laughed. "It's a famous aria from *Pagliacci* that we have on a record. I always get chills when I hear Caruso hit those high notes at the end."

"I heard that record once," she said, wiping her mouth with a paper napkin. "Auntie Laura Lee played if for me when I visited her in Memphis one summer; he laughs crazylike at the beginning of it. I didn't know what he was laughing about, but I liked it. I really did."

"That's great!" David said, wolfing down a forkful of scrambled egg. "I wish I had a copy of it right here so we could listen to it to-gether."

"That'd be nice," she said quietly, without conviction.

"Mary Deare," he began, unaware of her sudden coolness, "When we first met, you said I was cute . . ."

"Well, you are, Donny, you're very cute. Are you going to eat your grits?" she said, her fork poised over his plate.

"No, you can have 'em. What I was getting at—."

"I'll bet," she interrupted, "that you don't even know what grits are?"

"They're Cream of Wheat without the lumps," he said, putting a forkful in his mouth. "Mary Deare, do you remember that first time we met and you asked me if I had a girl?"

"Of course I remember. Her name is Margie, and she gave you that ring," she said, pointing to his finger, "that ring that you're not wear-ing. Where is it?"

"I took it off. Do you know why?"

"It was turning your finger green?" she joked, not wanting to hear his reason.

"Mary Deare, I took it off because I love you."

"Oh, goodness," she said quietly, closing her eyes and letting her chin fall to her chest.

"Now I don't expect you to say, 'I love you, too,' although I wouldn't hate it if you did. I just wanted you to know that when I found you in the balcony," he said, taking her hand, "I was looking for you to tell you how I felt about you."

"I want you to know, Donny," she said softly, "that I have those same feelings for you, and I've had them for a while now."

"Wow, that's great."

"Please let me finish," she said, holding his hand firmly. "Don, when you rocked me in your arms the other night and hummed that lullaby, I wanted to take your face in my hands and give you the biggest kiss."

"I'd have loved that!" David said, taking her other hand. "Why didn't you?"

"Because," she said, slipping both her hands from his, "I'm engaged to be married."

David might have been devastated by this information were it not for the sadness he detected in her voice.

"May I ask to who, I mean, to whom?"

"A navy ensign."

"When?"

"As soon as he gets a leave."

"Do you love him?" David dared to ask.

Her answer was a tear dropping from her right eye followed by a tiny head shake.

"So why are you marrying him?"

She remained silent but looked imploringly for David to ask another question.

"Do you want to marry him?" he obliged happily.

She shook her head vehemently.

"You don't?"

"No, I don't," she mumbled, "but I have to."

The stunning words "I have to" triggered a memory of a whispered discussion David had overheard his parents having about his cousin Phyliss. "Sam, she has to! Do you think she wants to marry that no-goodnik gambler?" "She doesn't have to, Bertha. She could get an abortion." My God, David thought, I'm in love with a pregnant girl whom I didn't even make pregnant. I was always so careful whenever I did it. "Who is this idiot?" David blurted out.

"His name is Prueitt Jackson Southerby, and he's not really an idiot."

"Huh?" David asked, shocked to get an answer to a question he thought he was thinking but had actually verbalized. "I . . . I didn't mean he was an idiot."

"That's all right. He does act like one sometimes," she said, dabbing at her eyes with a paper napkin. "Especially when he drinks."

"You can't marry a drunk!" David exploded.

"Prueitt is not a drunk!" she shouted back. "It's just that now and then he'll drink more'n he can handle, like his daddy and my daddy. They can't hold their liquor, either."

"Prueitt?" David asked suspiciously, having a delayed reaction to hearing her intended's name. "This Prueitt, Jack uh, something—?"

"Southerby," she interrupted. "Prueitt Jackson Southerby."

"Are you and he . . . ?"

"Yes"—she sighed—"we are related, but distantly. He's my second cousin, twice removed."

Strangely, this unnerving information did nothing to distance David from Mary Deare Prueitt in fact, his feelings for her became stronger. The girl he loved was in trouble, and even though he was not the cause of it, he would not abandon her.

"Mary Deare," David asked timorously, "did you ever think about getting an . . . uh . . . "

"Many times, but Prue's Catholic."

"Do you want his baby?" David dared to ask.

"I sure don't."

"Does Prue?" he asked, gagging on the name.

"If I can guarantee it'll be a boy who can catch a football. Prue was all-Conference in his senior year and won't ever forget it."

David could not believe that he was having this very personal and charged discussion with a relative stranger. He suddenly became light-headed, and images of his mother and father whirled though his head. He flashed on Margie, Mr. Foreman, Mr. Marlowe, Mrs. Skulnik, and his brother, Chuck, who supplied him with army condoms. He thought how shocked all of them would be to know that he was involved with a pregnant southern girl who was now asking him a real weird question.

"Don, would you get an abortion? I mean, what would you do if you were me?"

"If I were you?" he repeated slowly, trying to readjust his focus. "What would I do . . . ? Well, to start, I would never in a million years marry my second cousin."

"Twice removed," she corrected.

"Well, I would remove him entirely. Do you know that in ancient times," he said, remembering his father's lecture on incest, "the Jews forbade members of the same tribe to intermarry. They noticed that the tribes who took their mates from other tribes had many less retarded kids to take care of. In the desert just taking care of yourself was a major problem."

The look of wonderment on Mary Deare's face gave David heart to carry on.

"You mentioned that this Prue and your daddies had problems with alcohol. Well, that's gotta be hereditary, which means it's a good bet that this baby would have their problems in spades. Do you want to bring another drunken, retarded baby into the world? I sure wouldn't."

"Donny," she said, examining his face, "are you Jewish?"

"Am I Jewish?" he replied, taken aback. "I mean, that's a funny thing to ask."

"Are you?"

"Well, let's see," he hesitated, concerned about why she had asked. "If you mean, do I have Jewish parents, was I bar mitzvahed, circumcised, and beaten up by anti-Semites in Crotona Park on my way to junior high school, then I guess the answer would have to be yes. Why do you ask?"

"Don," she whispered excitedly, "if I can arrange to make an appointment with this doctor, would you go with me?"

"Oh, God," he shouted, and immediately shushed himself. "Abortions are illegal!"

"You didn't answer my question, Don."

"Well, it's a very hard question to answer, Mary Deare," he whispered, still torturing about why she asked if he was Jewish. "They say it's a very dangerous thing to do."

"What's very dangerous to do, roomie?" Gaylord interrupted, coming out of the diner.

"Lots of things . . . Uh, going onstage without knowing your lines, swimming after eating . . . "

"So you've heard the news?" Gaylord said, helping himself to a piece of David's bacon.

"We're going swimmming?" Mary Deare asked innocently.

"You obviously haven't heard," he said, smiling. "Our schedule has been changed. Raymond just spoke with his brother on the telephone and found out that one of the schools where we were to perform *The Shrew* complained that they had *The Shrew* last year."

"That's not a big problem, is it?" David said, thinking of Mary Deare's dilemma.

"Not for those of us who've done *Hamlet* before. We've got four days to bone up on it."

"Four days? We, we . . . we were told we wouldn't be doing Hamlet for four weeks."

"Well, it's four days now," Gaylord said, grabbing another piece of David's bacon before dashing off.

"I can't do it!" David moaned.

"I hope you're not talking about what I asked, Donny,"

"No, no, I was talking about *Hamlet.* Of course I'll go with you," David said distractedly, Mary Deare's problem having unexpectedly become a lesser priority for him. "Uh, where do we have to go?"

"Well, Donny," she said sadly, "there's this doctor I heard about in a little town not far from Decatur, where we'll be this weekend."

"That's in two days." David gulped.

"The sooner the better, honey."

Honey? he thought. I wonder if she called Prue that?

Behind the tailgate of Bo's truck, the actors gathered to receive their sides for *Hamlet.* Only the part of Ophelia was yet to be cast, and all three girls coveted the role. There was no question in David's mind that Mary Deare was the most likely choice, considering her brilliant performance as Adriana. Peggy could have done it well, and Helen, as far as he was concerned, should not even be considered for it. When Helen was chosen to play Ophelia, David reverted to his background and exploded in Bronxese.

"Jeez, c'mon f'chrissakes, whaddya doin'?"

Fortunately, Helen's scream of delight overrode everything, including David's derisive outburst. In the last few hours David had accumulated a host of problems that needed addressing, but for some perverse reason he chose to use his energy to fight this unfair bit of casting.

"I may be out of line, Mr. Selwin," David said as Raymond climbed into the cab of the truck, "but I think you chose the wrong girl to play Ophelia. Mary Deare Prueitt is—"

"Miss Prueitt is—watch your fingers, Mr. Coleman" Raymond barked as he slammed the cab door shut a second after David removed his hand— "not up on Ophelia's lines. Helen Troy knows them, and you have ninety-six hours to learn yours."

On the three-hour drive to Decatur, a wagonload of worried, subdued actors mumbled and mouthed lines from Shakespeare's greatest play. Only Raymond Selwin was able to relax and enjoy the scenic beauty of Georgia's lush countryside, for he had played Hamlet hundreds of times, and to prepare for a performance he needed only to comb out his blond wig and get an extra pint of gin.

Two days before having to perform King Claudius in *Hamlet,* David felt that he could ill afford to spend one full day of his free weekend riding in a cab for two hundred miles out of Decatur to a little no-name town for a clandestine meeting with an abortionist. He and Mary Deare had taken their sides with them and tried to study their lines while they bumped along a back road to the home of Dr. Z, a gynecologist who had lost his license for performing illegal procedures.

Since learning of the schedule change, David had spent every waking hour and at least two-thirds of his sleeping hours trying to memorize King Claudius's lines. When he rehearsed the king's speech that began "O Gertrude, Gertrude, / When sorrows come, they come not single spies / But in battalions!," Mary Deare, recognizing the irony of her being cast as his wife, Queen Gertrude, muttered, "You can say that again, honey!"

Since last night, the speech had taken on an importance for him that Mary Deare could not know. For the past two days David had been breezing along and had more than half of his part learned when a stupid middle-of-the night incident completely unnerved him. He had intended to tell Mary Deare about it and was surprised when she interrupted his studying to ask, "What'n the devil went on in your room last night, Donny?"

"What did you hear," he asked cautiously, "and who did you hear it from?"

"From Helen Troy, but I'd rather you tell me about it."

"How the heck did Helen find out?"

"What's the difference, Donny," she said testily. "What happened?"

"Nothing happened. Hey, you don't want to hear this now, do you? I mean, don't we have more pressing things to think about?"

"I want to hear anything that keeps me from thinking about where we're going."

"You're worried, aren't you?" He laughed nervously.

"Of course I am," she snapped, "It's my first abortion."

"I'm sorry, but maybe you ought to think about this some more. I mean, what do you know about this Dr. Z?"

"My friend Melanie used him, and he's Jewish."

"What's his being Jewish got to do with anything?" David said, stiffening again at hearing her say the word Jewish.

"My mama had a horrible car accident, and our family doctor, Dr. Pyle, said that if it weren't for Dr. Nussbaum in that emergency room she would have died. Nussbaum was Jewish, like one of those smart people in the desert you told me about," she said, taking his hand. "Just like you, smart and trustworthy."

"Thank you," David said, kissing her cheek, relieved to know that the girl he was mad about wasn't an anti-Semite.

"You're welcome, Donny," she said, squeezing his hand. "Now, tell me what happened last night. I don't think I believe Helen's version."

"I don't know what she told you, but this is what happened. About three A.M., I'm studying this darn 'O Gertrude, Gertrude' speech that I'm having trouble with, and I had the light on, and Gaylord—the lucky son of a gun is playing Fortinbras and has only a few lines—is sound asleep and snoring yet. We're in this double bed and he's facing away from the lamp, which is on my side— Mary Deare, why're you looking at me that way?"

"Because I'm fascinated. Go on, Donny!"

"Well, Christian's room is right next to ours, and he wakes up and has to go to the toilet. His room has no toilet, so we let him use ours. Well, this is the craziest thing; you're not going to believe it."

"I do so far."

"Well, right before Christian comes in, Gaylord makes a loud snort, rolls over on top of me, and starts humping me like a dog. I try to push him off, and I'm yelling his name when I look up, and there's Christian standing at the foot of our bed and staring at us. Gaylord is making these crazy moaning and grunting sounds while I'm trying to tell Christian that Gaylord is sound asleep. Gaylord is right on top of me so I can see that his eyes are shut tight. Then I say a really dumb thing to Christian, whose mouth is wide open. I say, he doesn't know what he's doing, Christian. Look, look, I say, we've both got our pajamas on. Well, the more I try to explain what the truth is, the more Christian looks at us like we're two queers, and he says I didn't see anything and scoots back to his room. As soon as the door slams, Gaylord stops moaning, rolls off of me, and starts snoring again. He still doesn't even know what he did, because he was asleep when I left to get you. Pretty wild story, huh?"

"I've heard wilder."

"Yeah, well, I gotta tell you, it was pretty embarrassing for me and for poor Christian. He never even got to pee."

"He did, too, in Helen's room. He told her the whole story, which she couldn't wait to tell me."

"What did she tell you?" David challenged.

"That she was really surprised to find out that you were a queer, too."

"T-too?" he stammered. "What did she mean, too? Who else is queer? Wait, I don't mean who else. I mean, who beside me. I don't mean that, either. I mean, who does she think is queer beside me?"

"David, where have you been?

"What do you mean, where've I been?"

"Didn't you know notice that Helen and Gaylord are no longer chummy?"

"Yeah, I noticed. So?"

"Do you know why, Donny?"

"Probably for the same reason Helen and I aren't. Gaylord found out that she's nutsy and can't act."

"No, dear Donny," she said amusedly. "Helen found out that Gaylord is a fairy and knew that Christian is one, too, and that's why she told him to sit with him in the front seat."

"I can't believe this," David said, shaking his head. "Mary Deare, I've been sleeping in a double bed with Gaylord since we've been on the road, and he's never once tried any funny stuff."

"Until last night."

"He was sound asleep!"

"If he was, he was dreaming about you, Donny, or maybe he wasn't really asleep."

David thought, I'm living with a bunch of sleepwalking sex maniacs! First Helen makes me feel her tits, and now Gaylord dry-humps me. What next? Oh, shit, an abortion!

"Mary Deare, maybe Helen was saying this about Gaylord because he dumped her. He doesn't act like a sissy at all. Look how manly he is onstage; he's got all that panache."

David stopped himself and thought, Yeah, maybe too much panache.

"What'll I do?" David entreated. "I like Gaylord, he's a very considerate roommate, he treats us to hamburgers and stuff, and except for the snoring and this one thing—"

"Before he does this one thing again, I think you should spend the extra fifty cents and get your own room or . . . "

"Or what? he said innocently.

"Move in with me."

"Oh, wow . . . I don't think I can do that."

"Why not? Peggy and Eugene share a room."

"That's true, but they're a couple, and I have this—"

"This Margie?"

"I haven't told her yet about you."

"What will you tell her about me, Donny?"

"Well, that you're very nice and that . . . I'm in love with you and that I really don't know how you feel about me. How do you?"

"How many girls have invited you to move in with them?"

"None."

"That answer your question, Donny?"

"Yes, it does, that's good." He nodded, wondering how many men beside him and Prue she had invited to move in with her.

As he hesitantly leaned in to kiss her cheek, Mary Deare, sensing his irresolution and desperately in need of his kindness and support, turned her head sharply and planted her mouth firmly on his. She held her mouth there for a brief moment before parting his lips with her tongue.

As they rode back to the boardinghouse from Dr.Z's, David knew that this long, hot day in Decatur, Georgia, was one of the turning points in his life. At thirteen, when he was bar mitzvahed, he felt nothing like a man, even though the rabbi decreed that he was. At seventeen, when he made love to Wanda Futerman in the churchyard for the first time, he thought he was a man. But today he knew that being a player in the illegal act of abortion qualified him for adulthood.

While Mary Deare, sedated and debilitated, nestled in his arms, his heart started to pound as he mentally revisited the entire trauma, from the thrilling moment in the cab on their way to the doctor when Mary Deare French-kissed him to when he escorted her into Dr. Z's waiting room. He relived the embarrassment and confusion he felt when the heavyset woman wearing a hospital gown brusquely asked, "Sir, do you and the young lady agree that the procedure be done?"

"Oh, absolutely," he answered, taking Mary's hand and patting it gently. "We agree, both of us."

Neither he nor Mary Deare had anticipated being asked that question, and David had jumped into the breach, as he always did, when a good lie was needed. He was rewarded for his gallantry with a hand squeeze from Mary Deare and a look of gratitude that almost made him cry. No one had ever looked at him in quite that way. The soul kiss and that look of complete trust on her face sustained him for the entire time he sat uncomfortably in Doctor Z's sparsely decorated parlor, waiting for the procedure and the recovery to be over. While nervously clutching Mary Deare's pocketbook as she was ushered into the operating room, David had caught a disturbing glimpse of the doctor and his quarters. Both were untidy and disheveled, but what was more disturbing to David was his suddenly recalling Aunt Martha's horror stories about all the death and disfigurement from botched abortions done "by those dirty, rotten butchers who call themselves doctors."

David had brought along his Claudius sides, intending to study lines, but there was no way he could keep his mind off the mysterious and terrible procedure he envisioned going on behind the door to the operating room. That door held his complete attention from the moment he heard the lock click shut until forty minutes later, when he heard it unclick.

"Your wife is doing fine, Prue," Dr. Z announced as he emerged. "She said that you have the money."

David, who was staring at Dr. Z's bloodstained apron and happy to hear that Mary Deare was alive, did not react immmediately to having been addressed as Prue and being asked to pay for the abortion. His panic, which came seconds later, was immediately relieved when he opened Mary Deare's purse and saw a wallet stuffed with bills. He had shocked both Dr. Z and himself when he asked, "How much will that be, Doctor?"

It was his mother's voice that had escaped from him. He had learned her philosophy well. When you pay for something, she instructed, always ask the price twice. Sometimes they lower it if they think you're going to walk out.

David stared out the cab window while gently stroking Mary Deare's hair. He chuckled to himself as he recalled the exchange he had with the nonplussed doctor.

"Two hundred and fifty is the amount your girl Daphne and I agreed to," the doctor explained.

"Daphne, you say," David said, controlling his urge to laugh at Mary Deare's choice of an alias, "agreed to the fee?"

"Yes, on the phone. Two hundred and fifty."

"Really? Gosh, I thought she said two."

"That's all you have?"

"Gee, I'm sorry, Doctor."

"All right, two hundred, but don't tell my missus. She doesn't approve of this work, and if she knew I was cutting my price, she'd leave me. A word of caution, Prue," he said beseechingly. "The next time, use a prophylactic! I may not be here to help you the next time."

David thought, Too bad I can't tell my mom about this. She would be so proud of me for the good price I got on an abortion.

They arrived back at the boardinghouse after nine P.M., and for the remainder of their Saturday an uncommunicative Mary Deare Prueitt lay quietly in her bedroom, staring at the ceiling and sighing, while David sat on a hard-backed chair next to her bed, keeping vigil and trying to learn his lines.

At eleven that evening Mary Deare sat up in bed and asked David for her sides and a bite of the American cheese sandwich she had packed for their excursion. Abortion notwithstanding, she was determined to be Queen Gertrude this coming Tuesday afternoon. Fortunately, the part was small, and she had studied hard in anticipation of her possible incapacity. David was amazed at her recuperative powers and envied the level of her concentration. Each time he started to study, his mind meandered back to Dr. Z and his bloodstained apron. He tried not to think about how the apron got that way or about the extra-large box of Kotex that he ran out to buy on their way home or what was going on between Mary Deare's legs. Each time he escorted her from the bed to the bathroom he hated that she locked herself in, because he imagined her fainting and bleeding to death before he could break down the door. By the time midnight rolled around, he had worn himself out imagining impending disasters, and all he could think of was the double bed he shared with Gaylord. It was only a ten-minute walk to his boardinghouse, but when he saw Mary Deare grimace with pain, he realized that he could not leave her alone. He was also aware that she had been using only a small portion of her large, soft bed and wondered if he dare ask permission to plop himself down on the unused part.

"Mary Deare, I am soooo tired," he said softly. "If I don't lie down somewhere, I'm going to die."

"Lie here," she whispered, patting the mattress beside her. "We'll die together."

"Yeah," he muttered as he lay down beside her, "just like Romeo and Juliet."

With that romantic reference buzzing in his head, David fell into a deep sleep, so deep that try as he could, he was unable to rouse himself, even when he saw Mary Deare, wearing her Adriana costume, get out of bed, open a Coca-Cola bottle filled with poison, and put it to her lips. He struggled to awaken from what he knew was a dream but succeeded only in making the dream seem more real. He heard himself shout, "Juliet, don't drink that! Romeo is not dead, I'm only sleeping, so you don't have to commit suicide! Those are not the lines Romeo says, but believe me, I'm not dead! I'll look up the real lines and learn them if you stay alive!"

A loud knock on the door awoke him from his nightmare.

"I'll stay alive," Mary Deare said, rousing him, "if you'll get up and see who's at the door."

David had difficulty focusing until he saw Mary Deare standing by the bed and putting on a brassiere.

"Huh?" a befuddled David asked as he watched her walk slowly away, wearing only her brassiere and panties. "Where're ya goin? How long did I sleep? How d'ya feel?"

"To the bathroom, eight hours, and I feel like having a sip of that poisoned Coke you were screaming about in your sleep."

"Oh, my god, eight hours! I only wanted a ten-minute nap!" David said, springing out of bed and opening the door to find a surprised and bemused Gaylord standing there.

"Whoops, so here you are, you devil. I was about to call the radio station and have Mr. Keane, Tracer of Lost Persons, go out and look for you."

"How did you know to look here?"

"Where else? You two were missing all day yesterday."

"Missing from where?"

"The high school auditorium. Raymond's arranged to use it for a blocking rehearsal. Tell your new best friend that we meet in fifteen minutes."

Gaylord gave David a sly, congratulatory wink and started to close the door.

"By the way, Don," Gaylord whispered, leaning back in. "I can ask Christian to take your place if you're planning to shack up with Missy Prueitt. Let me know."

"As Gaylord closed the bedroom door, Mary Deare opened the bathroom door and said, "Missy Prueitt has no objections if Massah Coleman doesn't."

"You mean," he said, still reeling from the newness of his lifestyle, "you really want me to share a room with you?"

"Unless you prefer rooming with Gaylord. You did say he was a thoughtful roommate."

"You're serious?"

"This is the second time I offered you the deal, Donny," she said, wincing as she attempted to put on her dress, "and it's rent-free. Yes or no?"

"I can't let you pay for me!" he said, helping her to slip the dress over her head.

"Yes, you can. My daddy has millions. How much does your daddy have?"

"Hundreds. I don't know about this . . . It just doesn't seem right."

"Neither does having abortions or falling in love with a Jew from the North."

"Did you?"

"Well, you were present at both events."

Once again Mary Deare beckoned David to her by holding her arms out and wiggling her fingers, and David hugged her gingerly.

"I don't believe this," he whispered. "Somebody pinch me!"

Mary Deare obliged and then kissed him.

The Sunday dress rehearsal of *Hamlet* at Decatur High went remarkably well for David, considering the amount of sleep and study time he had had. Gaylord had assisted David in becoming the aging king by lining his face with an eyebrow pencil, graying his sideburns with clown-white greasepaint, and powdering in a streak of cornstarch down the middle of his dark brown hair.

"I look like a skunk!" David complained, examining himself in a mirror.

"A dignified and handsome skunk, like Basil Rathbone," Mary Deare assured him.

At the dress rehearsal David managed to make his entrances on cue and to deliver his lines loudly, clearly, and with feigned emotion. The one important thing lacking was confidence. He visualized Claudius's lines sitting tentatively on the slippery part of his brain, where a good sneeze could jar the words loose and send them tumbling out of his ears. He was able to take some comfort when he measured his performance as Claudius against Bo's and Christian's as the two gravediggers and Raymond Selwin's slovenly nonrendition of Hamlet. David could not believe that this smelly, muttering old drunk, who barely remembered his lines, would think of getting up onstage.

"I have done Hamlet in college twice, Mr. Selwin," Gaylord Morley volunteered as he watched the actor foundering, "and I know the cuts, so if you're not feeling well—."

"Young man, I feel tip-top," Raymond hiccupped, "and even if I weren't tip-top, damn it, I *am* Hamlet!"

Pulling himself up to his full height, which was inconsiderable,

Raymond belched and staggered off, muttering, "I've always been Hamlet, 'n' I'll always be him!"

"The next morning, David and Eugene traded their concern over Raymond Selwin's capacities. "That stink of stale gin coming out of his pores almost made me throw up," David said, "He's worse than our wardrobe trunk. How the hell can he possibly perform today?"

"It is a little worrisome," Eugene granted, "especially that last-act sword fight he staged for us. If the drunken fart forgets to parry when I thrust, you may see me commit my first onstage murder."

"Mr. Selwin never forgets anything," Bo shouted angrily from inside the truck. "And if you damn Yankee smart-asses watch that old drunken fart do his Hamlet, you may learn something about actin'," he said, jumping down off the tailgate.

"Don," Eugene whispered as he watched Bo storm off, "do you know why Bo called us damn Yankees and smart-asses?"

"Because he hates us."

"No, because he's upset that Harold Selwin is going to be in the audience today and will blame Bo if Raymond forgets the words to 'To be or not to be.' It's Bo's job to keep Raymond sober."

All that David retained from Eugene's explanation was that Harold Selwin would be in the audience watching two actors screw up today. Spurred by this possibility, David recited his opening speech as he carried the King's throne into the auditorium. " 'Though yet of Hamlet our dear brother's death / The memory be green, and that it us befitted / To bear our hearts in grief, and our whole kingdom / To be contracted in one brow of woe, / Yet so far hath discretion fought with nature / That we with wisest sorrow think on him / Together with remembrance of ourselves.' "

Oh my gosh, David thought as he put the throne down. I know what Claudius means. He's saying that it's okay to mourn somebody's death for a while but it's only natural that you think of yourself, too. Impelled by this revelation, David went through all of King Claudius's lines looking for and finding meanings that had escaped him in the rush of learning the words. As he monkey-wrenched two lengths of pipe together, he was so elated that he allowed himself to believe that he would get through the performance without stinking up the stage too badly.

David continued to mouth his lines while applying his makeup and getting into King Claudius's regal robes. He was further heartened by what he saw in the mirror and, a few moments later, by what Eugene said to him as he took his place on the throne.

"Kid, you've already won half the battle. You look the part. Break a leg!"

Whenever an actor urged him to break a leg, David always thought of his mother and the first time she came backstage and heard another actor wish him luck in the theatrically traditional way.

"Break your own leg!" she said. "What kind of a thing is that to say to my David before he has to go act?"

Five minutes before curtain time, David went onstage, sat on his throne, and recited: " 'Though yet of Hamlet our dear brother's death the memory be green . . .' dozens of times, hoping to plant the lines so firmly on his tongue that he could say them without thinking. If he got over this first major hurdle, he felt there was a chance he'd make it through the rest of the play. Whenever offstage, he would refresh his memory for his upcoming scene by referring to his sides, which he had secured under his kingly robe. From a darkened corner of the wings, David heard someone going over lines and was happy to know that there was another insecure actor in the company. Moments later, he gleaned from the cigarette smoke that wafted his way that the other worrier mumbling his lines as tentatively as he had at rehearsal was Raymond Selwin. Christian calling, "Curtain up in one minute!" brought the coughing, bent figure out of the shadows. David stared in disbelief and watched the tiny black-hooded figure pass by, pinch out a lit cigarette butt with his thumb and forefinger, and jam it into a fold of his costume. As Raymond ambled to his position for the opening scene, David thought, This man looks as much like Hamlet as Rabbi Shmoloff.

The opening scene of the play, in which Hamlet sees his father's ghost, was performed in front of a heavy black drape, and David, who was seated on his throne behind it, could hear only muffled sounds. He continued to mouth his first line while worrying about Mary Deare, who looked tired and terrible when he visited her dressing room. As she now approached, he was impressed at how beautiful she looked. The pale girl he had seen a half hour before had somehow transformed herself into this luminous Queen.

King Claudius and Queen Gertrude's thrones were fashioned by draping crimson velvet cloth over two high-backed wooden chairs which sat on a raised platform covered with a large royal-blue velvet drape. Queen Gertrude squeezed the King's hand as the curtain rose. There were sounds of approval from the audience that David had not anticipated, for he had no way of imagining how striking a tableau King Claudius, Queen Gertrude, Laertes, and Fortinbras made when the amber-and-pink lights illuminated their beautiful costumes. Hamlet, who had settled himself downstage, just beyond the spotlight's edge, was barely visible. David spoke his first lines flawlessly and with an authority he had not rehearsed.

Eventually, David felt that he was out of danger and could rest comfortably, as the ball would then be in Hamlet's court.

" 'But now my cousin Hamlet and my son . . .' " David said, addressing it to the darkened area of the stage where he hoped Hamlet sat brooding and not in a drunken stupor.

" 'A little more than kin, and less than kind,' " a deep, pained voice that sounded nothing like Raymond's, responded in an aside.

" 'How is it that the clouds still hang on you?' " David asked, addressing the darkness again.

From the shadows arose a Hamlet that made David blink. Looking a foot taller than Raymond and with perfectly coiffed wavy blond hair, he made his way to the throne.

"Not so, my lord; I am too much i' the sun," the tortured, stone-cold-sober Prince of Denmark rejoindered.

David had become an audience member as he listened to an exchange between Queen Gertrude and Hamlet, ending with an impassioned Hamlet chiding his mother: " 'Seems madame! nay it is; I know not 'seems.' / 'Tis not alone my inky cloak, good mother, / Nor customary suits of solemn black, / Nor windy suspiration of forced breath, / No, nor the fruitful river of the eye . . .' "

Fruitful river of the eye, David thought, that's tears he's talking about, tears! By dint of Raymond's brilliance, David understood what Hamlet was saying to his mother, and when he heard his cue, David was so moved by Raymond's passion that the lines he had learned by rote suddenly took on meaning, forcing him to respond with a new-found attitude.

> " 'Tis sweet and commendable in your nature, Hamlet,
> To give these mourning duties to your father;
> But you must know, your father lost a father;
> That father lost, lost his; and this survivor bound
> In filial obligation for some terms
> To do obsequious sorrow: But to persever
> In obstinate condolement is a course
> Of impious stubbornness; 'Tis unmanly grief;
> It shows a will most incorrect to heaven."

David had been so mesmerized by Raymond's transformation from a drunk to the greatest actor he had ever seen that after this scene ended he remained in the wings to listen. The power of Raymond's performance so engrossed David that he delayed studying for his upcoming scene until Raymond delivered the last line of the soliloquy, "But break, my heart; for I must hold my tongue."

In the second act David rushed to the wings to hear Raymond deliver Hamlet's second soliloquy, "O, what a rogue and peasant slave am I!," which Raymond started by speaking softly and introspectively, slowly building in pitch and emotion until he reached a crescendo of fury that reverberated through the auditorium. " '. . . bloody, bawdy villain! Remorseless, treacherous, lecherous, kindless villain! OOOOOOOOOOOH, VENGEANCE!' "

Raymond's heartrending scream for vengeance had an even greater effect on David than Caurso's "Vesti la giubba," for besides his neck hairs standing up, David's arms and legs broke out in goose bumps.

As the performance progressed, David realized how badly he had misjudged Raymond and how wrong he was for pushing for Mary Deare to play Ophelia. Helen Troy's eerie, singsong delivery, which drove David crazy when she played Rosalind, made her Opehlia riveting. Helen's natural weirdness made her performance so affecting that during her mad scene David feared for a moment that she was actually flipping out.

About Mary Deare's talent he had not been wrong. Looking regal and beautiful, she played her part with such energy and skill that David wanted to shout to the audience, "Do you know how good she is? Just two days ago, Her Majesty had an illegal abortion, that's how good!"

By looking through his sides before each scene and forgoing the pleasure of watching Raymond's unbelievably brilliant rendition of "To be or not to be" and Hamlet's other soliloquies, David managed to get through the first four acts without a misstep.

The opening scene of act 5 had the troublesome speech that David fought to remember, and as he stood in the wings listening nervously for his cue to enter, he repeated his first line several times, "O Gertrude, Getrude, when sorrows come they come not in single spies but in battalions."

He girded himself now for this final challenge, took a deep breath, and strode onstage, where he joined Queen Gertrude and Ophelia.

Ophelia, who was now bereft of reason, singsonged her long, non sequitur responses. David listened to them, intently searching for his cues, which he managed to find without missing a beat.

The original play, performed in its entirety, which *Hamlet* seldom is, would require at least five hours, but to service the needs of the high schools, Harold Selwin had prepared a condensed version that could be performed during two consecutive class periods. With the hope of heightening student appreciation of Shakespeare's greatest work, all thirty drama students at Opelika High were seated in the first three rows and given copies of the cut version, which enabled them to follow along as the actors delivered their lines. Had David been aware of this, his unsureness would have trebled.

Playing Claudius with a proper amount of angst, David watched the mad Ophelia exit and then, filling his lungs with air enough for both Claudius and himself, he turned to his queen.

" 'O Gertrude, Gertrude,' " the King said confidently, " 'When sorrows come, they come not in single spies But in battalions!' "

Both David and Mary Deare breathed easily when Claudius successfully negotiated that first hurdle. Then, with a strong voice, he continued, " 'First, her father slain: / Next, your son gone . . .' "

After uttering the words "your son gone," David's eyes glazed over, and he, too, was gone. The remainder of the speech was stuck somewhere in his recalcitrant brain, which teased him by offering up small snatches of the sentences, such as, "the people muddied in their thoughts," "poor Polonius's death," "in hugger mugger," and "mere breasts." Knowing that if he hestitated, he'd be lost, David forged forward, interlacing these disconnected snippets of Shakespeare's writings with nonsense words, lines from other plays, and anything else that bubbled up from his panicked subconscious. David proclaimed this verbal garbage with such emotionally charged fervor that he convinced everyone in the audience and Eugene O'Neill, who was waiting in the wings for Laertes's cue to enter—"that all was well in Denmark." Throughout the rest of David's double-talk speech, there was much flipping of pages as the students searched their books for the page that contained "Here forsoothe the people muddied in their thoughts bespeaketh that which I, as t'were naught but falsity to thine falldasht, did here in thy nymphish orizons, bedraggle and naggle thy mere breasts. Breasts that hugger mugger claims of famitram for poor Polonius's death which I, O my Queen, my Gertrude, my wife, swear to thee by the inconstant and constant moon, that the antidisdamatory Thanes of Rosenkrantz and Glammis who have here, now yet to dispel the lippsnard or to delve drammmidly unto who is thou that hath annointed my soul and burderred it with the pale sweet, prunish of Dane!"

David prayed that his brain would stop sending up rubbish and transmit to his mouth some semblance of the entrance cue that Laertes waited to hear.

Though she knew David was circling the theater and desperately looking for a place to land, Mary Deare managed to stay in character and make it appear that the King had not gone berserk.

"OOOOOOOH, that thou wouldst in thy palatial nuditity," David continued, aping the impassioned tone of Raymond's first soliloquy, "now fail to candor in my framitol. It doth but speak of thy puny, forfeitures and craven carnaselot. Carnaselot! *Carnaselot!"* he repeated with heartbeaking intensity, staring into the wings where a helpless Eugene O'Neill stood transfixed.

"How they to the heavens stink! That I, King of Denmark, t'would in my domitage, suffer the stinks and wallowances of disgregious forsisisity and thus to my very marrow, quiver and quail!"

His voice, now hoarse from pushing it past its limit, David raised his arms above his head and, using what remained of his shredded vocal chords, roared, *"Slather all yon fraility and rail my raility, O nubellious stars! May aaall the feckless and detentioned heavens above be crushed and defted beyond the kindless, porous horizituuuuuude!"*

Exhausted and not knowing what else to do, David collapsed on his throne. Most all of the audience, who'd had difficultly understanding Shakespeare's words, were nonetheless impressed by the bravura performance and loudly applauded the actor who spoke them so powerfully and with such honest emotion. During the ovation, Laertes made his entrance and waited bemusedly for the applause to fade before saying his line " 'O vile King, Give me my father!' "

After this near disaster, David managed to get though the rest of the play without having to resort to double-talk except for one brief moment when, plotting with Laertes to poison Hamlet, he couldn't remember the line "whereon but sipping, If he by chance escape your venom'd stuck," and said instead, "So sip upon it, if he perchance scrape thy sticky blennom."

Luckily, he was able to rescue himself by delivering the cue line intact. " 'Our purpose will hold there.' "

After the curtain fell on the most sustained applause the company had received to date, Raymond, whose brilliant performance spurred this reaction, snatched the blond wig from his head and strode purposefully from the auditorium, brushing aside his fellow actors' sincere attempts to congratulate him. He climbed into the cab of the truck, took a long pull from the gin bottle he had stashed under his seat, and started the process of drinking to disremember how alcohol had destroyed his career.

Embarrassed and apologetic about his memory lapse, David was soothed by his colleagues, who assured him that he had not wrecked the play.

"Never in my vast experience, Don, me lad," Eugene offered, "have I ever heard anything as creatively stupid."

"Or funny!" Peggy added. "I bet you can't do it again."

While Mary Deare was trying to convince him that he should put off killing himself for a day or two, Harold Selwin climbed the steps to the stage and banged his cane on the floor.

"Under the thircumthantheth," he lisped, "I mutht admit that you all did remarkably well, and I congratulate you. However, in Thelma, Alabama, when we perform *Hamlet* again, I'd hope," he said pointedly, staring at David, "that you will uthe more of Shakethpeare'th wordth and leth of your own."

David, delighted to get off with a relatively small rebuke, smiled sheepishly and nodded.

Harold Selwin nodded back, dismissed the cast, and started to leave when he suddenly stopped and turned to David.

"Mithter Coleman," he ordered, banging his cane on the footlights, "if you will give me a minute of your time."

Uh-oh, David thought, preparing himself for a longer and more pointed censuring.

"Mithter Coleman," he said, clenching his jaw, "what in the world do you think you are doing?"

"I didn't do it on purpose, Mister Selwin. I just forgot the lines, and rather that just stand there, I—"

"Young man, I am not talking about your brilliant stage presence."

"You thought that was brilliant?"

"I have never theen anything like it, and I do not want to thee it again," Mister Selwin said unsmilingly, "but I am talking about your other talent."

"What talent is that?" David asked, unaware that he had two.

"Letth not be coy, Mr Coleman. What you have undertaken ith not only foolhardy but unactheptable. Do I make mythelf clear?"

"No, sir. I mean, I'm not clear what's unacceptable."

"Having your way with two women in the company."

"Having my what with who?" David asked, his eyes popping.

"Young man, are you not rooming with Mith Prueitt and at the thame time, to uthe a polite term, courting Mith Troy?"

Not having had sex with either of them, David was completely baffled by this accusation.

"Miss Prueitt and I are sharing a room," he admitted reluctantly, "but I have never, uh, courted her, or Miss Troy, for that matter."

"Thith kind of behaviour, Mithter Coleman, can dethtroy the morale of a company, and I will not tolerate it. You will either control your lutht or leave the company!"

"I'll control my lutht! I promise."

"Can you promith not to bother Mith Troy again?"

"I certainly can, Mr. Selwin."

"Now, young man, if you uthe your energy for learning your part inthtead of thcrewing my actretheth, you might avoid another onthtage dithathter."

For the next few days David studied hard, and at the Selma, Alabama, performance of the play he was letter-perfect. The drama students were able to follow along as he delivered King Claudius's lines, but at the end of his big speech he was disappointed that there was no big applause, as there was when he had double-talked his way through it.

"Face it, buddy," Eugene pointed out, "Shakespeare's words just don't have the zing that yours do."

The last night that David had eight hours of untroubled sleep was the night after the abortion, when Mary Deare invited him to lie next to her. Since then, the short, fitful hours he managed to catch were filled with nightmares that often featured Margie and/or her mother. Last night he had seen both of them: Margie standing on the train tracks, threatening to stab her eye out with a fountain pen unless he wrote more often and Mrs. Skulnik prancing around in her slip and promising to hit him with a baseball bat if he didn't dance with her. Added to these vivid nightmares were feelings of guilt, confusion, and frustration during David's waking hours.

That night, when Mary Deare told him how much she loved him while allowing him to watch her unself-consciously change her Kotex pad, David felt a shiver go through him. He had never shared a more intimate moment with any girl, and somehow her allowing him to see her this way made him feel more committed to her than ever. Resting on one elbow as he lay in bed, he thought how Margie's body, which he had seen nude many times, never looked as naked as Mary Deare's did now as she walked toward him wearing her short, peach-colored nightie. He loved everything about this girl, from her lilting southern drawl and her bouncy, wavy black hair to her smooth, sensuously bowed legs, which he was dying to caress. He had no idea why he found her legs so irresistible. He was similarly affected by girls whose eyes were slightly crossed. When he saw Norma Shearer for the first time in *The Barretts of Wimpole Street,* he did not think she was particularly attractive until her first close-up revealed to him eyes that were somewhat askew.

Mary Deare gracefully slid into bed under the sheet that David held open for her, kissed him, and then settled comfortably in his arms. They had lain together in five different beds in five different cities, and each night, when they cuddled, David, with superhuman effort, restrained the beast within him from touching her breasts or any part of her that might arouse either one of them. To ensure that her recovery from the abortion would not be compromised, even his kisses were circumspect and made with a closed mouth. David knew that one day Mary Deare would be well enough to make love with him, but his innate decency did not allow him to ask how soon that might be. That night as always, when David felt himself becoming erect, he told Mary Deare he loved her, rolled over on his side, and waited to doze off. The rigors of his job had blessedly made it possible for his weary body to supersede his baser needs and allow him to fall asleep rather quickly. In a delicious half-sleep, while fantasizing about the glorious day when he and Mary Deare would physically consummate their love for each other, David thought he dreamed that he felt a cool hand slide across his arm, down his belly, and come to rest on his penis.

"What have we here?" he heard a sweet voice whisper.

"My Birdie," a suddenly wide-awake David whispered back, using the name his mother called it when he was little.

"Hello, Birdie," Mary Deare said, taking his penis in hand and caressing it gently for a short time before it discharged itself.

"Sorry," David mumbled embarrassedly.

"Bless yo' horny heart." She giggled softly. "Poor little Birdie's been cooped up too long, and it's all my fault."

They kissed, and moments later David fell sound asleep and for five solid hours was free of visits from the ghosts of his former life. At six-thirty he woke up to find Mary Deare sitting at the edge of the bed, staring fascinatedly at his crotch.

"G'mornin'," David said quietly. "Whatcha lookin' at?"

"Yo' penis. It's the first circumsized one I've seen."

"Well, what do you think?"

"It's neat. Streamlined, like the new Chrysler. I like it."

"Thank you. And thank you for last night."

"It was my pleasure."

"Really? It sure felt like mine," he said, pulling her toward him and kissing her.

Later that morning, after he and Mary Deare enjoyed a compli-
mentary scrambled-egg and pork-patty breakfast that the boardinghouse owner, Mrs. Gayle, provided, David excused himself and went
out onto the porch to try to make some order out of his life. Sitting in a
wicker chair and recalling Mary Deare's sweet face telling him only
moments ago at breakfast how much she cared for him helped David
gather the strength to write the letter he had put off for too long.

Opelika, Ala.

Dear Margie,

*I hope you are well. I'm sorry that I haven't written more often,
but being on the road, we have little time for anything but
sleeping and doing the show. We did Hamlet again, and it was
quite an improvement over the last time, when I forgot
everything but the name of the play. I wrote you about that
disaster, but I don't know if you received that card yet. In your
last letter you asked about how I get along with my roommate,
Gaylord. Well, he's a really nice guy and a very good actor, and
we get along great, but he's not my roommate anymore. It's a
long story that ended up with Christian rooming with Gaylord
and me moving in with another member of the company, which
is an even longer story but one I think you have a right to hear.
My new roommate is a girl. I hesitated to tell you because I
knew you would be upset, but I think it's only right that you
know. I won't blame you if you never speak to me again, but I
assure you that even if this thing that happened didn't happen, I
don't think it's a good idea for us to get married. I never
thought it was, and I probably should have said something when
you were making plans for the wedding, but you were so
excited, and I guess I didn't want to be a wet blanket. Anyway,
in a year or so I'll probably be drafted into the army, and who
knows where I'll end up or how I'll end up or if I end up at all.
I'm really sorry for any pain I may have caused you and would
like for us to remain friends, but I know that maybe that's not
possible at this time. Margie, I want you to know that I have
always had great respect for you as a person and always will. I
hope you don't hate my guts too much even though I have given
you plenty of reason to hate them a lot.*

Sincerely,
David

P.S. Say hello to your mother for me.

P.P.S. After rereading this letter, I realize that I did not convey how really badly I feel about hurting you. If it's any consolation to you, I feel like a shit.

✦

Five days later, in the auditorium of Vidalia High, while he was hanging the backings for *As You Like It,* Beauregard handed David a letter. From reading the foreboding way Margie had addressed the envelope—David Kokolovitz, c/o Don Coleman—David knew that she was pissed off at him. He sequestered himself in a booth of the backstage toilet before opening it. By habit, he stopped to sniff the envelope even though he did not expect it would smell of Tweed toilet water. His heart pounded as he unfolded Margie's unscented letter and read:

David,

I can't say that the contents of your letter came as a complete surprise. In your last few postcards I don't think you realized that you had written more between the lines than on them. I want you to know that as far as I am concerned, you are free to do with your life whatever you want to. I could kick myself for not seeing you for the shit you admit you are. I wish you had told me earlier. All I can say is better late than never and good riddance to bad rubbish! I should have known that you couldn't be trusted when I caught you lying on the floor with my mother. Like a dope, I ripped up her best dress because I blamed her. Boy was I ever wrong about you, Mr. Kokolovitz! You must be a better actor than I gave you credit for. I thank my lucky stars that I learned what a person of low morals you are before I paid for my wedding dress. I hope your "roommate" isn't a dope like me and finds out what a two-timer you are before you ruin her life, too. By the way, I bet it's that southern girl who you only wrote about once. Well, whoever it is, she can have you with my blessings, and if you think I'm going to sit home and cry about you, you've got another think coming. You're not worth it! And David, don't try to get in touch with me by telephone, as I will not be home this weekend. I have accepted an invitation to go to Grossinger's with Milton Eisenstadt. You remember him, my boss's son, that tall fellow you met when I took him to see you

in your play. By the way, to show you that you didn't pull the
wool over my eyes, I accepted Milty's invitation long before I
read your last letter.

Drop dead,
Margie

P.S. I would appreciate it if you would return my gold
friendship ring. I intend to use it again; only this time I'll make
sure I don't give it to a snake.

✦

Reading Margie's vitriolic appraisal of him as a two-timing shit
and somebody whom she wished dead did nothing to help David's self-
esteem. Was he, in truth, all of the things Margie described, or had she
exaggerated his awfulness to make a point? He remembered now how
often he had dissembled and told Margie he loved her when he wasn't
sure he meant it. I am a shit, he concluded. Only a shit would lie to a
girl about loving her just to ensure that she continue to grant him her
sexual favors.

David went back to work thoroughly convinced that he was the
worst human being who ever lived. His self-flagellation was interrupted when Mary Deare came onto the stage and tapped him on the
shoulder.

"Donny, after you finish settin' up the stage," she asked, "would
you go for a walk with me? There's something I have to talk to you
about."

"Something good, I hope?" David asked nervously, fearing another assault on his self-worth.

"It could be, Donny, depending on how you look at it."

David finished his work quickly, declined an invitation from Eugene to join him for a cheeseburger, and rushed off to the football field
where Mary Deare had arranged to meet him. He had no idea what she
wanted to talk about but prayed that it was not about ending their relationship.

David found Mary standing under a goal post, lighting a cigarette.

"Hi," she said, holding out a package of Chesterfields. "Want
one?"

"I gave them up when I was twelve," David said, taking one, "but
I'll just hold it, makes me look suave. I didn't know you smoked."

"I do when I'm nervous."

"Like now?"

"Exactly!" Mary nodded, taking a drag and ambling down the football field.

"What are you nervous about?" David asked, catching up to her at the ten-yard line.

"My folks," she said, turning to him. "They're coming to see our show when we play Montgomery."

"That's great! I'd love to meet them," he said, breathing easily. "Is that why you're smoking?"

"Donny," she said, wrinkling her brow, "when I first met you, I flirted with you, but I never dreamed that I'd fall in love with you."

"So far, I love what you're saying."

"Please don't say adorable things," she begged, flipping her cigarette away. "It makes this more difficult."

"What is it that I'm making more difficult?"

"Don, this morning I called Mama and told her about you," she said, tossing her cigarette away. "That's why she and Daddy are coming to the show."

"Oh, boy," David said, nervously inhaling air from his unlit cigarette. "Guess they want to check out the actor-schnook you dumped a big football player for."

"Mama never liked Prue. She wasn't impressed that he was rich, good-lookin', and an all-Conference quarterback."

"Well, then, she should love me. I'm none of those awful things."

"No, you're not, Don, and I feel terrible."

"About what?"

"About not standing up to Daddy. When he asked me if Coleman was a Jewish name, I told him that it wasn't."

"Well, Coleman isn't, I don't think," David offered, hating the direction their conversation was taking. "It's the same name as Ronald Colman except that I added an *e* so we wouldn't be getting each other's fan mail. You know," he said, taking her hand, "if you had told your father my real name, you wouldn't have had to lie."

Mary Deare threw her arms about his neck and hugged him as hard as she could.

"Tell me," David asked after kissing her on the cheek. "Just how anti-Semitic are your folks?"

"Mama's not. Dr. Nussbaum is still her doctor."

"He's not your daddy's, though?"

"Oh, no."

"Would he disown you or something?" David asked, smiling sickly. "I mean, if he knew I was Jewish?"

"He doesn't have to know!"

"I can't lie about that."

"Why not?"

"Well, for one thing, that guy Hitler is saying how awful Jews are, and I think it's important that I show people like your father how really cute we are."

"He'd never notice or care."

"You know something? I don't think I should meet your daddy. How come you picked me to fall in love with. I mean, with your daddy being such an anti-Semite?"

Mary smiled strangely at David while deciding whether or not to burden him with any more of her problems.

"Oh, hell," she said, taking his hand and leading him toward the grandstand. "You have a right to know what you're getting into."

"Don't you mean, who?" David joshed, kissing her cheek.

David, happy that Mary laughed at his little joke, accompanied her up to the last row of the grandstand and sat down beside her.

"David, you must promise," Mary Deare said, her face now serious and her voice trembling, "that you will never repeat what I am about to tell you to anyone."

"I promise," he said, hoping her secret was not one he had to keep from the police.

"David," she said, lighting another cigarette and then tossing it away as if someone had forced it on her. "Daddy is not my real daddy, and he has no idea that he isn't."

"Wow, you mean"—David hesitated—"your mother, uh . . . ?"

"Yes, Mama was pregnant when she married Daddy but didn't tell him because he was a deacon in the church and she knew he needed his bride to be a virgin. Daddy's twenty-seven years older than Mama. She was eighteen, and the boy who knocked her up was someone she hardly knew. He was a trumpet player in a touring band who was playing a one-night stand in Charlotte. Actually, he played two one-night stands, one in the club and one in his car. Mama said that they were both pretty drunk and all she remembers about him were his eyes, the bluest she'd ever seen. His name was Pete, and she never saw him again."

"Gee, that's so sad."

"It really isn't, Donny."

"Sure it is. There's a trumpet player named Pete somewhere out there who doesn't even know what a beautiful, talented daughter he has."

"Don't make me love you any more than I do," Mary said, her eyes becoming misty as she put her lips on his. "Don Coleman, you are the sweetest thing ever."

They sat in the cold, empty grandstand, kissing and caressing each other with uncensored passion until Mary Deare suddenly jumped up and ran off. David followed her across the football field and to their boardinghouse, where, for the next half hour, in the comfort of their soft bed, with a mixture of hunger and passion, they explored and enjoyed each other's nude body.

As he withdrew from her and ejaculated on their bedsheet, Mary sighed and hugged him with all her strength.

"Someday, sweet Donny," she purred into his ear, "I'm gonna want you to leave your l'il ole tadpoles inside of me."

In the cubicle-size dressing room at Robert E. Lee High in Montgomery, Alabama, David, in an attempt to create a distinguished, non-Jewish-looking King Claudius, took particular pains in applying his makeup. Using an old toothbrush, he carefully blended the white greaspaint into his sideburns, and instead of using cornstarch for the streak in his hair, he gingerly daubed in some of the greasepaint. He had been told after that first forgettable performance that every time he ran his fingers through his hair, great poofs of powder swirled around his head. Eugene watched in amusement as his friend meticulously drew in and deftly highlighted the crow's-feet around his eyes and the age lines on his face and brow.

"Pretty impressive makeup, buddy," Eugene said, struggling to get into his damp tights. "Critics coming today?"

"Yes, Mary Deare's parents. And I expect a rotten review from Senator Prueitt. Mary Deare says he hates Shakespeare, and he's not too crazy about Jews. Look at me, Eugene," David ordered, turning his face to him. "Who do you see, King Claudius or King David?"

"Definitely Claudius."

"I hope you're right." David sighed, reaching for his doublet. "I've never had dinner with a guy who doesn't like Jews. Got any pointers on how to act Gentile?"

"Well, for one thing, don't show 'em your dick, even if they ask to see it."

"I'll try to remember." David laughed.

"Remember, too, buddy," Eugene said, pinching his cheek, "that the senator is the one with the problem, not you."

David appreciated Eugene's words, but they did little to relieve the anxiety he felt about his impending meeting with the Prueitts of Alabama.

Sitting with Mary Deare in the back of Senator Prueitt's shiny, black, chauffeur-driven Packard limousine gave David the rare opportunity to experience firsthand the advantages of being wealthy.

"You know, Doc," he admitted to Mary Deare, caressing the leather seat, "compared to riding in a New York subway, this is four hundred million times more pleasant."

"That much?" Mary Deare laughed. "By the way, who's Doc?"

"You, you're Doc, your initials. I could call you M.D."

"I like Doc."

"I love you, Doc," David said, leaning over to kiss her.

Riding in the limousine with the girl he loved might have been much more enjoyable for David had their destination been anywhere but the home of the Prueitts. His backstage encounter with the senator and his young, beautiful wife, though blessedly brief, was anything but warm.

"Can we make this a short evening, Doc?" David asked. "The less time I spend with the senator, the less chance he has of discovering my true identity."

When the limousine reached the bend in the road and the glorious splendor of the Prueitt mansion and its acres of magnificent green lawns and tall trees came into view, David imagined he heard a swell of symphonic music.

"We are home, Donny."

"Tara?" David joked, awe-struck at the grandeur of the antebellum estate. "You live in Tara?"

"It does look like Tara, doesn't it?"

"Spittin' image except for the slaves. Big Daddy give 'em the day off?"

David actually bit his tongue when he caught the light-skinned Negro chauffeur glaring at him in the rearview mirror.

"Your Mr. Lincoln made us free them," Mary Deare said playfully, sensing his embarrassment.

"Oh, that's right, I forgot."

The level of David's discomfort mounted when a colored butler appeared from nowhere to open the limousine door.

"Evenin', Missy Mary," he said in a basso-profundo voice. "Nice to have you home."

"It's nice to be home, George. This is my friend Mr. Coleman."

"How' do, Mr. Coleman," George said, bowing slightly.

"Howdy," David replied, unable to address this imposing gray-haired man by his first name. He remembered well how his father had once berated him for addressing their colored janitor as Willie. "His name is Mr. Mitchell to you," his father had pointed out forcefully during one of his after-dinner lectures on ethics. "Mr. Mitchell is an adult, and an adult, no matter what color his skin is, you will treat with respect!"

All David could think of now as he mounted the wide white steps and walked past the giant pillars toward the mansion's massive doors was how completely out of place he felt in this setting and also how great the food must be inside. David was famished and wondered how long it would be before someone offered him something to eat. Two-thirds of a Baby Ruth candy bar was the last substantial thing he had eaten since breakfast. Usually after a show he would go out for a hamburger, but tonight, to make himself ready to dine at the Prueitts, he raced back to the room, showered, shaved, cut his nails, and ironed the wrinkles out of his only suit.

As David entered the foyer of the Prueitt mansion, he felt as if he had been dropped into a Civil War movie. Positioned in the grand hall, on highly polished floors, were more pieces of elegant, antique-style furniture than he had ever seen outside of Mallory's Furniture Store in the Bronx. Walking down the hall toward the den, where they were to meet the senator and his wife, David learned that the gold-framed portraits of the distinguished people that hung on the walls were all Prueitt ancestors. David was particularly struck by the uncanny resemblance Senator Prueitt bore to his great-grand uncle, Civil War general William T. Prueitt.

"Mah great grand-daddy," George explained proudly. "He work fuh General Bill till the day he die. Mah great-granddaddy, he stay on after the war and help the general's widow rebuild this house, yessuh."

George ushered the couple into a wood-paneled den. Senator Prueitt stood beneath a flattering portrait of himself.

"Welcome and congratulations," he toasted, raising a crystal glass filled with bourbon. "You two young actors almost succeeded in making Shakespeare tolerable."

The senator moved forward, kissed his daughter lightly on the forehead, and then took David's hand and attempted to break every bone in it.

"Happy to have you in our home, Mr. Coleman," he said, holding David's hand in a death grip. "My daughter tells me that you have a grand sense of humor."

"And no sense of feeling in this hand," David said, wincing with pain.

"Sorry, young man," he said, releasing his grip. "Guess I don't know my own strength."

"I do. It's great, believe me," David said, nursing his hand. "I was thinking of cancelng my fall violin recitals, anyway."

"Do you play the violin, Mr. Coleman?" Mrs. Prueitt asked worriedly.

"Rowena, that boy was crackin' a joke. Weren't ya, son?" he said, turning to David, who nodded. "Now what're you drinking?"

Disappointed that he was being offered a drink instead of food, David answered politely, "What're you having, sir?"

"Bourbon."

"My favorite," David said, never having tasted any hard liquor in his life.

"George," the senator ordered, "a bourbon for Mr. Coleman and a whiskey highball for my daughter."

"Better make that a lemonade, George. I'm on the wagon, Daddy."

"Well, get off it, darlin'. Tonight we're celebratin' your homecomin'."

David took a sip of the boubon, and when his tongue and gums started to burn, he had no polite choice but to swallow.

"Ahhhh," he managed to rasp through constricted vocal cords. "Best . . . bourbon . . . I ever had!"

"The young man knows his spirits. Bottoms up, son," the senator commanded, offering his glass to be clinked.

David clinked it and watched the senator gulp down a quarter of a glass of the stuff without changing his expression. God, David thought, even Humphrey Bogart grimaced a little when he downed a shot of whiskey.

When David was eleven, after drinking a full glass of sweet sacramental wine at a Passover dinner and spending the night retching into the toilet bowl, he vowed never to drink again as long as he lived, and here he was, only ten years later, breaking his vow. Responding to the senator's order, David hoisted his glass and emptied its contents. As the fiery liquid made its way down his gullet and into the pit of his empty stomach, it took all of his acting ability to hide the fact that he thought he was going to die. Holding out his glass and sounding remarkably like Bogart, David managed to say, "May I have a refill, Senator?"

Mary Deare knew that he would have preferred a glass of milk and a slice of chocolate cake, but she admired how well her beau was playing the role of a good guest.

"Coleman . . . " the senator pondered out loud, pouring bourbon into David's glass, "is that English or German?"

From the pained expression on Mary Deare's face, David guessed what her old man was getting at.

"I think it's German," David said brightly, "but it could be either."

"Where does your father's people hail from?"

"Austria," David was happy to answer honestly.

"Austria," the senator mused aloud, sipping his drink. "Some good men have come from Austria."

"That's true, Senator," David agreed, thinking of Freud and Mozart. "Boy, I love this bourbon, Senator," he added, taking a sip. "I'd like to bring home a bottle for Dad."

David felt guilty referring to his pop as Dad, but he knew that if he did not change the subject, the dinner could go up in smoke.

"Sir, can I buy this in a store, or is this something you have blended for you personally?"

"Bourbon is not blended, son"—the senator smiled—"and you can buy it in a store. But don't bother to. I'll send your daddy a case with my compliments."

"Oh, no, no, sir," David balked, picturing his teetotaler-father dealing with a case of expensive bourbon. "I couldn't let you do that."

"I'm not asking your permission, son. Mary Deare, you get the address of the young man's folks. Now, as I was saying, Mr. Coleman, it was an Austrian who, in 1924, while he was in prison, wrote a book that contains ideas and a political philosophy that is more or less responsible for this awful war we're involved in. Now, I don't hold with most of what he has written, but there are ideas in it that are quite interesting. If Roosevelt had taken time to study this book and digested some of its truths, we could have avoided this damn war."

David took a big gulp from his glass and looked over to a seemingly impassive Mrs. Prueitt, who, during her husband's oration, stared into her lap and carefully folded and unfolded a small hankie. Mary Deare glared at her father and prayed that he would not start quoting passages from his favorite book.

"Don, young folks like yourself would do well to read this," the senator said, patting the copy of *Mein Kampf* he had retrieved from the coffee table. "It's a much-maligned book, and I can understand that.

There's a lot of garbage in here, but there are also some truths, and whoever wins this war, these truths deserve to be reexamined and taken seriously."

"Can I get a refill?" David said, holding out his empty glass to the senator.

"Listen to this, son," the senator said, ignoring David's request and opening the thick volume to one of the many pages that had been bookmarked with a strip of yellow paper, "and you may learn who your real enemies are."

David looked to Mary Deare for strength, but all she could offer was a sickly smile and a shrug.

" 'The Jew's life as a parasite in the body of other nations and states,' " the senator read, " 'explains a characteristic which once caused Schopenhauer . . . to call him the "great master in lying." Existence impels the Jew to lie, and to lie perpetually, just as it compels the inhabitants of northern countries to wear warm clothing.' "

"Does this make any sense to you, son?" the senator asked, looking up from the book.

"Oh, sure, Senator," David said, his senses reeling. "The inhabitants of northern countries need to wear warm clothing."

"Exactly!" the senator said, interrupting David, who was on the verge of blurting out that he was one of the perpetually lying Jews that Hitler was talking about.

" 'They lie in very cunning ways,' " the senator continued excitedly. "Did you know that the Jews have always been a people with definite racial characteristics but in order to get ahead they'd find ways to hide or distract attention from their unpleasantness? I'm paraphrasing," the senator admitted, searching the page for a quote. "He says it better in the book."

"That's okay, Senator," David interrupted. "You said it good enough for me."

Blessedly, George came into the den and, by announcing that dinner was being served, stopped his master from reading another inflammatory passage.

"After dinner," the senator suggested as they walked to the dining room, "I'd like to read to you a few other remarkable things this man we call a monster now discovered about Jews."

"I can't wait to hear them, Senator," David said, allowing his sarcasm to surface.

"Of course, I am aware," the senator said, taking his seat at the head of the massive dining table, "that I am in a minority at this time, but things can change."

"I can't wait," David said, crossing his eyes and staring at Mary Deare.

"David, I apologize for bringing you here," Mary Deare whispered as they took their seats. "I think we should leave. I can't believe he quoted all those terrible things to you."

"And I can't believe," David whispered back, sitting down unsteadily, "that I drank three full glasses of hard liquor and don't feel like vomiting."

"David, we should go."

"Absolutely, but let's eat first. I'm starved. I never met a Nazi before," David said, downing his drink. "It's very educational."

Had David not been drunk, he would have been intimidated by the amount of long-stemmed glasses and pieces of elegant silverware he found surrounding his gold-rimmed plate.

"Ooooh, Mrs. Prueitt," David gushed, picking up one of his three forks, "this is a great-looking fork. All the forks are great. And this plate . . . it's so beautiful, even more beautiful than the plates my mom got on 'Dish Night' at the Belmont Theatre. I can't wait to see how food looks on it. I know it's not polite," he rambled on, "but I gotta tell you, I could eat a horse. All I had today was a candy bar that Queen Gertrude here," he said, poking Mary Deare, "took a bite out of when I wasn't looking, which I don't mind, 'cause I am very fond of her, as she may have told you."

"She hasn't," the senator barked, glaring at him as he joined hands with his wife and daughter. "Let us say grace."

"Oooh, you're gonna say grace"—David giggled happily—"just like they do in the movies. I gotta see this."

Had the senator not been accustomed to dining with drunks, he might have been more annoyed by his guest's interpolations during grace and his verbal meanderings throughout the rest of the meal.

"Mrs. Prueitt," David said, putting a forkful of honey-baked ham to his mouth, "this is sooo good! Do you know how good? Well, I'll tell you how good. I have eaten Romanian pastrami in some of the finest delicatessens in the Bronx and New York City, but this, this Georgia pastrami of yours," he proclaimed, taking a slice from the platter and holding it up, "beats 'em all. I toast you, madam."

Mary Deare eyed David suspiciously as the senator and his wife exchanged reproving glances as David stuffed the piece of ham into his already full mouth and washed it down with wine.

"The cherry soda's warm, Senator," David remarked as he sipped the 1922 Lafite Rothschild. "Could use a couple'a ice cubes".

As the alcohol content in the senator's blood rose, so did his amiability and his acceptance of his young guest's antic behavior. He actually laughed out loud when the flaming cherries jubilee was served and David rushed to the phone to call the fire department.

"Fire!" David shouted into the wrong end of the phone, "Come quickly. Senator Prueitt's dessert's on fire! Looks like the work of a Jew arsonist!"

"A Jew arsonist," the senator repeated, roaring with laughter. "That . . . that is very amusing, young man."

"It might be amusing, Senator," David said, affecting a British accent as he strode unsteadily back to the table, "if the per . . . per . . . perperaperperatraitor were not in this room! There!" he said, pointing at George. "There's your Jew arsonist!"

David walked up to the senator and started to say, "Arrest that man," when a dense mixture of honey-baked ham, black-eyed peas, corn bread, and candied yams exploded from his mouth as if propelled from a cannon. By turning his head sharply, David managed to deliver the thick, foul, bourbon-soaked mixture directly into the senator's face. After releasing a second wave, which ended up on the senator's neck and vest and ultimately his lap, David ran from his blubbering victim to the powder room, where he retched the remainder of his meal into the toilet bowl. Miraculously, only two little specks of the regurgitated dinner splashed onto David's jacket. After spending almost ten minutes rinsing his mouth, washing his face with cold water, and rubbing his jacket clean with the end of a damp towel, an embarrassed but reasonably composed David returned to the scene of his crime. There he found George supervising the downstairs maid, who was working feverishly to clean the massive amount of half-digested dinner off the master's chair and the rug beneath it.

"Mr. Coleman," George said, a hint of a smile on his face, "Mrs. Prueitt asked me to tell yuh that the dessert 'n after-dinner brandy won't be served tonight, as she and the senator has real bad headaches and had to retire."

"The senator is mad at me, isn't he?" David felt compelled to ask.

"Well, suh, ah don' 'spect he gonna invite you back soon, leastways not for dinner," George said, shaking his head. "Mistuh Coleman, Missy Mary say to tell you she be waitin' for you out front. My wife, Ludie, give her a slice of bread 'n some lime Jell-o fo' yo' ride home."

"That was very nice of her," David said, offering his hand.

David knew that he had breached some southern rule of etiquette when he saw George hesitate and look around furtively before extending his hand.

"Thank you, George," David said, clasping George's hand in his.

"Thank *you*, suh," George responded, giving David's hand a single shake before moving off.

He thanked me for shaking his hand, David thought as he walked down the hall and passed the framed pictures of Mary Deare's family. It wasn't too many years ago, he thought, that the senator's ancestors owned most of George's ancestors. David was happy to leave the mansion and find Mary Deare waiting for him in the backseat of a cab.

"No limousine?" David joked as he climbed in. "The senator must think I vomited on him purposely."

"You did, didn't you?"

"Well, it could've been the hand of God. I think I felt him stick one of his fingers down my throat and then aim my mouth at that—Honey, we don't ever have to see that man again, do we?"

Mary Deare shook her head violently and patted his hand. After riding for a few moments in silence, David slapped his knee in anger.

"What is it, Donny?"

"I should have told the senator that I was a Jew. I want him to know that a Jew vomited in his face."

"My mother knows. I told her on the phone yesterday."

"Really? What did she say?"

"She asked if I loved you."

"What did you say?"

"I said I did."

"Do you still, I mean, after throwing up all over your dad."

"You didn't throw up on my dad. That was my mother's husband you did the job on. Donny, when we get back to our room," Mary Deare whispered throatily, "after you shower and brush your teeth, I'll show you how much I love you. But first . . ."

"But first what? I don't need any but-firsts."

"Oh, yes, you do. We are going to do something that'll make your whole body tingle with excitement."

A throughly debilitated David smiled, said a simple "Wow," and let his weary head fall against her shoulder. Within minutes he was asleep and dreaming of himself and Mary Deare doing lovely, wild things to each other.

He awoke with a start when he heard a distant voice sing out, "Wake up, sweet face, we're here!"

Squinting through watery, red-rimmed eyes, David saw what seemed to be the tails of a dozen small airplanes.

"Airplanes," he mumbled groggily. "Are we in an airport?"

"Yes, we are, darlin'."

"I thought you said that we were going back to our room, where you were gonna—"

"I am gonna," she said, taking his hand and pulling him out of the cab.

"Is this the thing that you said was going to make my whole body tingle with excitement?"

"Yessuh," she said, skipping excitedly down the line of planes and stopping at the propeller of a yellow Piper Cub. "Isn't she the most beautiful thing you evuh laid eyes on?"

"No, you are! Whose plane is this?"

"Mine!" she said, proudly patting its fusilage. "This is my baby."

"That's crazy," David said, shaking his head.

"What's crazy, honey?"

"Owning an airplane. Nobody owns an airplane. Even Lindbergh didn't. How come you never mentioned that you—"

"Because I didn't want you to think I was a spoiled, rich bitch. Oh, Donny," she gushed, taking his hand, "have you ever been up in a plane?"

"Never."

"Well, sugah, get ready for the thrill of your life."

"We're going to do it in a plane?" David asked.

"No, we're going up in it!"

"I don't know if I can handle it," he said, rubbing his stomach and looking around. "Who's going to fly it?"

"I am. I have a pilot's license. Please say yes, Donny!"

"Well, I'd really like to," he said, remembering that Amelia Earhart's body was still missing. "Maybe after the tour's over would be a better time."

"By then the plane won't be here. Please?" she pleaded as she opened the plane door.

"Uh, why won't the plane be here?"

"Because, even though Daddy gave it to me for a birthday present," she said, indicating the name *Missy Mary* painted on the door, "he really owns it."

"He's not going to take it away from you, is he?"

"He says he will unless. . . ." she began, unsure whether or not to continue.

"This has something to do with me, doesn't it?"

"Well, in a way," she said, taking a deep breath. "Tonight, after Daddy came out of the shower, he asked Mama if she had any idea what religion you were."

"Aha! And she told him."

"No, she said that she didn't know, but my Mama is anything but a good liar. Daddy called me up to his room and sort of told me that if I didn't discontinue my relationship with you, he'd sell my plane."

"What did you mean, he sort of told you? Maybe you misunderstood him."

"I don't think so."

"How do you know? I mean, what did he actually say?"

"Well," she said, taking a deep breath, "my dear daddy's actual words were"—she hesitated and then continued through clenched teeth—" 'L'il darlin' if you want to keep the Piper Cub, you get rid of that kike. You can't have both!' "

"I'm sorry I asked."

"I don't care what Daddy says. I will have both, and right now me and my Jewish lover are goin' for a spin!"

"My head's already spinning," he said, stunned at being called a kike.

Before he could mount an objection, Mary Deare climbed into the pilot's seat and shouted to a man in greasy coveralls who was approaching the plane, "Hey, Sparks, check us out!"

"Donny," she called, "get your butt in here!"

"Right," David said, making no move to join her.

"Please," she said, patting the seat beside her. "Once you're up in the air, you'll love it."

"Wanna bet?" he grumbled as he watched the man in coveralls duck down and jerk two wooden blocks from under the wheels of the landing gear. Against his better judgment, David yielded. He climbed into the plane and settled nervously into the copilot's seat.

"Buckle up," his pilot barked after kissing him hard on the mouth, adding, "Bastard senator!" as she pulled away. "I'll die before I let that son of a bitch come between us!"

David watched helplessly as his manic girlfriend fussed with things in the cockpit and exchanged strange but impressive hand signals with the mechanic. David felt a sudden rush of blood to his head when he saw the propeller begin to revolve and heard the fitful sound of the engine starting up. Mary Deare's oath was echoing in his head when the plane suddenly started to vibrate. The propeller blade become a blur as the airplane moved forward and picked up speed. Not since he had chicken pox and overheard his aunt Ida inform his mother that their cousin Rifkah died of chicken pox had David been as deeply concerned about his mortality. His body shook violently now as the the Piper Cub sped down the bumpy runway. He was about to complain about the rotten condition of the strip when the vibrating suddenly stopped. It took a moment for him to realize that the smooth road under him was air.

"We're off the ground," he yelped. "Omigod, we're flying!"

When Mary Deare banked the plane sharply to the left, he closed his eyes and whimpered, "Mama."

"Donny honey, are you scared?"

"Shitless! You're not going to do that again, are you?"

"Only when I need to."

"Could you please not need to. My stomach—"

"Donny, if you open your eyes and see how beautiful the world looks from up here, you'll forget you have a stomach."

David forced his eyes open and dared to look down. All of the diving, looping, and crashing in the movie *The Dawn Patrol* that he had watched while fantasizing he was with Errol Flynn in the cockpit of his World War I fighter plane had not properly prepared him for this real-life adventure. Actually, being up in the air and looking down on things he had always seen at eye level truly frightened him. He could hear his mother screaming at him, "Idiot, where are your brains? You go up in a plane because a girl asked you to? And if she asked you to jump out, would you jump out?"

David actually did jump when he heard Mary Deare ask, "Well, what do you think, Donny? Isn't it wonderful?"

"Oh, wonderful!" he lied. "I'm thrilled, I'm tingling just like you said I would, and I'm ready to go back to our room right this minute."

"We can't just yet," she said, grinning strangely. "First there's something I have to do."

With that Mary Deare put the plane into another sharp left bank and completed the 180-degree turn she had started.

"Hey, hey, hey" was all David could manage during the maneuver, but as the plane leveled off, he uncovered his eyes and asked, "Is that the something you had to do?"

"Part of it," she said, pushing the throttle forward.

"Well, you don't have to do any more of it for me," he insisted. "That was great; my body doesn't need any more tingling, I swear."

They were less than fifteen hundred feet in the air when David looked down and thought he recognized the grounds of the Prueitt estate directly below them.

"Isn't that your folks' house?" he asked, seriously concerned with her motives for flying over it.

"Yes, it is," she said, too coldly for David's comfort.

"Uh, why are we here? I mean, you said you had to do something . . . Is this where you're going to do it?"

"Yes, David," she said sweetly, making an even sharper turn than the previous one. When the plane leveled off, she pushed the wheel forward, nosing it downward and directly at the Prueitt mansion. The heart-stopping sensation in David's chest was beyond anything he had ever before experienced or wanted to experience again. Had she not pulled the plane out of the dive at the last horrifying second, they would have crashed smack into the gabled upper story of the house.

"We, we . . . we came close . . . to crashing into the house," David said, gasping for air.

"Not close enough." She smirked, pulling back on the wheel.

David yelped again when he found himself suddenly lying almost horizontily in his seat and looking up. In front of the nose of the plane, where a moment before there had been green treetops, he was now looking at a backdrop of billowy white clouds. On its climb Mary Deare steered the plane through a low-hanging cloud, leveled it off again, and flew straight ahead for five seconds before banking sharply and diving through the clouds. If there had been any food left in David's stomach, he would have heaved it onto the windshield. Once again, the small plane was on a collision course with the Prueitt mansion. Before Mary Deare pulled the plane out of the precipitous dive and headed for the clouds, David caught a glimpse of Senator Prueitt's terrified face peering through his bedroom window. It seemed to David, who was frozen with fear, that Mary Deare was maneuvering the plane for another daredevil pass at the mansion. When the plane leveled off after the ascent through the clouds, David decided that rather than die in a fiery crash, he had to try to talk her out of attempting a third and perhaps fatal dive.

"Mary Deare," he said, speaking as rapidly as he could, "this is so great, just as exciting as you said it would be. I really loved it. You're some great pilot, but I think we should go back to the airport now. You know we're doing *The Comedy of Errors* tomorrow, and we haven't done that show for a few days, so we should go over our lines. What do you say?"

"Good idea," she said distractedly as she leveled off the plane and made a gentle turn in the direction of the airfield.

"I really appreciate what you were doing, Mary Deare," David said, breathing a sigh of relief, "though I don't think your father did. Boy, those dives right at the house, whew! It was a little too dramatic for me, but I'm sure the senator got your message,"

"Well, if he didn't, he will when I give him back his plane," she said, taking her right hand off the controls and touching his face.

"Gee, hon, that's great." He laughed relievedly. "I'll bet I'm the first guy on my block whose girl gave up a plane for him. I feel like that Mrs. Simpson whom the Prince of Wales gave up England for."

"I love you," she said, leaning over to kiss him, "and I really appreciate your saying I'm a good pilot."

"Well, you sure showed me a lot today."

"Well," she said, banking the plane sharply and starting a 180-degree turn, "I'm going to show you one more thing."

"You don't have to," he insisted loudly, fearing for his life. "You really don't have to show me anthing more today. I mean it!"

"I have to show you how I land a plane, don't I?" she asked much too calmly for David's comfort as she pushed the steering column forward.

David froze as he felt the plane descend and saw that they were headed for the Prueitt estate. He could not believe that Mary Deare planned to use the front lawn as a landing field. The plane approached the small forest of pine trees that rimmed the property when Mary Deare decreased their air speed and deftly guided the plane over the tall treetops. They were less than twenty feet off the ground and descending when looming up ahead were two enormous trees that lay directly in their path. It was obvious to David that there was not enough space between the trunks to accommodate the plane's wingspan and that there was plenty of room on either side of the great trees for her use if she wanted to avoid a collision. Oh, God, David thought, she meant it when she said, "I'll die before I let that son of a bitch come between us!" She's going to commit suicide and take me with her. He prayed he was wrong and that she would do as she had done twice before—go full throttle and pull the plane up. She did increase the speed, but instead of pulling up the nose, she made a beeline for the trees. David saw the plane's nose glide between the hundred-year-old trees but covered his eyes and missed seeing the wings smash up against the trunks. He heard the sick, ripping sounds as the wings tore from the plane's body. He opened his eyes slowly and saw Mary Deare calmly steering the wingless plane toward the mansion. She taxied it up to the steps to the porch and brought the whirring propeller to within ten feet of the front door before cutting off the motor. She then unbuckled her belt, took the key out of the ignition, and jumped out of the cockpit just as her father burst from the house. His face was beet red, and his slack mouth and jaw were attempting to form words, but all they could marshal were a series of apoplectic coughs and indecipherable grunts. David scampered from the wreck, thankful to be alive and on the ground. Mary Deare sauntered up to her sputtering, shaken father and held the ignition key out to him.

"You take your Piper Cub," she said quietly, dropping the key into the breast pocket of his robe. "I'll keep my kike."

David had never heard the word *kike* said with such loving tenderness. To him she was Juliet saying, "A rose by any other name would smell as sweet?"

While Senator Prueitt was trying to compose himself, Mary Deare ran to David, took his hand, and started to lead him off. She stopped to look back at the house and found her mother peering sadly but resignedly through the curtains of her bedroom window.

"I'm sorry, Mama," she shouted. "I love you."

Mrs. Prueitt, raised her hand and, barely moving two fingers, waved goodbye to her daughter.

Marching hand in hand, the couple made their way to the back road that Mary Deare assured David led to the main artery, where they would have no trouble hitching a ride back to their boardinghouse. The only hitchhiking David had ever done was in the Bronx with his best friend, Milt Langsam. To save the ten-cent trolley fare to and from high school, David disobeyed his mother and bummed rides, trusting that he would not be robbed, kidnapped, or murdered and thrown into a ditch, as she projected he would. Because they carried schoolbooks, they never had to wait for more than a dozen cars to pass by before some Good Samaritan stopped to pick them up. Now, carrying no schoolbooks and being on a little-traveled side road, he suspected that their chances of bumming a ride were dismal. After ten minutes and only one passing motorist, David started to panic.

"Look, Doc, if another car ever does come by, why don't you show your legs like Claudette Colbert did in *It Happened One Night*. It worked for her and Clark Gable."

"You show yours," she demurred. "They're purtier than mine."

"Your legs are sexier, believe me," he shouted. "Quick, I hear a motor. Lift your dress."

As a small, beat-up farm truck came into view, David ducked behind a tree as Mary Deare lifted her skirt and held out her thumb. The young Negro driver gunned his motor and sped away.

"Well, I scared that poor fellow off," Mary Deare said, straightening her dress.

"Gee, I was sure he was going to stop."

"He might have if you hadn't been hiding. Colored boys aren't too keen about picking up white girl hitchhikers who show off their legs."

"Sorry. Next time we'll both use our thumbs."

However, it did not seem that there would be a next time. A half hour passed, and not one car appeared. As they walked down the dark, dusty, deserted road, Mary Deare promised a devitalized David that the main road was only a few miles away.

"And I promise"—David sighed, stumbling along—"that if I don't get something to eat, I will either faint or die. How far have we walked?"

"About a mile."

"And we're a few miles from the main road?"

"Yes, Donny. I hope you're not thinking we should go back to my house."

"No, I'd never suggest we go back." He spoke softly to preserve his strength. "I know how you feel about your father. What's the name of this road we're on?"

"Elm Way. What are you suggesting?"

"That I go back, sneak into the kitchen, grab a piece of that great ham, call a cab, tell him to pick you up on Elm Way, and then you come back and get me. I'll wait right outside the grounds."

"David, you're talkin' crazy talk."

"I'm not talkin' crazy talk. I'm talkin' 'if I don't get something to eat and drink right away, I'll faint' talk. I'll be back as soon as I get me a gallon of water and some of that great ham!"

"David, if you try to sneak into the house, you'll end up with a load of buckshot in you."

"I don't care. I gotta get *something* in me," he moaned, weaving drunkenly from side to side.

Mary Deare grabbed him by the shoulders and pulled him to her. Weak from dehydration, David offered minimal resistance and fell into her arms. Unable to support his dead weight, she toppled to the ground, taking him down with her.

"You see?" he asked with a silly giggle.

"See what?"

"How weak from hunger I am. I'm lying here on top of you and thinking about buckshot pancakes. Buckshot!" he repeated, giggling harder.

Within seconds David's silly giggle became a chuckle and then full-throated, contagious laughter that quickly infected Mary Deare. The two of them rolled around in the middle of the road, holding their sides and trying desperately to stop. Mary started to sober up when she realized that David's laughter had escalated to a point where it no longer sounded like laughter. Realizing that he was gripped by uncontrollable hysteria, she sat him up and slapped him hard. The pain in his cheek and the sound of a blaring automobile horn was all he needed to snap back to reality.

"Get up!" Mary dear shouted, tugging on his arm as she watched the car's headlights coming toward them.

"Leggo," he said, pulling his arm free and lying flat on the ground.

"What are you doing?" she screamed.

"Hitching!" he explained, holding up his thumb. "This is how Aaron Schwatt always got us rides."

The car came to a stop ten yards from David's body.

"Goin' my way?" David shouted from his prone position.

The headlights obscured their view of the driver, but they heard a voice say, "Yessuh."

"George?" Mary Deare screamed.

"Yes, Missy Mary. It's George. Is Mistuh Coleman all right?"

"I'm fine," David said, struggling to his feet. "You don't have a ham sandwich on you, do you?"

"No, suh, ah don't, but ah have what's left of the fried chicken my wife made fo' Sunday dinner. Yo welcome to it," George said, reaching back into the car and retrieving a paper bag. "She thought you might be hongry."

"Thank you, thank you, thank you," David mumbled, snatching the bag from George and tearing it open.

"George, what in the world are you doing here?"

"Well, Missy Mary, after ah give the senator his sleepin' pills, ah think of you and Mistuh Coleman wanderin' around in the dark, and I say to myself, George, on de road dose young folk are walkin' down, they have a no percent chance of hitchin' a ride, so ah fired up d'Packard, and here ah am."

"George, I love you," Mary said, throwing her arms around him. "You know that, don't you?"

"Yes, Missy Mary, I do know that," George said, patting her gently on the back.

"And I love you, too, George . . . and your wife," David mumbled, his mouth filled with chicken. "Tell her that I said this is the best chicken I ever ate in my whole life!"

David had already devoured two thighs and was ravenously biting into a drumstick when Mary Deare helped him into the backseat of the Packard.

"Is dat fried chicken gonna sit comfortable in yo' stomach, Mistuh Coleman?" George asked, hesitating to shut the door. "The senator don't know ah've taken the car, and ah 'preciate you not leavin' any telltale clues in it."

"Don't worry," David said, tossing a drumstick bone out the side window. "This is one meal I'm going to hold on to . . . and remember forever."

It was only when they were halfway home and he had devoured six pieces of the succulent, home-style fried chicken that David thought to offer Mary Deare the one remaining piece.

"Had your fill?" she joked.

"Nope!"

"Then it's yours, dear."

George watched amusedly as David popped the end of the chicken wing into his mouth and deftly denuded it.

"Mistuh Coleman"—George cackled—"ah can't wait to tell Ludie how much you enjoyed her fried chicken. You know, she say to me that you the favoritest guest we ever had at Prueitt mansion, yessuh."

"Even though I got drunk and threw up her whole delicious dinner?"

"No, sir, she didn't like that," George's said softly, his face breaking into a wide smile, "but she did 'preciate where you threw it."

George glanced into the rearview mirror and, though aware of Missy's feelings toward the senator, was relieved to see her smile back at him.

It was past two A.M. when George brought the Packard to a stop in front of the boardinghouse. The two tired lovers were sound asleep in each other's arms and snoring in counterpoint.

"Missy Mary, Mistuh Coleman," George whispered as he opened the car door. "Ah'm sorry Ah has to wake you, but—"

Having no idea where he was, David stood up quickly, simultaneously banging his head on the roof and sending Mary Deare tumbling from his lap. Thinking that she had crashed her plane, she crawled out of the car.

"Hurry, David," she shouted. "It could explode!"

"We're okay, we're okay," David said, scrambling to her. "Nothing's going to explode. We're back home."

"I'm sorry, Missy Mary," George apologized, feeling responsible for her confusion.

"Nothing to be sorry for." David sighed. "It's just been a very weird day, and it's finally over, thanks to you."

David offered his hand, which George took unhesitatingly, giving it two smart shakes.

" 'Bye, Missy Mary. Didn't mean to scare you," George said, climbing into the car. "May d'Lord keep y'and hep y'both to find all the things y'looking fuh."

"He's already helped me to find one of them, George," Mary

Deare said, encircling David's waist and drawing him to her.

Up to this moment David had felt only love, lust, and passion for Mary Deare, but after hearing her declare that he was one of God's gifts to her, he felt a knot develop in his stomach. At first, he thought it might be all the fatty fried chicken he had bolted down, but he knew intuitively that it had to be something much more serious, something he couldn't solve by heaving it into a toilet bowl. He felt that Mary Deare Prueitt, by irrevocably severing all connections with her family, had suddenly become his charge. He loved her but had no idea how he could possibly care for her in the lavish style to which she had become accustomed.

At seven o'clock the next morning Eugene rapped loudly at their door and shouted, "Hey, you two, a whole gang of us are planning to go to Sylacauga and do *Comedy of Errors.* They're all in the station wagon. Wanna join us?"

Because they had slept in their clothes, David and Mary Deare were able to toilet, pack, and leave their room in three and a half minutes.

"God, look at you two, all dressed up and looking like shit," Gaylord teased as they took their places in the wagon. "Are we going to hear what you two love birds did yesterday?"

"Oh, not much," David yawned. "I threw up on a senator, and then we crashed in an airplane."

"Pardon me for asking," Gaylord shot back with mock anger. "I was just trying to be friendly."

"No, really, vomiting and crashing is what we did," David said, removing his blue jacket. "Buy us dinner and we'll fill in the details."

In Sylacauga, David had one of his better days as an actor. Besides getting wonderful audience response for his performance as Antipholus of Ephesus, he later convulsed his friends at dinner by recounting how he spent his day off. While everyone was laughing and applauding David's re-creation of the final terrifying moments before the plane crashed, Beauregard entered and stole David's audience by shouting, "Mail call!"

At what turned out to be a momentous mail call, only August Shuttleworth, who received a veteran's disability check, was happy with what the post office brought him. David was handed another letter addressed to David Kokolovitz c/o Don Coleman, but the information in it, which he would not read until later that night, did not affect his life as dramatically as the greetings that Gaylord Morley and Eugene O'Neill received from the president of the United States through their draft boards.

"Oh, shit!" Eugene muttered. "Uncle Sam wants me."

"He wants me, too," Gaylord screamed, "and I can't possibly imagine what the hell for."

"To make a man out of you?" Christian joked sadly.

"You're a great fencer," Helen Troy offered. "They still use swords in the army, don't they?"

"No, not since the Three Musketeers retired." Gaylord replied, scanning his notice. "Oh, shit, shit, shit! I have to report in four days."

"Lucky bastard," Eugene said, throwing his notice in the air. "They want me there by Wednesday morning."

"No, no, you can't go," Peggy screamed, looking to keep him with her. "Tell them that you're playing Petruchio Wednesday afternoon."

"Oh, my God, you are! You can't go, Eugene, you can't!" Helen Troy insisted. "Mr. Ogilvie is coming Wednesday to see me do Katharina."

"Who the hell is Mr. Ogilvie?" Eugene barked.

"My drama teacher. He's traveling all the way from Canandaigua, and if you leave, they'll cancel the performance. I'm sure if you wrote them a note—"

"Great idea! How's this?" an annoyed Eugene chided. " 'Dear draft board, would you please excuse Eugene from the draft, as Mr. Ogilvie is coming all the way from Canandaigua to see me in a Shakespeare play. Your friend, Helen Troy.' "

Helen stormed out of the diner and went looking for one of the Selwin brothers. She found Harold Selwin in the lobby of the hotel, sitting dejectedly in a phone booth. Since early morning, after learning that his brother, Raymond, had been rushed to the hospital and diagnosed with pneumonia, nephrosis, and acute alcoholism, Harold had been struggling with the impossible task of rearranging a schedule that did not include the five contracted performances of *Hamlet*. On hearing Helen's news that two of his key actors would be leaving for the army, Harold's face suddenly brightened. With the impossible rescheduling problem now taken out of his hands, he immediately called for Beauregard and ordered him to assemble the entire company for "a meeting of utmost importance."

Drawn and defeated, Harold walked slowly into the Sylacauga High School auditorium, where, in an hour, the company was scheduled to perform. He tapped his cane lightly on the footlights and asked for everyone's attention.

"I have an announthment of import that affecth all of you. I am told that two of our printhipal playerth will be leaving to join the army. Thith, coupled with my brother thuddenly taken ill and unable to perform, leavth me no alternative but to canthel the remainder of our tour. Today'th performanth will be our latht, and you can all plan to leave for home immediately after it."

David and Mary Deare looked at one another in shock, each thinking of the consequences this bombshell would have on their lives. The entire company sat in stunned silence. August Shuttleworth, who had been stranded many times in his long, undistinguished career, was the only member of the company able to speak.

"Harold," Shuttleworth shouted, "we'll be given our return fares home and be paid for today's show, I trust."

"I apprethiate your trutht, Mither Thuttlworth," Harold said, sneering. "You all will be paid immediately after the thenery truck ith loaded."

Before turning to go, Harold Selwin scanned the somber faces of his players and nodded an individual farewell to each. As the bent old actor slowly made his way toward the wings, he stopped at the proscenium's edge, filled his lungs with air, squared his shoulders, looked out toward the balcony, and spoke. By a conscious effort, speaking and enunciating his words carefully, the old man managed to deliver Shakepeare's words with hardly a lisp.

" 'Life's but a walking shadow,' " he intoned, " 'a poor player that struts and frets his hour upon the stage, and then is heard no more.' "

No one stirred as the old man turned to leave. His last words still echoed as he disappeared into the darkened wings. It was clear that he was speaking not only of himself but of his brother and their repertory company, which after that day's performance would be heard from no more.

Only when Harold was out of earshot did Eugene O'Neill, the company's resident antisentimentalist, surprise everyone by rising from his seat and asking for their attention.

"Let us toast a wonderful man and a great actor," Eugene said solemnly. "I give you a man whom we have all grown to respect and love," he added, hoisting an imaginary glass. "Private Gaylord Morley! A fellow inductee who, along with myself, pledges to stop those German Nazis from invading our shores and conquering Broadway before we do!"

"Donny darlin'," Mary Deare whispered, "what's going to happen to you and me?"

"What's going to happen to you and me?" He repeated, painfully aware that Mary Deare had given up her home and her airplane for him. "I say, for Eugene and Gaylord's sake, that you and I go to Broadway and start conquering it!"

"You are so dear." Mary Deare laughed, putting her hand to his cheek. "It's going to be so exciting to live in New York. I can't wait to see all the things you told me about, and I look forward to meeting your mother and father."

"You'll like them," David said, imagining his mother saying, "A shiksa? You bought home a Christian girl?"

"Donny, do you think they'll like me?" a concerned Mary Deare asked.

"I guarantee one thing, honey. My father'll like you a lot more than your father liked me."

"What about your mama?"

"My mom will take one look at you and say '*Oi Gevalt,* a shiksa!' "

"What's that mean?"

"Oh, goodness, she's stunning!"

Traditionally, during the final performance of a play, some of the naughtier actors will try to break each other up by playing some kind of prank, preferably when the victim has important lines to deliver. When done subtly, the audience is most times unaware that anything unusual is going on. Tonight, for his final performance in *The Comedy of Errors,* Eugene, who was in a screw-it-all mood, kept the theatrical tradition alive by placing a large cucumber in his tights before going onstage for his first scene with David. As twin brothers, the two stood profile to profile and acted amazed at the similarities in their faces and bodies. David wondered why Eugene was being so generous and standing downstage of him, his back to the audience. It was more ususal for one actor to upstage the other, and here was his friend allowing himself to be upstaged. It was when the two brothers went to look at each other's legs that Eugene flicked up his gown and let David see his giant erection. Because of the way he had positioned himself, nobody in the audience could see Eugene's bulge and therefore did not understand why Antipholus of Ephesus suddenly looked shocked and then for no reason burst out laughing. The company, which was in on the gag, gathered in the wings to enjoy David's valiant struggle to stay in character.

After the last curtain call there was much hugging and crying and exchanging of addresses, except for Helen Troy, who made it clear to the company that she had no interest in ever again seeing or hearing from any of them.

"You are all self-centered, unprofessional egomaniacs," she railed at the astonished group. "And you, Eugene O'Neill," she screamed, pointing her finger at him, "you are the worst of all. Even after I told you how important it was for Mr. Ogilvie to see me perform Katherine on Wednesday, you made no attempt to contact your draft board and explain the situation! You, you . . ." she shrieked, rushing toward Eugene, "you selfish bastard!"

David instantly flashed to the incident on the train ride to Atlanta when Helen went berserk. Then it was fear that sent her screaming into the toilet. Now it was uncontrollable anger that guided her hands toward Eugene's throat.

"Oh, come on now, Helen," Eugene scolded, "you're not going to choke me . . ."

Before he could get his hands up to ward her off, Helen had her fingers on his throat.

"Hey, hey, hey," Eugene gasped, trying to pull her hands from his neck.

"Hey, bitch," Peggy screamed hysterically, scrambling across the stage, "get your hands off him!"

Gaylord and David sprang into action. Gaylord grabbed Helen by the shoulders and tried to drag her away, while David succeeded in peeling Eugene's fingers off Helen's, which left her hands on his throat and free to continue strangling him. Without thinking, David put his hands around Helen's neck and squeezed it hard enough to make her gasp.

"If you stop, I will!" he shouted in her ear.

Helen released her grip on Eugene's neck, fell into David's arms, and started to weep uncontrollably. Beauregard, who had been summoned, volunteered to take her to the infirmary, but when he went to gather her up, she kicked and cursed at him, screaming for David not to leave her. Why me? he thought. It could only be that she feels she can trust me. I may be the only one here who ever touched her breast. He knew he had no aternative but to escort her to the school infirmary. She kept a tight grip on him, and he hoped that ultimately she would get one on herself. She remained cradled in his arms until the ambulance came. He held her hand until the sedative took effect.

At the hospital she was diagnosed as having had a "psychotic episode due to an emotional trauma" and was released into the custody of her drama teacher, Mr. Ogilvie, who graciously agreed to accompany her back to her home in upstate New York.

The following morning in Sylacaugas was sunless and gloomy and mirrored the mood of most of the members of the Avon Shakespearean Company. By ten A.M., with packed bags and tickets in hand, the actors started to make their exodus. Only Mary Deare and David had not made any arrangements to leave town. They were still in bed, asleep in each other's arms, when Eugene and Peggy rapped on their door.

"House detective!" Eugene shouted. "Stop what you're doing and say goodbye."

" 'Bye, you two!" Peggy called out.

"Get out of here, ya rotten kids!" David shouted, flinging his shoe against the door. "We're trying to get some sleep here."

"I'll bet," Peggy trilled. "See ya' at Horn and Hardart's!"

"Ooooh, chocolate-pudding pie," David raptured. "We'll be there."

Besides not wanting to start the day by dealing with the problem of being out of work, David and Mary remained in bed because they were emotionally and physically drained. The previous night, after crawling between the sheets, a sadness overcame David, and he worried that something over which he'd have no control would take Mary Deare from him. Hoping to rid himself of this thought, David had suggested to her that they hold each other and make love all night long. She laughed and agreed that "it's a lovely way to spend an evening." The long, beautiful night of active sex and declarations of undying love was interspersed with pauses to pee, nap, and nibble on Baby Ruth candy bars. At four A.M., a spent, sweaty David rolled off Mary Deare for the last time and fell back onto his pillow.

"Oh, God, God," he announced breathlessly but proudly. "We've done it six times, an Olympic record!"

Mary Deare had not the heart to tell him that by her count it was not six times. Perhaps someday, after we're married, she thought, I'll tell him, but tonight, more important than coming to orgasm was knowing how deeply David cared for her. She loved his enthusiasm, his passionate grunting, and all the silly sexual chatter he made during the night, but what she cherished most was the sincere, tender things he said to her while they lay quietly in each other's arms. As dawn broke, David was deep in a nightmare, dreaming that his love, dressed as Ophelia, had gotten out of bed and flown off in a wingless plane to search for Amelia Earhart. On awakening to discover that Mary Deare was not in bed lying next to him, he screamed in panic, "Nooooooo, Maaaaarryyyy, come baaaack!!"

"I'm here, I'm here," Mary Deare shouted back, dashing out of the shower and to his side. "What? What is it, darlin'?"

"Oh, thank God you didn't drown," he said, pulling her wet body to him. "You didn't crash into the ocean."

"No, but I almost crashed in the shower when you screamed."

"She calmed him by inviting him to join her in the shower. They laughed, kissed, soaped each other's bodies, and agreed that they had just spent the most wonderful night of their lives and never wanted to leave the warmth and safety of their magical, two-dollar-a-night boardinghouse. Clean and concerned, they fell back into bed, snuggled in each other's arms, and quietly discussed their future. They were sure of only one thing, their love. They promised each other that no matter what the problems or pressures, they would find a way to be together forever and ever and ever and ever.

For the young lovers, however, "forever and ever and ever and ever" turned out to be a mere twenty-one days. On that day David received a letter from President Franklin D. Roosevelt requesting that David Kokolovitz join his millions of other young men in their valiant fight to save the world for democracy. On December 9, 1942, after David and Mary Deare reworded their promise and vowed to be together no matter how far they were physically separated, the draft board wrenched David from Mary Deare's arms and drafted him into the U.S. Army.

Part 2

Dec. 7, 1944

My sweetest of hearts,

It's been three years since the Japs attacked Pearl Harbor and it seems that long since we attacked each other. I don't know how much longer I'll be able to stand not being with you, dear Mary Deare. I'm lonelier than ever since last Wednesday when I discovered that my favorite photo of you, the one in the lacey white hat that I took when you visited me in Camp Crowder, was missing. I kept it in my footlocker and always looked at it before lights out—seeing your sweet, smiling face before I fall asleep helps me forget that I'm living with forty guys who snore and fart a lot. I'm not sure, but I think Henny Shwick stole your picture—he's that schmuck corporal I told you about. He drooled over your photo when he saw it. I never showed Henny your photo, but the sneak saw it when he went into my footlocker to borrow my nail clipper—he borrows things from everybody's footlocker. I kept it lying under my underwear. Oh, sweetie, I'd give anything to have you lying under my underwear right now, or in them would be even nicer. If you can find the negative, please make another copy and send it. Seeing your face before I go to sleep sort of jumps-starts my dreaming of you. Don't send the photo until I give you a new address—the army has plans for me and a few of my buddies. We've been assigned to something called Detachment 18, and we're told that we're moving off the island sometime tomorrow. I don't think I'm allowed to write about leaving tomorrow, but if this information is classified, you'll see gaping holes in this letter. Do you want to hear something unbelievable? Of course you do. Tonight Saul Marantz and I are going to the University of Hawaii to see a show, and I don't mean a FOUR JILLS AND A JEEP kind of show but a production of HAMLET with a big Broadway star, Evan Merritt. I'm curious to see how he stacks up against Harold Selwin. I don't see how Evan Merritt can do better than poor old Harold. I sure miss acting in plays, but I feel lucky that I've been able to work up an act. I really enjoy getting up at a mike and making guys laugh. I entertained again at the USO canteen in Honolulu, and among other things I did a double-talk Hitler routine, and the guys really loved it. Mine is a little different from the one we saw Zero Mostel do in that Times Square war-bond rally, so I don't feel like a complete thief. I've added some of my own jokes and a couple I borrowed from Eddie Cantor's radio show. I sure hope that wherever they're sending me has a recreation hall and a good microphone, and of course no Japs shooting at me.

Honey, I got a real thrill out of your last letter, the one where you told me how much you love me. You said in it that you were dying to kiss my sweet, curly lips—well I'm going to press them right on top of the x's at the bottom of the page—it's the best I can do for now. My darling M.D., I love you so much it hurts!

> *Your always loving and always horny for you, Donny,*
> *David K.*
> *XXXXXXXXXXXXXXXXXXX*
> *XXXXXXXXXXXXXXXXXXX*
> *XXXXXXXXXXXXXXXXXXX*

P.S. Shwick returned your picture. He borrowed it to compare it to his new pinup of Alice Faye. I saw it, no comparison, but her lips do look a little like yours. Oh, I need your lips! I love you.

✦

David folded the letter, placed it in an envelope, and sealed it even though he intended to write again that night after seeing Evan Merritt's Hamlet. He could have added it to this letter, but knowing how excited Mary Deare was about receiving his mail, he decided to put his critique in another envelope. He had once spent an entire Sunday writing letters to her and that night mailed off seventeen separate six-page letters. A week later, she received all seventeen letters plus four others he had written earlier that week. She wrote him back a ten-page letter telling him how touched, thrilled, and lucky she was to love a man who proved over and over again how much she meant to him.

"C'mon Dave," Saul Marantz shouted, standing at the open barracks door. "*Hamlet* awaits our presence."

Of all the members of his platoon, Saul Marantz was the only one with whom David enjoyed a genuine bond. The two had been best buddies since their induction. Besides doing their basic training together, they had both been assigned to the Army Specialized Training Program at Georgetown to learn to be French interpreters, then to the Signal Corps School at Camp Crowder, Missouri, to become teletype operators, and now to the 3117th Signal Battalion in Oahu. David cherished Saul's friendship and often wondered why this quiet, witty, intelligent fellow who had a master's degree in education had chosen to buddy up with a would-be actor who had barely squeaked through high school. He guessed that it was because of their shared interest in theater and sports and in avoiding all religious services. Saul was painfully shy and appreciated his friend's ability to get up on a stage in front of hundreds of people and make them laugh. Saul had once said that he'd trade his master's degree for David's guts, which David considered the highest praise he'd ever gotten for something he never thought he had.

Many soldiers had come to see the great Evan Merritt play Hamlet, but most came hoping to see a foxy actress or two strut about the stage. Saul Marantz had seen Evan Merritt do his celebrated full-length, five-hour version of *Hamlet* on Broadway and was anxious to see how he had adapted it for army consumption.

"*Hamlet*'s an amazing play," Saul said as they settled in the tenth row of the orchestra. "I read it in high school and then saw a college production, then again with Merritt, and each time I came away thinking about what a genius Shakespeare was."

"I played in four of his plays and each time I came away thinking about what an idiot I am." David laughed, perusing his mimeographed program. "I never understood half of what I was saying."

"I don't believe that. Hey," Saul said, referring to his program, "that actor in your rep company who did that song and dance after each show, didn't you tell me his name was Eugene O'Neill?"

"Oh, my God, that proves how dumb I am. I didn't notice it. He's playing Laertes; it's gotta be him. I had one letter from him when he was in basic training and he said he was going to try to get into Special Services, and the lucky bastard did."

Evan Merritt's production of *Hamlet* was done on a bare stage, with all of the actors, including those who played Ophelia and Queen Gertrude, wearing army-issue green fatigue uniforms. Remarkably, the lack of costumes and scenery worked to focus attention on the play. David was completely fascinated and reluctantly admitted that Harold Selwin's wonderful interpretation of Hamlet was nowhere near as powerful or stirring as Evan Merritt's, or as witty. David was surprised that there was so much humor in the play and was impressed with Merritt's comic timing.

As the play moved into the final scene, David concluded that every actor onstage except for the chubby actor who played Claudius and the tall redhead who played Fortinbras was superior to the actors in his old cast, and that included Eugene O'Neill, whose Laertes was now fuller and more exciting. The curtain calls were greeted with heavy applause and a scattering of bravos which David started. Both David and Saul were eager to go backstage, David to surprise Eugene and Saul to meet Evan Merritt, but when they reached the stage door, they were stopped by a burly M.P. and informed that they were off limits.

"But Sergeant," David protested, "Eugene O'Neill, the actor who played Laertes, is an old . . . der brother."

"I'm sorry, soldier, no one gets backstage," the M.P. barked. "Major's orders!"

"But you don't understand," David explained, his emotion building. "Gene and I haven't seen each other for two years. I'm shipping out tomorrow, and if we could just say hello, I'd be able to tell our mom that I saw him after his performance and that he looks great. Our mom's not well, Sergeant."

"Okay, Corporal, calm down. You wait here. What's your name?"

"David . . . Don Coleman," he said, quickly correcting himself.

"Coleman? I thought you said you were O'Neill's brother."

"I am, David Don Coleman O'Neill!" David explained, "I didn't think I had to tell my brother our last name."

"But you thought you had to give him your middle names? Wait out here!"

Eugene, who was by nature reserved, was beyond happy to see David and hugged him hard and long, repeating, "Donny, you old cock you!" four or five times.

"God it's good to see you, Don," Eugene said after releasing him. "So what brings you to our fair island? Wait, let me guess, you got drafted. Hey, I have a day off Sunday. Have you guys ever had saimin?"

"No, but before you tell us what is it, let me say that I thought you were sensational tonight!"

"You should have seen me last night. Saimin is Jap noodle soup, and it's great. If you're free tomorrow night, I'll spring for a bowl."

"Oh, shit," David groused. "I love noodles, but we'll be gone by tomorrow tonight. Are your noodles available for lunch?"

"Hey, Don buddy," Eugene said, looking quizzically at David, "you were a humorous sort of fellow, even made me laugh once. You wouldn't by any chance have worked up some kind of a comedy act?"

"I like to call it a comedy act, but some audiences—"

"Don't listen to him, he's great," Saul interjected. "Just this last Saturday night he killed them at the USO canteen."

"How many minutes do you have?" Eugene asked excitedly.

"Counting jokes, impressions, and routines, I'd say about thirty-five or forty minutes. Why do you ask?"

"One of our shows, a variety show, *Fire Away,* has a spot open. We have to replace the comedian."

"Why? Isn't he any good?"

"He's sensational, name's Fletch Jackson, but he's being shipped back to the States in a few days on a family-hardship thing. It's a long shot, but if you can come back here tomorrow morning and audition for the major . . ."

"Oh, God!" David said, his head spinning. "What shitty timing! We're shipping out tomorrow."

"What time tomorrow?" Eugene asked eagerly.

"At night, but what difference does it make? I'm officially assigned to this detachment, and I'm stuck!"

"What outfit are you with?" Eugene pressed on.

"Company D of the 3117th Signal Battalion, but believe me, it's too late to do anything."

"Think positive, Donny! Can you get here at nine tomorrow morning?"

"Can I?" David asked Saul as if he were his parent.

"Yes, you can," Saul answered. "After roll call they have nothing scheduled for us. Remember we talked about going to Waikiki? Do this instead."

"Okay, okay, I'll do it! Might as well find out if I'm any good. Who do I audition for?"

"Evan Merritt."

"Oh, no, Prince Hamlet's going to audition me. Does he know what's funny?"

"He knows everything. And he's *Major* Hamlet. He's our commanding officer. I'll pick you up in my jeep at 0800 hours."

"Saul, I can't do this," David moaned as they rode the bus back to their base. "I'm going to call it off."

"That's stupid, David. You've got nothing to lose."

"Except my mind. We're shipping out tomorrow night. If they say they want me, I'll want to kill myself, and if they tell me I stink, I'll still want to kill myself. Why should I audition?"

"Because if you don't I'll kill you. Look, if nothing else, you can tell Mary Deare that you met Evan Merritt."

"That's true, and he may be a good contact after the war. Okay, Saul, I'll give it a shot."

On audition eve, after writing a long letter to Mary Deare describing the events of the evening and of his impending audition, David lay awake in his bunk trying to decide which of his routines was the most likely to make a great classic actor laugh and concluded that he had no such routine in his repertoire. He then tried to imagine which would offend him least. His Hitler harangue? His impressions of Jimmy Stewart, Ronald Colman, Jimmy Durante, and Akim Tamiroff? Or perhaps his gooney-voiced Private Shtoomie, demonstrating how to roll a full field pack for jungle warfare? Would Major Merritt find it funny when he says he packs "a live carrier pigeon to carry uncensored letters to his girl back home" and also "a Coca-Cola bottle cap for the pigeon to use as a latrine to keep the field pack from getting messy"? Concluding that none of his routines were good enough, David replumped his pillow and said to himself, Do them all! You've got no problem. If you're great and they want you, then they're the ones with the problem.

Within minutes of giving himself this advice, he was fast asleep and dreaming of Mary Deare, naked and tiptoeing through the barracks, looking for him in every bunk but his. When she finally found him and started to get into his bed, the voice of Evan Merritt shouting, "To a nunnery go!" scared her off.

At eight A.M. sharp, Eugene drove into David's camp and picked up his jittery friend. On the ride, Eugene blithely outlined the many advantages of being billeted on the grounds of the University of Hawaii. While he was describing in detail the beauty of the campus and the coeds and the great college cafeteria where they ate their meals, David stopped him.

"Enough," David shouted. "I don't want to hear about how great this place is. It'll just make me feel more frustrated when—"

"Don't be negative! You'll do such a fantastic audition that they'll have to take you, I know it."

"Gene, you've never seen me perform comedy, so how can you know if I'll be fantastic?"

"Because if you're not I'll look the fool. I recommended you, and if you screw up, it'll reflect on me. Do you want that?"

"Oh, no." David laughed. "I'd hate to reflect on you."

"Seriously, Don, I have faith in you. You know, if you are accepted, you'll be the third most talented guy in the outfit."

"You and Evan Merritt are the other two?"

"Yes, but not particularly in that order. Yes, Donny me lad . . ."

"It's *David* your lad!" he corrected. "The army knows me by my maiden name, David Kokolovitz."

"Great name, Kokolovitz. I never understood why you changed it. Maria Ouspenskaya kept hers."

"And that's why she never got romantic leads."

"Speaking of romantic leads, you and Scarlett are still in touch, aren't you?"

"Every day."

"Sounds serious."

"And looks, feels, smells, and tastes serious."

"Oh, that's 'till death do you part' serious."

"I'd say so. Her father threatened to have me killed if I didn't stay away from her, and I'm still with her. The bastard disowned her because of me, and so may my mother when she finds out that Mary Deare's not Jewish and her father is a Nazi. How's Peggy?"

"Just great. A year ago, after she was sure that she'd never get a marriage proposal from Clark Gable, she accepted mine, and we got married."

"Oh, that's great! Congratulations. Is Peggy still acting?"

"Yeah, as a riveter. She got a job in a war plant catching hot rivets, and she loves it."

For the remainder of the forty-minute ride, David and Eugene commiserated with each other about the difficulty of living without the one person you can't live without.

As the jeep entered the university grounds, David thought about how in a few minutes he would be trying to make one of the world's most renowned classic actors laugh at jokes that he would probably neither understand nor like.

"Holy mackerel but this is an impressive campus," David said, rattling on nervously and starting to collect preperformance perspiration in his armpits, "but you know something, if it weren't for these big palm trees and the perfumy smell of those gorgeous flowers and those beautiful, exotic students walking around, I'd think I was at City College in New York, where, if I had listened to my parents, I'd be right now, studying to be a pharmacist."

"Boy, are you hyper," Eugene said. "How about a glass of water?"

"How about a ride back to my base?"

"How about proving that I'm a genius for recommending you."

Walking from the wings and out onto the same stage that Evan Merritt had trod the night before and then seeing the man himself seated in the auditorium flanked by two other officers sapped whatever resolve and confidence David had managed to muster. He considered calling the whole thing off but reconsidered when he realized that one of the officers who would be judging him was the awful actor with the flaming red hair who played Fortinbras. My comedy may stink, David thought, but nowhere near as badly as that second lieutenant's acting. While still deliberating with himself about which routine to do first, the decision was taken out of his hands by Major Merritt, who, speaking with an even more pronounced English accent than he had as *Hamlet,* asked, "Corporal, do you do any impressions of movie stars?"

"Do you like impressions of movie stars?" David shot back.

"Very much if they're accurate and funny."

"Then, sir, I don't do any impressions."

Buoyed by Major Merritt's smile, David admitted that he did a few.

"Then let us hear some of your more accurate ones, Corporal."

David did his very credible, hesitant Jimmy Stewart and followed it with a more than acceptable one of Charles Boyer and then stopped.

"You know something," David said, addressing his smiling three-man audience, "before I do my impressions of Ronald Colman and Jimmy Durante as the two Corsican Brothers, which are really very good, I'd like to do something I've been working on since I started this sentence"—thankfully there was a small laugh, which he rode over—"but before I put this bit in my act, I'd like to get your opinion of it, or perhaps I wouldn't. What the heck, you can't fire me. I've got a run-of-the-war contract with the United States Army."

A moment before, when David realized that Evan Merritt was enjoying his impressions, the name Cliff Nazzaro popped into his head. He had seen a stage show at the Loew's State where this comic did a hilarious recitation of a poem in double-talk. Since then he had thought about Cliff Nazarro and how he might incorporate double-talk into his act.

"With your permission, sir," David announced grandly, his adrenaline flowing, "and at the risk of being booted off the stage, I would like to give you _my_ impression of a sonnet written by the world's greatest playwright, William Shakespeare, recited by the world's greatest double-talk artist, Cliff Nazarro, doing _his_ impression of the world's greatest actor, Evan Merritt!"

David could see the heads of Major Merritt's jury turning to the major and to each other and could sense the major's body stiffen. David's ability to double-talk had saved him when he forgot King Claudius's lines, and now he hoped, as he took a deep breath, that the magic would work again. Closely approximating the timber of Evan Merritt's voice and its subtle tremolo while trying to recall some of the words of Cliff Nazarro's poem, David began emoting loudly and clearly,

> "When Portisan and Punahoe lilt the passing Chappaquar,
> T'is time to wend to Pippesnard and purpler fields of framitar.
> When ramparts of passa and plocks of polves,
> Shivell the shockles and
> timber the wolves,
> T'is time to pick petunias and pluck petainias,
> And say pip, pip, hail Britannia!
> Though seasons may come and seasons may go,
> Please Cliff me not the Nazarro!"

At the start of the poem David went into a small panic when he heard only an eerie silence in the auditorium. He was seriously contemplating a quick exit when the laughter started. His popping of his P's as he recited "P-Pick the p-petunias and p-pluck the p-patanias" sent sprays of spit flying over the footlights. David looked to the major and was happy to see that most of the laughter was coming out of him.

"Young man," the major said, wiping tears from his eyes, "that was a brilliantly funny bit, and if you're thinking of incorporating it into your act, don't!"

"I didn't mean any offense . . ." David mumbled.

"Oh, I doubt that," Major Merritt said, getting up and making his way to the stage, "but in any case, I advise you not to do an impression of me in your act. I found it quite amusing, as did my staff, but not one in ten thousand GIs will know who you're taking off on. Sadly, very few of them go to the legitimate theater, so you'd be better served by impersonating motion picture stars."

"I will, sir, thank you. I have other bits I could show you."

"I'm sure you have, corporal," Major Merritt said, coming up on-stage. "Perhaps some other time."

"I hope so," David said, surprised to discover that the imposing figure he saw onstage performing Hamlet stood a foot shorter than he.

"You're a very talented young man," the major said, eyeing David closely. "What is your situation?"

"Sir, I'm a teletype operator assigned to the 3117th Signal Battalion and have just been put on a small detachment that's scheduled to ship out tonight."

"Tonight?"

"Yes, sir!"

"Hmm, pity."

"Yes, sir, it is!"

"Corporal, you would prefer to join our company rather that shipping out, I take it."

"Oh, take it! I mean, yes, sir!" David answered, his heart starting to pound. "I'd much prefer that."

"Well, then, if you give your name and serial number to Captain Sullen," he said indicating the smiling, blue-eyed, blond-haired officer who had joined them, "we'll see what we can do."

"Thank you, sir!" David barked, bringing his hand to his forehead in salute.

Major Merritt nodded, then casually brushed his fingers against the bill of his hat. So jubilant was David at the possibility of a transfer, he snapped off a comically exaggerated return salute. It was one he used in his act and got big laughs when he said, "This salute is the most effective ass-kissing return salute a private can use to get a three-day pass, but be careful to use it only on officers who enjoy having their asses kissed. Fortunately, they are in the majority."

Since becoming commander of the Special Services unit, Major Merritt had never been saluted in this manner and was not pleased.

"What is your name, Corporal?" Major Merritt asked, staring disbelievingly at David.

"David Kokolovitz, sir," David answered smartly.

"Tell me, Corporal Kokolovitz, was that salute of yours meant to be serious or satiric?"

"Fifty percent serious, sir," David snapped back, "but I can make it a hundred percent with a very small adjustment."

"I suggest, then, that you make the adjustment!" the major ordered sharply. "Did you perhaps forget there is a war on, Corporal Kokolovitz?!"

"No, sir!" David answered, knowing he had destroyed whatever small chance he had for a transfer. Amazingly, he was still able to appreciate the elegance his name, Kokokovitz, took on when spoken by the great English actor.

David spent most of the ride back to his base either cursing his stupidity or bemoaning his fate.

"I know there was no chance I could get transferred, but if I didn't give him that dumb salute . . ."

"David, for chrissakes," Eugene exploded, "will you stop flagellating yourself!"

"No, it feels good," David argued. "I'm a putz! I alienated an important man in our business who thought I was brilliant. He said so, didn't he?"

"And he still thinks you are. I'll tell you what, Corporal Putz," Eugene said softly. "I'll bet you a sushi lunch that he gets you transferred to our company."

"I'll bet you two sushis that I ship out," David shot back. "Make that a dozen sushis, that's how sure I am! What the hell's a sushi?"

Dec. 8, 1944

My darling,

I love you so much, and I am so happy. The only way I could be any happier today would be if you were here beside me holding me and watching me write this letter to you. I have the most unbelievably wonderful news to tell you. I ate raw fish today! No kidding, honey, I ate slices of raw tuna, salmon, and halibut, and I loved it. It's called sushi, and it tasted a lot like lox but not as salty. The only cooked things I ate were the finger-size pieces of white rice that the raw fish sat on. I know you're asking, why is my eating raw fish such unbelievably wonderful news? Because, darling, I bet Eugene a sushi lunch that I'd never be transferred into his Special Services outfit, and I was! I was packing my duffel bag, ready to go off with the 3117th, when this call came to the post commander's office. It was like an eleventh-hour reprieve from the governor, only it wasn't the governor but Maj. Evan Merritt and Lt. General Matthew Richardson of the Central Pacific Base Commmand who pulled the right strings. I am now an official member of Army Special Services. Who could ever figure this one! Just nine hours ago I

*was a teletype operator auditioning to be a comedian, and here
I am, on the campus of the University of Hawaii and sitting in
my new barracks, which looks exactly like my old barracks
except this one smells a lot better. It all happened so fast, I still
can't believe it's true. The one shitty part of this transfer that
made me feel real sad and a little guilty is leaving my buddies. I
felt like a traitor when I watched all of my buddies in the
3117th packing to leave Oahu for God knows where while I'm
packing to go to a beautiful college campus. Saying goodbye to
Saul was especially difficult. We've been together for almost
two years, and he wouldn't be shipping out today if it wasn't for
me. I guess that's not exactly true, but that's how I feel about
not speaking up when this crazy thing happened a couple of
days ago. I didn't write you about it because I didn't want any
censor reading about it. Last week, at reveille, our captain read
off the names of guys who were assigned to something called
Detachment 18. My name was on the list along with Freddie
Miller, Milt Tepper, Manny Reff, Jimmy Concaron, and the
pain in the ass Henny Shwick. Shwick was the only name I was
sorry to hear called. Saul's name wasn't on the list, and we were
both surprised. He looked at me sadly and shrugged. He said,
"Looks like they're finally gonna split us up!" Honey, this next
part you're not going to believe. The Captain says that
Detachment 18 is one man short and asks for a volunteer. We
all learned the first week in the army that you never raise your
hand and volunteer for anything, so I never expected that Saul
would volunteer for Detachment 18, but I see a hand shoot up
and hear a voice shout, "Corporal Saul Marantz, sir!" The
captain says, "Thank you, Corporal Marantz" and adds Saul's
name to the list, only it wasn't Saul but Shwick who had
volunteered Saul's name. Saul asked him how the f——— could
you do such a thing, and Shwick says, "Your best buddy,
David, is on the list! Are you gonna let those bastards in the
Pentagon break up you and your best buddy?" I called Shwick
a dumb schmuck and said that if he didn't tell the captain what
he'd done, I would. Honey, I have never been so pissed off at
anyone, and I started to go to the captain, but Saul stopped me.
He said that if Shwick hadn't volunteered him, he probably
would have. His philosophy was that no matter where they send
him, the odds are that it would be someplace miserable, so he
might as well be miserable with guys he likes. Shwick, who
nobody likes, gave Saul a big hug and a kiss on the cheek. Saul*

can't stand Shwick, but he can't shake him, either. I think he's afraid Shwick might blackmail him. I never told you what happened when we went to teletype school, but I will after the war is over.

I really feel bad that Saul and I won't be together anymore. I owe him a lot. You know, if it wasn't for Saul, I wouldn't be in this new outfit. He really talked me into auditioning for Major Merritt. Honey, getting into Special Services is one of the two best things that has ever happened to me, and how I wish that the other best thing was here in my arms right now to help me celebrate. I can't wait for us good guys to win this damn war so I can go home and see your pretty face and kiss your sweet lips and any other parts of you that you care to make available to me. I love you so much, Mary Deare, that last night, when I looked at that new batch of pictures you sent me, I felt like crying. I mean it, tears actually came to my eyes. It's so terrible to love someone so much and not be able to tell her that to her face. I love you!

Donny

✦

The Entertainment Section of Special Services, presided over by Maj. Evan Merritt, was like no other unit in the armed forces. All the members of the section, which included actors, directors, composers, musicians, arrangers, singers, a choral director, stage managers, comics, a juggler, a magician, a harmonica player, a country singer, set designers, carpenters, electricians, and a still photographer, had been hand picked by Evan Merritt and transferred there from other army units. The unit always had one or two shows in rehearsal and at least three more touring the military bases on the Hawaiian Islands.

Assuming the role of David's guide and mentor, S. Sgt. Eugene O'Neill, who was the company's ranking noncom, was giving his protégé a tour of their quarters when a message blared over the loudspeaker. "Corporal David Klollowitzer report to Captain Sullen's office immediately . . . Corporal David Klollowitzer report to—"

David jumped. "Klolliwitzer! I think that's me they're calling. Who's this Captain Sullen, and why do you think he wants to see me?"

"He's second in command to Merritt, and I'm sure he'll tell you."

Capt. William Sullen's name in no way reflected his personality. He was blessed with a sunny disposition and a set of large whiter-than-white teeth which he kept on display for most of his waking day. He flashed his broadest smile when David entered his office.

"Corporal Cocklawits?" the captain said, extending his hand in welcome. "Did I pronounce that right? Cocklawitz?"

"Close enough, sir. Some people pronounce it Kokolovitz, but Cocklawits is fine. Nobody ever gets it right."

"I assure you I'll get it right if you stay with us."

"*If* I stay?" David said, feeling his world collapsing.

"I'm sorry, Corporal Cockclawsawits, but Lieutenant Yorby," he said, nodding toward the flaming red-haired officer who sat at a desk in the adjoining office, "informs me that our company roster has its full complement of corporals, so I am afraid that we're going to have to ask you to *either* give up your stripes *or*—"

"No *or,* Captain," David said, panicking. "I'll give up my stripes gladly! Bust me, make me a private, first class. It's actually better for comedy, being the underdog."

"I'm sorry," the captain said, his smile broadening, "but we also have a full complement of PFCs."

"How about a private? That's even better, more underdoggy."

Lieutenant Yorby nodded, pleased that his roster was now correct.

"I'm very happy that you're going to be with us. You're a very talented young man, Private Cocklawish?" he asked, smiling broadly. "Did I get it right?"

"Yes, sir!" David lied. "Private Cocklawish is perfect!"

Meeting members of the cast of *Fire Away* was not nearly as smiley an occasion as was David's encounter with Captain Sullen.

"Gene, I can handle a twenty-dollar cut in pay," David complained as they left the entertainers' barracks, "but I'm not sure about working well with people who don't like me."

"Donny, when did you get paranoid?"

"When you introduced me to that juggler—what's his name?— Parkinson. He barely said hello and never looked at me."

"He would have dropped his clubs if he had," Eugene said, starting for the cafeteria. "Parky's very friendly when he's not practicing, which isn't often. One time"—Eugene laughed at the memory—"I saw him juggle four apples while taking a shit."

"And what's with that magician who sat on the floor rolling a pair of dice against his footlocker. He didn't even say hello."

"He did, but you didn't hear him. That's J. C. Dandy; he has a great act."

"Rolling sevens and elevens?"

"He can roll any number he wants eight out of ten times, but that's not his act. He used to be a dice hustler, and he wants to keep his touch in case he doesn't make it as a magician after the war."

"A bit strange, isn't he?"

"No argument there," Eugene admitted, "but he's a good guy, an easy touch."

"And that husky blond private with that big voice? What's his story? I didn't get his name. He started to sing an aria from *Traviata* to me while you were introducing us."

"That's Lawrence Lawrence. He loves his voice and couldn't wait until tomorrow night for you to hear how beautifully he sings."

"Lawrence Lawrence?" David asked. "Isn't that a redundancy?"

"He's a walking redundancy. Actually, it's Lawrene *T.* Lawrence. He admires that baritone on the *Voice of Firestone* program."

"Thomas L. Thomas!"

"Right, so he became Lawrence T. Lawrence."

"And the T stands for Thomas?"

"What else?" Eugene said, leading David down a flower-bordered path to the cafeteria. "By the way, Bubba liked you."

"Bubba?"

"Lawrence's real name is Bubba Trippet. He's from Lubbock, Texas."

"How do you know he likes me?"

"He likes everybody. He's not sure why we're at war. God gave him a glorious voice, and to enhance the resonance in his skull, he decided to put in it the smallest brain he could find."

"Are there any regular-brained folks in this show?"

"There's a harmonica virtuoso, Dan Waller. He kills the audience. And another guy, Chicky Click Clack, who makes tap-dance noises with his teeth, and there's the company pianist, Sasha Manoff. He may be the most normal, but I'm not sure, because he only talks to himself."

"I don't know. Except for the brainless baritone, I felt a great hostility in there."

"Look, Donny," Eugene explained, "to them you're an unproven interloper. As soon as they find out that you're as good a comic as the guy you're replacing, they'll love you."

"How good is he?"

"Fletch Jackson is the best act in the show, but don't worry, they hate him for abandoning them to go back home."

David's discomfort about being in an unfriendly environment disappeared when he entered the cafeteria and was smacked in his face with the pungent aromas of anxiety-calming foods. After eating more that a thousand meals in the company of sweaty soldiers, the prospect of dining in a white-walled, spanking-clean cafeteria was almost too much happiness for David to handle. Waiting in line to choose their lunch from a long steam table were young college students, most of them female, most of them Oriental, exotic and attractive, some with flowers in their hair and all of them studiedly aloof, or so it seemed to David. The girls chatted among themselves, seemingly unaware of the dozens of smitten soldiers who unabashedly checked them out as they strutted by.

"I have died and gone to heaven," David admitted as he scanned the flower-bedecked room and breathed in the sweet scent of pineapple-glazed ham, gingered fish, and steamed fresh vegetables. "Do we get to eat all our meals here?"

"No. Dinners you eat at the company mess halls, where you're performing," Eugene said, handing him a tray, "but you can have all your breakfasts and lunches here if you want."

"I want, I want. Who wouldn't want?" David said, ogling the attractively presented food before him.

By the time David arrived at the cashier's station, his tray was overloaded with a plate of ham, beets, cauliflower, and mashed potatoes, a smaller plate with a tossed salad, a dish of sliced mango, a cup of tapioca pudding, and a tall glass of pineapple juice. He was lifting his tray to carry to a table when a soft female voice stopped him.

"Corporal," the voice advised, "that will be ninety cents."

There were two things that David had not expected. One, that he would have to pay for his food, and the other, that the cashier would be an Asian goddess with one of the most strikingly beautiful faces he had ever seen.

"Oh, I'm sorry," a flustered David joked, looking for Eugene. "I thought the cafeteria had a deal with the army."

"No," the unsmiling cashier responded curtly. "You have the deal with the army. Ninety cents, please. You're holding up the line."

David thought her attitude was unnecessarily unpleasant but decided to forgive her for her snottiness, as he would any girl of breathtaking beauty.

David handed her a dollar bill and followed her long, beautifully tapered fingers as they laid his bill into a cash drawer and fished out two nickels, which she offered to him with the grace of a dancer.

"Keep the change!" he said, pulling his hand away as the coins dropped into his mashed potatoes.

"There is no tipping!" she admonished.

"Whoops, sorry, my fault," David apologized, abashedly picking up his tray and slinking off.

He chose a table behind the cashier's station but proximate enough to afford him the opportunity to ogle her with impunity. Before sitting down, David spooned the nickles from his mashed potatoes, popped them in his mouth and sucked them clean.

"Stupid, are you trying to kill yourself?" he could hear his mother asking." Do you know where those nickels have been? Have you any idea how many people, with God knows what diseases, touched them?"

"Thirty-seven!" David joked out loud.

"Thirty-seven what?" Eugene asked, putting his tray on the table.

"People who touched these coins," David said, dropping them into his pocket. "I was just having a conversation with this person who lives in my head."

"Your father?"

"My mother."

"I got my father in my head," Eugene said sadly. "He was an Olympic-class walloper. Broke my nose twice and my mother's once."

"Wow, what did he hit you with?"

"His fists. Did you ever get hit?"

"Only with a yardstick. It would break before we did. Hey," David said, trying to sound casual, "that cashier over there has a very interesting face. Is she here all the time?"

"Who? Sooky?" Eugene said, glancing over at her. "Yeah, she's working her way through college, but if you're thinking of asking her for a date, don't bother. Better men than you have tried and failed."

"I wasn't thinking of asking her for a date," David said, not sure what he was thinking.

"Then what? To sit for a portrait?"

"She's beautiful enough to paint," David said, glimpsing her profile.

"Believe it or not, J. C. Dandy used that line, and it got him a stare."

"Did you ever ask her out?"

"Once, in a moment of weakness when I convinced myself that Peggy wouldn't mind if I went to a movie with a girl who every guy in our outfit wanted to fuck."

"She wouldn't even go to a movie with you?"

"She said no before I finished the question. I wouldn't have asked her, but I thought she was interested in me. When I paid for my meal, she smiled and called me back to speak to me."

"What did she say?"

"She said, You know, Sergeant, a sesame roll comes with your broiled Ahi dinner, but it was the way she said it. She's a Hawaiian-Chinese icicle. Having problems with Mary Deare or is it your groin asking these questions?"

"Mary Deare and I are great . . . I don't know what it is, but when I saw this Sooky's face, I couldn't catch my breath for a second. I don't know if she heard me, but I actually whimpered."

"Understandable. She's got a face and body that were built to make men cry. You know, you and I are lucky."

"How so?" David said, his mouth full of lettuce and his eyes full of Sooky.

"It's gals like Sooky that make it easy for us not to cheat."

Dec. 10, 1944

Darling Mary Dearest,

So much to tell and so little time. Just got back from the other side of the island where I saw this variety show, Fire Away, that I'm going to be in, and do I have a job cut out for me! The guy I'm replacing got a zillion laughs. Besides being the master of ceremonies and introducing all the acts, he did a monologue about a butcher who loved to hear the sound of meat being slapped on the butcher's block. He had a five-pound steak that he kept slapping on a table, and each time he slapped it down, he got more and more sexually aroused and kept screaming out, "Love to beat that meat!" It may not sound that funny, but the guys really loved him. Honey, don't be surprised if I'm back with my old outfit soon. I'd hate that to happen, because I could really get to love this place, especially the university cafeteria, where we're allowed to eat. Everything in it is so beautiful—the food, the decor, the students. Eugene and I talked a lot about you and Peggy today, and we argued about who misses his girl more. He won. He misses you more than I miss Peggy. Just joshin', sweetie. It's damn hard to keep a sense of humor about being kept apart. Separation is shitty! Hey, that's not a bad song title. Seperation is shitty, Oh, how I miss feeling your titty. I'd love to hear Dinah Shore sing it. Naw, I'd love to hear you sing it, right now, right in my ear. I love you so much, darling. I wish I could do something to speed up the winning of this damn war. Maybe if I had stayed with Detachment 18 I might have been able to do more to help. They tell us that entertaining the troops is important for morale, and I guess it must be. Bob Hope and Al Jolson and Martha Raye wouldn't be risking their asses for nothing. I don't know, though. It seems to me that angry, pissed-off soldiers with lousy morale would make better killers than happy, laughing ones. Tonight, before the show, I helped Fletch Jackson, the comic I'm replacing, to lay out the electric cable for the lights and the sound system. That job and making soldiers laugh every night are the things I inherited from this lucky stiff who's going back home tomorrow. I wish he'd stay one more day, because I don't know if I can handle tomorrow's show. It's scheduled to play the Honolulu Bowl, where a couple of weeks ago I was told that Bob Hope, Frances Langford, and Jerry Colonna played. I never played for more than a couple of hundred, and they tell me there are going to be about ten thousand servicemen out there. I am really, really scared, and if you don't get a letter from me tonight, you'll know an angry mob of soldiers rushed the stage and broke my fingers.

Eugene said to send you his love, but I'm not going to because I'm sending you all of mine, which is more than any one girl should be asked to handle in one letter. I love you and miss you more than I said in my last letter and only slightly less than I will in my next.

> *Yours till you yell stop!*
> *Donny.*

P.S. I can't wait to use my stage name again. I may change it legally when I get back. Kokolovitz just doesn't fit into anybody's mouth. Here's another one to add to the list. This guy who tap-dances with his tongue called me Cockalocka today . . . Whoever I am, I love you!

✦

The words *baptism of fire* jammed David's brain as he stood in the wings and looked out at the largest audience he had ever been asked to make laugh. Honolulu Bowl was Radio City Music Hall times four, and in a few minutes his name would blare over the loudspeakers, announcing him as the master of ceremonies, and he would have to smile and walk out onto this monstrously wide stage, stand at the microphone, and act as if he were not about to throw up. He was considering whether or not to heave into a fire bucket before going out when Lawrence T. Lawrence came up behind him and started making barking noises.

"Just warming up the voice," the singer said between barks. "Opens up the cavities in the head . . . woof, woof . . . It relaxes your whole body . . . woof, woof . . . Good luck tonight . . . woof, woof, woof. Try it, woof, woof."

To humor him David said, "Woof, woof," and miraculously found that his need to vomit all but left him. However, the queasiness returned when all the cast members gathered in the wings to wish him well.

While David was mentally digging through his material, searching for the perfect joke to start the show, fate intervened in the guise of 1st Lt. Owen Gorley. The officer in charge of events for the Honolulu Bowl strode erectly and confidently across the massive stage, tripped on the microphone cable, went flailing through the air, and fought desperately to keep his balance and his dignity. Adrenaline rushed through David's body as he heard the audience roar with laughter. There is nothing more enjoyable to a GI than the sight of a commissioned officer falling flat on his face. Lieutenant Gorley provided a another big laugh when, in trying to disentangle his feet from the mike cord, he pulled the microphone down on top of himself. Appearing unruffled and behaving as if no one had witnessed his ungainly fall, Lieutenant Gorley righted the microphone and deftly adjusted it to accommodate his six-foot-four height.

"One, two, three, testing!" Lieutenant Gorley repeated over and over again into a dead microphone. He stopped to cover his ears when the sound system was turned on and produced a blast of ear-piercing feedback.

"Feedback," he explained, his voice booming. "One, two, three, testing . . . Can everybody hear me?"

"They can hear you in the Philippines!" a GI screamed out. "Start the show, Lieutenant!"

"And so we shall, soldier. I am Lieutenant Gorley, and I bid you all welcome," he announced in a boringly nasal monotone. "Tonight we have a wonderful variety show for your entertainment entitled *Fire Away,* and it features members of the Entertainment Section of the Army Special Services unit."

David was shaken when the annoucement was greeted with boos and hisses, but the lieutenant did not seem to hear it.

"To get the show started," he continued gaily, "here is your master of ceremonies, a wonderful comedian, uh, "Corporal, uh . . . David . . . Kock . . ."

The audience roared when the lieutenant chose an inopportune place to hesitate.

"Now hold on, hold on," he entreated. "I want to pronouce his name correctly. It's Corporal David Kock . . ."

Another and bigger roar of laughter rolled in. David took it as his cue to rush out onto the stage.

"No, sir, it's not 'corporal'," David shouted, as he intentionally and violently tripped over the cable, closely mimicking the lieutenant's body language as he fell. "I have been demoted," David said, lying on the ground. "It's private, sir, and it's not Kock!"

The laughter rolled in and built when a rowdy, leather-voiced marine yelled out, "Hey, Cock, show us your privates!"

"I'd rather tell you my name, madam!" David shouted, the laughter growing as he stumbled to the microphone. "Lieutenant Gorley," David continued, snatching the paper out of the officer's hands, "the name is Kokolovitz, and I warned you, sir, about saying my name one syllable at a time! Shall we try it phonetically! Kokolovitz, sir. Just put the cock, the collar, and the vits all together. That shouldn't be hard," David said, addressing the crowd, "should it, men?"

"Shit no!" the rowdy marine hollered back.

"Shall we show the lietenant how easy it is?" David shouted.

"Shit yes!" a chorus of happy voices answered.

"Here we go, men," David ordered. "Say after me, Cock . . ."

"Cock," the men shouted back.

"Collar!"

"Collar!" the entire audience shouted.

"Vits!"

"Vits!" they screamed.

"Now put it all together and what do we have?"

"COCKCOLLARVITS!" shouted the charged audience.

One of the biggest thrills of David's life was hearing ten thousand voices scream in unison a version of his name.

David applauded their effort, told them that they would get a cluster on their good-conduct medal for superior efforts in elocution, and then asked for their undivided attention, which miraculously he got.

"Now let's see if Lieutenant Gorley can do as well as you did."

Lieutenant Gorley was obviously not at all pleased to be made the butt of a joke, but knowing that he had the audience with him gave David the courage to continue.

"Lieutenant, are we ready to say my name?" David asked as a hush came over the audience.

"We are ready." the lieutenant said, acting the good sport.

"Sir, please say after me, Cock-collar-vits."

Just as the lieutenant started to say it, David interrupted to ask, "Sir, would you like a sip of water?"

The lieutenant shook his head as David pressed on.

"A sip of green beer? A martini? Two fingers of gin? Two fingers of poi?"

By the time the officer shouted out, "Cockcollarvits," David had whipped the audience into a frenzy, and when it peaked, he shouted, "How about this Lieutenant Gorley here? Isn't he great? Why can't all officers have his sense of humor? How about a big hand for a terrific sport! Let's hear it for Lieutenant Owen Gorley!"

Lieutenant Gorley was grinning from ear to ear as he left the stage to the greatest undeserved ovation he would ever receive.

"Lieutenant Owen Gorley," David shouted, "come out and take a bow!"

When the officer returned and saluted, David snapped off his smart-ass return salute and thought, Hey, how about that. Two days ago this same stupid-looking salute almost got me court-martialed, and tonight it gets me big laughs and big applause.

Dec. 11 1944
1:00 A. M.

My sweet sweetheart,

Just a few hours ago I did my first performance in Fire Away and I got more laughter and applause than I'm used to. It was a great feeling. I wish I had the words to describe all the things I'm feeling tonight! Besides the aching in my heart that I will feel until I see you again, I feel relief. I feel proud and exhilarated but mainly worried, worried that I'll never again be able to do what I did tonight. I did better than I or the cast ever expected I would. The magician–tap dancer, J. C. Dandy, admitted that he bet Parkinson the juggler five bucks that I was going to stink. My routines went well, but it was my introductions to the acts that really tickled me. I found myself laughing along with the audience. That was the best part, the part that made me feel I belong up there. I hope I can do it again. I'll write you a more detailed letter tomorrow. I hope I can remember all the good moments. I'm going to sleep now, or I should say going to bed, as I doubt I'll fall asleep. My heart is still pounding, the same heart that pounds for you. I don't know how much more pounding it can take. I LOVE YOU, LOVE YOU, LOVE YOU!

> Yours forever and maybe even
> longer,
> David Cock*

*The most theatrically profitable mispronunciation of my name yet. More about that tomorrow.

✦

After his auspicious debut in *Fire Away,* David was invited to become a member of the Mutton Club, the recreation room named in honor of the venerated New York actors' Lambs Club. The Mutton Club sported an upright piano, a few tables and chairs, a supply of Cokes, and bottles of beer that contained only 3.2 percent alcohol, a formula brewed specifically to frustrate a soldier's need to get a buzz. The Mutton Club, open seven days a week, was the place where members came to fraternize, gripe, gossip, trade the latest filthy jokes, and receive their daily mail. Because of the amount of mail he received, David Kokolovitz had quickly become the most envied member in the section. Today he received three letters, one a V-mail from his brother, Chuck, who was with the Thirty-seventh Infantry, fighting somewhere in Europe. These V-mails were always eagerly awaited, as they attested to his undeadness, the word his brother used to describe his state after surviving the campaign in North Africa. In this letter he wrote, "Because some of the guys in our outfits got their uniforms dirty, we have been shipped to this nice cleaning-and-pressing facility run by Winston Churchill. David correctly gleaned from this that his brother had been slightly wounded and had been sent to a rest center in England.

On the envelope of one of the other letters he had received, the ink had run and only the letters, K, O, and Z of his name were legible.

"If this letter belongs to me," David said, showing it to Eugene, "then the cryptogragher in the post office deserves a promotion."

"It looks like it's floated across the Pacific."

"Holy shit, it must have! It's from Saul Marantz!" David shrieked, scanning the letter. "He's in Iwo Jima!"

"That's impossible. He just left Hawaii."

"Must have been flown there. Listen to this." 'Dear David, contrary to popular belief, there *are* atheists in foxholes! I am the living proof of it. I'm writing this from the only three-man foxhole on the beach. Robbins and I dug a perfect two-manner, but Shwick, who nobody wanted to pair up with, talked us into expanding it to accommodate him. We waded ashore this morning and dodged a lot of shells from an unseen enemy who we presumed to be of Japanese persuasion.' "

"Damn, that Saul is funny! He should be with our outfit," David stopped to comment. " 'There's little chance you'll get this letter, but if I don't write it, there's even less chance. . . . We were told to stay put until the marines secure the beach, which could be a messy job. I'm probably breaking all the rules of war by writing all this, but at this juncture I really don't give a shit. Hey, you may get this letter, after all. Two medics plopped a stretcher down right by our foxhole. There's a wounded marine on it, and they're waiting for a landing craft to take him off the beach. I asked the poor guy how he is, and he said, "I've had better days." I don't know what possessed me, but when I heard the medics say that they were going to fly him and a bunch of other woundees back to Oahu, I asked him if he'd mail this for me, and this busted-up marine with bloody bandages on his head says, "Finish it up and put it on my chest." So, having a wonderful time. Love, Saul.' Gene, this is great!"

"What, that your buddy is in a foxhole in Iwo Jima?"

"No, that he's alive and writing letters. Damn, Iwo Jima, that's where I would be. Gene, if it wasn't for you, I'd be in that foxhole with Saul. You saved my ass, buddy."

"Well, *c'est la guerre, c'est la* fucking *guerre.*"

David waited until the shock of learning about where his buddies were stationed wore off before reading any of Mary Deare's letters. He walked back to his barracks, lay back on his bunk, and opened the fattest one of the three. Mary Deare never wrote letters this long, so he assumed she had enclosed some articles of interest she had clipped from newspapers or magazines. His heart stopped when he opened the envelope and found that the enclosure was not a newspaper clipping but a letter he had written to her a year earlier. Oh, God, she's dumping me! he thought. She's sending me back my love letters. She's Dear Johning me with my own letters! He looked at the first page and recognized that it was the ten-pager he had written her when he was stationed in Missouri at Camp Crowder. He found her covering letter in the envelope and breathed easier when he read the salutaton.

Nov. 20, 1944

Hey, my sweet, darling curly lips,

You remember this letter? Not this one, sweetie. I mean, the one I enclosed. This Sunday I was doing what I always do on no-mail days, reread your wonderful letters. Well, sweetie, I came upon this one and started to chuckle. I was at breakfast, and dear old George came in with a pot of coffee. I'll be here visiting Mama for a another day or so, until the senator returns from touring army bases. Anyway, George asked me what I was giggling about, and I couldn't resist giving him your letter to read. Well, sugar, you should have heard George cackle. That letter sure tickled him. When that sweet, old colored man finished, he says, Missy Mary, that soldier boy of yours has got a head full of smarts and sure does know how to spin a yarn. I told him it wasn't a yarn but a true story, and he said, "Whatever it is, it should be printed somewhere," and you know what, darlin'? Old George was right. I showed your letter to my friend Sally-Lou Bethune, and she wants to publish it. She and her husband, who just got a disability discharge from the navy, have started a small magazine, and they're looking for humorous stories from our men in service. They loved yours and want you to trim it down to fifteen hundred words, and here's the best part. They'll pay you seventy-five dollars for it.

✦

Drunk with the prospect of becoming a published writer, David picked up his old letter and started counting its words. Eugene, who had just entered the barracks, stopped at the foot of his cot and stared at his friend, trying to guess what he was doing.

". . . Nine ninety-six," David mumbled, "nine ninety-seven . . . eight . . ."

"David, do you always count the words she writes you, or is it the number of letters you're counting?"

David waited until he got to a thousand before explaining what he was doing.

"I am impressed!" Eugene smiled. "May I read it?"

"Would you? Maybe you can help me cut it down."

"I'd love to. My wife sent me a short note today, and I need a letter to read," Eugene said, picking up the covering letter. 'Hey, my sweet, darling curly lips,' " he read. "You can definitely cut that!"

"Not that letter!" David said, snatching it from him.

"You do have curly lips. I never noticed," Eugene chided as he took David's year-old letter to Mary Deare and started to read.

Sunday, August 1, 1943

My dear, dearer Mary Deare-est,

I love you so much and am happy that I am still alive to write and tell you that. Remember that noncom school I told you they may send me to. Well, they sent me there, and that's why you haven't received any letters from me for almost a week. They worked our butts off, and we had no time to do any of the civilized things like reading a newspaper in the toilet or writing to our loved ones to tell them how much they are loved and missed. That first day at noncom school was one I'm never going to forget. Do you remember how scared shitless I was when we crashed in your plane? Well, this ran a close second. It started innocently enough in the latrine when I was urinating next to this big Negro master sergeant—by the way, this school is integrated, but not because the army has suddenly gotten democratic but because it's the only school for noncommissioned officers in Camp Crowder. We all live in the same barracks, the colored noncoms upstairs and us white guys downstairs. It's like an experiment. Well, this little guinea pig didn't enjoy a lot of today's experiment. It started okay with a friendly conversation I had with this colored master sergeant. We talked baseball. I told him how I admired Carl Hubbell and his screwball, and he told me about this Negro pitcher Satchel Paige who threw a hesitation pitch that made the batters swing seconds before the ball got to the plate. He was really interested in my being an actor and said that he had read a lot of Shakespeare. All the time I was talking to this colored sergeant, I was aware that a blond crew-cutted tech sergeant who was pissing a few feet from us was glaring at me. He must have been upset because he buttoned his fly and raced out of the latrine without washing his hands. When I got back to the barracks, I found him standing by my footlocker, looking at me with this crooked smile on his face. He announced that he was Sgt. P. Wallace Warrenton from Shreveport, Louisiana, and held out his unwashed hand, which I really didn't want to shake but I did to be friendly. Then, just as I start to say my name, he asks if I didn't think it was a fuckin' shame that we had to live with these fuckin' niggers. (Sorry, honey, but that's the way some of us talk in the army.) I just looked at him, and he says, "Now don't tell me you like that the damn niggers are living with us." I said that technically they weren't living with us but above us. I referred to the colored troops as "they" because I had a feeling that if I said negroes, he'd be more offended than he was, and boy was he offended! He asks, don't it bother me that they're putting their black asses on my toilet seats and usin' my fuckin' showers? I said it don't bother me unless they pissed on my seats and shat in my shower, but I'd feel the same if any of the white noncoms did that. Somebody laughed, and I tell you, hon, I never saw anybody look at me the way Sgt. P. Wallace Warrenton did. I felt as if I was standing in front of the grand dragon of the Ku Klux Klan. I was so happy that the one guy laughed. I figured I had at least one ally. Sgt. Warrenton stared at the guy who laughed and then walked up to me and asked if I thought that a fuckin' nigger was as good as a white man. I was scared but figured that the only way to avoid being lynched was to joke my way out of it. Sergeant, I said, using my King Claudius voice, if you are asking me to consider the possiblity that a fucking nigger might be as good as a fucking white person, then I would have to say that I honestly don't know. . . . "You don't know?" he screams at me. "You were chitchattin' with that big fuckin' nigger in the crapper, so you gotta know that he ain't as good as you!" I say, "Well, I'm not too sure of that. He seemed very smart, and I know he could beat the crap out of me in hand-to-hand combat, and maybe half the guys in the barracks, including you." I was afraid that I'd gone too far, but when I heard the guys laugh, I knew what I had to do. Get the guys to laugh and make them my allies! The sarge was really pissed, and he asks me if I thought that any nigger can be better than a white man, and I say it's within the realm of possibility that a particular nigger could be superior to a particular white guy. Well, I hit his racial nerve, because that statement paralyzed him. He stared at me forever before speaking to me as if I were a schoolkid who had missed a lesson. "Corporal," he says right in my face, "there ain't no fuckin' black-assed coon in this fuckin' world that's as good as me!" I was tempted to correct his grammar and say, "As good as I," but I wasn't sure it would get a laugh. I said that somewhere on the planet there may be one or two niggers who might be his

*equal, and he said, "Name one!" I wanted to laugh, but instead
I told him that this was a silly discussion. This got him really
mad, and he put his nose right up against mine and shouted into
my mouth, "You name one nigger as good as me and I'll kiss
your big, fat, dumb ass." I accepted his challenge but said that
if I won I would prefer he kissed someone else's ass. This was
my best moment so far. The guys howled, and while they were
laughing, I asked for volunteers who'd like to have their asses
kissed by the sarge. A few guys laughed and held up their
hands, which made the sarge double furious, and he yelled at
me, "Corporal, name a nigger! That's an order!" It was a
military command, so I clicked my heels and shouted back,
"Paul Robeson, sir!" I was really surprised when he asked,
"Who the fuck is Paul Robeson?" I said, "You're kidding," and
he said, "I never kid," and then he put his tobacco-smelling
mouth against my nose again and shouted right up my nostrils,
"Corporal, you tell me one fuckin' thing that this fucking
nigger has done in his life that's better'n what I have done!" I
knew we had something very entertaining developing, so I
played along. "Well, let's see," I said. "Paul Robeson
graduated as a Phi Beta Kappa from Rutgers University." The
sarge said, "I never finished high school and am proud of it!"
One of the noncoms laughed, and I said to him, "Okay,
Corporal, you keep score. One for the sarge and one for Mr.
Robeson. So far we're even." Then I said, "Paul Robeson was
fluent in five foreign languages," and he says, "Well, I speak
American, the language of the first president of the United
States and every president that came after him." I held up my
fingers, and the corporal yelled, "Two to two!" The guys now
started to gather around us, and I had myself an audience. I
hope I can remember the rest of our dialogue. I think I'll have a
better shot at it if I put the rest of our debate into play form.
We'll title it:*

ME AND THE SARGE

ME: Robeson was a four-letter man at Rutgers and was voted
all-American in football.

SARGE: (*smirking*) Before I enlisted, I ran a chain of grocery
stores.

ME: Three to three! (*holding up fingers*) Still even. Paul
Robeson has written a book.

SARGE: I never read a book!

ME: Damn, thought I had you on that one. Four to four! (*big response from the guys on that one*)

ME: Paul Robeson has a law degree.

SARGE: My daddy is a lawyer and has an office in downtown New Orleans.

ME: Damn, you got me again. Five to five! Okay, here's one. Paul Robeson has acted and sung on Broadway, in concert halls, and in motion pictures. . . . Beat that!

SARGE: I will. (*with a smile of superiority*) I am a Louisiana State board-certified embalmer and have worked as the assistant chief embalmer in the biggest mortuary in Shreveport.

Honey, here I really played it great. I threw up my hands and conceded defeat. "You win, Sarge," I yelled, and congratulated him on the brilliance of his strategy. I said, "You son of a bitch, you booby-trapped me. You waited for just the right moment to drop the bomb. Robeson couldn't embalm a dead man's pinky finger, and you knew it!" The guys were roaring, and he smiled at me with that kind of strange smile that villains use in westerns when they lose a round to the hero. You know that you're going to hear from them again, and boy was I right. That night, after lights out, I heard from him. I was lying in my bunk and thinking of you when the sarge's voice comes at me from across the barracks. He says, "Kokloko, or whatever the fuck your name is, why don't we take our carbines out to the drill field and settle our little argument like men." Honey, it was so quiet in the barracks that I was afraid the sarge would hear my teeth chattering. I actually clenched my jaw to make them stop. I don't know what came over me, probably adrenaline flowing into my tongue, but without missing a beat I said, "Look, Sarge, just for a few seconds of fun and excitement I'm not about to rot in jail for the rest of my life." The sarge asked me what the fuck I was talking about, and I said that I was an expert marksman with three medals to prove it (a lie) and if we faced off with carbines, I'd blow his head off before he could get his finger on the trigger. I said, "Why go through all that for a debate you've already won." Then I said my best line; it got me a lot of laughs and applause. I said, "What'll it be, Sarge? The choice is yours, wet dreams for you tonight or no dreams for eternity?" After a few giggles there was a stony silence. From the other end of the barracks I heard him call, "Hey, Cockwits, you a Jew?" Phonetically it came out Yew a Jyeeew? It was really scary. I said I was and asked him why he asked. Now here's the weirdest thing, which I didn't see coming. He says, "One of my best friends in Shreveport is a Jyeew, Goldfarb, Jessie Goldfarb?" He said his name like a question, as if he thought that all Jews knew each other. I said I didn't know him, and that was the end of it. He never said another word to me. I don't know what might have happened if I had been alone with him and no audience around to laugh. I think my stage training and doing comedy in the rec halls got me out of that in one piece. Honey, I'm going to send this letter off and then write you another one tonight that'll contain lurid descriptions of all the wonderful, dirty things I want us to do to each other when next we find ourselves in the same city.

✦

"Hey, Donny boy, where's that other letter? I'd rather critique that one."

"I know you would," David said, snatching the letter from him, "but this is the one I want your opinion about."

"I like it, but nobody'll print it with all the fucks and fuckin's you got in it."

"I'll change them to friggin', but that's not going to cut anything."

"How many words do they want?"

"Fifteen hundred."

"How many words is the letter?"

"About three thousand."

"Easy, cut every other word."

"You're very helpful, Gene."

"Anytime."

That evening, working diligently and actually using a variant of Eugene's formula, David managed to tell his story in 1,504 words. Eugene reread the cut version, gave it an A-plus, and told him to mail it in.

After months of traveling to every army base in the Hawaiian Islands, David and his good buddies gave their last performance of *Fire Away* at Schofield Barracks. David stood in the wings at that final show and rooted for his colleague Parkinson to successfully negotiate the four-club kickup, a juggling trick he had practiced and perfected months earlier but for fear of failure never dared to put in his act. He did it flawlessly this night and was roundly cheered by his fellow performers. The audience, unaware of the extraordinary skill it took to flip four Indian clubs into the air with his foot and then juggle them, did not applaud any more roundly than they did when he kicked up three clubs from the floor.

David watched for the last time his elegantly tuxedoed friend J. C. Handy dance out on the stage and do a graceful soft-shoe while producing out of thin air lit cigarettes, decks of playing cards, and finally, a couple of live doves. David appreciated and marveled at the virtuousity of Dan Waller, playing the famous violin solo Hora Staccato on his shiny chromatic harmonica, and he never ceased to be thrilled by the incredible power and range of Lawrence T. Lawrence's voice and his ability to make the pop song "Amapola" sound like an operatic aria. To David, the most amazing phenomenon of all was Chicky Click Clack, who, by putting his lips against the microphone and manipulating his tongue against his teeth, was able to simulate the sounds of Fred Astaire tap-dancing. To the dismay of his colleagues, Chicky Click Clack always collected the loudest and most sustained applause of the evening.

"Take away that fucking microphone," the envious and furious J. C. Dandy often philosophized, "and the fucking recordings of Irving fucking Berlin's fucking great songs and he'd fall on his fucking ass. It's the fucking songs that're getting the fucking applause, not that annoying fuck!"

At the demise of each show in the Entertainment Section, the performers, especially the legitimate actors in shows like *Hamlet,* would become depressed. With no play to act in, they became expendable and vulnerable for reassignment to combat outfits. New variety shows were easy to mount, and acts like Chicky Click Clack always had a place to do their thing. *Hamlet* and *Fire Away* shut down within days of each other, and with their closings came a great deal of scurrying and worrying. David spent that first day off writing letters. He knocked off an eight-pager to Mary Deare, a four-pager to his brother, and another to Saul Marantz, who was now working in a Signal Corps Message Center on a secured Iwo Jima. He wrote a three-pager to his folks and was about to scribble a couple of short notes to his old employers Messrs. Foreman and Marlowe when he heard the barrack's loudspeaker click on.

"Private Klokvitz," the voice boomed, "report to Captain Sullen's office. Private Klokvitz to Captain Sullen's office, on the double!''

David suddenly started to perspire. As successful as he had been in *Fire Away,* he did not feel at all secure about his future. He had just heard of a couple of fairly good actors being ordered to return to their original outfits, and he imagined that it might also be his fate. Why else, he thought, would I be ordered to Captain Sullen's office? A week earlier, the captain had asked David if he had any other comedy material, and foolishly he admitted that he had used up all of his best stuff in *Fire Away.*

Lieutenant Yorby, whose office was adjacent to Captain Sullen's, gestured for David to come wait in his office.

"Have a seat,'' the lieutenant said without looking up from the papers on his desk. "Captain Sullen is with someone.''

David looked through the glass partition that separated the two offices and was surprised to see a frowning Eugene O'Neill listening to a smiling Captain Sullen explain something that seemed to make both men uncomfortable. Reassignnent, David thought. Damn! David looked to Lieutenant Yorby, who was busy making notations on papers that were scattered all over his desk. The lieutentant's head was bent forward, giving David a clear view of the dark brown roots from which grew his weird flame-red hair.

"You're looking at the part in my hair, aren't you, Kockawish?'' the lieutenant asked without raising his eyes.

David jumped. "No sir. But I am now, since you mentioned it.''

"What do you see?'' he said, keeping his head down.

"Well, it seems to be a bit darker than the rest of your hair.''

"It is,'' he said, looking up for the first time. "You didn't think my hair was actually this color, did you?''

"I didn't know. I thought maybe the tropical sun had—''

"No, I hennaed it,'' he explained unnecessarily, "for my role in *Hamlet.* You saw the play, didn't you?''

"Oh, yes, it was wonderful! You, uh, you played Fortinbras.''

"Thank you.'' The lieutenant smiled, accepting a compliment that David hadn't proffered. "You know, Fortinbras is a rather thankless role and can be a boring one.''

"Yes, sir,'' David heartily agreed, "it sure can be boring.''

"Exactly. That's why I played him as a redhead. I thought that giving him this red, red hair would make him seem less bland, perk him up a bit. I think I accomplished that.''

"You sure did, sir,'' David said, playing the sycophant. "It made you stand out and helped give the scenes you were in a . . . a kind of focus. . . .''

"Exactly, a focus! It gave my scenes a focus! You're very perceptive," the lieutenant said, shuffling the papers on his desk. "But now that the show is closed, I'm thinking of letting my hair grow out to its natural color," he said, contemplatively tapping a pencil against his lips.

"That makes sense, sir. I mean, as long as you're not playing the role anymore, why walk around with—"

"Exactly! You're very sharp, Private Kockwish. However, waiting for my hair to grow out would take forever, and rather than having my roots be a topic of conversation, I've decided to bleach it back to my own blondish auburn."

"That's what I would do, sir, especially if my hair were blondish auburn," David said to the lieutenant, whose roots were clearly dark brown.

Lieutenant Yorby reached into his desk drawer and took from it an eight-by-ten framed color photo and handed it to David. "That's my wife, Karen, with our twins, Kiki and Niki," Yorby boasted. "They just turned two, and they are a handful."

"And Mrs. Yorby is an eyeful, if I may say sir," David said, shocked to learn that Yorby was heterosexual. He examined the photo of a buxom and very blond woman holding two girls who were even blonder. "And so are the twins. They're all so pretty and so . . . blond. A little like Jean Harlow's color."

"Very perceptive. That's exactly what my wife and I were going for. Do you like it?"

"It's very . . . arresting."

"Arresting?" David could hear his mother say. "They should both get arrested for baby bleaching!"

During this exchange, David kept one eye on Captain Sullen's office, hoping to hear what the captain might be saying to Eugene. From the broadness of the captain's smile and the heartiness of their handshake David surmised that Eugene's future with the company was in jeopardy. He would have loved to have talked with Eugene, but Eugene scooted as the captain bade him enter.

"Come in, come in, David. Have a seat," Captain Sullen gushed, using most of his thirty-two perfect teeth in a welcoming smile. "Did Lieutenant Yorby tell you why I called you in?"

"No, but I think I have an idea." David smiled back.

"What're you thinking?" Captain Sullen said, settling behind his desk.

"I'm thinking," David said, sitting stiffly in the chair opposite the captain, "that you're probably going to tell me what you told Eugene O'Neill."

"And what would that be?"

"Uh, about being reassigned?"

"Well, you're half right. I was discussing that with O'Neill, but what I want to talk to you about is a new musical review that Major Merritt has asked me to mount."

"You"—David actually gulped—"you want me to be in a musical review?"

"Yes, David," Captain Sullen said, bringing the fingertips of his two hands together in front of his face. "We want you to be in it, but we also want you to write the comedy sketches for it. You have written sketches before, I assume."

"You do? I mean, I haven't written sketches," David stupidly admitted, but quickly retrenched, ". . . lately! But I've been thinking of writing some new ones."

"From what we've seen of your work, the major and I feel that you would do a good job for us. We've already assigned a choreographer, a songwriter, and a lyricist to the project. I'll arrange for you to meet them this afternoon."

"That's great, because while I'm meeting them," David joked, "they can meet me!"

"That's the spirit. "The captain laughed as he beckoned Lieutenant Yorby to join them.

Equal amounts of pride and panic overcame David as he contemplated the enormity of the undertaking he had just accepted. Before he could give voice to his fears, the captain, who seemed to be reading David's mind, acknowledged that writing comedy sketches without a partner would be difficult to do.

"You are so right, sir! The Jack Benny and Fred Allen radio shows always use teams of writers."

"Is there someone with whom you would like to collaborate?"

"Yes, sir. Eugene O'Neill," David shot back without hesitation. "I'd love to work with him."

"That may not be possible," Captain Sullen said, shaking his head sadly. "He's going to be reassigned next week, and even if he weren't, he's an actor."

"And a very witty one. I've worked with him back in the States, and he used to crack me up. We once did a pretty funny comedy act together that he wrote," David half-lied, thinking of *The Comedy of Errors* and the *Pax Vobiscum* tap dance they did at the end of every performance. "Eugene O'Neill is the perfect one for me to write with. His name even sounds like a writer's name."

"Corporal, how is it that Sergeant O'Neill never mentioned to us that he did comedy?"

"That's typical of him; never one to blow his own horn. He's got this great Irish sense of humor. If it weren't for O'Neill, sir, we wouldn't be having this discussion. He brought me to the section, the man knows funny."

"I have heard him turn a snappy phrase now and then," the captain conceded. "All right, Kokolovitz, you got him."

David had always liked Captain Sullen, but at this moment he loved him.

David ran back to the barracks hoping to find Eugene there. He was dying to apprise him of his conversation with Captain Sullen and also discuss his meeting with Lieutenant Yorby. David still felt that the lieutenant was strange, married or not. From David's first morning in the company when he went to the latrine to do his morning ablutions and was greeted by the sight of soldiers wearing long, colorful, flowing kimonos, he suspected that he'd fallen in with a a company of merry, minty men, until he saw Eugene come flouncing in wearing one. He explained later that the kimonos had came from a production of *The Mikado* and were appropriated by the actors, straight and gay, who enjoyed wearing anything that wasn't government issue. Since discovering that his old roommate Gaylord was homosexual, David felt inept at determinining people's sexual orientation. Obviously, the army had the same problem, for the last he heard from Capt. Gaylord Morley was from London, where he was the lead pilot for a B-17 bomber squadron.

At his barracks, David learned from Lawrence T. Lawrence, who was in the middle of rehearsing, that Eugene had just left.

"Do you know where he went, Larry? It's important."

Lawrence T. Lawrence, who never let anything disturb his rehearsal, sang his answer to the tune of "Amor": "I think, I think, I think . . . that he went, that he went, tothecafeteeeriaa."

The cafeteria would not open for fifteen minutes, and David did not expect that Eugene would wait. More likely, a depressed Eugene would be at the motor pool trying to requisition a jeep to drive into Waikiki, his favorite place to lose the blues. Taking a shortcut to the motor pool, David walked behind the cafeteria and stopped short when, through some half-opened shutters, he glimpsed Eugene sitting in the empty lunch hall talking to someone who was hidden behind a potted plant.

"Eugene, Eugene?" David called excitedly, rapping his knuckles against the slats.

"I guess you heard the news, buddy," Eugene said quietly after rotating the shutters open. "Come through that side door and join us. We're having an intimate Hawaiian wake."

Making his way to the side door, David wondered who the "we" was that he was invited to join. Never in his wildest dreams would he have guessed that it would be Her Haughtiness, the Chinese-Hawaiian icicle, Sooky the cashier. He had never seen Sooky when she did not look elegant, composed, and ravishingly beautiful until this moment. She was a holy mess. Her ebony-black hair was hanging in wisps, and her eyes were red and teary.

"Donny, you know Sooky," Eugene said politely, as if everything were normal, "and Sooky, you know my friend Donny."

Sooky shook her head and did not look up.

"You can sit with us, Donald," Eugene said, pulling up a chair for him, "but only if you say things that will cheer us up."

David had no clue as to what had brought Sooky to this unhinged state and knew that he could never say anything cheerful enough to bring her out of it. She was trembling and making small, pitiful sobbing sounds. He ruled out that Sooky could be this upset by the news of Eugene's reassignment and assumed that her grief had to do with a death in her family. But if that were so, why would Eugene, a perfect stranger, be the one to comfort her? It didn't make much sense unless Eugene wasn't a perfect stranger but an imperfect one.

"Eugene, does this wake have anything to do with Sooky thinking you're leaving?"

"Yes, but I don't *think* I'm leaving, Donny. I *know* I'm leaving!"

"But you don't know about the musical review the section is mounting that I've been asked to contribute to," David said, smiling impishly, "or that I requested that you collaborate with me in writing the sketches?"

"No, I don't know that," Eugene said, squinting at David suspiciously, "but I know you hate practical jokes, so this eleventh-hour reprieve you've just handed me, it's no bullshit, is it?"

"Ask Captain Sullen."

"I will, but before I do, I think I should tell you," Eugene said, wincing as if in pain, "I have never written a sketch in my life."

"Neither have I, but we are actors and we will act like writers."

"Yeah," Eugene agreed, "Warner Baxter didn't produce *Forty-second Street.* He *acted* like a producer. Donny, you old thief, I owe you one."

Sooky was not sure what had transpired, but from the way the two friends shook hands and smiled, she knew she could stop sobbing.

The lunch bell sounded, sending Sooky to her feet. She blew her nose, smiled gratefully at David, whispered something in Eugene's ear, and hurried off. From the rapturous look on her face when she turned and waved to Eugene, David deduced that this formerly unapproachable Oriental goddess was out of her mind in love with Sergeant O'Neill.

"What the hell did you do to capture the ice maiden's heart, and why did you?"

"I didn't capture it; she surrendered it to me," Eugene said, collapsing into a chair.

"What do you mean, she surrendered it to you? You told me that when you asked her to a movie, she turned you down flat."

"She did, but the next day, when she invited me to her house for dinner, I didn't turn her down. Matter of fact, I never turn her down. Damn, am I in a sticky mess!"

"So that's why we haven't seen you in the Mutton Club lately. Look, Eugene I don't mean to pry."

"Sure you do, and the answer is yes, we do the Lambeth walk together, and it's just sensational, and I may kill myself if Peggy doesn't beat me to it."

"Peggy knows about Sooky!"

"Of course she knows."

"You wrote and told her?"

"I don't have to. Peggy will know by the way I dot my i's." Eugene moaned. "I really appreciate what you did for me, but under the circumstances I'm not sure it was such a big favor. Hey, whatever," Eugene said, getting to his feet. "Shouldn't I go back to the office and accept this sketch-writing detail you say I've been put on?"

"Excellent idea!"

"You won't believe this, Donny," Eugene continued as they hurried out of the cafeteria and to the captain's office, "but I was actually relieved when Sullen told me they were planning to transfer me out of here."

"Was that why Sooky was bawling?"

"Yes, I'm a bounder, not unlike my dad. I couldn't resist her; the girl's nuts about me."

"The girl may just be nuts. How the hell can anyone fall that deeply in love that fast?"

"She adores Van Johnson and would die for him."

"Yeah?" David asked, waiting for elucidation.

"She thinks I look like him. She's seen every one of his pictures three times. It's these damn freckles," he said, slapping his cheeks angrily. "There a curse, Donny. I'm in trouble, and you gotta help me."

"What the hell can I do?"

"Come with me to her apartment tonight for dinner. If we do the Lambeth walk one more time, I'm going to fall in love with her, I know it!"

"What are you saying?"

"I'm saying that if you saw that girl's naked body lying on a bed, you'd be in the same fix I'm in. Believe me, Donny, I need you to be with me at dinner tonight. If not for me, then for Peggy. I'd do as much for you."

"Would you?" David asked, suddenly sounding sarcastic. "I wonder, Eugene, if you have any idea at all what this lovely, exciting siren who you say captured your heart is making for dinner?"

"You sonovabitch." Eugene laughed, happy that David was still his friend. "She is making, among other gourmet delicacies, these fantastic Singapore noodles."

"I'll come."

"Sooky, these are fantastic," David gushed, heaping his plate with a third helping of the thin, curry-flavored Singapore noodles. "I am not leaving tonight without your recipe for this dish."

"You are being kind."

"No, I'm not, Sooky," he said, deftly popping some of the noodles into his mouth with his chopsticks. "When I get home the second thing I'm going to do for my girl is cook her some of these noodles."

"Donny, you are so funny." Sooky laughed, then turned to Eugene. "I am glad you brought your friend to dinner."

"Yeah, he makes eating fun," Eugene said distractedly, thinking of what he had to do sometime soon.

Earlier, on the jeep ride up the winding hills to Sooky's apartment, Eugene, searching for the gentlest way to break her heart, confided to David, "The best thing I can do for everyone concerned is to tell Sooky as soon as we get there and get it over with."

"I say after dinner is much better," David lobbied. "The poor girl must have cooked all day. Why ruin everybody's night."

"Okay," Eugene acquiesced, "in deference to your Jewish tradition, first we'll eat and then we'll talk, even though I think it's crueler."

"Face it, Gene, dumping a person is never not cruel."

"I know," Eugene sighed, "but it's crueler to eat, dump, and run. You win. I'll talk to her after dinner."

"After dessert!"

"No dessert. After dinner you'll excuse yourself and go for a walk. I'll signal you when to come back in."

"What should I listen for?"

"Probably the clang of a wok hitting my head."

At dinner, knowing what Eugene was planning made it difficult for David to fully enjoy her magnificent meal of savory noodles, tangy tangerine beef, and braised garlic shrimp. He had barely swallowed his last mouthful when he saw Eugene glaring at him.

"Great meal, Sooky. Now if you'll excuse me," David announced, "I shall go outside for my usual after-a-fantastic-dinner stroll."

Standing in Sooky's garden, David was overcome by an unsettling feeling as he breathed in the intoxicating aroma of her flowering plants. The exotic scents and the thought of his friend Eugene alone in the apartment with the love object of every serviceman who ever passed her cashier's station brought David to a state of arousal that was not unexpected but unwelcome. His guilty thoughts went immediately to Mary Deare and the boardinghouse bed in Decatur, Georgia, where she touched his penis for the first time. He looked up into the moonlit sky and wished upon the brightest star in a firmament of bright stars for his love to materialize beside him.

"I just want to see her face," he whispered to no one, "and give her sweet lips one soft kiss." I'm lying, he admitted. I want to see every part of her and kiss everything.

David paced back and forth on the deserted road in front of the house, waiting for something to happen. Maybe Eugene changed his mind, David thought, while leaning against a giant pandanus tree; maybe my friend succumbed to his baser self and is, at this moment, before breaking the goddess's heart, having one last fling with her. David could understand this behavior but could not condone it. He judged Eugene to be a cad for doing what most men, including himself, would kill to do. While pondering the ethics of out-of-control horniness, an ear-piercing wail shattered the stillness of the night and scared the shit out of him and a flock of startled birds who were perched in the branches of the pandanus tree. The volume and intensity of Sooky's keening compelled David to ignore Eugene's instruction and head for the house.

"Eugene! Sookey!" he screamed out, trying to be heard above the wailing, "I'm coming back in!"

Opening the front door a crack and using all of his considerable lung power, David bellowed, "DAMMIT, I'M COMIIING IN!"

David's maniacal shouting brought Sooky's wailing to an abrupt halt. Concerned that they might be in some state of undress, David cautiously made his way into the living room, where he saw a fully clad Sooky sitting on the floor, hugging her knees to her chest and silently rocking back and forth. Eugene sat on a couch looking contrite and helpless, his sad eyes, which were riveted on David, seemed to be pleading for help. David, ever the M.C., tried to think of something to say to help disperse the gloom and doom in the room.

"Great dinner, Sooky," David offered brightly, quickly realizing that she was in no mood to receive compliments. "So," he tried again, "is there anything I can do, for anybody?"

Sooky stopped rocking, raised her head from her knees, and studied David.

"Donny," she said eerily, "I would like to talk with you alone."

Mesmerized by the sad, beautiful face of this Oriental Bambi, David accepted her request. Sooky rose from her cramped postion in one graceful and effortless move and walked over to Eugene and whispered something to him. He nodded in agreement, took a pack of cigarettes from his pocket, and strode purposefully out the front door.

"So," David sighed, "what would you like to talk to me about?"

Sooky smiled and held out her hand, which David took. As she turned and led him down a hall, he wondered where she was taking him and why she gripped his hand so tightly.

"Please come into my bedroom. I wish to show you something," she said, answering his unspoken questions.

David had not been alone in a bedroom with a woman since the day, an aeon ago, when he and Mary Deare bid each other emotional and tear-filled farewells. The sensual aroma of Sooky's perfume hit David hard. His innate sense of decency clashed head-on with his natural, long-tethered animal passion. With every male gland in him screaming to be heard, David, who seriously coveted his friend's now former lover, swore that he would not compromise his integrity even if Sooky invited him to do so.

"Donny, look," Sooky said, pointing to the wall behind him, "and you will understand what I tell you."

David turned and beheld a wall covered with photos of Eugene, which included a glamorous one of him as Petruchio taken during their rep-company days.

"This is the man I love who does not love me," Sooky said, touching a framed photo of Eugene that sat on her dresser. "Don, you and Eugene are good friends, and I know he will listen to you."

"He never listens to me." David laughed. "Uh, what is it you want him to hear?"

"How very much I love him and how I will make him love me," Sooky answered, sitting at the edge of her bed and patting the space beside her. "Come sit here!

"Trying to make him jealous is not going to do it," David joked, backing away from the bed. "Making someone love you is not an easy thing to do."

"I can, Donny," she insisted. "If I can make you understand how deep is my love for Eugene and how I cannot live without him. I only want to make him happy," Sooky continued, her passion mounting. "Please tell Eugene that I want to be his wife and after the war I will go with him wherever he goes and do for him whatever he wants me to. Nothing would make me happier than to make a home for him and cook his meals. I would be honored to wash his socks and to bear his children. Tell him that I will never be a burden to him. If he does not get acting jobs right away, he does not have to worry. I will have my degree in chemistry, and I can get a job teaching or in research, and if I have to, I will do housework. You believe this, don't you, Donny?"

"Yeah, I believe," Donny admitted, thinking that if he were unattached, he would sign up for this deal in a minute.

As Sooky continued to enumerate the joys of Eugene's and her idyllic future together, giant tears rolled down her cheeks, and when she could no longer control her voice or her emotions, she flung her arms around David's neck, and hugged him with the fervor and strength of a woman possessed.

"No one will ever love him as I will! You must tell him all this. You must make him understand! Promise me you will make him understand. Please, promise me!"

Her sweet, warm breath blowing into his ear plus the feel of her soft, wet cheeks and lips pressing against his earlobe were more than a young, sexually deprived GI could be expected to handle.

"I promise, I promise, I'll tell him," David said, using all his strength and resolve to push her wonderful body away from his aching one. "I'll tell it to him right away, on the ride home," David said, backing out of the bedroom. "I'll tell him everything you said right now! 'Bye."

"Goodbye," Sooky said, sitting back down on the bed.

David was not aware at that time what was happening, but the pitiful image of Sooky sitting forlornly on her bed and wiping tears from her eyes with one hand as she sadly waved goodbye with the other was etching itself indelibly into his memory.

David left Sooky's house and made his way to the jeep, thinking, I am Ralph Bellamy playing the star's best friend. What a rotten role.

Eugene sat pensively behind the wheel and stared straight ahead as they drove back to the base. He smoked many cigarettes, made no comments, and asked no questions as he listened to David recall perfectly every emotional word that Sooky had charged him to remember.

Eugene remained silent for the remainder of the ride back to the university and did not speak until they started walking to their barracks from the motor pool. When they passed the cafeteria, Eugene stopped.

"Donny," he asked pensively, "did Sooky actually say that it'd be an honor to wash my socks?"

"And bear your children."

"You know, when Peggy and I roomed together"—Eugene sighed—"she'd often wash my socks."

"But was she honored?"

"No, she washed them in self-defense."

"You know, Gene, you might have avoided this whole mess if on that first date you'd let Sooky smell your feet."

"I did, and she found them intoxicating."

"You're funny." David laughed. "You're going to make a good comedy writer."

"Yeah," Eugene mumbled. "There's not going to be too much comedy in my letter to Peggy tonight. Our dinner at Sooky's wasn't a barrel of laughs."

"You're not going to tell her about Sooky?"

"I have to if I want to live with myself. Didn't know I had a conscience, did you? Well, neither did I until I met Peggy."

"Boy, are you sophisticated. What the hell are you going to tell her about Sooky?"

"Almost everthing. I've already told her that Sooky is a student at the university and works as a cashier in the cafeteria and we got friendly, and tonight I'll write her how both of us were invited to Sooky's house for a home-cooked dinner and how great the food was and how you pigged out on Singapore noodles. The only two things I have not and will not tell Peggy is that Sooky is a girl and that we had an affair."

"You told Peggy that Sooky is a guy?"

"Yes, a very handsome guy who's studying to be a chemist."

"That is so deceitful, Gene. Oh, yes," David said, nodding, "you definitely have a gift for creative writing."

"And for detail. Donny, you know that Peggy and Mary are in touch with each other, don't you?"

"Sure, why?"

"Well, did you perchance ever mention anything about Sooky in one of your letters to Mary Deare?"

"Do you mean, did I tell her about this girl Sooky who has the kind of face and body that every soldier in our outfit, would give a month's pay just to see naked and a year's pay to sleep with?"

"Yes, did you write her that?"

"No, should I?" David joked.

Eugene let out a small laugh and then fell silent. The two walked along the path and then, without either suggesting it, they headed for the latrine and ended up standing side by side, urinating into the tin trough. Eugene, who worked hard at hiding his sentimental side, stared straight ahead for a while before he spoke.

"Donny, I must tell you, I much prefer peeing in private, but until the war's over, there's nobody else I'd rather be peeing with."

"That's the nicest thing you've ever said to me, Gene."

"No, this is—I feel lucky to have you as a friend," Eugene said, barely making himself heard above the noise of their streams hitting the tin trough. "I don't think I can ever thank you enough for what you did for me today."

Straining to hear what Eugene was saying and not sure that he had finished saying it, David did not respond.

"Donny?" Eugene asked, buttoning his fly. "Did you hear what I said?"

"A lot of it."

"Good, because if I had to repeat it, we'd both throw up."

My only darling, now and forever,

Eugene and I started writing and tearing up sketches for this new show. Today, was our first productive one. We suggested some titles for the show, and everyone loved the one that we threw in as a joke. We hate it, but Mal Dradel, a songwriter who just got assigned to the outfit, said that he was going to use it in the opening song. The show's called, Four Gals for the Guys, and I bet you guessed that there'll be four girls in the show. (All ugly and they come with a chaperon.) Actually, honey, they're pretty; three sing and dance, and one sings and acts cute. They'll all do some parts in the sketches that Eugene and I are supposed to be writing but aren't because we both prefer writing to our beloveds. By the way, as soon as I finish reading it, I'm sending you a book of poetry called This Is My Beloved. It was written by my old company commander at Camp Crowder, Capt. Walter Benton. I wish I could write like he does, but when you read it, remember that what he says and how he says it goes for me, too. It made me want you so much. I love you, I really really do.

We're sitting in our new office, a dressing room at Farrington Hall (the University Theater), where we spent part of the day seriously trying to write but most of it examining our faces in the mirrors on the wall behind the makeup table we use as a desk. After hours of evaluating our faces and coming to no

*conclusions about them, we agreed that no work will get done
unless we turn our backs to the mirror while we write. It worked
well until Eugene had a need to know if his nose still tilted a
little to the right. While he was checking, I said, what the hell, I
might as well see if my hairline is a little more defined than it
was fifteen minutes ago. (I think it is, near the temples; lucky I
checked.) We both noticed after staring at ourselves a moment
ago that we looked like two guys who needed a break; hence,
this letter. Gene is writing to Peggy, which reminds me, in
answer to the question about those Singapore noodles Peggy
told you about. Yes, I did make a pig of myself at Sooky's, and
the reason I didn't write you about those noodles is that I
wanted to surprise you with them when I got home. After I
finish kissing and playing with every available part of your
magnificent body and using the most sensitive parts for our
mutual pleasure, (I can't wait to hear those cute, sexy sounds
you make), I was planning to cook the noodles and bring them
to you in bed. We did agree, didn't we, that for the first week at
home we'd do everything in bed but toileting? Well, I have bad
news about those noodles. I didn't get the recipe.*

✦

"Hey, Gene," David called out, "just so we keep our stories straight about Sooky's fantastic noodles, I'm going to say that I didn't get the recipe because Sooky enlisted in the navy and he got shipped out. Is that okay?"

"Good, and if Mary asks again, say his ship got blown out of the water by a kamikaze pilot."

"No, lost at sea," David suggested. "Why add to our own casualty lists? I just wish you hadn't written Peggy that I loved those damn noodles."

"I had to. That letter was so full of lies, I wanted it to have at least one sentence with some truth in it."

"I'll tell Mary Deare that I have the recipe. I could call Sooky and ask her for it. She's not mad at *me*."

"Eugene! David!" Captain Sullen called, breezing into the room and followed by a short, dark private, "How're the sketches coming?"

"Great," David lied, holding up his letter-writing tablet. "We're noodlin' around with two or three ideas here."

"Actually four or five," Eugene echoed, holding up his letter pad.

"They're all pretty good," David bluffed. "Would you like us to run them by you?"

"Later," the captain said, looking at his watch. "I really came to have you hear Mal Dradel sing his lyrics for the opening song. Mal's going to sing it for you two. There's a piano just down the hall," the captain said, leading the way. "I think it's very good. I'd like your opinion."

"And I think, sir," David said, using a farcical, high nasal voice, "that I am going to think exactly what you think."

"I agree with Private Brownnose," Eugene said, trailing behind."

"That's one of the things we're working on," David explained in his natural voice, "Private Brownnose and Corporal Asskiss, two GI jerks."

"Sounds promising, boys," Captain Sullen said, smiling broadly. "I have a great feeling about this project."

"Now, fellows, if you have any suggestions . . ." Mal said, sitting down at an old upright and putting a lyric sheet in front of him, "please feel free."

Under a vamping introduction he noodled on the piano, Mal announced, "I'm using your title *Four Gals for the Guys,* and I think it'd be effective if the four girls in the show each made a solo entrance and sang a line of the verse. They'd then be joined by the guys wearing army, navy, and marine uniforms."

"Wonderful!" Captain Sullen said, clapping his hands. "Having all branches of the service represented is good thinking. We'll probably play some navy and marine bases."

After clearing his throat, Mal, accompanying himself on the tinny, out-of-tune piano, sang with a voice thinner than Irving Berlin's,

> "Guys, if you're lonely and blue,
> And miss your Janie or Sue,
> We say get happy, get wise,
> Here's four gals for you guys.
> I'm Dolly, I'm Bitsy, I'm Lolly, I'm Sissy.
> We are the Four Gals for the Guys,(thump thump)
> The four gals for guys, the
> Four ready, willing and avail-able, gals for guys."

Before anyone could tell him how bad his song was, Mal Dradel crumpled the sheet of paper and bolted from the room, muttering as he went, "I'm a graduate of Juilliard. I can't write this shit!"

"Maybe Dradel can't write songs," David said, "but he's a damn fine critic."

"It *was* awful, wasn't it? I don't have very good rhythm and I'm tone deaf. Well at least I have a sense of humor and I read well enough to judge comedy material," the captain admitted. "You fellers keep plugging away. Dradel will come through. He's written songs for dozens of shows in the Catskills."

Three weeks later, after obscuring their reflections by applying Bon Ami window cleaner to their dressing-room mirror and allowing the chalky white residue to remain on it, David and Eugene were able to concentrate well enough to write five comedy pieces. Also helpful in maintaining their discipline was their periodically reminding each other that if they goofed off they could end up on some remote Pacific island either killing or being killed. From David's standpoint, the most important sketch they wrote, besides his comedy monologue, was a solo pantomime sketch that David insisted Eugene demonstrate. Eugene performed it so well that he was invited to join the cast. Short of hearing that Germany and Japan had been defeated and that he'd been ordered to go home, nothing could have thrilled David more than having Eugene in the company.

On the last night of rehearsal, Lieutenant Yorby unveiled the poster he had designed for their new show. It was now called *Shape Up!* The poster featured the four girl members of the company wearing scanty costumes in a pose that displayed their fine bosoms and shapely legs.

"Well, what do you think?" a freshly bleached-blond Lieutenant Yorby asked eagerly." Rather attractive, isn't it?"

"I'd like it better if it had my picture on it," Lawrence T. Lawrence, who was as vain as he was honest, said. "This here poster only says that there are four pretty girls in the show."

"Exactly. Just what I designed it to say!" Lieutenant Yorby said through clenched teeth, angrily rolling up the poster. "Attention, everyone. I believe Captain Sullen wants a word with the cast," he said, nodding toward the captain, who had just entered the auditorium. "Captain?"

"First off, I want to congratulate you all on the fine work you've done in a very short time. Tomorrow night will be your one-and-only dress rehearsal for *Shape Up!* Unlike most dress rehearsals, there will be an audience present, a very special audience, I might add. Along with a few hundred servicemen, Major Merritt has invited as his guests the distinguished actor/playwright Hart Milton and the cast of his play *Dinner at Home With Maud.* To reciprocate, Mr. Milton and his company, who've just arrived from the States, have graciously agreed to give us a special matinee performance of their play before starting their tour of Hawaii."

A wave of paralyzing fear overcame David as he contemplated

performing his untested comedy material for a Pulitzer Prize–winning playwright. How could Major Merritt do this to me? he asked himself. How can he expect me to be funny in front of this wit who lunches at the Algonquin round table and trades barbs with Oscar Levant, George S. Kaufman and Groucho Marx on their weekly radio show. David looked to Eugene for comfort, but Eugene, who was undergoing a gut-disturbing reaction to Captain Sullen's announcement, was rushing off to the toilet, where he often went in times of unmanageable stress.

David found Eugene standing over a toilet bowl and giving up his lunch.

David could feel his heart skip a beat as he peered through a hole in the curtain and saw Hart Milton and Major Merritt sitting in the third row. The sight of these two theatrical giants and the sound of the drumroll starting the band's rousing overture quickened David's pulse precipitously and brought him close to experiencing the first fainting episode of his life. The opening song-and-dance number preceded his first appearance in the show, a two-man sketch that he and Eugene had never performed for an audience. Eugene stood beside him in the wings looking pale and deathly calm, which only made David more anxious.

"Hey, budddy, break a leg!" David said, punching his friend on the arm in the hopes of energizing him.

"Do that again, Don, only harder."

"Why?"

"Because I saw you punch me, but I didn't feel it. I think my body's numb."

David obliged with a quick, sharp jab.

"*Oooh,* that felt good," Eugene said sighing.

"I enjoyed it, too," David said, the level of his own terror abating.

They smiled weakly at each other and then stood quietly in the wings and watched the three leggy dancers, Dolly Pastori, Bitsy Kane, and Loretta Yung perform their simple but effectively choreographed opening number. Eugene had once described the song they sang, "Shape Up!," as having the singularly most distinguished lyrics since the classic "Bibbity Bobbity Boo."

With broad smiles on their pretty painted faces, the three girls, moving sensually and singing the insipid lyrics with such verve and ingenuousness that only the most discriminating would not be moved to smile, which amazingly, David noted, this audience was doing. He was heartened to see smiles on Milton and Merritt's faces as the girls sang,

" 'Now hear this! Jill, Sally and Sue!
This is yo' Mama talkin to you . . .
You gottaaaaaaaa . . .
Shape up! . . . Shape up! . . . Shape up!
Shape up! . . . Shut up! . . . or Ship out! . . .
Until Johnny comes march, march, marchin' home.' "

Eugene and David got into position behind a flat that depicted a corner of a barracks and waited for their cue. From what David could sense from the happy hoots and wahoos that greeted the long-legged, short-skirted girls who were prancing around the stage, this was going to be a tough act to follow.

The short sketch, which was more like a blackout, was based on an incident David witnessed when he was at the Signal Corps school in Camp Crowder. It was a Sunday, and his friend Saul Marantz was sitting on his cot writing a letter when Gino Tarantelli, a New York recruit who spoke with a slight Italian accent, had came into the barracks one Sunday carrying a box of Oreo cookies. Gino walked the full length of the barracks, sat on his bunk, opened his box of Oreos, ate one, and then called out to Saul, who was engrossed in writing his letter. "Hey, Marantz, you can go fucka you'self!"

"You talking to me, Tarantelli?" a confused Saul had asked.

"Yeah, I'm talkin' to you, Marantz, and in case you didn' hear me. I said, You can go fucka you'self."

"What the hell's wrong with you, Tarantelli. I'm sitting here minding my business, writing a letter, and you attack me for no reason."

"It's not for no reason, Marantz, and just so my message is clear to you, I say again, Marantz, You can go fucka you'self."

"Tarantelli," Saul said, projecting across the long barracks. "Please tell me why I should go fuck myself?"

"Because I know human nature. I just come from the PX where I bought myself a box of chawclate cookies, and when I came in, you didn't even look up to say hello."

"I was busy writing."

"You wanna hear, or you wanna interrupt?"

"I wanna hear."

"So listen! I walk across the barracks and sit down to eat my chawclate cookies. In a coupla minutes, you gonna finish your letter and look up, and you gonna notice that Tarantelli is munchin' on somethin', and you gonna say, Hey Tarantelli, whatchya munchin', and I'm gonna say, Chawclate cookies, and you gonna say, Can I have one of your chawclate cookies, and I tell you now, Go fucka you'self!"

In this first of the series of short blackout sketches, which they referred to as "Life in the Barracks with Tarantelli." David played Tarantelli, and Eugene played Marantz. By order of the high command David had been ordered to delete the word *fuck* from the sketch and replace it with the less offensive and less funny *frig*.

As the new comedy team walked off after their debut performance, neither member was happy.

"Aw shit," Eugene muttered, "we're getting half the applause those friggin' gals got."

"And no marriage proposals," David groused, "but we did get a couple of good laughs. Whaddya think, a B minus?"

"C plus."

The two old Shakespearean troupers stayed in the wings to hear Lawrence T. Lawrence belt the hell out of Cole Porter's "Begin the Beguine." The audience ate him up, applauding during the song when his soaring voice pleaded, "So don't let them begin the beguine."

Every number in the show seemed to be working, but the biggest reactions came when the three girls came out and sang or danced to Mal Dradel's uninspired but serviceable songs. He had written four original songs for the show and a big comedy song, which was sung by the whole company, "Send a Pastrami to Your Men in the Army," which he swore he didn't steal from the guy who wrote "Send a Salami to Your Boy in the Army." David had heard the salami version when he was stationed at Georgetown. It was written by one of the guys in his French class for a Christmas show that he put on in Gaston Hall. When David told Dradel of the song's origin, he laughed it off.

"David," Dradel argued, "they're similar, I'll give you that. I heard about it, and I could sue, but my philosophy is, live and let live."

The dress rehearsal proceeded along rather smoothly, with an acceptable blend of good, fair, and excellent reactions to the songs and sketches. Eugene's pantomime of a hungry soldier, at home on furlough, raiding the refrigerator to build himself a skyscraper-high sandwich received so many laughs that it surprised David and put Eugene in shock.

"What was that?" a stunned, sweaty Eugene asked as he came off the stage. "What the hell were they laughing at?"

"You, you dope. You were great!" David said, squeezing his arm, "You see, all that vomiting paid off."

David had a mixed reaction to Eugene's success. He was happy for him, but he was more concerned that it had made his job more difficult. He had been given the next-to-closing slot, which historically was reserved for the star of a show. As the star, his turn was supposed to generate the biggest response of the evening, and he had no confidence that it would. He was not even sure that the audience would buy the premise of his monologue. He had never done it for any audience but Captain Sullen and Lieutenant Yorby, two men devoid of humor who thought it good enough to carry the spot before the finale.

David remained in the wings and rehearsed the opening lines of his monologue, using the technique that stood him in good stead since the days when he fought to remember Shakepeare's words. With half of his brain and one ear he listened to and watched Alicia Santana sing. He looked at her in amazement and wondered how a five-foot one-inch mite could look so statuesque. The long, flowered, tight-bodiced dress she wore and the three-inch heels she stood on were not the full answer. It was her carriage and attitude, he decided. There was no question that she was the most talented of all the girls, and besides being attractive, she was different, having been blessed with the best features of the four ethnic groups that made up her gene pool. Her shiny, wavy black hair and her large blue-green eyes made her face something to stare at, which most everybody found themselves doing.

Alicia had been brought up in Ewa, a small farming town on the other side of the island. Her home had no indoor plumbing, but it did have electricity, which gave her a chance to hear all the great American singers on an old radio that she kept glued to her ear day and night. David was present when Alicia auditioned for the show, and before she sang eight bars of her first song, he knew she would be hired. The two songs she sang at the audition, "Cow Cow Boogie" and "Don't Sit Under the Apple Tree With Anyone Else But Me," she had just finished singing for the dress-rehearsal audience, and they were going wild. She was Dinah Shore and Ella Mae Morse all rolled into a new and original Alicia Santana package.

As David stood in the wings listening to her sing an encore, "Dream, Dream, Dream," backed by the Four Surfers, a talented close-harmony group, he was not sure he wanted to do his new act. He actually considered going to Ben Possie, their stage manager, and requesting that they cut his turn and go straight to the finale when the number came to an end and he heard Possie's radio-trained voice announce, "Ladies and gentleman, please welcome Monty the Talking Dog and his manager, Don Coleman."

For the monologue that Eugene and he had written, David had built a wire-mesh frame which he covered with a dog's sweater that had the name Monty embroidered across it. Attached to the frame was a dog collar onto which a dog leash was hooked.

Just as he was being announced, David picked up the dog leash, adjusted the position of the wire-mesh frame, straightened the lapels of his houndstooth blazer, and checked his fly. The ripple of anticipation that went through the audience was loud and clear enough to let David know that they had bought his premise. Of course, he thought, who wouldn't want to hear a dog talk, but how will they react when he tells them that Monty the talking dog had just died? He waited four or five seconds, took a deep breath, and shuffled slowly onto the stage, dragging behind him his dead dog's collar and sweater. There was a smattering of laughter and some applause as he made his way to the microphone. A fleeting moment of panic passed as he worried again that the audience would prefer to hear what a talking dog had to say.

David stared at the audience for a long time before he tried to talk, and when he did, it was with a voice so choked with sorrow that he was forced to stop. Tears actually welled up in his eyes, and he waited for one drop to fall before he attempted to explain just why he was in this emotional state. He had the audience's rapt attention.

"Ladies and gentleman," he announced his voice quivering much like Harold Selwin's did, "Monty, the world's only talking dog . . . died in his dressing room exactly three minutes ago."

Here David stopped to wipe the tears from his eyes and attempted to compose himself.

"Before Monty passed on, he whispered to me how badly he felt about missing the opportunity to perform for you and after the show chat with the great classic actor Major Evan Merritt and the brilliant Pulitzer Prize–winning playwright Mr. Hart Milton."

The first solid laugh and applause started when he mentioned the names of the two celebrities and nodded toward them. Immediately, David asked himself how he was going to get that kind of big response when there's no Major Merritt or Hart Milton in the audience, and he answered himself. The same way Bob Hope does. I'll use the names of the commanding officers who are present.

"While lying on his doggy deathbed," David continued, choking back his emotion, "Monty heard Alicia Santana's encore, and when he heard the ovation you gave her, he whispered to me, 'They sound like a wonderful audience . . . and then he closed his eyes and passed on.' "

David was aware while he was performing that the reaction of the audience was good but strange, different from any he had ever before received, and he was enjoying it.

"Before I leave the stage," David said, picking up the wire frame and unhooking the leash from Monty's empty dog collar, "I'm curious to know how many of you never had the opportunity to see Monty the Talking Dog perform? May I see your hands?"

Hundreds of hands shot up, including Major Merritt's and his distinguished guest.

"None of you ever saw Monty?" David said, feigning shock. "Perhaps you heard him on radio?"

"Never, no!" The audience laughed and shouted back.

"Well, that doesn't surprise me. Monty did only a few weeks on the *Edgar Bergen Show,* but people thought Mr. Bergen was talking for him like he did for Charlie McCarthy, so he quit radio. Well, those who did get to see him know what an artist he was. I can't do for you what he did, but as a memorial to Monty, I would like to try to recreate his act for you. I managed him for fifty-six years of his life—that's eight of mine—and I know every word of his act. He didn't do what most dog entertainers do—jump through hoops and walk on his hind legs up ladders. No, he was an actor and one of the greatest makeup artists since Lon Chaney. His acting and makeup were so convincing that you may not be aware that you have been thrilled many times by his performances on the screen. So, with his blessings, which I'm sure he'd give me, I will attempt to do his act."

As the audience applauded, David snatched up Monty's sweater and tossed it offstage. He was in such a hyper state that he did not feel the nick on the underside of his thumb that he got from a wire protruding from the mesh frame.

"Monty was going to do for you a scene from one of his greatest roles, as Mr. Smith in *Mr. Smith Goes to Washington.* Many people think it was Jimmy Stewart who played Mr. Smith, but it was Monty. It was just one of the many roles for which other actors received the credit and the glory."

David then launched into a series of very credible, satiric impressions of movie stars in scenes from their movies. The ones that got the biggest applause were his Akim Tamiroff as Pablo in *For Whom the Bell Tolls,* Paul Muni in *The Story of Louis Pasteur* (David revealed that to play Louis Pasteur, Monty grew his own beard), and Roy Roger's horse, Trigger.

"Playing Trigger," David explained, "was the most physically demanding role he had ever attempted. Besides the tons of makeup required to make Monty look like a horse, he had Roy Rogers sitting on his back. Few people are aware of something, because Monty gave his word never to tell, but now that he's left us, I think it should be revealed. Roy Rogers can't sing. He lip-synched to Monty's voice."

David then proceeded to sing "Empty Saddles," moving his mouth like a horse might and keeping time by pawing the ground with one foot.

The audience started to applaud loudly in the middle of David's singing impression of Roy Rogers. It was during this final bit in his act that David relaxed enough to notice something strange happening to him. Whenever David was nervous, his hands would become cold, but his palms were never sweaty, so why did his right hand feel clammy and sticky while his left hand was dry and cool. He continued to sing and paw the ground but glanced down once and saw a dark red pool of water beside his right foot. His looked at his clammy red palm and realized that he had been dripping blood from a small puncture in the base of his thumb. David finished his act and ran off to the kind of applause that he was praying to get but never dreamed he would.

Inexplicably, no one in the audience or any of the company noticed that anything was amiss. Only Eugene, who was watching David carefully, knew that his friend was leaking blood.

"Your act killed 'em," Eugene said, using his hanky to wrap David's thumb, "and if it lasted ten minutes longer, it might've killed you, too."

As the applause for David subsided, the band started to play the introduction for the finale and curtain call. Each of the cast members had been choreographed to dance out, or if they danced like Lawrence T., Eugene, and David, to march out one by one to sing a line of the song, receive their applause, and stay onstage, to be joined by the next dancing or marching cast member. The reception was loud and more than anyone could have asked for, the applause peaking for Lawrence T., Alicia, Eugene, and David. The finale went smoothly up until the moment when the whole cast, lined up across the stage, locked arms to sing the last line of the rousing song "Stand Firm!"

> " 'We stand firm!
> We stand tall!
> And we stand for
> Freedom . . . for . . . aaaall!' "

With arms locked tightly and marching smartly foward, the company sang full out, with Lawrence T. Lawrence's voice soaring above the rest. On the words "for . . . aaaall," Lawrence T. stepped in David's blood and slipped on it. To keep himself from falling, he held tightly onto the arms of the performers on either side of him, who in turn tightened their grips on the arms of the persons next to them, which resulted in the entire line cascading to the floor. The audience screamed with laughter at the sight of the whole cast falling down in a heap. A second, bigger explosion of laughter followed when Lawrence T. struggled to his feet, slipped in the blood again, and fell off the stage.

The band was still playing the exit music when Lieutenant Yorby rushed backstage.

"Brilliant, brillant," he gushed to the stunned company. "Whoever came up with the idea for that crazy burlesque ending to the finale deserves a medal. Are you responsible for that, Kocklawish?"

"Well, it was really a group effort," David mumbled, amazed that Yorby would think that they had planned the mass flop. "All I did was bleed a little."

Captain Sullen, Major Merritt, and Hart Milton made their way backstage and thrilled the cast members by taking the time to compliment each one individually. David collected more than his fair share of kudos and was surprised when Hart Milton called him aside.

"Young man," he said, studying David's face, "unless I am terribly mistaken, and if I am, it will be the first time in my life, I predict that you will have a wonderful career in the theater."

David controlled himself from saying, Are you bullshitting me? Instead, he said, "Gee, Mr. Milton, I don't know what to say."

"Say thank you."

"Thank you, sir."

"You think I'm handing you a lot of bullshit, don't you, Private Kokolovitz?"

"No, sir, not since you asked me that question and pronounced Kokolovitz correctly."

"I really enjoyed your talking-dog routine. Monty was a most ingenious device to do impressions of stars, which, by the way, you do very well, but it was your talking about your dead friend Monty that really impressed me. You have done a lot of acting, haven't you?"

"Yes, sir, I've done some."

"Where?"

"No place you would know about, sir."

"Try me."

"Well, I spent a year at the Marlowe Theater. It was on—"

"Sixty-third and Broadway, formerly the Daly Theatre, run by John Marlowe and his daughter, Angela?"

"Boy, you're amazing Mr. Milton."

"I know. What other stages have you graced?"

"Well," David said, flabbergasted that Hart Milton was giving him this much attention, "I spent two summers at the Rochester Summer Theatre."

"In Avon, New York, run by Leonard Altobell and his wife, Saralie Bodge. Continue, Private Kokolovitz."

"Have you ever heard of the Avon Shakespearean Company?"

"Based in Atlanta, the Selwin brothers, Harold and Raymond?"

"Holy shit! I mean mackerel sir, but you sure know your show business."

"I *am* show business, and I reiterate, Private Kokolovitz, when you get out of the army—"

"Mr. Milton," a solemn Major Merritt called out, "may I have a word with you?"

"Certainly, Major," he answered, then turned to David. "As I was saying, when you're discharged, look me up. I'm in the New York phone book."

"David made an aborted attempt to tell Hart Milton how thrilled he was by his words of encouragement but was frustrated by a dour-faced commanding officer spiriting off his first major Broadway contact. David could not hear what the major was saying, but whatever it was, it sent Hart Milton reeling.

"Oh, Major, no!" Hart Milton groaned as he fell back against the wall. "Dear God, it can't be true."

The eyes of every member on the company, especially Eugene's, had been riveted on Hart Milton ever since he walked up to David and started to chat with him. All had been curious to know what they were saying, but now they were more than curious.

"Major Merritt has a message to read to you," Captain Sullen announced to the company with quiet digity, "so please give him your attention."

"This bulletin just came in from Central Pacific Base Command," Major Merritt said, his voice quivering, "and it reads, 'At four-fifteen P.M. President Franklin D. Roosevelt died at his summer home in Warm Springs, Georgia.' "

The cast, which seconds before had been ebullient over their successful debut, now stared in stunned silence at their commanding officer. David thought immediately of his father and mother and how stricken they would be. They idolized President Roosevelt and boasted how fortunate and proud they were to have had the chance to vote for him in all four elections. A concurrent thought flitted through his mind that he knew made no sense at all. Now that his leader and savior, President Roosevelt, was dead, David worried that there was no one to care whether or not he was shipped back home after the war.

"I am sorry to have brought you this terrible news on the night of your triumph," the major said, his voice getting stronger, "but there is a great war going on that has taken yet another victim. President Roosevelt was resolute in his determination to win this war, and he would expect us all to be no less determined to do the jobs we have been assigned. As long as this filthy war goes on, our shows must go on! May God go with us all."

All eyes were on their leader as he stared at the death bulletin in his hand and then, invoking a line from *Hamlet,* said simply, "May flights of angels sing thee to thy rest."

Eugene and David stood together and watched Major Merritt step off the chair and leave the stage.

"Boy, does that old ham know how to make an exit," Eugene commented.

"Frchrissakes, Gene, the president just died. The last thing we need is a review of the major's performance. I found it very moving . . . what he said."

"I'm sorry, buddy. I agree, the words were moving, but I guess I didn't like hearing them from a guy who hated Roosevelt."

"Is that true, Gene?"

"Yes, I half-expected him to say, 'May flights of angels sing thee to thy rest and good riddance!' "

Strangely, it was not till sometime later, when most of the members of the section gathered in the Mutton Club, that Chicky Click Clack thought to ask, "Hey, who's going to run the country?"

"The vice president, you jerk" was the answer he got from a few of the members.

"I know that," he screamed out, "but what's his name?"

Most of the members of the section were overseas during the last election and had not followed it. They knew Roosevelt would be re-elected, and it really didn't matter who the vice president was. Roosevelt had been the country's president since they were kids, and he was going to be it forever. His dying was simply out of the question.

"It's Harry S. Truman," Lawrence T. Lawrence offered when he realized what the discussion was about.

"The man's right!" Eugene concurred. "Lawrence T., howdya know?"

"Harry and Bess were our neighbors in Independence. We lived two houses down from the Trumans on Independence Drive." Lawrence T. offered ingenuously, "My sister and their daughter, Margaret, used to play together."

"What do you know about him? I mean, is this guy going to be able fill President Roosevelt's shoes?" David asked. "I can't believe that you actually know our new president."

"And I can't believe," Eugene whispered to David, "you'd ask cement-head for his opinion about anything except throat lozenges."

"I tell you one thing," Lawrence offered, "Harry Truman's a real, honest, down-home kind of person, and I for one am glad he's gonna be our president."

"That's good enough for me." Eugene clucked. "I'm going to sleep a lot better tonight knowing that you approve of him."

"Glad to be helpful," Lawrence said. "Well, guys, I gotta go get me some shut-eye. We got us a show to do tomorrow night."

"What?" David said, aghast. "President Roosevelt just died!"

"You heard what the major said," Lawrence T. reminded him. "As long as the war goes on, our shows must go on."

Many members of the section remained in the Mutton Club long after Lawrence T. left. Their need to share with someone the sadness and frustration they felt about losing their president was overwhelming.

"Shit," Eugene growled, "just as the war is going our way. Why couldn't he have held on for just another few months?"

"Who knows, maybe this new guy can get it done," Chicky said hopefully.

"That'd be nice but not likely," Eugene answered. "I don't know anything about Harry Truman, but I know he's no Roosevelt."

"How can you say that, Gene?" Ned Smith, the tenor member of the Four Surfers, shouted, his tenor voice rising an octave. "We didn't know Roosevelt was Roosevelt until he closed the banks and got us out of the Depression. Maybe this guy will come up with something."

May 11, 1945

Dearest "only girl in the world for me" Mary Deare,

Please do not read the last page of this letter until you've read the preceding pages, as you will not be able to concentrate on them fully, and I want you to. There's a lot of news in them. I was going to send that last page to you tomorrow in another envelope, but I want you to have it now. You'll see why when you read it. Did you read it already? You probably did, because I'm making this so mysterious. Well, if you have, I won't be upset, but if you didn't, don't!

I got the sweetest letter from you today, and it made me so happy and so sad and so hot. When I read that you want to feel my arms about your body, I was sad that your magnificent body and my aching arms are three thousand miles apart. We have just flown back from Maui, where we did our last show on the Hawaiian Islands. In the last nine weeks we've played every military installation there is on Maui and Oahu, which means that finally we'll be flying off to the central Pacific and its lesser known but heavily populated islands. As you well know, I am a bona fide fearful flier and am not at all thrilled that for the next few months we'll be flying over billions of gallons of salt water. We're told that in some instances we'll be doing this for guys who haven't had any live entertainment for over a year. I guess compared to what those guys have been through, my crapping in my pants is a small sacrifice to make. I'm afraid that there's still a lot of fighting to do before the war is over and won with. By the way, you thrilled my folks. They wrote that you sent them a note introducing yourself as my friend from the Avon Shakespearean players and that you enclosed a picture of me as King Claudius. I didn't know one existed. Where did you find it? They said that you made a copy and are sending one to me. Among a million other things, you are a very thoughtful person. I can't wait for them to meet you. My father will be a pushover, as he loves movies with girls who speak with southern accents. My mother'll think that your're putting it on to make yourself sound cute. You keep amazing me, darling. Just when I think you're the sweetest, dearest person in the world, you do something like this and prove again that I underestimate your sweetness and dearestness, which brings me to page three of this letter. If you haven't already read it, take a deep breath and turn the page. . . .

Mary Deare-est,

When I learned that the army was planning to fly me farther away from you, I broke out in a cold sweat, and I knew immediately that it wasn't my fear of flying that panicked me but the fear that I'd never see you again. I also worried that distance might not lend enchantment but estrangement. I might have reacted like this because of a dream I had the night before. It really scared the hell out of me, coming right after the one I wrote you about where I was walking on the wing of your plane and you were doing loop-the-loops, trying to shake me off. This one was not as spectacular, but it was awful because it was so real. I dreamed that I had just been discharged from the army and was walking down a street in Atlanta and you were coming toward me. You were wearing that chiffon dress you wore when I first saw you walking across the ballroom floor of the Hotel Tallulah, and I got all horny seeing your darling sweet legs, backlit though your dress. In the dream I was so happy to see you, and I ran toward you, but you ran right past me and down the street. I ran after you, but I couldn't catch you. I raced to your house and knocked at your door and your cousin Prue opens it and says, "Come in, Jew-boy, my wife, Mary Deare, will be so pleased you dropped by to say hello." Ordinarily, I don't give too much credence to dreams, but when I woke up and thought about it, it scared me. I know how you feel about

Prue, but imagining him in that role made me realize that I wanted to be him in that nightmare and the daymare that followed when I recalled it. I want to be the one to open the door to our Bronx apartment or Atlanta apartment or Hollywood apartment or wherever apartment and be able to say, Come in, my wife, Mary Deare Coleman (or Kokolovitz, your choice), will be so happy you dropped by. So . . .

Mary Deare Prueitt, will you marry me?

My darling, except for a deep and growing love for you, I have nothing tangible to offer, but if we're to believe what Hart Milton wrote to me on that autographed photo of himself, I know that material things will come. If Mr. Milton believes that I am going to be a force in the theater, then who am I to argue. Just give me five years, sweetheart, and I'll give you, besides love and devotion, a new home and a new airplane. The moon will take a bit longer. Darling, I know I'm repeating myself, but I love writing these words:

Mary Deare Prueitt, will you marry me?*

> *Your loving and, I hope, future*
> *husband,*
> *Don Coleman (née David*
> *Kokolovitz)*

*When? No later than the day I return.

*Where? At a city hall or a justice of the peace or in a synagogue or a church, or both if necessary, or onstage at a theater or under a mighty oak tree in the Bronx or 'neath a flowering peach tree in Atlanta.

P.S. I just reread this letter and wish I'd made a stronger case for myself. I should have mentioned that I'm getting big, big laughs every night and getting more and more confidence in myself as a performer, and besides, Hart Milton has faith that I'll make it. Lieutenant Yorby said he'd like to do a play with me when I return from the tour—that's another reason I want the war to be over!

P.P.S. Darling, I await your answer. Please say yes.

◆

The four-engine B-24 bomber that was pressed into service to transport the members of the *Shape Up!* company to the Mariana Islands in the Central Pacific was a renovated and reconfigured long-range bomber that had been on more than its share of bombing missions. These Liberators, as they were called, were slowly being replaced by the B-29, a sleeker, faster bomber that could fly farther and was capable of carrying a heavier payload. On this sunny June morning, in lieu of bombs, the ground crew at Hickam Field loaded aboard the entire company, which included the cast, the nine-piece band and their instruments, the sound system and scenery, and Mrs. Abigail Furst, the company's chaperon. It was Mrs. Furst, a tall, attractive thirty-five-year-old churchgoing Christian, who was responsible for the conduct and behavior of the four female members of the troop.

It was apparent to all after boarding the plane that the Army Air Corps had spent little or no time on refurbishing the plane to carry passengers. A baby-faced officer who looked to be no more than eighteen climbed aboard and hurried toward the cockpit.

"That's not our pilot, is it?" David said, grabbing Eugene's forearm in fear.

"He's wearing flight wings, and he's a captain," an equally uneasy Eugene answered, "so he may very well be our pilot."

"He couldn't be," David argued. "Look at him, he hasn't started shaving yet."

"Donny, a pilot doesn't need face hair to fly a plane."

"May I have your attention," the young officer called out, his voice cracking. "I am your pilot, Captain Tom Neely, and we'll be taking off shortly for Johnston Island."

"I'm getting off," David whispered to Eugene in a panic. "His voice is changing."

"No, Private," Captain Neely said, clearing his throat.

David jumped. "No what, sir?"

"No changing planes," the captain answered. "You were asking about changing planes, weren't you?"

"Changing planes! Yes, sir, absolutely! That's what I was asking about. So we won't be changing planes?"

"You will, but not till we get to Saipan."

"Right," David said, as if aware of the plan, "that's what I thought. We change planes in Saipan."

"Two C-47s will be waiting there," the captain said, clearing his throat. "They've been assigned to your show for the whole tour."

"Oh, right, those two C-47s that've been assigned." Relieved, David sighed, "Thank you, Captain."

"You're welcome, Private."

"Good recovery, Donny!" Eugene muttered as the captain looked away, "but work on your stage whisper."

"We'll be making two stops, one at Johnston Island and another at Kwajalein, each for about an hour," the captain said shyly, facing in the girls' direction but not looking at them, "to refuel the plane and to let some of you unfuel yourselves."

"Unfuel ourselves?" David, still in shock that his life was in the hands of a blushing teenager, asked the question that all on the plane were thinking. "Sir, are you saying in a cute way that this plane has no toilets?"

"I'm afraid so. Sorry, gang, but these planes were built for carrying bombs, and they didn't anticipate we'd be carrying female passengers, or any passengers for that matter."

"So where do we, uh, if we have to before we get to Johnston Island?" Mrs. Furst inquired.

"We have no toilets," said the pilot, smiling embarrassedly, "but we do have accommodations."

"And what are they, Captain?" she asked.

"A milk bottle and, uh, a funnel, for whoever needs one, and a blanket for privacy. I'm sorry, but this plane was pressed into service last night. I'm sure you've noticed that there are no seats."

"Captain, you can't be serious!" Mrs. Furst said."

"I wish I weren't."

"You're not suggesting that we stand for the entire flight?"

"No, ma'am, not for twenty-one hours."

"Twenty-one hours on an airplane?" A very distraught David screamed out. "That can't be right."

"Good gosh," Lawrence T. said, interrupting his quiet, close-mouthed vocalizing. "Twenty-one hours seems like an awfully long time to be over water!"

"Being *in* it would seem even longer," Eugene quipped. "Keep humming, Lawrence."

Only the captain and his equally juvenile looking copilot, 1st Lt. Bill Tusher, found this ghoulish remark amusing.

"Except for weekend dips at Waikiki Beach," the young captain offered with a smile, "neither my copilot nor my navigator, Smiley Sims, has ever splashed around in the Pacific, and we do not plan to on this trip."

"Captain Neely, you still haven't told us where we sit." Mrs. Furst asked curtly.

"Right where you're standing."

"On what?"

"On the plywood, I'm afraid," Captain Neely answered apologetically. "Of course, it'll be covered with a pad. Sorry, that's the best we could do on short notice."

The entire company grumbled their disapproval but settled down when Eugene quietly reminded everyone what their mission was. David mentally slapped himself in the face for grousing about not having a comfortable place to sit when he thought of all the muddy foxholes his brother, Chuck, had slept in.

"I guarantee you two things," Captain Neely shouted, leaning out of the cockpit. "One, we'll get you to Johnston Island on schedule, and two, you'll never have a noisier or more uncomfortable flight."

"That's reassuring," David quipped nervously as he sat down next to Eugene. "How can you guarantee that?"

"Easy. The C-47s you'll be using on your tour have bucket seats to sit in and two less motors to rattle your sinuses."

"It's stiflingly hot in here, Captain," Mrs. Furst complained. "Can you do something to cool it off a little bit?"

"Yes, ma'am, fly you to a cooler climate."

With that, Captain Neely pushed his throttle forward and individually revved up each of his four idling motors, bringing each to maximum rpm's before idling them back down. When all four motors checked out, he shouted, "Prepare for takeoff!"

The two rugged crew members who had just finished lashing all of the show's baggage and equipment to the plane's naked metal interior donned their headsets and acknowledged the captain's order. The plane started taxiing to the end of the landing strip, and when it turned to position itself for takeoff, one of the crew members came forward.

"I'm Sergeant Judd, and we're getting ready for takeoff!" he screamed through cupped hands over the noise of the motors. "Can everyone hear me?"

The nine cool musicians and the twelve jittery show folk who were now all sitting on the plywood floor nodded that they could.

"Okay, now, everybody scoot back against the fuselage and find yourself a holding-on place. Just grab on to any solid piece of metal that's attatched to the plane and hold on to it until I tell you it's okay to let go."

The group obediently scurried like crabs to find holding-on places. Sergeant Judd then went about checking to see that no one was using a duffel-bag strap.

"Ready to take off!" the sergeant shouted. "Everybody holding tight? Nod your head if you heard me!"

All nodded. The sergeant nodded back, gave a thumbs-up sign, and shouted, "Bon Voyage!"

The sound of the four motors on open throttle was so deafening that half the group covered their ears with their hands. Sergeant Judd jumped up and pantomimed that they take their hands from their ears and regrip the fuselage. As the plane picked up speed, it started to vibrate. The faster it rode over the bumpy airstrip, the more fiercely it shook. Immediately before takeoff it vibrated so violently that David feared it would break apart and that he would die without knowing if Mary Deare had accepted his marriage proposal. He stared unblinkingly at the line of rivets that held the fuselage together, and as the fully loaded plane struggled to become airborne, David fantasized that the rivets on the panel he was holding on to for dear life would vibrate themselves loose and he'd be sucked out of the plane and plummet into the ocean. Within minutes the vibrating stopped, and the noise abated enough for David to fight his way back to reality.

As the plane climbed to its cruising altitude, the temperature in the unheated, uninsulated cabin went from oppressively hot to freezingly cold. No one but the crew members, who wore fleece-lined flight jackets, were dressed or prepared for this precipitous drop in temperature. Wrapping themselves in the wool army blankets which the crew tossed at them helped, but not enough to stop their teeth from chattering.

Sergeant Ben Possie, the company stage manager and a problem solver par excellence, rummaged around in the back of the plane and gathered up two large, quilted cargo pads.

"Keep your blankets wrapped tight around you and then lie down and get as close together as you can," Possie shouted. "We're going to do like the Eskimos, share our body heat with each other."

"That's an order I can dig," Drago, the trumpeter, screamed out. "C'mere, Dolly, bring your fine body over here. We are going to share our heat."

The girls giggled, the men laughed, and Mrs. Furst frowned as Drago grabbed Dolly Pastori in a bear hug.

"Drago," she shouted, "behave yourself!"

"Just following orders, ma'am," Drago said, hugging Dolly harder.

Jim Drago was a jazz trumpeter of renown who had no idea why he was in the army. The only thing that kept him sane was an occasional stick of marijuana and the opportunity to, as he put it, "Rile, annoy and unhinge every square individual who comes within my purview."

Mrs. Furst, who had lived all of her life in Hawaii and was more affected by the cold than the rest, nevertheless felt it imperative to act as chaperon. She pulled back the tarp and went about rearranging the company so that the men's bodies would not be touching the women's. Because of the number of bodies and the size of the mat they had to lie on, it was an impossible task, made more difficult by giggling girls and obstreperous boys.

"Alicia, if you will climb over Private Lawrence and settle next to Bitsy and Loretta, and uh," Mrs. Furst said, tapping someone whose head was covered with a blanket, "whoever this is, if you raise up your legs and let Dolly slide under, I think we'll have the problem solved?"

"It was nice while it lasted, baby," Eugene joked as he raised his legs to let Dolly slip by.

When Mrs. Furst was satisfied that the configuration of bodies made middle-of-the-night fraternization unlikely, she wriggled herself in between Dolly Pastori and Drago and became a human bundling board. Drago immediately turned to David, who was on his other side of him, and winked.

"D-D-David," Drago said, his teeth chattering, "in the m-m-middle of the night, if I get a call from L-L-Lou Costello and he says, Who's on f-f-first, tell him Who's on second and Drago's on Furst." With that the jazz player started to climb on top of Mrs. Furst.

The furious chaperon pushed Drago off her, called him "incorrigible," and ordered him to change places with anybody immediately or be reported for insubordination. She then pulled her blanket around her and moved to the other side of the pack. Everyone continued to shiver with the cold until Possie threw a second cargo pad over the group and tucked them in for the night. It did not take long for the warming effect to take hold. Within minutes everyone was comfortable enough to think of things other than how freezing cold they had been. The members of the band, who had passed a joint around before boarding, fell asleep in minutes and stayed immobile for most of the night. The offensive roar of the motors had, under the padded cover, become a muffled, sleep-inducing drone that had the effect a running vacuum cleaner has on an infant.

After lying quietly for a few moments monitoring the sounds of the four giant engines and deciding that they were all operating efficiently, David turned his attention to the two people lying on either side of him, a very still Eugene O'Neill and a quiescent Loretta Yung. He could not understand how anyone could be this calm, or were they calm? Maybe, he thought, they're just as frightened as I am about flying over the ocean and the pilot's not being able to find that dot on a map called Johnston Island. Maybe everybody is hiding their terror from me as I'm hiding it from them. David was so petrified about the possibility of crashing into the ocean that he started to question his commitment to show business. At this moment, he decided that if he had to choose between flying across the Pacific in an old bomber plane or going back to work for Mr. Foreman, he'd choose Mr. Foreman. When he heard Eugene start to breathe heavily, another paranoid, mortal fear struck him.

"Gene," he called out while shaking him, "wake up!"

"Where am I?" a groggy Eugene asked.

"You're lying under a tarp, and I think we got a problem."

"What problem?"

"You fell asleep too fast; everybody fell asleep too fast."

"You woke me to tell me that?"

"I woke you because I wasn't sure you were sleeping or that they were sleeping!"

"What the hell do you think we were doing?"

"Suffocating!" David explained, slightly hysterical. "We're all breathing each other's carbon dioxide. We could all be asphyxiated."

"Donny, there is plenty of air leaking in from all the untucked corners. "C'mon, now," Eugenne begged as he lay back exhausted, "instead of thinking about suffocating, think of pastrami sandwiches, the war ending, think of Mary Deare, think of me kicking your ass . . ." his voice trailing off, "for waking me up . . . when I was . . . dreamin' about . . . having my . . ."

Eugene dozed off, leaving David to consider his suggestions. David thought of Mary Deare and actually conjured up her scent. It was so real that he imagined she was lying beside him and that he was smelling her perfume.

"Every time you put this stuff on," he had once whispered to her while nibbling her ear, "it makes me want to do lewd things to you."

The scent that David thought he was imagining was now too real and present to be a sensory illusion. The moment he turned and faced away from Eugene, he knew he was not fantasizing. Mary Deare's enticing scent was emanating from Loretta Yung who lay next to him, enshrouded in an army blanket.

"Loretta? Loretta, are you sleeping?" David whispered quietly.

"I think so," she whispered back. "Who is this?"

"David. Mrs. Furst put us back to back, remember?"

"Oh, yes," Loretta said, changing her postion to face him. "Was I kicking you?"

"No, no, Loretta, I don't mean to get personal, but are you wearing Shalimar?"

"No."

"You're not?" David asked, getting concerned about his mental health. "I could swear I smell Shalimar."

"You do, I put some on my blanket to try to kill its musty odor. Do you want some?" she asked, holding out a tiny flask. "It might help you to relax."

"I don't think so. Shalimar doesn't work on me that way"—David sighed—"but thanks for the offer."

The perfume's aphrodisiac effect on him was heightened by knowing that Loretta Yung's lithe, desirable body lay inches from him. Only his deep love for Mary Deare and the two dozen sleeping chaperons who surrounded Loretta and him made it possible for him to subdue his baser instincts. With the scent of Shalimar in his nostrils, he mentally revisited each boardinghouse bed in each Southern town where he and Mary Deare had slept. He drifted off to sleep trying to remember the names of all the towns in which he and Mary Deare had made love . . . Atlanta . . . Opelika . . . Birmingham . . . Greenville . . . Wadesboro . . . Decator . . . Columbia . . . McMin . . .

David's mind shut down after McMinnville and dropped him into a deep, dream-free, body-repairing sleep. He remained comatose until the plane bumped down on Kwajalein for refueling.

Kwajalein bore no resemblance to anyplace David had ever seen. The island, a refueling stop, was originally a Japanese possession and had been captured after being unmercifully pummeled and denuded by bombs.

"Whaddya think of my home away from home?" a ground-crew member asked David from atop a ladder while refueling the plane. "Neat, isn't it?"

"Incredible," David replied, squinting as he made a 360-degree scan of the island. "Only the floor of a volcano I saw on Maui has it beat for neatness."

"Admiral Nimitz used a lot of bombs to get it to look this way."

"This is amazing. There isn't a thing growing here."

"Except my resentment for the brass who sent me here," he said, wiping the sweat from his forehead. "Lucky it's only a three-month gig."

"I hope Saipan's got a shade tree or two," David said, feeling the tropical sun beating down on his head. "This is one unlush-looking island"

"It's not an island; it's an atoll," he corrected. "The biggest atoll in the world. Look at all this unused closet space. I'm gonna buy me a coupla million acres of it and peddle it to people who live in New York."

"Put me down for four yards," David said, laughing. "I'll send it to my mother in the Bronx."

"The Bronx? Where in the Bronx?"

"Arthur Avenue and 180th Street."

"Hughes Avenue and 179th," the crew man shot back.

"I used to live at a 179th and Belmont," David said excitedly.

"What's your name?"

"Kokolovitz."

"Your first name David?"

"You know me?"

"Yes, I know you, David Kokolovitz! I've seen a picture of you in an album."

"What album?"

"My sister's album. You were wearing a full dress suit and had a mustache."

"What's your name?" David asked, staring at the man's suddenly familiar face.

"Alexander Futerman."

"Your sister is Wanda Futerman!?"

"Yeah, she's my kid sister!" Alexander shouted, almost letting go of the wide-nozzled refueling hose.

"This is crazy!" David screamed. "I went with her for a year."

"When I was away at college, in Ithaca. She wrote me about you. You still an actor?"

"More like a comedian. I'm in this revue *Shape Up!* We're on tour of the army bases. Kwajalein isn't on our itinerary."

"Kwajalein isn't on anybody's itinerary," Alexander grumbled.

Suddenly, David stopped and looked around at the bleak, treeless, grassless, barren land that surrounded them, and he started to laugh. Alexander Futerman knew exactly why and joined him. Both were thinking, If this isn't the weirdest conversation for two Bronx boys to be carrying on in the middle of the Pacific Ocean. David thought, Should I ask this guy who's pumping gas in the middle of the Pacific if he knows the answer to one of the great mysteries of my life? Why not? Whatever I find out can't hurt anymore.

"Alexander, Wanda and I had a date one Sunday to go to the Bronx Zoo, and when I get to her house, she tells me that she thinks we shouldn't see each other anymore and won't tell me why. Do you know why she dumped me?"

"Yeah. She met this really handsome, rich guy at a cousin's wedding and married him."

"How did it work out?"

"Both are very happy. She divorced him three months later. You still available?"

"Sorry, I never let a girl shit on me more than once."

The two Bronxites laughed, shook hands, and simultaneously said, "See ya'."

David's discovery about Wanda and the mind-bending experience of learning about it from her brother on bombed-out Kwajalein, plus the fact they had just landed in Saipan without incident, put David into a maniacally joyous mood.

"I love Saipan! I love this airfield," he shouted, stepping off the plane and falling to his knees to kiss the tarmac. He stopped short when he heard his mother's voice admonishing him, "David, are you meshuga? You're going to put your lips where a dog makes kaka?"

"Whoops," David said, leaping to his feet and faking a cough. "Better not kiss the ground. I got a cold. Hate for your airstrip to catch it."

An officer who had been standing nearby ran up to David, his hand outstretched and an ear-to-ear grin on his deeply tanned face.

"I'm Lieutenant Rendina, of Special Services," he said, grabbing David's hand and shaking it vigorously, "and I take it you're the comedian in the show. Welcome to our island."

A smiling Lieutenant Rendina shook the hand of every exhausted member of the cast as they deplaned, lingering a bit longer and smiling more broadly when he welcomed the weary female members. The long hours they had spent lying under cargo mats did nothing to help them look like the sexy, attractive women they were, but the lieutenant, who had not seen any women for almost a year, fell over himself being attentive and charming. His ebullience did not sit well with Drago, who winked conspiratorially at his bass player, Broody Hale.

"Brood, that lieutenant's zestful enthusiasm should not go unpunished."

"I'm not going to make a speech," Lieutenant Rendina announced, "but I must tell you how much we've all been looking forward to seeing your show. Let's see, now," he said, looking at his watch, "it's four-thirty. Approximately how long does it take you to set up your show?"

"Show?" the whole company moaned in unison.

Everybody then spoke at once, paraphrasing what Possie finally said after he restored order.

"Lieutenant Rendina, I think there's been some mistake," Possie said, pulling out a folded paper from his pocket and offering it to the lieutenant. "We're not schedluled to do a show until tomorrow night."

"I know, Sergeant, but that schedule was incorrect. Somehow this battalion of engineers was omitted on your schedule. We radioed Lieutenant Yorby about it, and he said that adding this one show would be no problem."

"No problem for Yorby," Possie groused.

"Is doing this show going to be a problem, Sergeant? I know you're all tired, but these men would be very disappointed. Let me show you something."

There is no better way to rally a group of tired actors than by showing them pictures of themselves printed in a newpaper under a banner headline that read: *"Shape Up!* Most Exciting New Show to Visit Marshall Islands Since Bob Hope!"

Three Mars Bars, a bag of potato chips, and a couple of Cokes were what David and Eugene had for dinner while setting up the lights and sound system for the show. Besides fatigue, disorientation from flying though time zones, and the worry of doing a show that they had not performed for almost four days, they were futher hampered by a hard, steady rain that fell on them as they worked.

"Don't worry about the rain, boys," Lieutenant Rendina exhorted them. "Our boys don't mind getting wet as long as you don't."

"The stage is covered, so we'll be all right," David said, water dripping off his nose as he unwound some cable, "but the musicians, they play in front of the stage, right below it."

"How about setting them up on the stage?" the lieutenant suggested.

"If we put the band onstage," Possie explained, covering a speaker with a tarp, "there'll be no room for the girls to dance. All they'll be able to do is stand there."

"Standing there is all they'll have to do to make our boys happy," the Lieutenant snorted. "Wish we could do something about this rain."

"Eugene," a giddy David called out, "m'thinks 'tis time for our traditional stop-the-rain dance."

With the rain splashing down on his face, David looked heavenward as he chanted in mock Latin,

> "Raino, rainas, ranat.
> Away, awas, awhat.

Immediately, Eugene joined in, and the two went into their old routine, tap-dancing and singing "Pax vobiscum, et cum spiritu tuo, ite missa est."

Miraculously, that evening at five minutes to curtain, the rain stopped. The musicians took their places in the pit, and the company gave a performance of *Shape Up!* that was, from the first note of the overture to the last note of the finale, something they could all be truly ashamed of, and they were. It was, hands down, their sloppiest and worst performance to date. But the audience could not have been more demonstrative in their appreciation. The applause and laughter throughout and the standing ovation they gave the cast at the curtain calls were louder and longer than any they received on their two-month tour of the Hawaiian Islands.

"I think we all learned something today," Sergeant Possie said after the audience filtered out.

"I know I did," Broody the bassist spoke up. "If you eat two cans of cold Van Camp's beans before a show, you won't stop farting until right before the finale. Wait"—he paused—"I was being premature."

"That's disgusting," Mrs. Furst scolded.

"That's exactly what I'm saying, ma'am," Broody replied and farted again.

What the company did learn was that the further they got from civilization, the more appreciated their efforts were.

After striking the show, Lieutenant Rendina, Mrs. Furst, and the entire company gathered in the mess hall and reviewed the highlights of their wonderfully terrible show while downing platefuls of scrambled eggs, bacon, sausages, home fries, Cokes, and beer. It was two-thirty in the morning when the pooped group agreed that it was time to turn in for the night.

David and Eugene trudged into their Quonset hut, sat on their bunks, and yawned in each other's face.

"You know what?" David volunteered, attempting to untie a shoe-lace.

"What?" Eugene said, falling back on his bunk.

"What, what?" David said, his head dropping on his chest.

"Huh?" Eugene mumbled, and started to snore.

"Think I'll . . . write Mary . . ." David murmured, reaching for his duffel bag and falling flat on his face, his head at the foot of his bed.

After the company performed for two weeks at the various encampments on Saipan, everybody, from regimental commanders to the lowest-ranked GIs, agreed that *Shape Up!* was, among other things, "the finest entertainment we ever had on this island."

". . . better than any show you could see on Broadway and a whole lot funnier!

". . . full of the the prettiest gals dancing on legs sexier than Betty Grable's."

". . . as good as the *Bob Hope Show.*"

". . . better than the *Bob Hope Show*

". . . something I want to see again just to hear that cute gal singer who sings like Dinah Shore and looks like Judy Garland."

It was difficult for most soldiers to believe that there was no sexual hanky-panky going on between the male and female members of the company, and David explained many times to his inquisitors, using their language, that there was absolutely no boffin', bangin', bonkin', shtupin', screwin', or dippin' the ole wedge going on.

"The girls have a chaperon," David advised the skeptics, "who's been given orders to shoot the balls off anyone who tries to use his dick in an illegal fashion."

Prior to finishing their run on Saipan, the show was scheduled for a couple of performances on Tinian, one of the three islands in the Marianas that was equipped with stages large enough to accommodate their show.

David was not too anxious to fly anywhere on this particular morning for fear of missing the mail that was rumored to be coming in later that afternoon. Since leaving the section, there was no longer a daily mail call, and company members had to be content with getting one, two, or sometimes three weeks' worth of mail at one time. David was still waiting to learn Mary Deare's answer. He had not proposed again in any of his subsequent letters and wondered now if he should have.

"Eugene?" he called to his friend, who was cramming socks and underwear into his bag for his trip to Tinian. "You're smart."

"Yeah? So how come I'm a sergeant and Yorby's a lieutenant? Sorry," he apologized, seeing serious concern on David's face. "How can my smartness be of help to you?"

"Answer me this. If you were Mary Deare and I sent you a letter asking you to marry me . . ."

"I'd say yes. That was an easy one. Hey, Donny boy, did you do that, or is this hypothetical?"

"I did that!"

"That's great!" Eugene said, reaching over and slapping at David's shoulder. "When did you do this?"

"Over two weeks ago, and I gotta know what she said."

"Well, judging from the sheer volume of mail you do get from her," Eugene said, wrapping a can of beer in his shorts and jamming it into his duffel bag, "I'd be shocked if she said no."

"I don't know."

"Donny, don't you read the stuff the girl writes in those letters to you?"

"Yes! Hey, how many letters of hers have you . . . ?"

"Just a couple to check her literary style. Boy are you insecure," Eugene said, closing up his bag. "Been rejected a lot of times in your life?"

"Once, and I hated it."

"Not this time," Eugene said, hoisting his bag onto his shoulder. "Jeeps are here, let's go!"

David hurriedly stuffed some dirty socks into his duffel bag and started to follow him out.

"Where are you going, Donny?" Eugene said, stopping at the door.

"To Tinian, where else?"

"Without your bucket and your pillow?"

David ran back to retrieve them. It was because of Chicky Click Clack that David carried these two items.

"David, trust me," Chicky had implored him. "Take your pillow and this bucket on the tour and you'll thank me."

When David had first boarded the plane carrying a canvas bucket with a feather pillow stuffed in it, everyone derided him until they found that pillows are not issued on any of these islands. During those first two weeks away, David's pillow had been stolen from him often, but it was not difficult to track it down. The thief's head was always lying on it, and David would cruelly snatch it out from under him while he slept. David had wisely thought to bring two pillowcases, enabling him to play the altruist by lending out his pillow whenever he was not using it. He often used the bucket to rinse out his socks and pillowcases.

Flying to Tinian in a C-47 was a breeze. The cast had barely buckled themselves into their bucket seats when they heard the pilot announce, "We're landing."

"Now, that makes sense," David said, looking out the window at the island. "That's how long all flights over water should be."

The audiences on Tinian turned out to be the most appreciative yet. The cast kept learning that the hungrier the guys were for entertainment, the more demonstrative they would be.

On their way to Guam, Capt. Andy Riley, the pilot of their C-47, reminded everyone to keep their seat belt buckled during the present turbulence as he calmly went on to describe Guam as the largest and most beautiful island of the Mariana chain.

"Who gives a shit," David muttered to Eugene. "Just get us there fast!"

With the plane bouncing around like a Ping-Pong ball on a water jet, David's short honeymoon with flying was over, and he reverted back to being a reluctant passenger. He had been sandbagged, lulled by the smooth-as-glass, twenty-one-hour flight from Oahu to Johnston to Kwajalein to Saipan.

David became his jovial self again when, after landing safely on Guam and eating a lunch of breaded pork chops, mashed potaoes, peas, and the sweetest papaya ever, he was handed three letters from Mary Deare. None of the letters was in answer to his big question, but their contents boded well. The letters were chock-full of declarations of her love for him and gave no indication that she loved him any less than she told him she did in her previous batch of letters. It was heartening to read:

> *Donny, every night before I go to bed I kiss the picture of you*
> *as King Claudius that Mr. Selwin sent me a few weeks ago, the*

*one I sent a copy of to your folks. By the way, I received the
sweetest letter from them thanking me for it and telling me that
I "must be a nice person because my son has good taste and if
you chose him as a friend, you must have very good taste, too."
The rest of it is just as darling. I can't wait to meet them.*

That night, David decided that he was going to propose marriage
to her again in his next letter just in case the first letter was lost or
wound up in enemy hands, like her father's.

Guam was an island that David would never forget. Besides being
a tropical paradise that rivaled the Hawaiian Islands, it was where he
met and worked with a great Hollywood star, his mother's all-time favorite. He could not wait to write home about this megastar, which he
did that night.

Aug. 1, 1945
Some very pretty place in the Pacific

Dear Mom,

*I am writing this letter to you because, well, you'll see why if
you keep reading. Of course, after you finish it, you can let Pop
and the rest of the family read it, too, or read it out loud. I'm
feeling fine, eating well, sleeping well, and apologizing for not
writing more often (Ma, insert here my excuse from the last
letter I sent you), but anyway, last night we did a great show on
this big island we arrived at yesterday, and this morning at
breakfast, the officer in charge calls me into his office and asks
me if I'd like to act on a radio show that's broadcast from this
island. No, Ma, you won't be able to hear it in the Bronx. Well,
at the radio station I meet this other fine actor who plays Sam
Spade on the radio, Howard Duff. He saw me in Shape Up! last
night and asked me if I'd be interested in doing a series of
comedy skits with another actor for this weekly show. Guess
who this other actor turns out to be, Ma? I'll give you a hint, he
starred in Lloyds of London, Suez, and The Mark of Zorro,
and you once told Papa that he would be the only man that you
would run away with if he asked. That's right, Ma, he's the
actor Papa says is too good-looking for a man and should be a
woman. Yeah, Ma, Tyrone Power! I must really take after you,
because I almost fainted when I walked into the studio and saw
him standing there. He stuck out his hand, and do you know*

what he said to me, Ma? He said, "Hi, I'm Tyrone Power," and do you know what I said? I said, "I'm David Kokolovitz," and he said, "I know, I saw your show last night, and I thought you were just wonderful, David." Did you faint yet, Ma? I'm quoting him exactly, Ma, he didn't say, "You were wonderful, David." He said, "You were just wonderful, David." It was the way he said "just"; you had to hear it to know how great it sounded. I'm writing this to you at two o'clock in the morning because I know how much of a kick you and Pop will get out of this. I'm sorry to have to tell you, Pop, but he's even handsomer in person than he is on the screen, and as nice as he is handsome. We did this little two-man radio sketch where I played this goof-off soldier, Private Peepsight, and he played my commanding officer. I had him autograph the script, which I will send to you when I finish showing it to everybody. He's a marine pilot, and boy, do the guys like him. We walked out of the studio together and signed dozens of autographs. Howard Duff is also a great guy. He knew I would want a picture of myself with Tyrone Power so he had the photographer snap one of us standing on either side of the sign that says Radio Guam. First Hart Milton says I'm good, and now Tyronne Power tells me I'm just wonderful. Hey, Ma, maybe you were right when you embarrassed me on my first opening night by yelling out during the curtain call, "That's my son . . . and he was the best one!" Hope you're all well, I miss you, my love to everybody in the family. If Chuck gets home, give him a hug for me. I haven't heard from him since that last letter he sent on V-E Day.

Love,
David

P.S. I don't want to jinx anything, but things are looking good. Some people are saying that the war in the Pacific may be over soon.

✦

It was on Guam that the public relations officer dubbed *Shape Up!* the army's miracle show. It had rained every day, all day, during the time the show was touring the islands, but the rain had always stopped at curtain time and allowed the show to go on before starting up again. That the show was never rained out was attributed to Eugene and

David's antirain dance. A photograph of the two actors doing their dance was snapped by a Signal Corps photographer and printed in the Central Pacific Base Command newspaper along with a great review of David and of the show. David grabbed up a dozen copies of the paper and sent the photo and review to Mary Deare, his folks, his brother, John and Angela Marlowe, and his old boss, Mr. Foreman. He wrestled with his conscience about sending one to Wanda Futerman, the girl who four years ago had, without a reason, unceremoniously dumped him. He decided that it was a stupid, childish, "look at who you coulda had if you weren't so stupid" kind of behavior, but he sent it, anyway, to her old address, and let fate decide whether or not it would reach her.

The twenty-first and final performance on Guam was a memorable one, and Lieutenant Rendina, their Special Services officer, added a touch of mystery and excitement to the evening by his touching farewell announcement.

"I just want to say, gang, that this last month," he began in an unsteady voice, "has been the most enjoyable one for me and that I want to thank you all. I have never met a nicer, more giving bunch of people, and we're going to miss each and every one of you."

"Especially," Drago muttered to David and then hummed a few bars of "Don't Sit Under the Apple Tree."

"Tonight, for those of you who still have any energy," the lieutenent continued, "I have arranged to have a truck standing by for anyone who wants to join me for a most special event."

"Does it involve extra rations of beer," Drago asked, closing his trumpet case, "and either Hedy Lamarr or Lana Turner?"

"I'm afraid not, Drago."

"Then the event ain't special enough. See ya' in the A.M."

"Hey, Drago," David whispered, "when you hummed 'Don't Sit Under the Apple Tree' down and dirty, you weren't suggesting . . . ?"

"Kocky, what Lieutenant Rendina will be missing will be Alicia Santana and *her* apple tree, from which he's been swiping fruit."

"You're making this up, Drago, aren't you? You shouldn't spread this kind of gossip."

"I am not a gossiper, I am a disseminator," Drago said as he lit a cigarette and strolled away.

Eugene, David, Alicia, Mrs. Furst, and the Four Surfers—Fred Smith, Matt Lowery, Jeff Binns, and Kyle Black—were the only company members who opted to climb into the truck to join Lieutenant Rendina for the special event. With the sound of planes taking off as a backround, the trucks drove off the main road and started up a steep hill. Thinking of what Drago had told him, David kept glancing at the lieutenant and Alicia. Besides a lot of eye contact between the two, David observed an exhange of subtle smiles. There was no question that the smile he gave Alicia wasn't a casual one. That smile, he thought, had teeth in it! Ole Drago was right. These two are having an affair. But how and where?"

"What is it, David?" the lieutenant asked suddenly.

"What? What is what, sir?" David answered, almost jumping out of his skin.

"You were looking at me as if I were playing a prank on you." The lieutenant shouted to be heard above the roar of a low-flying plane.

"You read me right on that one, sir," David shouted back as another plane roared overhead. "This special event is a practical joke, right?"

"Anything but," he said, his voice filled with emotion. "I can assure you all that what you are about to witness is something you will long remember."

And write home about if I were allowed to! David thought as he climbed down from the truck and looked out at the awesome sight of the airfield below him. Lined up and stretching from here to eternity were row upon row of shiny B-29 bombers waiting their turn to take off.

"My God," David shouted to be heard. "I've never seen so many planes in one place."

"Few people have. There are three hundred of them," Lieutenant Rendina shouted through his cupped hands, "three hundred B-29 bombers on their way to drop their payloads on Tokyo. It's our biggest bomber raid ever."

"This is *it!*" Eugene exploded, jumping up and punching the air with his fists. "If this isn't *it,* then there is no *it!*"

Eugene then punched David on his arm hard enough to make his friend wince.

"Hey, hey?" David screamed. "I'm your ally, remember?"

Eugene then raised his arms in victory and, sounding like Jimmy Cagney, shouted, "I'm coming home, Ma!"

The unprecedented, out-of-control behavior of his reserved friend and the incredible sight of the sleek, silvery, cigar-shaped bombers taking off one after the other, convinced David that this could indeed be *it.* This massive bombing raid on Tokyo could signal the beginning of the end for Japan—and possibly for Lieutenant Rendina if Mrs. Furst looked behind her and caught him groping Alicia Santana.

The members of the company who opted to miss watching the bombers take off boarded the C-47 all talkative and chipper; the others dragged their bodies on and fell into their seats.

"Captain Riley, is there any news about last night's bombing raid over Tokyo?" Eugene asked.

"Successful, I hear; all but three planes returned safely."

"Any talk of surrender?" Eugene asked, guessing from the captain's attitude what the answer was.

"Didn't expect there would be. We've been hitting them regularly since that first 117-plane raid from Saipan almost a year ago. Those Japs are stubborn little bastards."

"Captain Riley," David asked, "before I buckle myself in my seat, a few questions. How many miles to Palau, and will there be any bumps?"

"Lot of miles to Palau," the captain said, humoring him, "and only one big bump when we land."

"Then I'll stay on board," David said brightly as he buckled up.

"You been into my bennies, pal," Drago asked, noting the change in David's flying persona, "or has your mind made a natural left turn?"

For most of the smooth flight to the Palau Islands, David kept his mind off the fact that they were flying over water by writing a series of short essays with long titles which he addressed to Mary Deare and put in separate envelopes. The first one he entitled "Twelve Reasons Why Anyone in Their Right Mind Would Have to Fall in Love With Mary Deare Prueitt," followed by "Five More Good Reasons," "Ten Feeble Attempts at Humor and One Really Good Dirty Joke," and the longest essay, "What I Did and Saw Yesterday and How It Made Me Love You More Than Ever, Which I Didn't Think Was Possible."

In this last letter David apologized for his rambling, bumbling attempt at trying to describe his feelings about life and how sad and terrible it would be if taken from you while you are still living it.

Peleliu, the largest of the Palau Islands, was the site of one of the fiercest and most publicized battles in the Pacific War, Bloody Nose Ridge. David had read about the enormous loss of life and the extraordinary heroism displayed by a tough band of marines who secured the blood-soaked hill. On their way to setting up their first show, their driver stopped to point out the landmark. In the time that had passed since the battle the tropical rains and sun had hastened the regrowth of the hill's lush foliage, efficiently covering all signs of the horror that had transpired there.

"Gee, it reminds me of a hill we have in Crotona Park," David commented. "We called it Pike's Peak, and we used to play a game called king of the hill. We'd choose up sides and try to push each other off the hill."

"The Japs and the marines played king of the hill here," the driver offered, "and the hill won."

The audience reaction to the show that first night on Peleliu rivaled anything that it had gotten before and, if there was a meter to measure it, probably bettered it. The rule of thumb about distance lending enchantment held firm. After five days of blockbuster shows, their new Special Services liaison officer, Captain Codd, asked Possie to hold the performers onstage after the show.

"What's happenin', Possie?" Drago asked, encasing his trumpet. "My time is limited. I'm in the middle of very important negotiations with my stubborn friend David here, and we're at an impasse."

"What's the impasse, Drago?" Possie said while rolling up cables. "Maybe we can help."

"Do you know how to readjust a man's taste buds?" Drago asked.

"No, I don't."

"Then butt out!

It was David's taste buds that Drago wanted readjusted. David had stopped trading away his daily can of beer for Drago's two Cokes. He had struck this deal with Drago before he tasted beer and discovered its magical properties. At first sip he wasn't sure he liked it, but by the time he emptied the can, he knew he'd found his new beverage of choice. Every beer drinker in the company admired David for his ability to get stupid and silly on one beer.

"May I have your attention?" Sergeant Possie called out. "Captain Codd sent his apologies and this note. It seems we're such a hit that they've added to our schedule. Tomorrow we'll be flying to Mog Mog."

"Mog Mog?" David asked, "not a long flight, I hope?"

"Fifteen minutes or so. Mog Mog's a tiny island; only one installation to play there."

"Sounds like one Mog would have sufficed." Eugene quipped.

"Where do we go from Mog Mog?"

"We come back to Palau for a few days, and after that it's still open, but," Possie said, checking the note, "there's a possiblilty we'll play an island that should make you happy, David."

"Manhattan Island?" David shouted. "They're starving for a good show there."

"You're close," Possie teased. "It's that island you keep telling us that you were supposed to invade."

"Iwo Jima?" David screamed. "You're not shitting me, Possie?

They said that we couldn't play Iwo Jima because it's under a different commmand."

"Things change. Yesterday there was no Mog Mog in our future."

"Oh, that would be great!" David shouted. "When will we know?"

"Probably when we get back from Mog Mog."

"Then on to Mog Mog!" David yelled. "I wonder if Mog Mog ever gets fog fog."

"I'll pretend you didn't say that." Eugene offered.

"Thanks."

It wasn't until they arrived at the Peleliu airfield that the company learned that their two C-47s had been requisitioned for a mission more important than flying *Shape Up!* to Mog Mog. The two planes were replaced by one fat, graceless C-46, which, because it was wider and heavier than the C-47, was able to carry both the company's personnel and the show's equipment. The cast was not happy with their new, ugly plane or with having to share leg room with the scenery and sound equipment crammed in the aisle, and they let Sergeant Possie know about it.

"Look, folks," he barked as he buckled himself in, "I don't give the orders. If anybody is unhappy, then write President Truman!"

They all booed loudly but quieted down when their new captain came on board.

"G'mornin', gang. In about five minutes we'll be taking off for Mog Mog," the young captain said, removing his cap to wipe perspiration from his prematurely balding head. "It's a short flight and should be a smooth one. I've flown into Mog Mog often, but I must say this is the most interesting load I've ever transported." He chuckled self-consciously. "By the way, I saw your show, and I thought it was something to write home about, and I actually did."

Everyone applauded, and David shouted out, "Three cheers for our wonderful pilot, Captain, uh—"

"Spaulding."

"Captain Spaulding, a likely story," David said as Groucho Marx, and then sang,

> Hurrah for Captain Spaulding,
> Although he may be balding,
> I have no rhyme for balding,
> Fa lala lala la.

The captain laughed, as David prayed he would.

"Hereditary," he said, pointing to his scalp. "Even the tires on my landing gear are bald. Ha, look who I'm telling jokes to," he apologized as he started toward the cockpit, then stopped. "Oh, one thing, as a rule we don't usually fly the C-46 into Mog Mog, but for you folks we're making an exception. Happy landings!"

Fifteen minutes after takeoff, Captain Spaulding announced that they would soon be preparing to land. As the Captain banked the plane, David managed to get a glimpse of the island.

"Now, that is one tiny island!" David told himself.

In preparation for touching down, Captain Spaulding throttled back and decreased the plane's speed, but the second before the wheels were to hit the ground, the captain pulled the throttle back, causing the plane to shudder violently as it strained to stay aloft. With great physical effort the captain managed to abort the landing. The plane climbed steeply, and as it banked to the right and started a 360-degree turn, David experienced an exquisitely clear déjà vu. He was with Mary Deare in her Piper Cub and about to crash on the lawn of the Prueitt estate.

David looked to the crew member for an explanation of what had just happened, and the man obliged.

"Mog Mog's landing strip is about a hundred feet shorter than the length of the island, and unless the captain sets this baby down at the very tip of the runway, almost at the shoreline, he's gonna run out of room at the other end."

"And what? Crash into the ocean?" Eugene shouted.

"Nothing there to stop him. Hold on, he's going to try it again."

As the captain decreased the plane's speed and lined up the nose of the plane with the landing strip, Eugene grabbed David's canvas bucket.

"Take my pillow out first!" David shrieked.

Eugene yanked the pillow out of the bucket and tossed it aside, but instead of using the bucket to throw up in, he put it over his head and sat stock-still while the plane descended for another attempt at a landing and an even more terrifying abortion. On this pass some of the tied-down scenery broke loose, which caused the girls to scream louder than they did on the first attempt. The band members and Eugene remained eerily silent. When the plane leveled off and started its turn, the screaming subsided, and Drago raised his hand.

"One mo' time!" he shouted, putting his trumpet to his lips and starting to play "When the Saints Go Marchin' In."

David looked over at Eugene behaving like an ostrich and then at the Four Surfers, who were singing along with Drago, and knew for sure that everybody's number was up. The only sensible thing he could do was to sing along.

" 'Ohh, I wanna be there in that number, when the saints go marchin' in . . . When the saints . . .' "

The singing cut off abruptly when Captain Spaulding made his third attempt to put the plane's wheels down at the water's edge, and when he aborted the landing again, the heavenly choir picked up the song exactly where they had left off.

" 'go marchin' in . . . When the saints go marchin' in . . .' "

When the captain readied his fourth landing attempt, David shouted, "Why don't we fly back to Peleliu and write a nice letter of apology to Mog Mog!"

"We don't have the fuel to fly back," the crew member responded. "We took only enough to get us here."

On the fourth pass at a landing, the captain succeeded in setting the plane's wheels down at the exact point where the soft, sandy beach ended and the airstrip began. He quickly reversed his engines' thrust and brought the ungainly C-46 to a lurching stop just feet before the strip ran out. A mighty roar greeted Captain Spaulding when he emerged from the cockpit.

"Routine landing," the captain said, looking like he had been doused with a pail of water. "Hope y'all enjoyed the little flourishes I threw in for your enjoyment."

"You okay, buddy?" David asked, lifting the bucket off Eugene's head.

"Fine, thank you," Eugene said, feigning boredom. "Have we landed yet?"

"You son of a gun." David laughed. "Did you ever look stupid sitting there with a bucket on your head."

"Looking stupid," Eugene said calmly as he rose to leave, "is a small price to pay to keep the plane from crashing into the sea."

"Gene, what the hell are you talking about?"

"A plane will never crash if one passenger is wearing a bucket on his head."

"You're a nutcake."

"It worked, didn't it?"

As the two friends stepped from the plane, David asked, "You were scared, weren't you?"

"Shitless!" Eugene whispered, and walked on.

The potential for a second big disaster on Mog Mog came to light while the crew was setting up the show. As David was laying down electric cable between the rows of seats, he noticed that spaced about fifteen feet apart were neatly arranged pyramids of small green papayas. At first, David thought, Hey, how civilized and nutritious, fresh fruit for the GIs to munch on during the show. Always ready for a snack, David picked one up and found it to be at least a couple of weeks from ripening. He looked around for Sergeant Piles, the gloomy, uncommunicative one-man welcoming committee who met the plane and greeted them with "Welcome to the asshole of the Pacific!"

On every island there were men who hated being where they were and treated everyone as if they were responsible for sending them there. Mog Mog, per capita, seemed to have gotten more than its fair share of smoldering malcontents.

"Hey, Sergeant Piles," David called, spotting him sprawled out in the front seat of his jeep, "these papayas aren't ripe enough to eat, are they?"

"The guys like 'em that way." Sergeant Piles said, smirking.

"They're hard as rocks."

"They're perfect," Sergeant Piles said, gunning his engine and driving off.

Eugene, who had been working onstage setting the speakers, came trotting toward David with a young, bespectacled PFC in tow.

"There they are," the PFC said to Eugene, pointing to the pyramid of papayas. "They got 'em in every row."

"So they have," Eugene said, picking one up. "Hey, Donny, know what these are?"

"Papayas, but they're not ripe enough to eat."

"According to our friend here," Eugene said, nodding toward the PFC, "they're not eating papayas, they're throwing papayas."

"That's right," the soldier explained hastily, fearful that he might be caught snitching, "Mog Mog has not had a live show since Eddie Downey brought his one-man show here seven months ago."

"I love Eddie Downey," David offered, "but I didn't know he did a show. What did he do?"

"We never found out. He told some jokes that some guys didn't like, and they heckled him, and he said, 'If you think you can do better, why don't you come up here?' One soldier did and grabbed the mike from him, and he shoved this guy. In couple of seconds a big fight broke out, and they wrecked the place. The colonel said no more live shows until we all learn some manners."

"It doesn't look like they learned them yet," David said, hefting a small, rock-hard papaya.

David and Eugene alerted Possie to the possibility of being bombarded by papayas, and Possie in turn alerted the company. In trying to determine if the members of this audience looked any more hostile than those in other audiences, the worried cast kept sneaking peeks at them as they filed into the theater.

"They all look like potential papaya pitchers to me," Jeff, one of the Four Surfers, noted.

"Hey, 'Papaya Pitchers of Peleliu.' Nice song title," Matt, the bass Surfer, added. "Could be a hit."

"Naw," offered Don, the alto, "too similar to 'The Princess Papuli Has Plenty Papayas.' We'll get sued."

"C'mon, guys, enough about papayas," David pleaded as the band tuned up. "Look, we know we've got a great show. Let's just do it, and if worst comes to worst—"

A loud, resounding thwack interrupted David.

"It's come!" David yelled. "Let's get out of here!"

Someone had heaved a papaya and hit the body of the bass fiddle with a force that should have shattered it but miraculously didn't. The girls, moments away from making their first entrance, looked to Sergeant Possie for help, which came, surprisingly, from a couple of guys in the audience and Broody the bassist. The soldiers subdued the papaya thrower, while Broody, the three-time winner of *Downbeat*'s Jazz Bassist of the Year Award, got a huge laugh by disappearing behind his instrument and continuing to play with only his hands visible. From a mock cowering postion, he played through the overture, and when he finally emerged from behind his bass with a big smile on his face, the audience cheered him.

Impelled by Broody's good humor and a joyfully demonstrative audience, the cast, still charged by that morning's near disastrous landing, gave one of their more spirited and animated performances. Every sketch and song was received with the kind of ego-boosting enthusiasm that makes performers happy to have chosen show business as their career. Lawrence T. Lawrence's singing and his leading the cast in their slipping, sliding, falling-down finale, brought the audience to its feet. The curtain calls were topped by someone in the audience having a sense of pageantry. He hurled a papaya high over the top of the stage's proscenium, and in a flash hundreds of small green papayas were flying through the air and landing harmlessly in the empty field behind the stage.

The company's takeoff from Mog Mog's short landing strip was as routine as their arrival was terrifying. It was a quiet, reflective flight for David, who fantasized that when he stepped off the plane in Peleliu, good things would be awaiting him, like a packet of letters from Mary

Deare or news that the show would continue on to Iwo Jima. Over the past few months he and Saul Marantz had been corresponding regularly, and each time David would write describing their show, Saul wrote back and said how great it would be if it came to Iwo Jima.

On arriving back at Peleliu, there was no packet of letters awaiting David, but there was news about Iwo Jima. Major Merritt had once again pulled some strings, probably the same ones he pulled to get David transferred to the Entertainment Section, the result being that permission was granted for *Shape Up!* to fly to Iwo Jima and tour its army and marine bases.

On learning this news, David leaped in the air, pounded Eugene on the back and let out a loud "Yahoooo!"

"Let us not get carried away, my friend," Eugene warned. "May I point out that you were yahooing alone. A lot of us do not cherish the idea of stretching this tour for another couple of weeks by flying to a charmless, bleak island."

"Visiting charmless, bleak islands is our business," David argued, "because that's where the servicemen are who need pepping up!"

"Donny, there are plenty of servicemen on bleak islands that we can pep up on our way back to Oahu."

"C'mon, Gene, my old outfit is on Iwo. It could be exciting."

"For you, maybe, but I'd prefer wending my way toward Oahu."

"Oahu, Oahu!" David shouted, losing control. "What the hell have we got in Oahu?"

"Mail!" Eugene shouted back. "The possibility of getting some fuckin' mail from our fuckin' loved ones!"

David did not respond, and Eugene looked away sheepishly.

Both were embarrassed. Never had they raised their voices to each other in anger, and they quickly realized that it was the frustration of receiving no mail for weeks that had provoked them.

Feeling guilty about pushing to go to Iwo, David apologized. "Hey, Gene, I'm sorry I got angry."

"I am, too," Eugene said contritely. "You know, you're not one of those people who are beautiful when they're angry. I don't know why I sounded off. We don't have a choice about going to Iwo; we've been ordered to go."

"Right, and you know what, Gene? Maybe our screaming woke up whoever it is who's holding up our mail. I'll bet it catches up with us in Iwo."

"For how much?"

"A month's pay!" David shouted.

"You're on," Eugene said, offering his hand.

That afternoon, after setting up the first of the three remaining shows scheduled for Peleliu, the two men, with the idea that a walk was what they needed to calm them, took off for a three-mile hike back to their Quonset hut.

"Hey, Gene," David asked, "when you don't get a letter from Peggy for a week or more, do you think that she may be sittin' under the apple tree with another guy?"

"No, I think she's lying in the back of a car and screwing her brains out with a handsome athlete who's classified 4-F because of bad knees."

"C'mon, Gene, you know Peggy's not like that."

"Everybody's who's not been laid in over a year is like that. That's why I didn't resist Sooky, and that's why every time I watch Bitsy Kane dancing in the opening number and her skirt swirls up, I want to jump her bones."

"But you don't!"

"Only because Mrs. Hawkface is on duty. Peggy doesn't have a chaperon keeping her faithful."

"That's ridiculous, Gene. Peggy is . . ."

". . . a very hot lady who loves to do it, and if she doesn't have a cop watching her like I do, she'll do it! I want to go home, god-damn it!"

Eugene used the Lord's name in vain just as an army chaplain emerged from his quarters.

"Sorry, sir," Eugene apologized, "but I'm very upset today."

"As we all are, I fear. Would you like to accompany me?" the chaplain said, indicating his jeep. "I'm on my way to the chapel if you care to discuss today's event."

"Father, I'm a fallen Catholic, but I haven't fallen so low that I'd blaspheme in front of a priest, and, sir, in the army cursing isn't really an event."

"Hold it, Eugene," David said, seeing the confused look in the priest's face. "I don't think the chaplain heard you curse."

"I didn't, but I daresay there will be much swearing today and I hope even more praying. You boys obviously haven't heard the news," the chaplain said, searching their faces, "have you?"

"What news?" they asked in unison.

David, remembering the shock of Roosevelt's death, asked, "President Truman didn't die, did he?"

"No, but many, many people did," the chaplain said sadly. "Our air corps dropped a new and terrible bomb on Japan today. The news came in just minutes ago."

"What kind of new bomb?" Eugene asked.

"A brand-new one, reported to have the explosive power of twenty thousand tons of TNT. It was referred to as a special bomb."

"Wow!" was all David could say.

"Wow sums it up, Corporal," the chaplain said, getting behind the wheel of his jeep. "It was dropped on Hiroshima and purportedly leveled the entire city. I'd best be getting to the chapel. I know that members of my flock will have some questions. You're welcome to join us."

Without hesitating, they scrambled into the backseat.

David tried to imagine what twenty thousand tons of anything looked like, and the only thing he could think of to use as a comparison was the ton of coal that as a kid he had watched being delivered to his Bronx apartment building. Trying to imagine twenty thousand trucks each loaded with a ton of coal was asking too much for a mortal brain to visualize, so he moved on to thinking about Mary Deare and how this special bomb might speed up his chances of seeing her sweet face again.

On the road to the chapel, the Chaplain slowed the jeep down as it approached a tall, gangly, rawboned corporal.

"One of my flock," the chaplain explained. "Probably on his way to see me."

"Going to the chapel, Abner?" the chaplain asked.

"Yup."

"Wanna lift?

The corporal nodded and climbed into the jeep.

"Hear about the new bomb, Abner?"

"Yup."

"What do you think of it?"

"Quite an improvement," the taciturn midwesterner said, speaking slowly. "Yessiree, quite an improvement."

For the rest of the day nobody talked about anything but the special bomb and what it meant to their future. The details of the awesome destruction the bomb wreaked spread quickly, and many met the reports with skepticism.

"I say it's propaganda to calm everybody down because the generals are embarrassed that the war is lasting too long," offered Broody. "I bet there's no such place as Hiroshima."

"You'd win, Broody," Drago said, sipping his beer, "because it's not there anymore."

"I agree with Broody," Lawrence T. suggested, "it's a publicity stunt. Where did they get a plane that can carry twenty thousand tons of dynamite? It'd have to be a mile long."

Most people believed that all the reports about the bomb were true because they wanted them to be. David believed it with all his heart. That night he wrote:

August 6, 1945

    My Darling,

By the time you receive this letter, I predict that the war will be over. That special bomb we dropped today had to get their attention, and unless the Japanese are a whole nation of kamikaze pilots, they should be surrendering soon. I can't believe that with the war in Europe over, they're still hanging on. Whatever happens, I'm assuming that you still love me as much as you said you did in your letter of June 20th, which is the last one I got from you. To remind you, you said that you ache to see my face again and that when I come home to you, you're going to kiss it and keep kissing it until I yell for help. You said a few other things that you plan to do to other parts of me, and frankly, honey, I prefer that to your giving me a hickey face. I, too, have plans that involve your lips, mouth, and other sundry parts of your magnificent body that I will not discuss in this letter, lest the censor read it and have me arrested for corrupting the morals of a southern belle. Honey, not only do my arms ache to encircle your torso, but my legs ache to be around your hips. Hey, hey, Kokolovitz, calm down! Every time I write things like that to you, I worry that I'm saying them to somebody who has rejected my marriage proposal. I don't know why I assume that your answer was yes. You could have said, "Maybe," or, "I'm flattered, but I'll have to think about it," or, "Mr. Coleman, this is so sudden," or, "You'll have to ask Daddy fo' mah hand," or, "I don't believe in marriage," or, "I've decided to a nunnery go!" or, "Ask me again when you're wealthy or at least have a paying job!" or, "Tyrone Power asked me first," or, "Me? Marry a Semite? Are you mad?"

Honey, I think by now you realize that I suffer from acute insecurity and not so cute loneliness. I really do know that you love me, and I know you've said yes, but until I read it in your own sweet, dear handwriting, you can expect to get these self-deprecatory letters from me. ("Self-deprecatory" I learned from Eugene when he told me to stop being it.) We were promised that there will be a mail delivery before we leave for Iwo Jima!

I love you today more than I did yesterday, but not nearly as much as I will tomorrow and every day after that until you holler Uncle!

> *Your Uncle Don,*
> *forever,*
> *Don*

P.S. Holy shinola! I didn't tell you about our going to Iwo Jima. Isn't that great, honey? I'll get to see Saul Marantz and all the guys in my old outfit. How could I forget to tell you that? It's that damned bomb, it's unhinged everybody.

♦

Four days after the bomb was dropped on Hiroshima, a second bomb devastated the city of Nagasaki, and the world learned that the awesome instrument responsible for the complete eradication of two large cities was an atomic bomb. With rare exceptions, everyone felt that this atom bomb was the greatest thing that had ever been invented.

"This is going to end the war," David said confidently as he sat at lunch with the cast, "and maybe all wars. Hirohito has to know, unless he's not been reading the newspapers, that if he doesn't surrender soon, Japan will evaporate. I don't know what he's waiting for."

"Do you think that maybe," a frightened Loretta Yung, asked, "he also has such a bomb and is preparing to drop it on us?"

"If they had it, they would have used it, believe me," David said, picking up his tray. "Well, gotta get back."

"David," Loretta asked sweetly, putting her hand on his arm, "please sit with me for a bit. I like talking with you."

For months now, since the flight from Oahu, where he spent an entire day lying besides her under cargo pads, David had assiduously avoided being alone with this petite, attractive dancer. The arousing scent of Shalimar that always hung in the airspace around her, coupled with the inhumanly long period of celibacy the war had imposed on him, made David particulary vulerable to this delicate Eurasian beauty who more than once had asked if he had a steady girl back home. David was painfully aware that if he hadn't been strong, there is no way that Mrs. Furst could have managed to keep him from this girl.

"Sure, I'll sit with you," he said, feeling relatively safe from himself in an army mess hall. "What would you like to talk about?"

"About what you think of me," she said, shyly sipping her coffee. "I see you looking at me sometimes."

"You do?" David said, getting caught off guard. "I didn't realize I was. No, that's not true. I do realize that I look at you. I like looking at you; all the guys do. You're very beautiful, you know. I guess you've heard that, haven't you?"

"Yes, I have, many times," she said, her sad brown eyes looking directly into his blinking ones, "but never from you, David."

"Sure you have," David said, looking around for Eugene, who, along with the rest of the company, had eaten and run. "Haven't you?"

"Never."

"Well, let's remedy that right now. I think you are very beautiful."

"I'm sorry, David," she said, moving close to him. "I did not mean to drag it out of you."

"You didn't," David said, the scent of her Shalimar starting to do its job. "Hey, listen, you were voted Miss Waikiki this year, so it's not just my opinion."

"It's your opinion that matters to me," she said, taking his hand. "I think you are the most talented man in this company, and the nicest and most honest."

"And the most modest. Let's not forget that," David joked, making a minor attempt to retrieve his hand. "And I think that you are terrific."

"Do you, do you really?" she said, staring into his face.

"Yes, really," he said, her perfume and her proximity getting to him. "You sing and dance great, and you're sexy, and boy do you smell good."

"Thank you," she said, becoming emotional. "You are kind, but tell me, do you think if after the war I came to the mainland . . ."

Oh, shit, he thought, she's going to propostion me; she knows I'm getting hot. I better remind her about Mary Deare. "Loretta Deare," he started. "I mean, just Loretta . . ."

"Do you think, David," she pressed on, tears in her eyes, "that an American producer would hire me? I see all these movies, and I never see an Oriental girl singing or dancing in them. Oh, maybe once in a while in the chorus, but never in a real part. I am foolish to think of going, aren't I?"

David was surprised and mildly disappointed to learn that she wanted his opinion and not him.

"Loretta, when I look at you, and you caught me doing that many times, I don't see an Oriental girl. I see a very beautiful and talented girl and if I were a producer, I would hire you in a minute and feel lucky to have you in my show."

Loretta looked into his eyes and, seeing that he was sincere, started to cry. She leaned toward him, whispered, "Thank you, David," then put her plump red lips on his, kissed them firmly, and ran off.

David watched her move gracefully across the mess hall and sighed for what might have been had he not had his friggin' scruples. He would like to have gotten up and left, but had to wait until the scent of her Shalimar dissipated sufficiently to lose its power to arouse. It took a little while before David was in a condition to stand up and walk erectly out of the mess hall.

At six-thirty A.M. on the morning of August 14, 1945, just as David had finished packing for the flight to Iwo Jima, Sergeant Possie, carrying a big canvas bag over his shoulder and behaving like Santa Claus, burst into the quonset hut.

"Ho, ho, ho, mail call!" he shouted at the top of his healthy lungs. *"Mail fucking call!"*

While those wonderful words were still echoing, an obstreperous group that had too long been denied news from home came racing toward him. David, one of the fastest in the gang, wiggled his way to Possie's side.

"I'm volunteering to be Possie's assistant!" David shouted.

David tossed out a few packets of mail to the group before finding his.

"We need another volunteer to assist!" David yelled, and ran off.

The letter on top of the packet was a V-mail from his brother, and even though he was dying to open all of Mary Deare's letters to find the one where she reacted to his proposal, he had to know what his brother's status was. The war in Europe had ended months before, and men were starting to be discharged. David ripped open the letter and read:

July 30, 1945

Dear David,

Well, my unlucky draft number 158 now turns out to be my lucky number, first ones in will be the first ones out. The way it

*looks now I'll be back in civilian clothes before this reaches you.
I didn't tell Mom and Pop when I'm coming because I'm not
sure of the exact date yet. They hate surprises and
disappointments, so I'll wait. I read that great review your show
got. You'll have to do your talking-dog thing for me when you
get back. It can't be too long before the Japs get the idea that
the war's over. I got a very nice letter from Mary Deare. She
appears to be as sweet as her name. Can't wait to meet her.*

Love,
Chuck

✦

By checking the postmarks on each envelope, David had managed
to put all of Mary Deare's letters in chronological order and had just
opened the first one when Possie barged in.

"Hate to do it, gang," he announced, "but you're going to have to
continue reading those on the plane. We have a show to do on Iwo
Jima tonight, so let's move out."

"How far from here to Iwo?" David yelled out.

"From-Kwajalein-to-Saipan far," Possie answered.

"I can handle that as long I have this," David said, grabbing his
bucket.

The company had not flown since their return flight from Mog
Mog, having toured Peleliu in trucks, but as they boarded their C-47
and settled into their regular seats, even David was pleased to be
where he was. The sound of the revving motors had somehow
become comforting to him, and he was looking forward to a flight
where he could stop worrying that the engines were malfunctioning
every time he heard their pitch change. As the plane taxied to the end
of the strip, it stopped short suddenly, jerking everyone sharply forward and then backward. The motors shut down, and wild screaming
emanated from the cockpit, which triggered higher-pitched screams
from the girls. Both the pilot and copilot bolted from the cockpit and
ran up the aisle.

"The war's over, the war's over!" they shouted, jumping in place
and waving their arms. *"Japan has surrendered!"*

Within seconds the aisle was clogged with happy, laughing, jumping, hugging people yelling, "The war's over, we did it, we did it. I can't
believe it! The damn war's over!" The only member of the company
who did not join in the celebration was Drago, who was still buckled in

his seat and casually fingering the valves of his trumpet.

"Hey, Drago, Drago!" David yelled, "why don't you join the celebration?"

"I would," he said casually, "if I had a reason to."

"For God sakes, Drago," Mrs. Furst said, screaming in his face. "Isn't the war being over reason enough for you?"

"Is that what happened?" he asked ingenuously.

"Yes, yes, Drago, Japan surrendered!" everyone shouted at him, knowing that he was toying with them.

"Japan surrendered!" he yelled as he sprang from his seat and threw his arms around Mrs. Furst and grabbed her ass firmly with both hands. While passionately kissing her on her neck, he bent her over and lowered her to the ground.

"Oh, Mrs. Furst darling," he moaned as he started to dry-hump her, "now that the war's over, we can be ourselves again! No more doing this where people can't see us!"

Of all the strange things Drago had done, this was the most bizarre, and given that he was doing it to the girls' chaperon, the company was reluctant to react too loudly. Most just stared and giggled until Mrs. Furst shouted, "Drago!" and then violently grabbed his head by the ears, planted her tongue in his mouth, and soul-kissed him hard and long. The group exploded, laughing and clapping their hands until Drago came up, gasping for air.

"If you all don't mind," Drago said disapprovingly, "my chick and I would appreciate some privacy?" He then turned and went back to dry-humping her.

"That will be all for now, Drago," Mrs. Furst said, tapping him on his shoulder and then slipping out from under him.

"I really enjoyed that, Mrs. Furst," he said politely while escorting her to her seat. "We must do this again sometime."

"We will, Drago." She smiled, "Every time we're in a plane together and hear news of a world war ending."

Drago kissed Mrs. Furst's hand, and the company broke out into spontaneous applause in appreciation of their beautifully executed victory improvisation.

David did not get back to his letters until after the plane had taken off and climbed to its cruising altitude. In contrast to the extraordinary high-decibeled celebration moments before, the only sounds that could be heard now were the drone of planes' engines. Everything the cast members had to say to each other had been said loudly and with much emotion. David had hugged everybody in the plane at least once, Eugene three times, and Loretta Yung twice. The second one she initiated, and it ended in her kissing him again.

"Hey, Antipholus," Eugene asked as they settled back in their seats. "Art thou leading a life of which I, your dear twin brother, am not privy to?"

"Oh, the kiss." David laughed. "it was nothing. She was thanking me for some advice I gave her in the mess hall the other day."

"Must have been some powerful advice," Eugene teased. "For two months no guy has gotten more than a smile out of that girl."

"Because they all wanted more than a smile," David said, dismissing Eugene's comment and reaching for his precious packet of letters. "Don't you have some reading to do?"

Before opening one of Mary Deare's letters, David pulled out his hanky and blew his nose hard, hoping to weaken or lose the scent of Loretta. It worked, but he decided to hold off reading any of her letters for at least a couple of hours, realizing how really long and miserable this flight would be if he learned that his marriage proposal had been rejected. He would try exercising the kind of self-control he rarely ever called upon himself to use, for when he did, he usually failed. He began by reading every letter but Mary Deare's, starting with a short surprise one from his old girlfriend Margie Skulnik, who was now Margie Feldsher. It read:

Dear David,

Just a note to let you know how happy I am. I hope that you, too, will be happy to know that I have remarried and have just given birth to a darling nine-pound girl whom we are calling Justine Danielle. My husband, George, is a C.P.A., so when you become a big star, which I heard from your mother you've already become, you'll know who to call to do your taxes.

Your old dear friend,
Margaret (formerly Margie)
✦

The next letter made David sit up and exclaim, "Holy moly!"

"Look at this!" he said, handing it to Eugene. "It's from Iwo, and it's dated eight days ago."

Eugene read,

"Dear David,

Well, Shwick did it again. He's got us both up for a court-martial. There was a radio-voice message I received in the

*Message Center that said the Japanese surrendered
unconditionally. I couldn't get authentication on it, so I refused
to send it out, but our buddy Shwick, who outranks me, ordered
me to send it. So I teletyped this false report to Guam, who sent
it all over the world. Someone who picked it up in the
Philippines started to celebrate and blew up a munitions storage
depot. Six guys were killed. If your show ever comes to Iwo, I
won't get to see it unless you do it in the stockade. Hope all's
going well for you; all's going shitty for me. Wanna trade
buddies, your Eugene O'Neill for my Henny Shwick?"*

> *Love,*
> *Saul*

✦

"Explain something to me," Eugene said, handing the letter back. "What did you tell Saul about me?"

"Just that you're the least schmucky person in our outfit and I'm lucky to have you as a buddy."

"Likewise. Now explain this to me. How come Shwick the schmuck got to be in charge of Saul? You said Saul is so smart."

"He is; that's how he got in trouble. When we were all in Signal Corps school, Shwick got the highest marks ever recorded at the school on the teletyping and procedure tests, and Saul Marantz came in second."

"How the hell can that be?

"Saul took both tests, that's how," David said, shaking his head at the memory.

"Henny Shwick could barely type, and he knew shit about Message Center procedures, so he begged Saul to take the test for him. Saul and I had taken the tests the day before, and . . ."

"When your buddy Saul took the test again," Eugene laughed, "he got a better score because he was familiar with the questions."

"Right. He forged Shwick's name, and if he'd have gotten caught, they'd have fried his ass. I told him that, but he said that if Shwick had been sent back to the infantry and got himself killed, he'd have felt guilty."

"Now that's what I call a good soul."

"You'll tell him that when we visit him in the stockade," David said. He was about to open another non–Mary Deare letter when a strange feeling came over him. He looked about the plane and saw everyone quietly reading their letters. Their behavior, he thought, was not reflective of the great news they had just learned about the fate of the civilized world. He felt an obligation and an uncontrollable urge to address the company and make them aware of this observation.

"Hey, everyone, may I have your attention," he said, speaking just loud enough to be heard over the roar of the motors. "I just want to remind you that, today is V-J Day!" he screamed as loudly as he could. "This lousy war is over, and we won! . . . Oh, I loved saying that, and I hope you liked hearing it again!"

They responded with loud cheering and applause and made "V for victory" signs with their fingers.

"I'm glad we agree. Hey, here's an idea. How about every half hour or so somebody yell out a reminder that it's V-J Day."

"Folks, I think that David's idea of people jumping up and yelling," Drago said, sounding deeply sincere, "is to me thoughtless and repugnant. I have used the last two of my special cigarettes to ensure I sleep through this flight, and I am serving notice now that if anyone dares to wake me up to tell me news that I already know, they will be severely punished and then spat upon. David, I know your heart's in the right place, but your brain is up your ass! However, having said that . . ."

Drago then put his trumpet to his lips and started to play a slow and unbelievably stirring version of the "Battle Hymn of the Republic." Before the last sweet trumpet note faded, Broody called out, "One mo' time," and the whole company responded by joining him in singing a rousing chorus of the hymn, the Four Surfers weaving in their exquisite four-part harmony. It was so thrilling and perfect that Broody called, one mo' time, "One mo' time!"

Lawrence T. Lawrence, who had only been humming along because he was uncertain of the lyrics, suddenly sang out, " 'Mine eyes have seen the glory of the coming of the Lord,' " his powerful baritone voice never sounding more beautiful, soaring to vocal and emotional heights of which no one dreamed he was capable. Mrs. Furst wept openly, and many fought back tears. David felt the hairs on the back of his neck stand up higher ever. When the song ended, all were smiling, the girls throwing kisses and others making victory signs toward a nonchalant Drago, who nodded, looked to David, and said quietly, "Need we say more?"

Then, cradling his horn in his arms, Drago lay back in his seat and closed his eyes.

With a thick packet of unopened letters in his lap, David flashed on a line he had heard in a movie when he was very little. A kind, bespectacled, avuncular character had told someone, "Count your blessings, my son!"

David had no idea what this meant, and he asked his father, who explained, "Every once in a while it's not a bad idea to make a list of all the good things in your life."

Every time that phrase popped into his head, he would count his blessings and always start by thinking, Let's see, now . . .

1. My brother is alive after five years of fighting.
2. My folks are both alive.
3. Hitler is dead.
4. Japan has surrendered.
5. I've got a leading part in a great show.
6. Maj. Evan Merritt, the Broadway star, said I was good.
7. Hart Milton, the great American playwright, says he expects great things of me.
8. In a few hours I will see Saul Marantz and all my old buddies of the 3117th Signal Battalion.
9. I'll get to do the show for them!
10. I have a girl whom I love and who keeps telling me that she loves me and who, if the army remembers where I am and how to get me home from here, I will marry!
11. Hitler is dead!

David told himself, That's the longest list of blessings you ever compiled. Five more than you had when Carl Hubbell pitched the New York Giants to a pennant.

David went through all this in preparation for reading that his proposal of marriage was rejected. He checked the dates on the postmarks and tried to divine the one that would be most likely to contain her response. He chose one that she had written two weeks after he had written to her.

His hands trembled as he ripped open the envelope, but they stopped when he picked out a single folded page of notepaper with no writing on the back, the kind of note she sent when she didn't have time to write but didn't want David to go without some message from her. He opened it, and it was her shortest note yet. "Yes, yes, yes. Letter to follow."

David let out a loud and piercing "Yahooooo" that awoke the sleeping Drago.

"If your aim is to be maimed," Drago growled at him, "you're going about it the right way."

"I'm sorry, Drago, but I just got some great news."

"I warned you, butt brain, about waking me up to tell me things I know."

"What is it, Don?" Eugene interrupted. "She say yes?"

David, smiling from ear to ear, thrust the letter into Gene's hand and nodded his head violently.

"Hey, gang," Eugene shouted to the company, "David's getting married!"

"Kid, from a man who's been married twice"—Drago sighed, pulling his blanket around him—"welcome to World War Three and don't wake me when that one's over, either."

David went through his stack of letters looking for one of Mary Deare's dated after the one with the scriggly block-printed yeses. He wondered about that lettering and the answer came in a typewritten letter, dated two days after the scribbled acceptance letter.

> *Oh, darling, sweet darling Donny,*
>
> *What must you be thinking! When you read why this letter is being written by my cousin Ellen, you will understand why I wrote you that crazy-looking answer to the dearest, most wonderful question anyone has ever asked me. But before I explain, here is how my answer to your proposal of marriage looks on a standard Royal typewriter. YES, YES, YES! I'D LIKE VERY MUCH TO BE YOUR WIFE. I can't wait for the war to be over*

✦

"It's over darling, it's over!" David shouted at the letter, and went back to reading it.

> *and to have you in my arms again, which should be healed by that time. There, now, I've managed to sneak in the reason for this letter being written by my cousin. Darling, I had the stupidest accident the day I got your letter, which I read on my way to the hospital. I wrote that scribbly note right before I went under anesthesia. It was the best I could do with two broken wrists, but I wanted you to know that I'm yours forever, although you may not want me now that I'm damaged goods, but I'm sure by the time the war is over, honey*

✦

"It's over, the war's over!" David barked as he continued to read.

"Who're you talking to?" Eugene asked.

"This letter!"

"Well, hold it down, Donny. You don't want to wake up a sleeping Drago."

"Oh, poor darling," David said, referring to the letter. "She broke both her wrists in a plane crash. You know, she works as a civilian flying instructor for the Army Air Corps."

"Yes, so how did it happen?"

"Let me finish reading this and I'll tell you," David, shushed him, and read on:

> *So, darling, after soloing for the first time, this student pilot makes a perfect three-point landing about ten feet to the left of the landing strip and hits a parked jeep. I'm lucky to get away with two broken wrists. He was a bloody mess. They say because I'm a fast healer that I'll be as good as new in six weeks. Now, about our wedding, my sweet husband-to-be but not soon enough. I loved all your romantic and goofy suggestions, and any one of them would suit me fine. You choose, honey, and I'll be there. You know what, honey. I was thinking that when the war is over,*

✦

"It's over! It's over!" David said, annoyed at the letter's ignorance.

> *the beach at Waikiki might be nice to get married. What do you think?*

✦

"I'd love it, I'd love it!" he exploded, then mumbled to himself, "But my folks would never come . . .''

"Say, Donny," Eugene interrupted, "as long as you're talking to your girl's letter, tell her I said hello."

The flight to Iwo Jima was more than half over when Sergeant Possie came over to David with a piece of paper in his hand.

"This may be of interest to you, David. They just radioed this list of the installations that we'll be playing on Iwo Jima. Looks like we'll be there for six days."

"Is the 3117th Signal Battalion listed? Hey, wouldn't it be sensational if I played for my old oufit on V-J Day."

"There's a chance you will, Dave. The 3117th is listed for tonight."

"Tonight? Are you shittin' me, Possie?" David interrupted, snatching the list from him. "Oh, my god, it's true! This is unfuckingbelievable! Hey, hey, hey, gang!" He stood in the aisle, shouting. "We're going to be playing for my old outfit on V-J Day! V-J DAY!"

A stoned and sleepy Drago awoke to find his tormentor standing directly above him and still screaming about V-J Day.

"David, the only reason I'm not kicking you in the balls," Drago moaned, "is because it would prolong your screaming."

"David, you may be wasting a lot of good energy," Possie advised, calming him down. "I spoke with the captain and, well, have you been listening to the engines?"

"I knew it," David shot back excitedly. "We're losing an engine, right? It started sounding funny about and hour ago. I told Gene—"

"Told me what?" Eugene said, looking up from the letter he was reading.

"About the engines sounding funny. Remember, Gene? I said that, and you said I was being a nervous Jew?"

"*You* said you were being a nervous Jew. I said you probably had wax in your ears."

"Oh, yeah, but the engines did sound funny," David insisted.

"There is nothing wrong with the engines," Possie stated calmly. "That's not the problem."

"Problem?" David said, his ears pricking up like a bird dog's. "So I wasn't being a nervous Jew. What's the problem? Don't tell me we're low on fuel?"

Possie's slight hesitation in answering was proof enough to David that he had guessed right about the fuel. Instead of falling apart, as Eugene had expected, David sighed, and quietly said, *"Oy vey!"*

"Hold the *oy veys,*" Possie advised, starting for the cockpit, "until the captain explains it."

"If the captain has to explain it," Eugene offered, "then perhaps, David, your *oy veys* were not premature. What's the exact translation of *oy vey* anyway?"

"It's short for *Oy vey iss meir,* Oh, woe is me."

"I hope we've no need to use, either. *Oy vey!*" Eugene said on seeing a serious-looking captain emerge from the cockpit.

Capt. Ed Pecora was the pilot assigned to them for this leg of their tour. He was a short, compact man whose dream, after flying transports for three solid years, was to be handed his last assignment and news of his disharge on the same day. Half of his dream was being realized on this flight to Iwo Jima, and the other half he exected fulfilled on his return flight to Peleliu.

"Hi" was all Captain Pecora had to say to get everyone's rapt attention. "I'd like to explain some things you might be wondering about. An hour ago, some of you may have noticed a change in the sound of our engines."

"Wax, huh?" David said, whacking Eugene's arm.

"The engines are fine, but as a precautionary measure, we've reduced their speed."

"If they're fine, Captain Pecora," David asked, raising his hand as if he were in school, "what are we taking precautions against?"

"Running out of fuel."

"Nervous Jew, huh?" David muttered, hitting Eugene again.

"Private," Captain Pecora addressed David sternly—"I don't consider your remark either appropriate or accurate. I am not nervous, but if I were, I'd be a nervous Italian, not a nervous—"

"He was talking to me about himself, sir," Eugene said, rising to David's defense.

"Sorry, Corporal," Captain Pecora apologized, "but being cautious is what we are right now."

"So you have enough fuel, sir?" David asked.

"Probably. The fuel gauge might be faulty," Captain Pecora said calmly. "If we keep flying at this reduced speed, getting the most mileage out of what we have left in the tanks, we'll get you to Iwo, but probably too late to do your show."

An assortment of reactions greeted the captain's announcement, ranging from pleased to extremely pleased to displeased, the lone dissenter, saying, "Shit!"

"C'mon, David," Eugene reasoned, "so you'll reunite with your buddies a day after V-J Day. Think how much worse you'd feel if you told Captain Pecora to push this plane and we run out of gas and end up crashing in the—"

"Gene! All I said was shit, a sentimental outpouring. I may be corny, but I ain't crazy."

As long as the plane was moving smoothly through the air, most of the company was content to sit back in their seats and relax. The religious members of the group, led by Mrs. Furst and including Loretta Yung, Lawrence T., Alicia Santana, and two of the Four Surfers, now all joined hands as Mrs. Furst offered a quiet prayer for their safe passage. David was mildly envious of their faith in prayer and was sorry he saw no reason to join with them. He listened to Mrs. Furst conduct their little service, and when he caught Loretta Yung's eyes on him, he decided to please her by saying amen when the prayer ended.

David lay back in his seat and closed his eyes, his mind lingering on Mrs. Furst's prayer asking God to keep their group safe from harm. He wondered how many people in the world, immediately before a bomb fell on them, had made that exact request of God. As David started to nod off, he puzzled, What does God do when he hears good people praying to Him to keep them safe when at the same time other good people are flying over them in planes, praying their bombs hit their marks. How does He figure out which good people's prayers to honor? Maybe it's like a competition and the ones who get their prayers in first win and stay alive. Too many people in the world making too many requests of God at one time, David mused, and conflicting requests at that. Boy, I wouldn't want His job. He must fail as many times as He prevails, maybe more. He must hate that. Probably tells Himself, Can't win them all. He's sure right about that , . . . I wonder what He thinks of the atom bomb, or maybe He doesn't know about it yet. Four hundred thousand tons of TNT? He must have at least heard a little bang up there, wherever *there* is, or maybe He was out of town, or out of planet, like on Mars . . . just floating around . . . floating around . . .

David fell asleep and dreamed that he was floating on air, flying alongside the plane and urging it to fly faster. It refused and spat oil at him, so he flew on ahead. He loved the feeling of flying and looped-the-looped around before spotting Iwo Jima. It had no landing field and no trees or buildings on it. The only structure on the barren island was a coliseum-like theater that was filled to capacity with soldiers, who sat quietly, their hands folded in their laps, quietly waiting. They looked up at him as he flew over and beckoned for him to land. He became frightened and . . .

David awoke with a start—and a plan. He quickly looked about and, satisfied that he was where he was supposed to be, unbuckled his seat belt and staggered to the accommodation. It had been improved greatly since the early days on the B-24. In place of the narrow-necked milk bottle was a wide-necked mayonnaise jar. After defueling himself, he hurried to search out Possie to learn if the plan he awoke to was at all possible. Possie listened and shook his head, but suggested that they both talk to Captain Pecora about it. Eugene, who had eavesdropped on their conversation, joined the trek to the cockpit.

David entered first and was taken aback by the sight of Captain Pecora sitting in the pilot's seat, his head slumped on his chest and appearing to be either sound asleep or dead.

"Is he okay?" David asked the young copilot, Lieutenant Schaefer.

"He will be if you let him sleep." Schaefer said, looking around to see Possie and Eugene squeezing themselvles into the cockpit. "What are you all doing up here?"

"We had a question for him."

"You got me scared for a second," he said, laughing. "I thought it was a mutiny and you were commandeering the plane."

"Who's commandeering the plane?" Captain Pecora said, his eyes popping open.

"Sorry, sir, we just wanted to ask how far we are from Iwo?"

"At our current air speed, we should be there in three hours," the captain said, checking his instruments.

"Two and a half, sir," the copilot corrected. "You dozed for a half hour."

"That should get us to Iwo at about eight-thirty," David said, checking his watch and getting charged up. "It's six-thirty now, the show was supposed to start at seven, that means—"

"That means," Eugene interrupted, "that if you're thinking of doing a show tonight, forget it! What're you going to do, ask an audience to sit from seven o'clock to ten while we set up?"

"Captain," David said, ignoring Eugene's question, "where's our scenery plane?"

"They're five minutes from landing, sir," Lieutenant Schaefer offered. "They radioed a few minutes ago."

"That's great," David said, keeping his enthusiasm under tight control. "Sir, is it possible to contact the pilot after he lands and have him relay some instructions to the Special Services officer who's meeting our planes?"

"That should be no problem," the captain said, absorbing some of David's energy. "What'll I tell him?"

"Excuse me for one second, sir," David said, turning to Possie, who knew what he was thinking. "What do you say?"

"I say," Possie answered quickly, "what Major Merritt said to me when he put me in charge of this show. Get the show on no matter what it takes!"

"And I say," Eugene interjected, "you better talk to the company. They were planning on a day off."

David rushed into the cabin and quickly got everyone's attention but Drago's, who slept through David's entire impassioned presentation.

"Look, gang, we can't let a busted fuel gauge do us in. It's V-J Day. It's a day for celebrating!" David exhorted, aware that he was sounding like Mickey Rooney trying to convince Judy Garland that her barn was the perfect place to put on a big musical. "Those guys on Iwo are waiting for our show to help them celebrate, and we can if we all just bend a little."

The cast, reluctant at first, started to catch some of David's fervor.

"But the show is scheduled for seven," Alicia spoke up. "We won't be landing until eight-thirty."

"They'll be happy to wait a couple of hours for it!"

"What about setting up the sound?" Lawrence T. asked.

"When we get to the theater, the scenery, lights, and sound will all be set up and waiting for us to adjust. Any more questions?"

The cast popped questions that David was able to handle easily, some in mid-pop.

"Who's going to set up all the—?"

"Volunteers!"

"What about our makeup? When will we—"

"On the plane, if anybody didn't carry their makeup with them, borrow someone else's."

"What about taking a shower before the show?"

"Take it after the show. You'll enjoy it twice as much!"

"When do we eat?"

"Right now! We'll divvy up the snacks we've stashed. I'll contribute two cans of pork and beans and a Baby Ruth."

"Private," the co-pilot cut in, tapping David on the shoulder, "the captain has the Special Services officer on the radio. What'll we tell him?"

"That I need to talk to him."

"Hello, sir," David shouted into the radiophone. "I'm Private Kokolovitz, and I'm with our stage manager, Sergeant Possie . . ."

For the next few minutes, the Special Services officer in Iwo Jima listened to Possie describe to him, in detail, exactly how to set up the stage for the show.

"And if you need volunteers, sir," David interjected, talking fast, "get in touch with Corporal Saul Marantz at the 3117th Signal Battalion. He'll round up a batch of guys for you."

"Hey, Possie," Eugene asked, "do you feel like you're in a Dan Dailey movie?"

Captain Pecora, whose father was a first tenor in the Metropolitan Opera chorus, found himself empathizing with these show folk's dilemma.

"Hey, Private," the captain whispered as David started from the cockpit, "I think I can get us to Iwo earlier than I estimated?"

"Could you do that?" David asked excitedly. "I mean, without jeopardizing our lives?"

"See that?" the captain said, tapping a gauge on his instrument panel. "The fuel gauge unstuck itself and it shows that we have ample fuel. Happy V-J Day, Private!!"

When Captain Pecora set his C-47 down on Iwo Jima, he had trimmed almost an hour from his flight time. It was that and a flawless landing on a bump-free airstrip that got the captain his first-ever applause for piloting a plane.

With the kind of precision the army is ofttimes capable of, the plane taxied to where two trucks were waiting, and in less than three minutes the company was out of the plane, into the trucks, and off to the theater. The girls never looked lovelier and the men never looked seedier but were too excited and tired to care. The thousand or more soldiers who had been waiting for almost two hours to see a show with girls in it let out a deafening roar of welcome when the trucks rolled into view. Possie instructed the girls to get into their costumes as soon as they were dropped off behind the stage. He jumped off while the truck was still moving and ran about adjusting lights and repositioning speakers, amazed at how well the volunteers had followed his radioed instructions. Even the drums had been set up properly.

It was exactly sixteen minutes after the plane landed when Possie called, "Places for the opening number! Overture!"

During the girls' opening number, David stood in the wings and looked out into the audience, hoping to spot Saul Marantz or any of the guys in his former detachment. He zeroed in on a recognizable face in the very first row that was leering up the dancers' skirts as they kicked and pirouetted above him. It was Shwick in all his glorious unattractivenes. The only reason David was relieved to see Shwick sitting there was because it meant that Saul wasn't in a stockade, but it also meant that while performing, he'd have to concentrate on not thinking about the idiot in the first row whom he disliked so intensely.

Compared to the the hundreds of performances David had done of *Shape Up!* and *Fire Away!,* none were quite like this one. From the opening number on it was apparent that this audience had checked their critical senses and behaved as if this were the best show in history. Their reactions made every sketch, every song, every dance, into a showstopper. By the time David came onstage to bring out Monty the Talking Dog, the audience was one homogeneous, happy, howling, cheering group, and David did nothing to disturb their euphoria and might have even kicked it up a notch. David had still not been able to spot Saul Marantz or any other familiar faces in the audience, and he was dying to know if Saul was present, so instead of taking his bows and running off, he picked up the mike.

"Thank you, thank you," David said, humbly acknowledging the thunderous applause and holding up his hand for silence, which they gave him, no doubt sensing from his demeanor that more fun was coming. "Before we go into our finale, I wanted to boast about something that may come as a surprise to all but eighteen of you. For more than a year, I was a member of the greatest signal battalion that ever existed, the 3117th!"

If the show had been playing indoors, the roof would have blown off. This simple announcement provoked the loudest and most prolonged mix of screaming, feet stomping, and whistling since the girls made their first entrance.

"I had the misfortune to be plucked from the 3117th," he said after finally restoring order, "one day, one lousy day, before you and my lucky buddies left ugly old Hawaii to invade this beautiful island of Iwo Jima."

More laughter, applause, and screaming, but they quieted down quickly, apparently anxious to hear more.

"While my old buddies were having fun invading and securing this beautiful island, I got stuck with these new buddies," he said, getting a howl as he pointed to where the girls were peeking out of the wings, "new buddies who don't drink beer, don't smoke, won't trade dirty jokes or talk baseball or horse around in the shower room with you, snapping towels . . ."

More laughter and lots of wolf whistles.

"Fellers, because I haven't seen my old buddies since before the invasion of this eight-square-mile volcanic island, which I gotta tell you from the air looks like a pile of coal"—David stopped for a huge laugh and continued—"I wonder if the following guys would stand up if they're here. Naturally, if they're not here, they can remain seated. Here we go. Is Saul Marantz out there?"

About ten rows back, a thinner, tanner, but still shy Saul Marantz stood up and waved.

"Oh, great, Saul, you're here. Last letter I got from you, you thought you might be otherwise occupied."

The few dozen who knew of his impending court-martial laughed, but Saul shook his head and gave David an okay sign. David then continued calling out names. "Frank Robbins, Freddie Binns, Tony Caputo, Milt Tepper, Jim Cavanaugh, Carmen Costanza, Manny Reff"—each got applauded as he stood up. "And," David continued, "any other of my old buddies from Detachment eighteen whose names I forgot or never wanted to know."

For the misery he had caused Saul, David intentionally omitted calling Henny Shwick's name, a small gesture that Saul noted and enjoyed.

Seeing all his buddies standing there, David had an idea which, if implemented, could easily have started a stampede, so he quickly ruled it out, then even more quickly ruled it in. Screw it, he decided, today is V-J Day, and whatever happens will be for a good cause.

"It's really great to see you guys," David said, smiling and waving at them, "and I was just wondering if my old best buddies would like to come up onstage and meet my four new best buddies and join us for the finale?"

Miracle of miracles, the audience, which contained many serviceman who had been drinking since they heard of the victory, sprang to their feet but did not rush forward; instead, they cheered wildly and made way for Saul Marantz and the rest of the designees to sidle out from between the tight rows of seats. Son of a bitch, David said to himself as he watched Henny Shwick be the first to climb onto the stage and charge him like a rhinocerous.

"Kokolovitz!" Shwick screamed, bear-hugging David harder than any bear would and then kissing him on the cheek to the delight of everyone in the theater who didn't know him to be a con artist.

"We missed you, baby!" Shwick said, releasing him. "You did great tonight! Wasn't he great, gang?" he asked the audience, which applauded loudly. "I taught the kid everything he knows."

David, with a frozen smile on his face, acknowledged the audience and then, without moving his lips, whispered to Shwick, "Get the fuck away from me, you bastard."

Shwick, who was uninsultable, playfully patted David on his behind as he moved away to embrace Saul Marantz. Ironically, David's and Saul's tentative embrace generated a much smaller response from the audience than Shwick's flamboyant bullshit bear hug.

After warmly greeting each member of the group, the Signal Corps photographer, who wished to preserve this emotion-charged reunion for posterity, quickly posed them for a group photo, with David and Saul in the center and their arms around each other's shoulders. Just before the shutter clicked, Shwick made himself the focus of the shot by wrapping his arms around both Saul and David and smiling right into the camera. Had there not been an audience vocally approving Shwick's behavior, David would have strangled him.

"Well, so much for show and tell," David said, addressing the audience. "Back to just show. I'd like to return our stage to my four beautiful new buddies and the whole company for our rousing finale!"

"That pain in the ass," David whispered to Saul as they walked off the stage. "I'm surprised Shwick didn't get into the photo when the marines raised the flag on Suribachi."

"He did," Saul whispered back. "A week later, he conned a bunch of guys into re-creating it for a gag, with him holding the flag. He sent the picture to his mother and signed it: Your son the hero."

"What an idiot," David said, herding his group into the wings where they could watch the finale. "Did his mother know it was a gag?"

"No, he didn't tell her. He boasted that when she showed it to the neighborhood merchants, they'd give her extra ration stamps for meat and butter."

David kept Saul at his side, waiting for his cue to enter.

"Hey, Saul, how about coming onstage with me for our finale?"

"Why not," Saul said to David's surprise. "It can't be as scary as being court-martialed. What do I do?"

"Just take my arm, move your lips, and march in time to the music."

"I don't know if I can, David."

"Sure you can, Saul. It's like falling off a log," David said, putting his arm through Saul's and marching him onto the stage to join the chorus line of actors and dancers singing "Stand Firm!" Never had Lawrence T. Lawrence sung the last line of the song, "Freedooom . . . for aaaall!" with more sincerity, and never had he taken a bigger, more reckless and hysterical-looking flop as he hit the last note. It inspired the cast to outdo themselves singing and flopping around with such joyful abandon that Broody was moved to yell out, "One mo' time!"

During the frenzied second chorus of "Stand Firm!" the actors were joined by the wild, screaming drunker members of the audience, who threw themselves on the ground, pulled themselves up, and bounced up and down for two whole choruses. Had the band not stopped then, there might have been more bloodied kneecaps, twisted ankles, bumped heads, and scraped elbows, but there couldn't have been more laughter and uninhibited, good-spirited insanity.

David was excused from striking the show so that he could visit with Saul and his friends of the 3117th. The moment Saul and David arrived at Saul's barracks, they found Shwick waiting there, armed and ready to barrage David with stupid questions.

"Hey, Doovid," Shwick yelled out, "tell me about that Chink broad. Anybody shtupping her?"

"The Chinese girl's name is Loretta, and she's a nun," David said, glaring at him. "Look, Shwick, Saul was just telling me about how you almost got him court-martialed? Did your really order Saul to send out an unauthenticated message?"

"Look, if you guys are going to talk army shit, I'm going to bed."

"Go to bed, Shwick . . ."

". . . we're going to talk army shit . . ."

". . . David wants to hear how you fucked up . . ."

"Bullshit!" Shwick barked, and stomped out.

"You did it, David," Saul laughed. "You embarrassed the unembarrassable."

"I didn't think it possible." David shook his head, "Anyway, how come you're not in jail?"

"Dumb luck. You know how in the Message Center there's always supposed to be a commissioned officer on duty? Well, when the fake surrender message came in, our lieutenant was goofing off somewhere. It was pretty hairy there for a week. I think the atomic bomb dropping got us off the hook. It sort of put things in a different light. Now, tell me about this Loretta? I hope you were kidding about her being a nun, because I think I love her."

At five-thirty in the morning David and Saul were the only two who had remained awake, and after covering every subject about which they had not written to each other, they decided to end their all-night bull session. Saul drove David to his Quonset hut, where they said their penultimate farewells, having made plans to see each other again before the show left Iwo.

Lying in his bunk that early morning, completely drained and hoping to get a couple of hours of sleep, David felt a sense of serenity and satisfaction as he recalled the exchange he had with Saul just moments before.

"David," Saul had said, "the fellers were talking about you one of the times you went to piss."

"Bet they were surprised to see me drink beer."

"Very, but they were more surprised that with this big success you're having, you still seem the same."

"Still a jerk?"

"No, still a person."

Aug. 17, 1945

My one and only future wife,

SHAPE UP! is no more! We did our final finale of the show last night, and it was a happy/sad experience for me. Happy that we did a good job and sad because I had to say goodbye to Saul and the guys. They don't know how long they're going to have *to stay on ugly Iwo before being sent home. I'm not being sent home, either, but at least I'm flying to Hawaii, which is beautiful and closer to where you are. By the way, we're flying to Honolulu in a converted B-29, and even though I am not a fancier of things that fly, I have to admit that if I can't get there by car, my second choice would be a B-29. By the way, you know that it was one of these B-29s that dropped the bombs that won us the war. Don't tell your dad, but they say that it was Einstein and that $E = MC^2$ thing he formulated that made the development of the atomic bomb possible. I was sorry to hear that the senator had a stroke. No, that's not quite true, darling, because when I read about Hitler committing suicide in his bunker, I thought of your dad and what a big fan he was of that Nazi bastard. I thought, too, of how I threw up all over him at dinner. Ah, what fond memories. I'd give anything to throw up on him again, not because I enjoyed it that much but because it would mean that you were nearby. I wouldn't be writing all this if you hadn't written me so much about how much you despise the old man. I guess it's my way of getting closer to you, loving all the things you love and hating all the things you hate. I really shouldn't be kicking the old Nazi when he's down, but then again, if not me, an American Jew, then who? I was so happy, darling, when you told me that you aren't his natrual child, although it should have been obvious to me.*

Two hours later, somewhere between Kwajalein and Johnston island and very high up in the sky.

My darling, I just ate a K ration dinner, and guess what I'm doing? I'll give you a hint. It has to do with a photo of someone smiling so sweetly while wearing a tight two-piece bathing suit with a bare midriff and standing in such a way as to emphasize her lovely, lovely bosom (one "lovely" for each breast) and the darlingest, sexiest legs anyone has ever been blessed with? I'll give you another hint. I'm staring at this photo, and guess what it's making me? Right! Hot! It's getting me hot, so hot that I had to turn it over so I won't embarrass myself. Oh, darling, darling, I can't stand not being able to see and touch you. You know, sweetheart, now that the war's over, it makes no sense for the government to keep us apart. If I had any guts, I'd go AWOL when I get to Hawaii, stow away on a boat to the States, find you, and spend the rest of my life making love to you whenever I'm not running from the authorities. Whoops, darling, we just ran into some turbulence, and even though I'm not a big fan of turbulence, this one just helped me get rid of my erection, meanwhile, know that I llllooovvve yyyooouuu, MMMaaarrryyy Deeeaaarrre,

Don *

* The turbulence stopped.

◆

L ess than three months after the capitulation of Japan, the disso-
lution of Maj. Alan Merritt's Entertainment Section was well
on its way. Whereas David, who had been in the army for a
little over three years, had not accumulated enough points for his discharge, many of his colleagues who had been in for as many as four
years were being mustered out every week, Major Merritt being the
first to leave, followed by Captain Sullen soon after, which left the section in the eager and extremely incapable hands of Lieutenant Yorby.
Eugene's leaving was the most difficult one for David to handle, for
now he had no ally with whom to laugh and play and gossip about the
latest of Lieutenant Yorby's follies. For weeks now David had single-
handedly tried to discourage Lieutenant Yorby from mounting a new
play entitled *Boys Will Be Boys*. It was an inordinately bad comedy-
drama, in three acts and thirty scenes, written by one Edmund Rys
Dante. It depicted the goings-on in an Entertainment Section similar to
Major Merritt's. Lieutenant Yorby had cast David in the lead, and because the company's ranks were constantly being depleted by untimely
discharges, open auditions were held for actors to fill the twenty roles.
Luckily, the play was never done, and David did not have to dye his
hair blond to play the part of Lt. Darnell Cornell, the fictional character fashioned after the playwright, Edmund Rys Dante, a.k.a. Lt.
Theodore Yorby.

Soon after learning that he would not have to play the part of Lt.
Darnell Cornell, David was informed that his days of playing a private
in the U.S. Army were over. His discharge had come through, and unless something untoward happened, he would be home by Christmas.

Within twenty-four hours after learning that he was going to be honorably discharged, David went from delirium to despondency.

Prior to receiving an honorable discharge, every serviceman was required to undergo a complete physical examination to determine if the soldier, while in service, had sustained any injuries or contracted any diseases that would make him eligible for disability benefits and medical treatment.

As David lay on the deck of the SS *Wyndham Bay* listening to the powerful engines of the former aircraft carrier propel him and his thousand fellow dischargees toward San Francisco, he wondered if he was the only one who had been told that he had contracted gonorrhea. He was too embarrassed and too ashamed to share his guilty secret with anyone. David had thought of remaining in Hawaii for the results of a new test and/or treatment, and he might have if Mary Deare had not already received a letter from him that ended with

> *. . . and so, my love, if on Christmas morning you find a naked soldier with a fine tropical tan lying asleep under your tree, check his dog tags, and if they have my name and blood type O, then roll him over on his back and place your entire, wonderful, warm body on top of his eager one and say, "Wake up, Donny, you're home! What can I do for you?"*

✦

For five whole days and nights he had run over in his mind everything that he had done and everywhere he had been in the last few months and could not imagine how, where, or from whom he could had contracted gonorrhea! He was the only one he knew who had ever gotten this dread disease. None of my friends, he thought, had ever had the clap or even crabs.

He could not shake the memory of the white hospital room and the reed-thin nurse explaining to him the reason why he had been called back for a second blood test.

"You tested positive for gonorrhea, Corporal," the nurse said, coldly.

"You're kidding!" David laughed.

"We don't kid about venereal disease, Private."

"But it's impossible," David had argued. "I couldn't have a venereal disease."

"I know," the nurse repeated the admonition from the army sex film. "She looked clean."

"No!"

"Then why didn't you use protection?"

"There was no *she* who looked clean," David yelled. "I was responding to your saying—"

"You don't have to explain yourself to me. Roll up your sleeve, Private. I'm just here to draw blood."

"What for?" he said, reluctantly rolling up his sleeve.

"To confirm the lab's findings," she said, tying the rubber tourniquet on his forearm. "Make a fist!"

"By 'confirm' are you saying that the lab might have made a mistake?"

"No, I am not," she said, pushing a needle into his vein. "Relax your hand."

"But it's possible, isn't it?" David said, getting panicky.

"When's the last time you had sex?" she said, drawing his blood into the syringe.

"Sixteen months ago!" David answered forthrightly.

"Are you married?" she asked, retrieving the needle.

David shook his head, trying to think of how he might explain to Mary Deare that he had a venereal disease.

"And you're an actor?" she said, shaking her head and smiling knowingly.

"Yes, what's that got to do with anything?"

"You tell me, Private." She sneered while putting a Band-Aid on the small puncture wound in his forearm. "We'll contact you when the results come in."

"When will that be?"

"Approximately five days," she said, tossing David's blood-filled test tube into a wire rack that held dozens of other blood samples. "We'll notify you."

"Five days? That's impossible, nurse. I'm shipping out tomorrow! "I wrote my girl that I'll be home in two weeks."

"Then go, but your medical records will go with you. You know that the army will not discharge if you have an active venereal infection."

"But, what if—?"

Before David could frame another question, the nurse grabbed the blood samples and rushed from the room.

The blue Pacific was unusually pacific, but David, who had puked his guts out hanging over the rail of the Liberty ship on his way to Honolulu, was fearful of reliving that nightmare and avoided doing anything that would make him queasy, like standing up or eating anything but cold apples. Even though it had been explained to him that the SS *Wyndham Bay* was equipped with a gyroscopic stabilizer, unlike the jerry-built Liberty ship that had taken him overseas, he could not risk getting deathly sick again. This time he might succumb to the urge and jump overboard to drown himself.

He looked up at the cloudless blue sky and thought how pleasant this trip could be if he could just forget that his body, the one he had promised to Mary Deare, was being ravaged by gonorrhea.

David opted to stay upside and do all of his living on the flight deck, which included sleeping, eating, and straining his mind to remember every event and every person with whom he had contact and who might be responsible for his condition. The only sex he had had in months was with Loretta Yung and Bitsy Kane on an empty stage in his mind after a show, but he knew that however exciting and real those erotic dreams were, they were not infectious. Damn it, he asked himself, how the hell did I catch this? A contaminated toilet seat? I have sat on a lot of strange toilet seats in my army career, but you can't catch a venereal disease from a toilet seat—unless you kissed it. He laughed at the absurdity of the thought, but it suddenly got him to thinking about all of the girls he had kissed at the emotionally charged and singularly uninhibited farewell party for the cast of *Shape Up!* David, allowing himself to drink more than his usual safe limit of beers, had found himself involved in saying long and overly affectionate farewells to the four girls in the show and to Mrs. Furst. A tipsy Bitsy Kane was the first to kiss him goodbye, and when she discovered something about David that she thought her duty to share with the world, she did.

"Girls, listen, listen! I have some lovely news for you," she announced, giggling, her arms around David's neck. "This corporal here has the softest lips I have ever kissed!" To confirm her diagnosis, she kissed him again.

"Try them, girls, this man's got lips like little, downy pillows."

One by one the giggling girls tested David's lips, and all came away believers. He was more than a willing participant, and when Loretta Yung approached him for her kiss and looked up at him with her lovely brown-green eyes, he felt that he was more than an object of her research. She was only one of two who kissed with her mouth open and welcomed his tongue, which he had not planned on using. She kissed him long enough to let him know that she was not offended. Mrs. Furst was the last to kiss David and attest to the mushiness of his lips. In that one kiss, Mrs. Furst forgot she was a chaperon and unleashed all her pent-up frustrations by trying to give David a tonsillectomy with the tip of her tongue. Because David decided that Mrs. Furst was legally drunk, he gallantly rejected her offer to meet him behind the cafeteria, although he seriously considered it for a long moment.

David knew there was no possiblility that he picked up anything that night other than the sweet memory of Loretta's mouth and a pain in his groin that lingered for hours.

The ten days it took for David to travel from Honolulu, Hawaii, to Fort Dix, New Jersey, were the longest days of his young life. He had spent most of the trip thinking of Mary Deare and trying to decide how, what, or if he would tell her about his disease. The night before the SS *Wyndham Bay* docked in San Francisco, he played out in his head the telephone conversation he might have with her if he decided to call. He was aching to hear her voice, but he did not trust that he was actor enough to hide his anxiety. But why should I? he reasoned. I'll just tell her the truth. I'll say, "Darling, I think that our love for each other is strong enough for me to be able to tell you that I caught this thing." That's a good idea, he thought. I'll just refer to the disease as this thing. "I swear, honey, I have not had sex with anyone since our last night together sixteen months ago, and I have no idea how I caught this thing. The doctors are stumped, too. It's a real medical mystery, like an immaculate infection."

David concluded that he would tell Mary Deare nothing that would ruin her part of their happy homecoming. He wanted so to call her and tell her that he was on his way but feared that when she heard the quiver in his voice and the beating of his telltale heart, she'd know that all was not well. He settled for a Western Union telegram.

MARY DEARE-EST, ON WAY TO FORT DIX WHICH IS NOT FAR FROM YOUR LOVING ARMS—WILL PHONE TIME OF ARRIVAL SO YOU'LL KNOW WHEN TO OPEN THEM TO RECEIVE, YOUR LOVING DON

✦

Of all the ignominies that he had to endure, the worst presented itself when he arrived at Fort Dix. The officer in charge of his group of returnees informed them that the process for honorably discharging them would take no more than two days. Before David could feel any joy over this piece of sensational news, he heard a voice boom over the speaker: "David Kokolovitz, David Kokolovitz, please report to the infirmary immediately."

Oh, damn, he thought, my damn medical records have followed

me across the sea. David could feel two thousand eyes on him as he left the staging area and could hear their owners thinking, Poor bastard, wonder if he's got syphilis or gonorrhea.

David hoisted his duffel bag onto his shoulder and found the infirmary, where he encountered a smiling, plump, compassionate-looking army nurse.

"I'm Sergeant Fine, and you are Private Kokolowitz," she said, looking at his medical record. "Have a seat, and I'll be with you soon."

Now came his second stigmatizing event of the morning.

"Uh, Sergeant Fine," he asked shyly, "is there a latrine I can use?"

"Right around the corner," she said sweetly, "and please use the red-painted seats."

God, he thought, those seats are for guys with VD.

David had rarely broken a sensible law, but this morning, as he looked at the bright-red toilet seat, he said to himself, No, sir, David, if you don't already have a dread disease, sit your ass on that and you'll catch one. David sat down on a regular seat.

"So, Private," Sergeant Fine said brightly as she prepared to draw blood from him, "I hope you didn't spend a lot of time worrying about your last test."

"Not a lot," he said, "only all day and night for six days and three hours today so far."

"Oh, that's awful. We get false-positive reactions all the time," she said, sliding the needle into his vein. "Didn't anyone tell you that?"

"No, nobody told me that," David spoke slowly, a mixture of rage and relief flowing through him. "I was told just the opposite."

"Hmmm," she said, drawing blood from his arm, "did you tell them that you'd been promiscuous?"

"No, I told the nurse that I haven't been with anyone for sixteen months, that's what I told her, and that's the truth!"

"Well, then, she should have told you that a positive test result was an impossibility," she said, withdrawing the needle. "I'd say that you you can stop worrying now."

And David did, but not until the following day, when the test results were as predicted.

The telephone rang in Eugene and Peggy's cozy two-room apartment in Greenwich Village, and Eugene picked it up on the first ring.

"Donny?" he asked expectantly.

"Hey, Eugene, I'm out!"

"Oh, shit!"

"Oh, shit? Not congratulations, buddy, welcome back to civilian life?" David said, standing in a freezing phone booth at a bus station in New Jersey. "Is Mary Deare there? She said you had invited her to stay with you this week."

"No, she's not here. That's why I said, 'Oh, shit.' She and Peggy went out to walk Yorby. Did I tell you we got a dog?"

"Oh, damn, not about you getting a dog, about Mary Deare being out. When do you expect her back?"

"Should be very soon. Since she's been with us, she won't leave the apartment. She was afraid she'd miss your call. Weren't you supposed to be discharged yesterday?"

"Yeah," David said nonchalantly. "They kept me an extra day to make sure I didn't have gonorrhea."

"Are you kidding?"

"I wish I were. I don't, but this sadistic nurse in Honolulu—"

"Whoa, a beautiful southern belle with red cheeks just walked into my apartment," Eugene shouted, waving her over. She may want to say hello."

Mary Deare screamed, "Donny!" ran to the phone, and snatched it out of Eugene's hand.

"Donny, is that you, darling?"

"It's me! Oh, boy, is it ever me. How are you, Mary Deare? I missed you. Did you miss me? What a stupid thing to ask."

"Nothing you can say is stupid. It's so good to hear your voice. Where are you? Have you been discharged yet? When will I see you? Of course I missed you." She rattled on, struggling not to cry. "I think I'm going to cry," she said, losing the struggle."I'm sorry, but I'm so happy. I love you so much, Donny . . . I can't wait to see your face. I loved your telegram, and I'm ready for you. Did you get my last letter?"

"I don't know, honey. What was in it?"

"Plans for your welcome-home party," she said through sobs of joy.

"I didn't get that letter. When were you planning this for?"

"The day you were discharged. Today!"

"That's great, but isn't it short notice? I mean, nobody knows I'm home yet. I didn't even call my mother and father."

"I was hoping, darlin', that you'd call them after the party," she said kittenishly.

"Where is this party going to be," David asked, catching her audacious drift, "and who exactly will be there?"

"Well, it's going to be the Hotel San Moritz in room 940, and it'll be a very, very intimate party. I'm planning for just one other person besides me."

"I love you!" David shouted. "That's the kind of party I've been dreaming about every night for sixteen months!"

David buttoned up the heavy wool army coat he had just been issued and stepped out into the December air. He had not breathed cold air for so long that it shocked his nose and lungs. He hailed a cab, opened the door, and tossed his duffel bag in.

"Max Zussman," David said, reading the cabbie's license as he climbed into the backseat, "if you can beat the existing record driving from here to the Hotel San Moritz on Fifty-ninth Street in New York City, I'll double what's on the meter."

Without breaking any laws or records the garrulous cabbie deposited David at the entrance of the Hotel San Moritz in excellent time.

"Put your money away. The ride was my welcome-home gift," the driver said as David went to pay him. "You'll give me a free ticket someday when you're on Broadway. What's your name again? Never mind, I won't remember it. Go, go to your dearie, she's waiting."

David hoisted his duffel bag to his shoulder, entered the lobby of the San Moritz, and raced to the bank of elevators, just managing to squeeze into one before the doors shut.

"Nine, please," he called, praying that the elevator did not have to stop to leave any guests off before the ninth floor.

Since learning that his blood test had come in negative, everything was going his way, and the ninth floor was the first stop. David become aroused the moment he stepped off the elevator and saw a sign with an arrow, indicating that rooms 900 to 950 were to his left. He started off walking, but after passing 904 he broke into a dead run and did not slow down until he reached 936. David stopped in front of 940, dropped his bag, and with his heart pounding much harder than it normally would after running the short distance that he did, he took a deep breath and rapped on the door. Mary Deare opened it immediately and threw herself into his arms. They held on to each other tightly and rocked back and forth saying each other's name, as if checking to see if they were dreaming this moment. They hugged, then kissed, then hugged again, then kissed again, and continued until Mary Deare suddenly stopped and stepped back.

"Hey, Donny," she said, laughing, her face wet with tears, "let me look at you. I heard you and I felt you, but I have't seen you yet."

"Here I am!" David said, taking off his wool coat and presenting himself like a male model. "The latest version of me."

"Oh, Donny," she said wiping her tears. "You're beautiful, so beautiful!

"Look who's talking," he said. "Have you any idea how beautiful you are? You're—" He stopped and studied her. "Is that the same chiffon dress you wore when we first met?"

"I had it shipped from home," she said, whirling around. "You remember it?"

"Remember it? When you walked across that ballroom at the Hotel Tallulah wearing it that morning, I wanted to—"

"I know, I saw you looking at me. I don't know if you remember this, but I wanted you so bad and knew you wanted me, but you said you were taken."

They laughed, rushed into each other's arms, and danced around the room and over to the bed.

"Oh, Donny, I missed you so, so much," she managed to say when her lips were free of his. "Would you please make love to me?"

"That's one of the reasons I'm here tonight," David whispered. "I just hope I remember how to."

"Does this help?" Mary Deare whispered throatily as she took his hand and placed it on her breast.

"It does, dear, it really does."

Mary Deare and David fell back onto the big double bed and started fulfilling their promise to love each other forever and ever and ever and ever . . .